Island

D. Bolland

This book is dedicated to my wife, Christine. I have sailed the southern oceans, been part of forests thousands of years old, lived on islands alone, wandered through coral reefs and existed in the largest of the cities. There is nothing that will ever bring more wonder than each morning being with you. For everything, for all time; I thank you.

Island

This is what happened as I saw it.

These words and the journey I took in this space of time are now history. But the effects are ongoing, like a memory reaching out from a shallow grave. We all have them, buried, waiting.

Each of us has our own truths. Our perspective is a personal view through one's own eyes; I see you therefore you exist. I see what you see but I stand in a different place and have a different view.

Perspective is self-centric by its nature. How can it be any other way?

I have made decisions that had consequences far beyond what I thought were possible. But I have now seen the impossible. My perspective. But the one question will always persist. Why me?

Start

We, that is my wife Barbara and I, live in what can be described by some as a summer haven from the city but for us, a sea laced paradise. The spit of sand dune that the houses here are built on is a designed summer place, a carefully planned and developed suburb-by-the-sea. There is an 'old end', where the first arrivals built and then there is the rest of us. Those who came later. The original developers went broke and this little beach front village languished through the years until the next upsurge of the property market.

We really came here because of the sea. The sounds, the smell, the ever moving life. Here we get both types; a small inland harbour protected by a sandy bar at the entrance and a five kilometre ocean beach. I particularly wanted the smell of the salt and the sound of waves on the beach at night. We had moved through the country a lot and we needed to gather some moss. Barbara as a Nurse and I a Park Ranger. Some houses on our journey were government owned, others we bought. These were fine but nowhere really to just be. To call home.

We weren't getting the same fire within the job. The smart systems that clever people created, with their dynamic solutions, to reinvent a cyclic wheel had become simply, a bore. Where lots of highly University trained people sat behind computers who actually have little understanding of the practical part of the job. Ticked boxes were being filled in, with real answers forgotten. Politicians got closer as we moved up the ranks. Wheels of differing policies and budgets up or down with each voting round, brought challenges that had worn thin. So we chose a small house over a man-made lake looking towards rugged forested hills that float on the small inland harbor which shimmers in the sunlight. The habor is tidal. Sand flats at low tide are dotted with feeding birds tip toeing in tidal pools on the sand. As the channel fills with the incoming water, mullet splash and stingrays sweep in the shallows on butterfly wings. Pods of dolphins come and go, playing their way through the sand bar entrance.

Summer multiplies our population by ten. Boats, jet skis, electric scooters, dog walkers and the various city dwellers rush to grab sun, sea, sand. Some play golf on the course, walking frowned on, electric carts a must have. Some take boats filled with tackle out on calm seas to catch fish to show their hunter gatherer skills off at the local fishing club. Mine is bigger than yours, I guess. We have come to rather like the ebb and flow of the summer rush. People bring a holiday mood to pass on. Parties are held and gossip swapped, BBQs lit and meals shared, just nice.

While the summer people are here the beach is well used. Surfing, swimming, cooking in the sun. Children dig holes down and sandcastles up. They jump over wave ripples and are watched by their parents from sun shades, in the nicely named Helicopter Parenting mode, where the kids are within calling distance in ankle deep water. Adventure stifled, fears instilled, rules applied.

The one café is over joyed to see the summer crowd, as is the single grocery store. The store staff remain friendly even at summers height, when the rushed city dwellers are at their most painful, the mostly widows smile and chat as people wander in and out. Lots of widows here, retirement seems to remove men quickly to the next world, their male self-worth dissipated with the loss of the job, and therefore who they are as people. But I guess after a lifetime this becomes indivisible. The lack of planning for the so called 'next phase of life' is very obvious in the grey wanderers.

As the summer wanes, houses become silent. The birds and rabbits appear. The small population that is left at summers end, are either retired, work on the next phase of the development or are building beach holiday homes on carefully grassed sections of ground. Some of the retired got bored and started mowing grass. There is lots of grass here. Hardy African grass to stand the lack of water in summer.

The development is curious in one aspect: The ground level is too close to the sea level so the land for buildings is raised, the ground level is now higher for houses, the earth stolen creates lakes and ponds. Global warming, a new earthy catch phrase. At council level it has found its way into the developers requirements: build up or don't build. The fact that it may well be too late isn't considered. Rules are rules. Our views across the little machine made reed lined lake are always changing, the inhabitants come and go. Flights of ducks, gaggles of geese and snooping moor hens on the edges. Their scream like calls can be heard late at night reminding me of the natural world that is still very close.

Chapter 1

The summer rush is over. I walk through a sparse grove of pines with rough mown grass that is peppered with golden needles then through a few yards of low sand hills scattered with salt grasses. It is late afternoon when I arrive at the beach, just as the tide reaches its low. I come here with my metal detector to give reason to wander aimlessly along the beach.

The beach is nearly empty. A couple walking with their dog are just visible in the salt haze a mile or so down the beach. The air is cool and a slow breeze off shore has kept the locals at bay. The sea is chopped and restless. Oystercatchers black with orange beaks stand on one leg looking bleakly at the waves. The breeding season some months away, they stand singly at the waves edge, watching for titbits. A Black Backed gull floats towards me on stiff wings. The cold eyes inspect me for food options then tilts away, drifting along the beach, black and white against a dulled sky.

The sky is a Turner delight. Grey and white glints of sunlight rays stream down and merge with the sea salt haze. White caps rise and collapse on the harbour sandbar a kilometre out. The breeze is strong enough to hold the spray in a spiralling curl, sweeping the fine drops backwards in reverse waterfalls.

The sea has been part of my life for all time. My first memories were watching ships in the shipping lane from our house as they delivered their load to their city berth. The island protected beach, at the end of our road, was where I learnt to swim and be taught how the sea worked. Waves of each size bringing great joy, going under, over and through, body surfing and eventually crouching on boards of fiberglass. Swimming for hours, warmed by the fine brown sand before going back to the water.

I had always been a beachcomber. From a small child the sea thrown treasures have always amazed me. Shells varied shapes, similar just not the same, all with differing colors, big ones that are whole; a favorite. As time passed I got to know the place of each creature of which shells are the discards of their lives. I swam, learned to snorkel, then dive. I sailed and capsized small yachts, crewed on big ones. Fished for most things that swam day and at night. The sea is life to me. The ebb and flow of the tide and the roll and snarl of waves make a simple sense. Time passed, my world expanded with my career, then I moved on.

One day metal detectors and their obsessed operators appeared on my computer. Even the mundane treasures they uncovered, were a delight, like beach combing underground. My computer ran hot with my own snooping. Videos watched of people finding the past at their feet. Old lost coins or just lost coins, horseshoes, buttons, even old bottle tops have their story. I learnt that people who detect are detectorists.

Strange metal left from by gone ages, some treasures but mostly random bits let loose from ordinary people doing ordinary things: just living. A lot of people detecting were driven by the value of what they found, others the simple value of past lives. I rather fancied myself as a purist; seeking historical artefacts that look back in time. The reality is finding anything was a leap to the pulse. Touching the past. We live in a relatively 'young country' at the end of the world where metals didn't arrive until the late 1700s. While the chance of finding Viking relics or pirate gold, sadly is very limited, there is always hope.

As time passed I have worked out a walk/stride pattern with the detector. Foot forward, swept left, foot forward sweep right. A slow march for treasures and rusted bottle tops. Beer-can pull-tabs surface more than you would like. A few coins emerged. Nails. Cheap bracelets if lucky. One earing, never two.

U-tube abounds with startling finds. My reality as a treasure seeker is different and often repetitive. Foot forward, swept left, foot forward sweep right. But there are treasures on the surface to scan and wonder at.

Tangled dry seaweed sea and sun greyed driftwood take on snake shapes. Shells pure white against a cool wind dried sand, sometimes a dry brown fish or a pearl white bird bone. These shore treasures come into view and are passed with the ongoing foot forward, swept left, foot forward sweep right.

A rising whine from the detector stops my routine. Shift the head right, sound lowers. Shift it left, sound rises. Stop and pin point where my target is and I take out my trowel, bend and dig. Lost it, damn. Now use the small pin pointer; a hand sized detector. I grab a hand full of sand and try again and again, now on the fourth try, a beep from the pin pointer. I smooth the hand full out on the sand in front of me. A small round silver coin shows its self. Treasure. A 1962 sixpence that I rub clear of sand. Our country went decimal in the late 1960s, dollars became king and part of our colonial past fractured from Europe. Sixpences are becoming less common. Hardly rare but the find does take me to a childhood of shillings and 3 lollies for a penny. Age makes touchstones out of memories.

A dog barks down the beach and a gull calls me back to my find and I fill in the hole with a pushing foot. Even in the world of

Detectorists, there are ethics: Fill in all holes is number one, take away found rubbish is number two. The pin pointer goes into its bag with the trowel and my silver hoard.

I have been working my way along the high tide mark. This is generally where people sit, laze, set up beach umbrellas, shade tents and drop small pieces of loot for the hunter to find. The tide is just about fully out and the six-hour run in will soon begin again. A dark lump in the wet shine of the sand 100 meters towards the waves calls out to me. Odd things should be investigated. Curiosity is the simple driver of the beachcomber. I wander towards the lump stepping and sweeping as I go. The closer I get to the object, other tide washed gems appear. A large shell, a feather, an orange crab claw with no owner, a small black pebble. All are eyed and left to lay, awaiting the endless flow to come.

The movements of the waves go from a minor roar to individual movements of sound. Hissing, crashing but lightly, this is no storm, with thumps of weight and crossed water, yet the noise has a constant individual pounding which differs with each arch of salted water. Harmonious in its diversity, the wind is adding to the shift of intensity.

From a distance, the lump, I think is wood. Dark from the water, slightly squared to my mind but I can only see about a few inches protruding from the sand. The rest, if there is a rest, buried. I give the lump a push with my foot and it moves minutely, the sand glistens with water from the pressure. I am satisfied that it is wood but unsure if it has been shaped by hand.

I bend and dig around one edge balancing the detector in one hand and push my hand into the sand and pull. The wood lifts and turns. The wood is about two foot long, a hand span across; heavy. Shaped and squared and in the centre is an old greened bronze nail. This is old. The nail creates the thought, part of a shipwreck I wonder? In the surface of the darkened timber is another hole but no nail. I brush the wet sand away from the length of the wood and another nail hole revels its self. I turn the timber again and again inspecting looking for clues from this part of a jigsaw.

I had been kneeling on the sand holding the detector in one hand. I now stand, shift the piece of wood aside and turn on the detector. I am hoping for the lost nails. I stand and shift back to allow for the sweep of the coil to target the depression where the wood has lain. No signal. A move sideways and the alarm shouts at me. The digital dial has rolling numbers.

There are slices of time that stay in one's memory: A breath of wind on the face. The first scene of a new place as a child, the smell of hot sun cooked dust from a gravel road in the summer. Recalled in clarity at the edge of your world to be inspected at will. Why these are held is not explainable but they rest in the jumbled archives of the mind. These seconds before me are now tattooed into my soul for the rest of my days.

I move the coil again, again the same response. I can tell by the dials reaction this isn't iron. I fall to my knees, using the trowel and carve away the sand. I touch something hard. I scrape gently. It is shiny. It is gold colored. I put the trowel aside not wanting to damage anything. Now I am shocked at the possibility of actual treasure. There is more shine. The curve of the object shows as I rub the sand from its length. Characters are etched into the golden surface. I reach one end of the tube and feel a lip under my fingertips.

Gently I pull. It breaks free of the clinging wet sand. It is a tube, smaller at one end than the other, holes at either end, a little under a foot long maybe. It is a bright almost translucent gold but not heavy. Aluminium? Not sure. It reminds me of a piece of armour. There is a gap, narrow at the smaller end wider at the other, which runs from round end to round end. The textured characters are unknown to me.

I am in awe of what I have found. I place the detector on the sand and walk to the shallows to wash the sand off my find. The water makes the piece glisten. I wonder about this. Gold or silver rings don't hold their high polish, they tend to slowly dull with use. The highly polished surface is enhanced by the hieroglyphic raised marks that run the length of it. The full edge is slightly raised and rounded. Looking inside the tube there are similar marks to the outer. Three rows of small indents run the length from one end of the tube to the other. In between each of these rows are a series of more raised marks. All the same size. Swirls. Dots, curved dashes, lines that are zigzagged that end with a curl.

I turn the piece in my hands, completely fascinated. I am struck that the inner hieroglyphics are in a different orientation to the outer. The designs are not pressed from the inner to the outer. They are either carved to create relief or maybe it's been cast? There are more questions at each look. No matter, the finish is beautiful. Polished, crafted, totally captivating in its form. I am reminded of a book from my youth: The gabbled ravings of a creature underground and his precious. Precious. Yes, no matter what this is; it is precious to me. I am oddly uncomfortable with the thought but it fits. This is a real treasure.

A small wave brings me back to my surroundings. The tide is on the move and is just about to reach the detector where it lays on the damp sand. The breeze has slowed and the sun straining through clouds is getting close to the hills. I go back to the detector and bag, which I sling over my shoulder. The detector in one hand and my find grasped tightly in the other, I head to the gap in the small sand hills towards the truck and home.

The couple with the dog that had been on the edge of my vision down the beach are now only 100 meters away. We are on a convergent line. I change direction slightly. I am in no mood to discuss anything. All I want is to get home and further examine this stunning find. The dog heads towards me, tongue flopping in welcome.

My find will not fit in my small carry bag. I stop turn away from their sight and with little thought try to slip the object up the left sleeve of my sweatshirt. It slips over my wrist and on to my left forearm; the sleeve a cover against the curious.

It has slipped on to my arm. It feels strangely warm. It fits my arm. As I recognize this, with surprise, the dog reaches me. A happy Labrador cross thing, curious to meet a new friend.

'Harry, come here.' The owner calls and is ignored. A tongue sideways resting on pink gums. He calls again. The dog looks at him and wags a sandy tail.

'He doesn't bite.' As a Park Ranger I had heard this mantra a thousand times. Mostly true. But every emergency room in the country has customers that are bleeding and torn from dogs that their owners trust. Mostly kids pay the price.

I give a wane smile, step around the dog and keep walking. The owner walks over reaches out to the dog and clicks a lead on to its collar.

'Have any luck?' he calls, a conversation gambit. He has stopped and is facing me.

At a glance I know him; or at least there are plenty of his kind here. He is a touch older than myself. He has the intense eyes of the lonely. Modern house with nothing to do to it, gardens sorted, grass carefully mowed and the only sight on each morning's horizon is waiting. I sometimes wonder whether I am one in the same but not now, not today.

'Nothing much, normal bits of rubbish.' I answer. My gait is paused. His wife has stopped and is watching from a distance.

'I have been thinking about buying one.' He nods towards the detector. His eyes flash from the detector to the dog to hide the untruth. Anything to talk and prolong contact, the loneliness is palatable. My arm is now being warmed by its large new bracelet and the warmth is increasing.

'Sorry, need to get back. We are heading out.' I fidget a reply. My arm is now uncomfortably hot. The dog man nods but his eyes narrow with annoyance. At me, or himself I can't tell. He pulls on the dogs collar with the leash and turns towards his wife.

I walk another fifty meters and a bolt of pain reverberates through my arm. The bracelet is crushing it. Heat. Pain. Fire. I am stiff with utter surprise and shock. The detector hits the sand. Sweat explodes from my face and rivulets down my chest and back. I sink to my knees panting small gasps of breath. My arm feels like it is in a boiling cauldron of molten metal encased in a vice. I am now shuddering and then vomiting into the sand. The pain gets worse and I am trying to scream but there are no words, no sound. I shake with the pain.

A light stream of blood is dripping from my fingers into the sand and I have instinctively cradled my arm in the other. My vision is starting to blur. I lunge to my feet and stagger towards the shoreline. The dog man calls something out, I don't know what. Beyond caring, I pull wildly at the bracelet. Bolts of pain respond to my tugging, the arm is still encased, the bracelet will not budge. I stagger on towards the edge of the beach. Each step a journey to be mastered. Then another. Then another. The trees creep closer at last, the soft sand cutting before the small set of dunes my target. The pain has easing I think, or it may be my concentration on just moving.

The path through the dune set is well trodden and I lurch from side to side in the soft sand, balance erratic. My arm is a burden to cradle. The blood has slowed. But enough has run down my arm and on to my sweat shirt and I can feel my Tee shirt is soaking enough blood to look as though I have been gutted.

The pine trees, brown sentinels on the grass, rough dark brown weathered skins, brooding, waiting. I make my way to the first and lean against it, the sharp bark biting but welcomed. I didn't think I would make it this far. I tug again at this bloody manacle that has caused this nightmare. Less pain than before but also less movement, I strangely feel skin, it feels buried into the arm. As I go to investigate further. Harry and his owner hurry up to me. Harry's tail wagging in welcome.

'You dropped this.' Lifting the detector towards me in his hand, quickly inspecting me with an open mouth at the same time. The target of blood becoming the centre of his stare.

'Are you alright?' Eyes glued to the red. The inquiry is genuine but not wanted. Over the years injuries came with the territory of the job. Mostly minor, others not but I had learnt I coped better doing my own doctoring. I hated the fuss and I also the mistakes that well intentioned amateurs made, which were often painful.

'I don't know, but I think I am OK. I will head home. Thanks.' I try to be emphatic. I just want to be left alone. He looks unconvinced, head shaking.

'I can ring for an ambulance.' This idea makes me twitch with some humor. We are tens of miles from any medical base. Had my bleeding been really bad I would be long gone.

'No. No thank you. I will sort myself out.' Looking into his eyes, shaking my head in turn, trying to end this conversation.

'I really think...' He starts off trying to be forceful. I cut across him with a hard stare.

'No, don't think. I am not well and in pain. Just go away. Thanks.' I stare quietly.

His mouth opens to reply but then snaps shut. He tosses the detector on the grass and stiffly walks away back towards the beach in anger, pulling Harry with him. Harry looks back over his shoulder at me with a tongue hanging grin.

I have now realized I am feeling better than I was. The concentration of trying to be polite was a focus that I needed. I am starting to chill with drying sweat and blood. The breeze is moving the pine branches above me. The surf sounds run in the background. I sit on the grass back against the tree to try to make sense of what happened. The pain has been subsiding. The intensity has left me feeling weak and rattled. I lift my sleeve carefully, gingerly, frightened of what I am going to discover.

The bracelet appears buried in the arm. I flex the arm, the bracelet seems to move with it. I am amazed, shocked and horrified all at once. I have had leeches on me in the past, very unpleasant. A similar feeling is welling in my mind. I flex my arm again and the ridged hieroglyphics seem to move as though part of my skin. The edge where it joins the wrist is flat and I struggle to feel where the skin joins the bracelet.

Fascination begins to overcome my horror. The bracelet runs up the arm to just below the elbow. Again, I think it has embedded in the arm but pain fogs my thoughts. It feels oddly elastic. The translucency I saw earlier on is strangely dissipating. The hieroglyphics are still pronounced with the overall color; a deepening red, the gold has changed and dulled. As I touch it, I feel the presence of my fingertips. I take my fingers away then lightly touch the raised marks. I can feel them as though I am touching skin. I realize this should not be possible, but I can. I rub the surface of the bracelet. Yes, I feel the rubbing on my arm.

The pain has become a throbbing solid awareness that underlines my movements. Not nearly as acute as before but more amplified, it disrupts my thoughts. The sky is darkening and chill is creeping into me. I need to get home. I push to my feet and pick up the detector in my right hand. I am shaking slightly. Left arm clutched lightly across me I walk slowly through the pines to a path that runs between houses to the road, the overhanging bushes create a shadowed tunnel past silent closed beach houses. A blackbird is scattering leaves and hops away as I pass.

The truck is waiting on the edge of the cul-de-sac. I put the detector onto the tray on the back and click the opener. I slip the bag off my shoulder, open the door and ease into the seat. As I struggle to close the door it slams my arm into the steering wheel and my body. Pain beyond pain; I pass out. Black.

Chapter 2

In front of my eyes are moving spheres. They curve across my sight, some slow, others blindingly fast. One of a red heated desert, another a blue touched with green, yet another glowing white-hot. They slide around me then pass away to let more come in to view. I am moving in a stream of silent gliding bubbles. Flying? Unsure. There is thought, no sound, just being. I then hear. Noise. I am being called.

'Bill, Bill are you all right? Bill...' I can hear the fear, concern and caring in my wife's voice. All at once, my eyes open and I am still in the driver's seat, head against the rest, the windscreen is black. Car lights are reflected in the mirrors. The door beside me is open and my wife is standing there with a flashlight in her hand. The cold air brings more awareness. I move my right arm instinctively, waiting for pain. Nothing. No pain comes as a surprise. Odd.

'Sorry. Yes. I think I am OK. What time is it?' I am asking, still trying to gauge exactly how I am.

'It's after ten. What happened? I've been really worried. Are you all right?'

Her face frowned with concern and I can feel the under laying fear. The concern and questions are more than fair. I would have been the same or worse. We had met later in life. Our previous marriages hadn't worked. Some don't. But ours does, very well in fact. We know each other. We know what works in the intertwining of our lives. Our respective older children like each other or at least get on well enough. Grandchildren from two differing family's go to the same school. They get together for barbeques. This acceptance has underlined our harmony. Kids echoed bitching in the background of a new life does not help. We were lucky.

'Yes. I hurt my arm, worse than I thought. I can't understand it, it's bazaar.' I am still waking, trying to work out actually what did happen. Explain the unexplainable. Barbara shifts the torch in her hand and the stains of dried blood leaps out at her.

'Bloody hell!' The shock is obvious. But I laugh at the poor unintended pun. What else does one do?

'You cut yourself with a detector?' She shakes her head with the ludicrous nature of the question or a husband's stupidity I am not sure. But I certainly can't argue that one.

'Let's get home. I can drive. I'm feeling OK, seriously, I can drive. I am cold.'

She looks doubtful but nods, glasses glinting in the torch light. She knows through experience how I feel about injuries and turns back towards her car, which is parked behind my truck. The keys are in the ignition where I had left them. I go to start the truck and then remember my arm as I lift it automatically to the steering wheel. No pain. I can't feel the bracelet, nothing, just skin. I rub my hand up my sleeve again, just skin. I want to turn on the light to check what happened but Barbara's lights behind me make me turn the key and put the vehicle in gear.

I have scared her enough. I suspect I have scared me enough. You fear what you don't understand. As we drive the empty streets, a rabbit is caught in my lights. I drive slowly around it, Barbara's lights follow suit. I wonder about the rabbit in the lights as I finish the short distance home. Is that me? An odd thought that I leave to rest.

Home. Our small house started as a beach cottage. As we moved from house to house we had always made a specific point of making our environment, ours. I had started my working life as a carpenter. We would spend months remodelling, painting, tiling, not for resale, just to make our small world completely us. I had worked on a number of historical sites in my job, which underlined my interest in history. Barbara had come from a farming family where one made or built, not buy. Both our family's histories were touched with pioneer traits that we carried as part of the fabric of our lives. Our countries past is the shadow of our ever-growing book selections.

I get out of the truck. The lights are on in the house. Barbara arrives behind me. The door is unlocked which reminds me of Barbara's fear. I stand still in the kitchen and try to plan.

'Do you want food or shower?' The ever practical, Barbara with head tilted queries me. She will wait for the story but now things need to be done. She is searching my face intently.

'Where is the wound? How bad is it? Is it still bleeding?'

'No, don't think so. Shower first. I will call you to have a look once I get this gear off.'

She bobs her head in agreement and turns towards the kitchen. I can see the tension in her stance but also know that it is easing. I am annoyed at creating this situation but still can't understand what has happened.

The bathroom fan whirs as the light is turned on. I turn the shower on and strip my sweatshirt and tee off in front of the mirror. Now there is real shock.

The bracelet is gone. Dried thick blood has crusted on my hand and wrist but there is no wound. I turn my arm and look closely and I can just see the ridged marks that I saw on the bracelet are all rather minor but there. At least that is something I think. I had fancied I was either dreaming or worse going slightly mad. But then there are the remnants of blood; proof but proof of what?

Barbara comes in and peers at my arm where my gaze is directed.

'Where's this wound?' She looks intently at the arm. There is nothing there that would allow such a residue of blood.

'I don't know. It's gone. The bracelet has disappeared...I don't understand it.' I shrug my shoulders in frustration.

'Bracelet? You don't wear one.' Again she is perplexed. Wanting to believe but not understanding. That, I get.

'I'll have a shower and tell you what happened. It's weird. I don't get it either. Can you make something to eat? Starved.' She grimaces, shakes her head and reaches out to touch my arm.

'OK. You Ok?'

'Yes, but confused. Very tired. Anyway, shower.'

She turns away as I turn the shower on. I give way to the heated water. Bliss. As I wash the blood off my hands and wrist I can feel the small raised ridges. They seem to be under the skin. I press into my arm and now I know where the bracelet is. The meal is simple but as always thoughtful and tasty. It is one of Barbara's real talents. Making great meals and that only comes with real thought and understanding the ingredients. In short, love.

'That's what happened. I don't understand it.'

I shift myself in discomfort on the couch. It is very dark, the curtains are open to the black night, the sound of the surf on the beach is just discernible. The meal is finished. Barbara had been patient waiting for the story to come out. I can see she believes but doubts. I doubt too. I doubt my remembering then rub my arm. And feel the residue that is left. The evidence of the blood and the ridges on my arm are not disputable. I note the ridges are lessening.

The bracelet can be felt under the skin. Now it appears to be a part of me. A mental horror I can't really grasp and why I am scared of this I am unsure. As I tell the story Barbara feels my arm and the intruder. Her hand snaps back in disbelief, then returns gentler. Eyes concentrated intensely on the proof in front of her. Barbara believes what she sees but has struggled to take it in. Logic is defied, which I understand.

'Not possible but.....So what now? Any ideas? How is the pain?'

Barbara is a plans person. A problem solver, isolate the issue and resolve it. Which I value and agree with. I have been surprised and amazed over the years how many of my peers at work and in their personal lives put such little thought into looking ahead. Their lack of forward thinking I have never been able to understand, houses of cards that live on an edge. I like a simple life and planning seems to me to make things so.

'No, no pain, thanks. I have been thinking about seeing Gary.... maybe an X-ray? Find out what we are dealing with?'

It's not much of a plan but I am throwing this pebble in the pond to see what Barbara's opinion is. I use word 'we' particularly. We have always been a team that worked towards our life collectively.

'Hmm.' She makes considering noises. Her feet are up on the couch. I can see her staring at the arm. Lips pursed in thought, light red hair cups her face. There are the lines that come with age, an open caring face with bright curious eyes. Natural and not ravaged by years of masking foundations that need thicker and thicker layers to create a false state of beauty, if beauty comes from a French laboratory that suggests almost eternal youth. It is a good face that has done well through the seas of time and reflects the inner attractiveness; a face that I love.

'Maybe.' She is balancing thoughts. ' You can't exactly go to an A&E. I mean you could but......' I have played with this idea myself. If they find an implant and what else do I call it? It. My unknown. Then what happens? I am scared if what I have is a parasite. I dislike the direction my thoughts are heading.

'Yes. Then what? Surgery? Cut it out? I may end up with no arm or becoming an experiment. And of course there will be the questions of how it got there. I can see me in a hospital forever.'

Barbara nods, eyes fixed on a non-horizon across my shoulder. I can tell she has worked through these options as well.

'Well, at the least an X-ray for a start, find out what exactly we are dealing with and where it sits.' She is thinking out loud looking for a plan. Option delving.

'OK but who and where? Something simple, not a large hospital, I don't want to be someone's specimen. If this is seen by X-ray, I could become a toy. Difficult to keep quiet really, doctors are human too.' I am eluding to the ever present media. Strange things get talked about then get reported. Seconds of fame appeal to a lot of people.

My fear and distrust are obvious and we have both had enough brushes with the news media over the years that have left professional bruises. A small sign came to mind that I had on my desk. 'Nothing is off the record!'

I am a private person. I have no interest in media, of putting my story into the mouth of the news monster. Where truth is an interpretation made to suit the interviewer, the subeditor, the editor and, of course, the avid readers who mostly don't read but take their bites from titles. I had had my share of misquotes, utter lies and reediting from local papers to national TV, to know to stay away from them. It was part of the job, but I had been burnt enough to still have the invisible scars. News stories are generally that: Stories.

Barbara's head bobs in understanding what leads me to this.

'So what about Gary then? His surgery has an X-ray and he works with his wife. Provided he doesn't send a copy to a radiologist. I guess we underline the patient confidentiality...I don't know.' She stops the sentence but not the wondering.

She is right. Gary is newish doctor in the town that acts as our local centre. They live here but commute the 20 minutes to his clinic. Barbara had met Di, Gary's wife, via the local book club. A new doctor needs patients and the clinic we were signed up with was oversubscribed. Battling to get an appointment via the snarling receptionists was unpleasant. So we changed. We found Gary to be personable, interested and efficient, a good combination for a GP.

'Hmm...OK I am ready to drop. Let's discuss it again in the morning, I have to sleep. Not thinking. But seems like an idea.....and then what are the choices?' I shrug and stand up. I am swaying slightly.

'You go to bed. I will just clean up a bit.' This is her way of saying I need to process this. I nod dumbly. The bed is cool. A haven. Tired. Sleep.

The dreams that come are strong, lucid, colored, frightening and remembered. I see a semi-mirrored cube, like but not ice, semi- transparent. It is on our beach at the edge of the waves, perfectly square. I am standing close to it looking up. I am looking at me, looking at it. Some times my height; it sits with the waves washing around it but oddly not touching it. It is there but the waves show no interest, odd. A gannet patrolling for food drifts behind the cube. Beak directed down towards the water, searching. The bird I can see clearly through the structure.

Now I am looking at the cube that is not ice. I see sky and ocean through the cube and yet it is more than a mirage. I 'feel' the internals of the cube, there are layers, places, and things. It is a building of light but not of light. I 'know' this place. But how I know I cannot grasp. It is visible but not visible, a drift of fog. A 3D drawing, come to life from a screen. I walk over the water and into the cube. The sea, the sounds, the breeze, is gone. I wake. The bedroom is in half-light, I am in bed and I can hear water running in the bathroom. The door opens and closes. Barbara comes into the room.

'Hi, awake? Feeling OK?' A statement and question.

'I think so. Strange dreams. I can still remember them. I.....' She cuts across my thoughts.

'Yes. You had a busy night.....lots of talking, mumbling, but no sense...' She smiles at the jibe.

'No. Not surprised. Hard to find that at the minute.....coffee I think.'

Her head bobs and she turns and heads towards the kitchen. I sit up on the side of the bed. As I rub my arm and I can feel my intruder. The reality that it is still there, a disappointing awareness. The dreams had rolled into the past hours. I had thought that ......damn. My yesterday world isn't a dream. Damn. I stare at nothing and minutes pass.

'It's ready.' Brings me back to the now.

Tee shirt, shorts and hot water on the face. There are two poached eggs on toast with off black coffee on the table. I get the salt and pepper. Over the eggs we discuss the plan for contacting Gary. I make a phone call and set the ball in motion.

Chapter 3

I find it interesting how you never make a wrong decision. At the exact time of deciding a course to take, you evaluate your choices. Balls go into the air, one is caught, peered at, then you move on with what you believe is the right one. Given all the facts in front of you the decision is made and you walk into the future on that course. Until a later glance over your shoulder brings clear twenty, twenty.

As luck would have it Gary had to be at his clinic this morning, a Sunday.

'I have an issue with another patient, an extra few minutes won't matter, with the weather as it is.' Was the vaguely glum reply, I am pleased, no staff, no wife, I feel privacy without other people is better.

Gary is fishing mad. The weather is the one real brake to his passion. His knowledge of fishing gear, boats, species, water temperatures, when to fish and what time is well known and respected, even in a town where most people have fished from childhood. Di, Gary's wife, I suspect rather enjoys the enforced companionship of a stormy winter.

As we arrive, a stony faced middle aged stout woman is leaving the clinic door. She looks over my shoulder and stiffly marches down the ramp to the only other car in the car park, with no reply to my 'Morning'. Not happy. Barbara is about to press the buzzer when Gary opens the door into the reception area.

'You didn't make her day.' I quip as way of a greeting, a statement, not a question.

He jerks a grin. 'No. Hypochondria is difficult to cure.' His eyes move, he has said too much. Gossip is poison for a small town doctor. I nod, as does Barbara. Case closed.

Gary is taller than I am. Starting to grey with a tanned skin, blue grey eyes, surfer style more than doctor. He has the ability to seemingly exclude everyone in the room bar you, with his intense look, a 'friends against all trials' gaze. There is a comfort in being the subject of his scrutiny. The perfect GP doctor's tool.

'OK. A Sunday visit, must be important.' He waves us into his office.

His desk is against a wall and the two chairs are facing his from one end, which is armed with a computer and small printer. Behind him on a set of shelves is a range of doctoring gear. Along one wall is the patients examination bed. I sit in the seat closer to him and Barbara the other. He leans back and waits for the story. All prognoses start with information. I recount the last 24 hours, Barbara adds continuity and pieces I have forgotten.

As the story rolls out, the gaze falters. His eyes shift from mine to my arm then to Barbara's gaze, his disbelief is obvious.

'OK, let's have a look?' he nods at my arm. He moves his chair and feels my arm over my sweatshirt. The hardness of the bracelet is felt. He then pulls the sleeve up. As he feels my forearm, his look intensifies, reality deepens. I think vaguely that could have been amusing once but not now.

'Hmmm. Not possible!' His eyes boring into my arm. 'Any pain?'

'No, not possible, but there it is. No pain. Not now. Not pleasant at the time.' I shake my head.

'We thought an X-ray it may give a better idea of what's going on.' Barbara offers, a step to a plan.

'Take your sweat shirt off and lets have a proper look.'

He nods towards the examination couch. A blue platform covered with a raised end. I slide off the shirt and sit on the couch. He takes my arm, feeling, turning, examining, manipulating. Some of the pressing is odd. I twitch in pain.

'Hmm...sorry.' Gary's eyes are fixed on the arm.

He straightens and stares past the curtains into the garden of the clinic. Minutes tick.

'OK, X-ray...let's see what we can see.' He turns to Barbara. 'I'll get you to wait here....radiation.' Hardly misunderstood given her occupation but Barbara nods a smile at me. Nice. He leads the way to an X-ray room at the end of the clinic. The room has a bench couch and a small X-ray machine. There is a cubicle in a corner with a small glass window. This is the lead lined retreat for the operators to protect themselves from excessive radiation exposure.

'So how are you?'

The question is asked as his gaze settles on me. Some people in the community find Gary's intensity unnerving. I am neutral. He and Di have been to our place for dinner a couple of times. More than a patient, but not friends, his way of interacting with the world is simply, his way.

'OK I think. Disturbed. Shocked but coping mentally, if that is what you are asking. I don't understand what happened or how. I don't want to think about why. I have too many questions I guess and no answers that I can see. Scared I suppose but not sure of what.'

I have stopped feeling the truth of the words. And a little surprised at my own self-diagnosis.

Gary settles me into a chair next to the machine and puts a board under the arm. As he shifts the head of the X-ray a cross of light is aimed at the centre of my arm and he goes into the cubicle to check the screen. He returns and shifts the machine slightly and goes back to the cubicle.

'All set, don't move.' A rolling hum. He comes back, shifts the board, rearranges the arm, then the head of machine and repeats the process. He moves to the cubicle end of the room. More noise.

'Come and look.' Gary is looking at a screen that is set up on a desk. Standing beside him I see my internals; bones and misty bits I have no name for.

'Jesus.'

'Yes' Gary is slowly nodding, eyes glued to the screen. 'Yes.' The bracelet is there wrapped around the bone. No, not wrapped. Floating around the bones of my forearm, muscle not visible. In the black and white of the x-ray the ghostly image of the bones, are contrasted to the very solid image of the bracelet. I am oddly relieved what the image shows, that I wasn't going mad. A dream that is reality or a reality gone wrong. I still struggle with what the screen is showing. I have never been a fan of X-rays, they make me too mortal somehow. Seeing my own bones seems to underline the human state; here today, gone tomorrow.

Strangely, the hieroglyphs are visible in the image; a sign post to the unbelievable. There is a tapping at the door: Barbara calls. I go to the door and open it.

'Hi, how's it going?' Her face concerned questioning.

'Come and have a look...not sure. Just very odd.'

Gary is still standing staring at the image, hand out stretched tracing the bracelet as we move beside him.

'Oh wow.' Barbara is glued to the screen. Gary dips his head in agreement.

She is obviously stunned. Mouth open, a small sideways glance towards me tells me she is frightened. But I am pleased she can see what I saw. The bracelet is real. Jesus.

'The symbols were there when arh...you found it?' Gary's question opens unpleasant thoughts and I shrug them off.

'Yes. I thought of Egypt. Hieroglyphics. I only got a brief look. The guy with the dog turned up, so I hid it. Too well by the look.'

Barbara glances at me. 'Ha ha. You gave me a hell of a fright. More the amount of blood.' She isn't laughing.

I nod wanly in agreement. 'Both of us.' And she takes my hand.

Gary presses buttons saying 'I will print these out. I presume you want a copy printed? I'll send one as well to your email. The printed copies won't be that good. The days of x-ray film are gone. Screens give better resolution.' He twists a smile and pushes a button.

'And tea. I think better with tea.'

We follow him into the small very clean tearoom. Everything very neat, magazines piled, coffee, tea and sugar containers, very clean, in a row on the bench. There is a small table surrounded by four neat chairs. Three cups are filled with boiling water, drowning tea bags. One window on to the very quiet Sunday street.

There is lots of quiet thinking staring into nowhere, but going everywhere.

'So what are your thoughts? Can this be removed?'

Although I think I know the answer, I am asking anyway. The images reality has deepened the fear that I don't want to acknowledge but feel drifting in the back of my mind.

'I don't know. Surgeon's territory, metal buried in the arm is one thing but this......is no accident. I mean it looks surgically added. I don't know if it is possible to actually to remove it, even if they could. I am surprised your body isn't trying to reject it. Lot's we don't know.'

He pauses and stirs the tea, small amount of milk, no sugar. Barbara and I are still. These thoughts embedding themselves.

'Removing it? There is the question of how attached is it to the arm. Just under the skin? Or is it situated as part of the muscle, bone, or the arms structure now? Arms are complicated. Lots of tests and some they can't do because we don't know what it is made of. An MRI may rip it out of your arm. Magnetic. So many tests before any idea of removal and, of course, can you live with it?' The stirring stops and Gary looks at me directly and holds my eyes.

'The real question that will be asked again and again is, how did it get there?'

He shifts his gaze across to Barbara then away out the window, as he shifts his chair to lean back with his feet out, hands behind his head: thinking position.

'What happened, happened! The proof is on your screen. There aren't any stitches to show surgery......anyway who the hell would want it...Jesus!'

I am stung by the question and have a sinking feeling that Gary doesn't really believe my story. There is doubt in the tone. What more proof could he need? What more reminder could I need? The rebuke is heard and he turns the gaze in my direction, unblinking, staring.

Barbara puts her hand on my arm.

'OK. I know you are angry and trying to sort this through but....'
'Hmm sorry Gary. All a bit much to take in really.'

Gary shrugs and stands.

'Look, go home. Take it easy. There is nothing more we can do here. Given what has happened, you are fine. I need to consult with a surgeon and....actually, I am not really sure what to do or if anything can be done. Don't get this too often.'

His grin is shot at me as way of a minor apology but the eyes are cooler. The shutters are down. Barbara feels the cooling but just gives her thanks and a 'hello' to Di. Gary gives me the printed copies of the X-rays, which are average quality but the images are good enough. Too good for me, I think. We head to the door of the clinic, Gary opens it on to the bright day.

'I'll ring a surgeon I know and see what he says. I will email the X-rays to him. That will be an interesting conversation.' He shakes his head.

'No further than him please, I want this kept quiet. I don't like my information spread too far. This is too.....' I struggle with what to say. But I feel uncomfortable about spreading this news too far.

'Strange.' Barbara interjects. I laugh. She just gets it and my situation. I am so pleased to have her on my side.

'Yes, strange, you are really right!' Gary looks from Barbara to me, seeing the team at work.

'OK, I will try to keep this quiet but....yes, it is strange. This is a first, you know. I mean I don't think anyone, anywhere at any time, has had....this.' A hand gesture follows his eyes to my arm. The synopsis of my situation is simple, direct and quite probably true. A car passes in the stillness of the statement.

'Alright, thanks.' Gary is unmoving, watching us from the door, he raises a hand as we drive away. The trip home is very quiet. Lost in our lack of knowledge, we travel the familiar route and sit for a few seconds after I stop the car.

'So what now?' I am wondering out loud not really looking for an answer, a question of the future with no solution.

'Gary made an interesting point. You aren't rejecting it....that is really odd. I mean that's what the body does to protect its self. Rejects foreign bodies......and so much metal, if it's metal.' Staring into nothing Barbara is asking questions of her training that give no reply. 'That your body isn't rejecting it, is important. What this thing is made of and how it got there. That's important. On a wider scientific and medical stance, it's important. I mean this is really big!' She stops, still staring through the windscreen into her questions.

'Hmm....so I become what? Important but a guinea pig?' My answer and question send my own thoughts scrambling into areas that I hadn't had time to delve into. Now what has happened is proven, it has made things far more complicated and real in my mind.

She turns and looks at me. Her brown eyes are searching, seeing the confusion and at the end of that, the fear.

'Sorry. It's just .....just so strange... you look tired but hardly surprising. OK, lunch.'

The ever-practical solution; food is an answer which comes from a farming background and to be fair, does seem to work. We leave the car in the drive and unlock the house. Jug filled and water boiling. Meal preparation noises, fridge opening and closing, pantry door squeaks slightly. Rustle of paper. Normal sounds but we are both very quiet, consuming odd thoughts.

I lay down on the couch and peer at the copies of the X-ray Gary gave me. The hieroglyphics are obvious on the bracelet but the picture chills me. The ghost bones are mine. This picture has become very personal. I rub my arm gently absently, the ridges and dashes of the lettering I feel under the skin. I am aware I have become use to the bracelet. This disturbs me and yet, I am surprised how I have accepted the intruder. Part of me now and as I think this, sleep drifts me away.

There is a flickering of light and I am in the clear cube. The translucency of the last dream has gone. I am standing in a corridor. I turn and see a strip of water, beach, sand hills and trees framed in a square doorway. The walls are a neutral color they glow with a gentle light. I turn away from the door and walk down the corridor. At the end of the corridor a door opens. There is no sound. I enter and wait. The door behind me closes. Time passes. A door in front of me opens.

The curved room that greets me glows lightly. The ceiling is the color of a new dawn. There is a chair. The chair has wide formed rolled arms and is the color of a green sea. Small lights, half domes are buried in the arms. A controllers chair, a captain's chair. The left hand arm is contoured. I sit and my arm sinks into the chair. The curved wall shimmers with a colored night sky.

I am wrong, this isn't just a night sky it is THE night sky in minute detail. A real-time map that is distinct with moons, planets, stars in a diorama of colors beyond grasp of thought. Where my eyes focus I see layers of further planets, more black of space, further stars. There are places beyond places. I am the seer of the unseen. I know where I look, I can see the detail, how I know this I cannot fathom.

My arm feels heavy, it seems to bury its self into the chair. I am locked into the chair, in mild panic I try to lift the arm, it does, but with difficulty. I return it to its place on the chair. My arm settles in to its place. Hieroglyphs launch themselves across the wall faster and faster. Colors stream with stars, planets, gases and worlds that merge into bright laser cut shapes. I can read them.

I can read them.

My waking is difficult. I feel I have left one reality to another. The dream is too real, detail too clear. I push them away, time to deal with the real world, I think.

'Hi. Its 5.30. I didn't want to wake you. You have been talking but no sense.' Barbara puts a cup beside me on the coffee table, a pile of sandwiches are also there uneaten.

'Hi. Yes sorry.' I am struggling to come back to now.

'Wow, strong dreams, Sci-fi stuff, so real.' I stretch and sit up.'5.30? slept for hours.'

I rub my arm and the bracelet is still there. Barbara watches me. I can see she is disturbed by this new habit. She says nothing but her eyes are wary and questioning, which in turn, makes me ask myself if I am changing. I think I am. I wonder how, still no answers.

'What were the dreams?' The question holds both concern and annoyance. Barbara is scared of what has happened but there is nothing for her to reference for answers. Our team 'sense' tells me this.

'OK, this is what I saw.' She settles into a red lounge chair and studies me as I relate my sleeping world. Each detail is easily recalled. The minutes move away as I speak. I talk for an hour. The first question is:

'What did you read?' Eyes still deeply intent on my face.

Her question startles me and prods me back to the dream. My mind floods with new knowledge. My phone rings. I automatically answer but also wanting to somehow avoid the question.

Gary's greeting is friendly but somehow guarded. Whispers of unease pass my sixth sense. A knowledge picked up from countless conversations with intense colleagues at work. Agendas are often hidden in bright clean sentences of quarter truths.

'I contacted the surgeon I know. He has put me in touch with a guy from a medical school. Jeffery Shanes he is a Forensic Pathologist and a surgeon he....' I interject.

'Pathologist? I don't think I am dead yet. Is he a lecturer? What exactly is he?' My questions and tone display my disquiet. I am also concerned that yet another person is being given information that I don't understand myself. My voice raises and the questions rattle across the airwaves.

Gary's short silence is used as an admonishment; I am the doctor, naughty boy. Gary didn't say it but it is there just the same. His words are slower and stilted as he carries on.

'Well, given your situation is so...different...Jeff seemed the best fit. He has worked in prosthetics and robotics. And yes, he is a senior lecturer at the medical college. Anyway I sent the images to him and he wants to see you as soon as possible.' Gary stops, his annoyance at having to explain himself, crystal clear.

Barbara is watching me closely only getting one side of the conversation, with bites she can pick up from Gary. She is concentrated on the black of the mobile.

'Look Gary, from my point of view you have involved another person without discussing it with me. Sorry but I am the patient here. You went outside your brief.'

I am now angry. I want to remind him of his professional ethics. I have never liked people making decisions for me without at least discussing them with me first. Now that I am completely outside any work constraint I don't have the barriers I used to have to adhere to. I don't like being caged by others reasoning; my world, my choice. Barbara wears a slight frown.

'You have spread this too far Gary. Where this will go now, I don't know. Neither do you. Bloody disappointing. I now have three people, you, a surgeon and a pathologist, whom I don't know, with information that can obviously go anyway they decide.'

Barbara puts a hand on my arm. The 'be careful' sign is up. I nod at her concern but ignore it. She sits down still watching the black square of the phone.

'Your judgment here may well cost me. Barbara and I have discussed I could become a guinea pig and you may have set me on that track. Great. Thanks.' I stop before I head towards the word of trust but the implication is out in the open.

Gary's snapped reply has the sting of the wronged but I also hear the lacing of appeasement. He knows he has over stepped the patient mark but his back tracking puts me on alert. I am unsure why.

'Jesus! Just trying to help. Yes, I get your point but I doubt if anyone ever has had this.....umm..issue. Who does one contact? He seemed the best guy given his background. He's from the states. Really bloody qualified. I mean world leading....here on sabbatical. The Med school was lucky to get him. His wife is from here...loves the slower pace. He fishes.'

A man to be trusted then. In Gary's world there are two types of people, those who fish and the others, I am not quite sure where I fit.

'Jeff is amazed at the X-rays. He is on his way......I actually thought you would want some advice on this soon....and..' He slows and stops.

And I thought, you would make points with a world leader at the med school. Ego networking. Just what I needed.

'So you gave him my address...wonderful. Goodbye Gary.' My voice dripped sour as I clicked the end on the screen.

I flop on to the small couch opposite Barbara and stare into space.

'Self-serving bastard.' An observation of my ex doctor. Barbara passes me a glass of water and we sit quietly.

'So we are getting a visitor?' She has followed most of the conversation and I nod.

'This guy is meant to be the Bees Knees.' Barbara catches my sarcasm and arches her eyebrows but says nothing.

'Senior guy at the Med school. American, his wife is from here. Knows robotics and medicine. His field. Not that I have heard of the mix. Didn't know there was.

Anyway Gary has him fired up and he is coming here.' I shrug.

'Not happy about Gary not asking but too late now, there is something with Gary's attitude, I frankly don't trust. Gut feeling really. Anyway we will see what happens.' I shake my head and stare into space. Surprises can be unpleasant.

Barbara stands and goes to the fridge, opens it and peers. Over her shoulder comes.

'OK, let's see what this guy comes up with.....dinner? Any thoughts?'

'Something simple?' An OK is followed by fossicking and stuff is placed on the bench. She stops, faces me with a tomato in one hand and a knife in the other.

'Are you OK? I mean are you in pain? How are you doing?' Barbara has worry lines around her eyes and I know she is actually asking about my mental state. I stand and put my arms around her holding her quietly.

'I am OK, honestly. Sort of concerned about how this may get complicated. I don't understand how Gary thought this was OK. Let's see what this guy says. Am I too big to be a guinea pig?' With a quick kiss she snorts at my question and turns back to the bench. The meal is something to concentrate on rather than more questioning.

Chapter 4

After an omelette and small talk, just as the sun is creeping redly behind the darkened hills to the west, a large imported utility pulls in the drive and parks behind mine. It has a double cab and two people get out. I can see shaded figures in the rear seat. One of Barbara's quirks with houses: she wants to know who is coming, being prepared or no surprises I have never been quite sure. But it works.

The first person has bright eyes that are directed into mine as I open the glass door. Casually formal dress, expensive with a controlled style, to place the owner. Fiftyish, thinning hair carefully trimmed with deep grey eyes. No smile lines, humor not natural I suspect. He twitches a smile in greeting then the face falls its normal watching brief.

'Bill? Gary spoke to me and sent some incredible X-rays. Unbelievable...sorry. Doctor Jeffery Shanes.'

His handshake is mild and he grips the ends of my fingers rather than the whole hand. Doesn't like touch I wonder? The 'doctor' emphasized, status underlined.

As I nod, my eyes turn to his companion standing to his right. Tallish, ex something, army or police. The eyes stare then dart surveying for threats, I know this look and stare. I had worked enough with people like him within my job doing what the bosses labelled, interdepartmental compliance. Administering poorly written laws that had little teeth. I had spent long hours and days with police, fisheries and customs on so called training exercises, with all of us following orders but wishing we were back doing the 'real' job each of us had been trained for. He wears a street uniform, dark clothes non-descript, light boots, no collars to grab, ready for action.

'Hello, another doctor? I didn't realize I was that special.' My question and quip I cover with a smile but the doctor's friend sees through the jibe and his eyes narrow slightly. No doctor, ex police maybe or some sort of army boy. Interesting.

'Dan Bridges, a college.' The doctor nods and flickers another smile but the question remains unanswered. No hand to shake. No words, a nod. I look at Dan Bridges a little too long then stand aside. I pretend welcome.

'Come in. My wife, Barbara.' Introductions made again, seats taken and offers of coffee or tea refused. The doctor is in a hurry, his hands move continuously. Finally he asks the question.

'Can I see your arm?' He can't quite still his excitement. A dog at the bone, I slip the sleeve of my sweatshirt up and he manipulates my forearm.

'Good God!'

His fingers run over the ridges of the hieroglyphs then feeling the start and end on the bracelet at the wrist and the elbow. From a slim case he has pressed glasses on his nose. The type that are designed to show cool, money and intelligence all at once, but often fail.

'Yes, what I thought.' His eyes shift to mine but ignore my levity. Dan's eyes are glued to my arm. Even he can see the ridges as the flesh is pressured. Barbara is watching but I can see her amusement masked by a serious stare. Minutes pass and I bore with the pressing hands, now not so mild. The doctor pushes too hard at my wrist and I jerk in pain.

'OK, enough.' I take my arm away and slide the sleeve down.

The doctor says sorry but he has the look of a cat losing its mouse. His eyes are still enthralled with my arm, his fingers are twitching, he laces them across a knee. Dan senses the fixation and has the grace to look slightly uncomfortable. Barbara allows a half smile.

'Let's have some tea.' There is silence as I fill the kettle and collect cups. The two visitors are nonplussed but I have learnt that control often comes with action. Even a small action focuses people. Barbara takes over the task collecting milk from the fridge; team work.

'So what are your first thoughts?' I ignore his title. Bitchy, but I don't like this guy. There is too much self-importance in the room for my liking and I have concerns on why he needs his companion. Odd again, more people that I don't know. I am damning Gary as he formulates his reply.

'Well, lots we don't know of course. I mean, we really need to run further tests, such a curious and irregular situation really, just so unknown. A complete run down first. But yes, further tests at the medical school laboratories. Maybe the university, include the nuclear sciences of course.' Barbara sets mugs down and tosses in a question.

'Biopsies of course?' he stops and peers at her.

'My wife is a nurse.' I watch as he takes this idea in.

'Ah, well yes, of course, biopsies. Not sure if this can all be done here, may need to try a bigger medical university....the Mayo Clinic possibly.' Jackpot. I think, the researchers Holy Grail. I raise my hand in a stop motion.

'Barbara and I have spoken about guinea pigs recently and I am not going to become one. I have no idea what has happened. And it is very plain to me, neither do you.' His head moves with glasses glinting and starts to cut across me but I keep going. His mouth is open, face annoyed.

'Doctor, the X-rays show a foreign body. Biopsies aren't going to change that. What you actually want is a sample of the bracelet right?' I ask again more forcefully.

'Right? Yes?'

His head bobs in agreement and glasses shift, soft hands move to fix them back in place. His gaze darts to his companion. The power balance moves courts. The doctor is the first layer but there are more layers in this. Dan is the director of play in their game, here on the ground, I see. His eyes flicker from me to the doctor and back, then to Barbara.

'So who exactly are you Dan, and who are you from?' I ask.

Dan squares himself slightly and meets my gaze. The smile comes easily as he leans forward, hands open. A classic police interview stance. We are all friends here. I have used this technic myself. It's the 101 of body language school. I am disturbed at what this manoeuvre tells me. I note this isn't lost on Barbara. She watches him intently. Dan's American accent is light, controlled, educated, East Coast I would guess. Clipped orders have been given with this voice, I can hear the training. For now though charm sweeps the room.

'I happened to be in the country visiting. I work for the US government, an off shoot of NASA. Doctor Shanes received the information about you from your GP and invited me along. Your situation is, well, as the doctor said, a first. So different, that we figured it would be good to meet with you to see if we could help.' He leans back, hands placed open on his knees.

A friend in a time of need, just here to help and I don't believe a word. His eyes are too tense, body too stiff, too acting casual.

'So no one from our government? Bi-lateral co-operation, all that stuff.'

Dan leans forward into my question. The doctor's head shifts from quiet observer to alert, eyes very still.

'Your folks here thought with the doctors expertise and my offices networks, we would be best placed to offer advice.'

The lie is so smooth and said with such charming sincerity that Barbara nods her head. Dan smiles at this acceptance. I smile and watch his eyes.

A ranger in our small country is a jack-of-all-trades. As part a small national team I covered most parts of the job, search and rescue, medical assistance, fire fighter, even customs on islands. I up held the various laws that applied to public lands. I worked with most government agencies including the military over the years. Lessons on border control and who does what, were I learnt through simple on the job experience. Small countries means small departments, which means we help each other, cooperation teaches lessons.

Countries are very careful with borders and who works within them. Nobody works on another's patch and interviews citizens without a minder. Nobody. It's the rules of the game. One of my lessons learnt, trust is as far as one can see. Often a lot less.

Two things are at very obvious to me. Dan is lying. And worse, Barbara and I are very much alone. I make a decision.

'OK, excuse me. Bathroom stop.' Dan nods as if in allowance. The doctor watches his mouse walk away. There is silence as eyes follow my exit to the hall.

My return, minutes later, is all most comical, but not quite. As I come through the door, the shotgun that I have levelled at Dan, says most of what I want to know. A hand jumps to his side. I had wondered if he was armed, fits the type. At my shouted stop! He stays still. The doctor has hardly moved completely stunned, mouth in a circle.

Barbara has twisted towards me 'What the hell?' shocked but calm, good.

'Trust me here.' My eyes don't move from the main threat. Dan is right handed, his mug of tea taught me that.

'Left hand, take the gun out very, very slowly. This holds 8 shots, I use it regularly. Doctor, not a word or movement.' The shotgun is steady.

'Home invasion people with guns get shot, even in this small country Dan. I warn you just once.' His left hand moves slowly and places the small black automatic on the coffee table in front of him. Barbara's eyes widen. The doctor looks stunned.

'Hands behind your head, you too, doctor.' In a louder voice I snap 'Do it now!' The gun stays steady as they both comply. Dan's face is blank but the gears are moving. Surprise gone, just angry. A dangerous man.

'Barbara slowly, please pick up the pistol, put in my pocket and ring 111. Police. Let's get some help here, enough lies. They can test the truth of things.' My words are precise and clear, a sensible path.

Barbara nods steps forward and grabs the pistol keeping eyes fully on Dan, then slips it into my right pocket. She picks up her cell from the bench top, happy to see a plan in action and starts tapping. As Dan shakes his head his hands shift and I twitch the barrel of the gun upwards. Hands return to their place.

'No, look we can work through this misunderstanding.' His tone calming, but intense, ignoring Dan I motion with the gun.

'Shut up! Doctor stand up and go and stand with your back to the door. Now please. Now or I will shoot you.' The doctor shakily stumbles to his feet and does what I ask. There has been movement outside, an internal light has come on and the other people in the vehicle are moving.

'Dan very carefully take out your phone. You will tell your friends to get back into your car. No sharp movements.' I move, so that Dan and the doctor are blocking me from line of sight of the door.

'Do it or I remove your leg.' I have dropped the barrel of the gun. Dan is tapping numbers, face cold anger. He has dropped the ball, a professional caught by an amateur.

'Bill, police want to know what is happening.' Barbara looks scared eyes wide with the scene in her lounge but is still in control.

'Tell them we have armed intruders and that I have them at gun point. We need immediate help.' She nods and relays the message. 'On their way.'

Dan's people have answered. He is snapping answers. I listen.

'He has us covered. Get back in the car. He can see you. Local police are coming. Yes.' I motion with the gun.

'Enough! Stop now!'

Dan looks at me and quickly rushes one word. 'Confirmed.'

The blast of the shotgun is very loud. The blue couch takes the shot and filling explodes into the room, a white cloud of dust surrounds the blast area. The doctor squeals, hands jump to his face. Dan is on his feet but stock still, face pale. He taps the phone.

'Jesus. Bloody. Christ!' Barbara is angry and has turned towards me. Face flushed in shock. I haven't moved, eyes fixed on Dan. He is silent.

'He came here armed. This is no game. This bastard and his buddies are dangerous. Now they know we are too.' She listens, still angry, I flick her a glance. She is still shocked but gets it. The doctor is white and shaking now leaning against the closed door.

Dan's phone hums in his hand.

'Tell them you are fine, that it was a warning shot. Nothing else or you do lose that leg.' He nods and he does as he is told. Lesson learnt, maybe, I think.

'Doctor slide down and sit on the floor, before you fall down.' He is looking very unwell. He simply bobs his head sinks to the floor, back against the glass. I move across the room slowly, the gun focused on Dan and sit on a dining chair, away from the view from outside. Dan watches me warily.

'Sit down. OK, now we discuss what to do with you. The police are coming and not just police, Armed Offenders are like your SWAT teams, they know their job and they will lock you up. Maybe me as well but you have more to lose than I do, I would guess. At least two foreign nationals armed and attacking people.' Dan snorts shaking his head.

'Who will they believe? You did bring a pistol. Not legal here. The doctor will break under questioning, you know that.' The point is made. Dan shifts a look at the doctor. Not much to see. I look at Barbara she is unsure and stretched but she gets the logic.

'Jug on, eh?' She looks at me, sees the calming that I am looking for and starts the simple process. As I continue Dan has relaxed slightly but still tense.

'This is about to become an international incident, your bosses won't be pleased. You never know, you may even get jail time and you will be on your own. The doctor may be sent home, he's probably too famous. The cops aren't far away, if I let you go then you are in the clear. You have minutes. So I ask again. Who do you work for and why are you here and what did you confirm?'

Barbara is watching and shaking her head. She pours water into cups.

Dan shrugs and sits back in his chair. He knows the time is ticking and he needs to move, he also thinks I will push further if I have to.

'OK. I do work for NASA and yes it is an offshoot, we were put together to find any solid actual real evidence of outer space life forms, Unidentified Anomalous Phenomena. Check google. We monitor as many places as we can. I was in Australia at a monitoring station. A message came through and we got the Gulf Stream to bring us over. We picked up our contact, the doctor, and here we are.'

The Gulf Stream is one of the fastest private jets in the world, lots of money. "Us. We". A team in other words. Dan is being very careful with his information.

I nod.

'OK, what did you confirm? Be quick.' Dan shifts in his seat but the "in for a penny" in his eyes is enough for him to answer.

'I confirmed that this, you, what you have in you is real.....umm' He tappers off reflecting on my arm his eyes resting on it, questions obvious. Again I nod.

'One last thing before I let you go. Why the little task force? Why not just be up front? Why not just ask me if I would help, be cooperative? Surely that would be simpler?'

My anger is showing. Dan's eyes are very direct he leans forward, honesty for the first time maybe I think. His voice is cold, the soldier watching his guinea pig, the sniper on his target.

'You are the very first person ever, ever to be the proof that others, aliens call them what you like, exist. Anything that needs to be done to study you, will be done.' Now here's the truth of it.

Barbara drops a cup from her hand and it shatters on the tile floor. Then her phone rings. I sit the shotgun across my lap. Dan moves in his seat. I gesture with the barrel of the shotgun. Listening takes place.

'OK here are the rules; you won't come back. If you do, bad things will happen. Simple.' The phone is still ringing.

'That is the police call, I suggest you go.' Dan starts to speak. 'No, nothing to discuss. Just leave.' I stay seated but level the gun again. Dan stands turns and puts a hand under the doctor's armpit.

Barbara answers the phone. 'Hello, yes?' And listens.

Dan pulls the doctor to his feet, opens the door and glances at me as he pushes him through the doorway, an unhappy man. Doors open and then close. Lights come on and they reverse rapidly down the driveway. I am wondering if that was wise. Barbara walks over bits of foam and stuffing and hands me the phone. She is shaking her head, at a loss on what has happened, close to break down but holding up.

'Yes?' I ask. I start the first of long explanations. Our police are not gun tolerant.

Finally, after many assurances of being unarmed the police come up the drive, we are told to lay on the ground and are roughly handcuffed under torch light. We are pulled to our feet. We wait as the house is searched, then we are brought inside. Handcuffs are removed. Barbara glares at the policeman and snaps.

'We are the bloody victims!' He has a no care look.

The shotgun that I had unloaded is confiscated. My gun safe relieved of more ammunition. The questions are ongoing. We are taken to each end of the house and separately interviewed. Statements are taken. Barbara and I had quickly discussed what to say: People came with a gun. I confronted them with the shotgun. I fired a shot but missed. They ran. I was in shock so didn't follow. Dan's pistol is waiting in the compost bin under potatoes peelings and tea bags, this I don't pass on to the police.

The senior sergeant is unhappy. I can see why but I am not in the mood to help. He doesn't believe our version of events. His gut feeling is; something is wrong.

But our stories match and we just keep repeating the same mantra. His dark grey eyes are intense as we sit watching each other.

Gary arrives, the village grapevine of 'lights and police' has made him feel guilty I think. He has obviously been through the "who are you, sir'" at the police cordon. Those magical words "family doctor" still work in our rural areas. The senior sergeant has a sour look as Gary explains who he is and that we are his patients. Thought he might be able to help. I say Barbara could use some of that help with her shock. Gary looks at the sergeant who snaps an OK. Gary heads to the other lounge where Barbara is under guard.

The foam flecks of the couch look very white against his black police issue boots.

'I believe you are lying to me Bill.' He is looking into my eyes from another seat at the dining table. I shrug but say nothing.

'Something happened here that you won't explain,, I think you should. Home invasions don't just happen here. Not here. Not for no reason.' He says, very quietly, steadily. His eyes are boring.

'I think you know the people that were here. They may come back.' I am blank at the suggestion and inadvertently yawn. It really has been a long day and my exhaustion is showing.

'OK. But I don't like being used and I think that is what has happened.' He studies me quietly, waiting.

'Right, I am thinking about charging you with reckless discharge of a firearm.'

I almost laugh, having been in his shoes I know that proving this in court will be almost impossible. But I look back and just nod with the gravity required.

'Nothing to say?' There are four other police in various states of disguised boredom in the room waiting as well. I shake my head and stare back. Minutes pass. He then nods, stands and issues pack up orders. His men head out the door towards their vehicles. After the last one has left, he motions to the couch.

'That could be you soon. Yeah, I know you pulled the trigger. But they will come back and I have your shotgun.' his eyes are mocking and we both look at the damage, he turns and walks out the door. The room is still as the sound of vehicles leaving comes through the open door. I turn and go in to the lounge at the end of the hall. Barbara is on a couch looking washed out. Gary sits on the other. I sit down beside her and put my arm around her. She leans into me.

'Sleep I think? What a bloody night.' Her hair brushes my cheek as she nods agreement.

'I'll head off.' Gary stands and looks at me. Was this to do with me?' He asks quietly, his stance humble.

'Yes. You put us in the shit. Thanks.' I stop, it's too late, I am too tired. He opens his mouth then closes it, nods dumbly and walks up the hall.

'OK, bed.' Half order, half talking to myself, I stand and Barbara joins me. She goes to our bedroom. I do a careful round of locking everything. Lights are turned out. In the dark I retrieve Dan's pistol from its compost bed, wipe it and as Barbara goes into the ensuite, I slip it under my pillow. I twitch as Barbara gets into bed. I had nodded off, sidelight on.

'Sorry I scared you so much today. Not sure I went about it the right way. Too bull headed and too late now.' She moves her head on the pillow getting comfortable and slowly replies.

'Hmph, yes, scared the hell out of me. I know why, I know how you work. The doctors face was a treat.' She laughs softly.

'Dan was lying, I saw it in him. I wondered what you would do. You never liked that couch.' I laugh and then hear her breathing deeper into sleep. As I also head into oblivion I thank the gods for such a woman. Sleep.

Chapter 5

I am back in the curved room, back in the chair. My arm locked into its seat. The Hieroglyphs seem to pulse with the speed as they move around the wall. They slow then speed up again, the wall behind them is a backdrop of hundreds of thousands of stars, galaxies, clusters of clusters in rainbow colored darks and lights, the everything of everything seems on show.

My mind is an empty well. The little drop of all my life experiences in my world, is at the bottom, a lining of knowledge as the flood pours in. The pulse of the Hieroglyphs is a message in itself. A world thousands of light years away has gone. This is their accumulation, this is the vial of knowledge passed to whomever, in the vastness of universes everlasting, ever expanding. Time passes and their reasoning fills me. I remain as I was but changed. I know the why. This knowledge I am given is a minor prologue of what is stored.

Millions of years of evolution, they were the same as us but different, better and worse. But how does one compare in the incomparable? The stream becomes a river of knowledge flowing into a pool. The pool is deep, swirling and finally still. I am the pool. My surroundings are now clear as I sit in the chair. I see and I know some things, but not all. There were sailors at the tiller of a lifeboat that belongs to a long lost people. The opening key to this boat is the bracelet I wear. Left by the last of his people on a tiny grain of sand in the universe's sea. My planet is the grain. This boat sits unseen waiting on the tides edge and I wear the key. This boat is a library of the people. I have the key but I am not the keeper. The bracelet is the bridge but there are things that don't match. We are not what they expected. They did not expect humans with their deep flaws and scared emotive reasoning.

'Bill, Bill are you awake, Bill?' The concern in Barbara's questioning is obvious. As the world around me clears, I know it is different. I am different. Right now I am oddly groggery and slow to respond. My body is not functioning well.

'Uhmmm yes sorry. Sorry just bit slow, slept in?' My reply is slurred. I am on one of the couches in the lounge. I don't understand.

'Slept in! you've been asleep for 3 days. We moved you for better care. I had Gary here. He talked about hospital and coma.' Her agitation and relief are mixed. I struggle and sit up. She sits on the bed and we hug rocking slightly. We both need reassurance against the unknown. My bodily needs shout at me. I struggle to my feet and am shaky. I sit trying to get myself to upright.

'Bathroom. Shower and food. Sorry I have scared you, again.' She looks deeply steadily into my eyes.

'What happened? The bracelet, right?' I nod and disentangle myself from her and the bedding and head to the bathroom. As I towel myself off I see the ridges are now a tattoo of golden hieroglyphs translucent on and in the skin, I read them:

All paths are a circle. Knowledge is the key.

Barbara comes into the bathroom.

'You've lost weight, oh.'

She is checking to see if I am OK, the last few days have been hard on her. As I dry myself she sees the tattoo, she runs her fingers over it. She peers at me, her eyes questioning and curious. Her eyes flicker to mine and back to the tattoo, a stillness takes her. She looks into my eyes.

'You know what it means!' A realization, her eyes widen as they shift from mine to the hieroglyphs and back.

'The dreaming.' She stops again and asks the question.

'What does it say?'

'All paths are a circle. Knowledge is the key.'

I speak the words in English then in the language of a long lost people I will never meet. The strange sounds hang in the air. I am conscious that this maybe a first on this planet. Barbara stares, mouth open, shock obvious. Tears run down my cheeks in a depth of loss that gripes my soul. I shake with the grief. Barbara holds me in non-comprehension but knowing through instinct it is the right thing.

'Get dressed, your lunch is on the table.' She says it softly, leaves and closes the door. She understands I need moments to just be. I am certainly hungry. Simple salad sandwiches with tea, I notice Barbara has sugared the tea. Old wives tails do work, I think. Barbara's phone hums and she answers.

'Hi Gary. Yes he is awake. Yes, seems fine. Just a little slow from being in bed so long.' She makes 'do I want to talk' gestures, I shake my head and wave the idea away, she nods.

'No, he does seem OK. I'll get him to call later. He's in the shower.' An old reliable excuse.

'OK. Thanks very much for your help. Bye.' She taps the phone. 'He is OK you know. He has been to check twice.' I nod. I don't necessarily agree but Barbara has a point. Anyway she had support while I was comatose, a good thing I suppose. I let my thoughts about Gary ride.

'Any visitors?' I am asking about Dan and his crew. Barbara shakes her head with a, no just Gary, but she knows exactly what I am asking. I carry on.

'I need to tell you what happened in the dream. It's important for you to know. Things will really change now. I may make decisions that don't really make sense or I don't have time to explain. I need to try to give you context, at least, I hope it will.'

My tone is serious, she turns, agitated, to the bench and tosses a 'tea first' over her shoulder. I quietly walk up the hall and settle on the couch looking into the far hills and wait. Barbara brings two cups in, passes me one and puts her feet up. I start.

It is a journey of re-describing the dream, how it felt. Barbara says little apart from the occasional nod and a hum. I continue, balancing my words. It is important to me she has some understanding.

'So these people sent out lifeboats, not full of people, but of knowledge. Their knowledge, millions of years of it. The part that I now hold, is how to open the door of the cube, where there is a guardian of the knowledge.' I pause, tired but somehow clearer in my explanation to her and me.

'The boats are a gift to the universe and whoever can use them. But the guardian does the choosing.'

Barbara shifts, reaches out for her half-drunk cold tea and sips.

'Guardian? Alien?' I shake my head slowly, trying to understand and explain.

'No, I think more the other side of the link to the information, yet oddly part.......' I falter with lack of understanding. Barbara watches but doesn't push.

'Where were these people from?' She uses the word people like I do, Alien doesn't seem to apply. I reflect on this briefly but then I know them as not human but not alien.

'A long way, 100,000 light years, maybe more. They could move through space a lot faster than we have dreamed. Space is very, very, big. Beyond imagining. Our closest system is four and a half light years.' I watch a duck floating on the lake.

'Their home world was a long way from anywhere, this stopped their move from their planet. Their sun was dying. By the time they reached the industrial point so that they could move into space, it was too late. The population was too large with not enough resources, distances too far and they hadn't found a world that they could actually live on. We have exactly the same problem. We can't live on another planet in our solar system without huge infrastructure or some way to limit radiation. The issues humans face are immense. We can't even put a base on our own moon.' I shrug at where we are as a race.

'How many boats did they send and what happened to the person in the boat?'

'They sent five hundred and fifty five boats to all points, some to closer galaxies. Some to far ones, some to further star clusters, others straight into the deep black of space. Some are still travelling and may do forever.' This thought saddens me, forever travelling to no destination.

'The number is part of their solar systems rotation. Their year, five hundred and fifty five days around their cooling star.' I speak the name and Barbara shakes her head in wonder.

'Thinking and knowing their world has gone. I just ....Odd.' She finishes lamely but is right, it's so hard for the mind to grasp.

'The person on the boat arrived long ago. Before humans arrived here on this part of our planet. He was old. Their life support slows but doesn't stop aging indefinitely. This planet they could have lived on. He came ashore here. And I guess died, I don't know what happened to him. His last entry was his going to walk on this new world. I presume he buried the bracelet. Who knows. You cannot enter the boat without it.'

'Why take it off?' Barbara gives a quizzical look. I continue but for me, us, the hardest part of this explanation is yet to come. I am dreading this and torn over my next words.

'The boat, what I see, is a transparent cube. It is a place unto its self. It has stayed stationed above our planet for over 1000 years. Every 3 months it comes and waits for its sailor to return, unseen, by the people who live here. Once the bracelet is worn the boat comes alive. There is a type of symbiosis. The sailor is the last part of the puzzle. The boat knows another being may come. That being may have needed programming to the boat and to see if they were worthy.' Barbara finishes the sentence.

'And that being is you, Oh worthy one.' There is slight grin on her face and she grimaces.

'What do you mean taught? Programmed? Is it a robot?' She is curious but unhappy as things are turning unpleasant for her. This is reflected in her eyes. I get it, she echoes my feelings.

'The principles I don't know. The new knowledge I have is a lot but it is also partly unconnected, some stuff just doesn't match. It isn't robotic or programmed more like a gel in a battery, organic but not alive. That's the storage system. The knowledge I have been passed doesn't cover the make-up. What I have been given is part of their reasoning and but little context. I do know it needs its sailor as the part of the process. The bracelet is the first bridge to the memory bank and the boat. I know I am being simplistic. It's rather like a person driving a car. You know to a degree how it works but not the detail. But that will be in the library. Countless years of a peoples' knowledge. I do mean vast. There are other things that the boat can do but this feels like it's veiled. I have an awareness but not full understanding.'

I stop, waiting for her comment. She is staring at an old oil painting given to her by an aunt who has since passed away. An old man caste in shadow with his hands bathed in light. She starts to speak slowly then gains momentum.

'So what you are describing, is a place where every piece, vestige and spark of knowledge was held, from earliest mankind to right now and you could ask it any question. Is that pretty close?' I nod, great synopsis.

'But this is the complete knowledge of a whole people that is new to human kind. There will be things that we have never imagined. Look, their science is way beyond our knowledge, maybe medical advancements, space travel .....I mean everything, just everything will be different. The possibilities are huge and ......' She stops as she sees it. The danger. I nod and put words in her mouth.

'Who gets this? Who controls it? Control is power and who do you trust?' I stop, then gather the threads of thought.

'Governments are nationalist by their very make up. Their people put them in power to protect their own countries interests. The United Nations isn't a world body, its controlled by a handful of so-called super powers. Humanity's goodwill has always been limited to personal ends. If this was given to one power, what is the likelihood would they use it for their own ends?'

I slow and stop as we examine the dilemma. The mountain on the horizon. She hums as she gazes at the old man and says.

'Ultimate power corrupts ultimately.'

'Yeah, exactly, again who does one trust?'

The day is over-caste and the light is fading. As I watch through the window a duck lands on the lake on out stretched webbed feet, announcing an arrival with one loud quack. I go into the kitchen, get a beer and pour it into a glass, it tastes better in a glass, Barbara a lime and water, she rarely drinks alcohol. I place the glass on the small table next to her. She is still looking at the old man but I know her mind is wandering to places she won't like. She looks at my arm.

'I am beginning to hate that thing. We had an easy life, a simple one.' Her wane look says it all and we sit quietly as the room darkens, sipping from our glasses.

'One more thing.' I speak carefully aware of my words as if speaking them brings more reality to our situation.

'The bracelet has the power to protect its self and the wearer.' Barbara's head shifts quickly in my direction.

'What? What do you mean? What? Makes you a superman or something? Come on!' Her disbelief is obvious, her voice slightly hollow, sick of trying fathom so much change.

I get up and turn on a sidelight. I am not sure exactly what is going to happen. In my head I know parts of what it will let me do. I think, but stepping into the enormity of what I have been shown is another. I touch the ridged tattoo in the prescribed sequence.

'Well, what I learnt should be, this:' I am standing in front of a large mirror we have to reflect the view, side on I can see Barbara and my reflection. I disappear. Strange. I am still in the room and can see but there is no reflection. Invisible? Yes! Wow!

'Christ! Bill! Where are you? Are you here?' She sits back in in shock trying to take in the impossible.

'Yes, I am here and yes. I am fine.' I tap the tattoo and reappear. Shaking my head. I stand looking at her. 'That's so bloody strange. I felt nothing but I just can't see myself.'

Barbara is looking at me in complete wonder.

'Come and stand beside me.' I ask her. There is fear in her eyes but she complies.

'Hold my hand.' As she does, I tap the tattoo and our reflections disappear. I wait for a couple of minutes, tap the code again and we are back. Complete magic!

We sit on our couches contemplating this. Barbara is the first to speak.

'I've seen it but still can't grasp it.....can't believe it. Real Sci-Fi. Strangely, really frightening but unbelievable.' Her eyes are glued to mine.

What else, I mean what else is there? What can, it...ummm you, actually do?

'Well, the bracelet should let me defend myself. Laser thing really. I need to try this stuff. I guess I need to play with it. In the dream I walk into the water but I was walking, on it. Well that's how it felt.'

I am feeling stupid and strangely embarrassed. I feel that I am lying to her but I aren't. I can't. The world we have been forced to enter is playing with my mind. So much has happened I feel I need more control. I look at her.

'I need to go to the boat, it is waiting on the beach and I need to be awake. I need to take charge of what is happening to me, to us. Does that make sense? What do you think?'

Barbara's opinion has always mattered to me and us. She has a way of reviewing my ideas, giving them the correct form or screwing them up and putting a stupid idea in the bin or just laughing at them. Reality bites! Whichever way, we get a consensus, we have a path to follow, again it's teamwork. A partnership that works.

'OK when? I mean what time of day. If walk you into the water, disappear and someone sees you?' She shrugs her shoulders, point made. I nod in agreement.

'Well, I will use the bracelet so no one will see me.' She raises her eyes with an I forgot look. Hardly surprising.

'But you make a good point. I am very new at this thing. I will make mistakes. OK, early morning?' We both nod ascent, a plan is made. Small steps.

We have a trying-to-be-normal night, salad from the garden, steak on the BBQ. Simple things that have been the flow of our life in this place. Forced change creates unpleasant ripples on one's pond. We watch a game show with a smooth host, slipping his banter into the contestants dropped thoughts, oiling the programs wheels. The world news reminds me there is a world outside our little town. Our own issues are part of another whole. And I wonder about the overhanging truth. Things will never be normal again.

I pour another handcrafted beer into a frosted glass.

It is early morning, there is a misty rain falling as we leave our back gate. We have dark raincoats on. I wanted Barbara with me. The lack of contact from Dan and his friends has left a warning in my mind. He, or people like him, will return or they will be here somewhere, watching. Angry men are dangerous.

Our plan is simple enough. I go, find the boat and explore it to give reality to what the dreams have delivered. While I believe, given what I carry, I really need to see. Humans are strange things or maybe it is just me I wonder, as I close the gate quietly. We turn into a cycle path that runs between the houses, one of the many that cross our neighborhood. Most of the houses are empty. The owners in the city paying mortgages. Where we cross the road from one path to another, a dark vehicle sits a hundred meters away.

The watchers really are watching. A door opens and a figure slips out. We disappear from their view in the bushes surrounding the path but he won't be long. I take Barbara's hand and pull her off the path.

Quickening steps can be heard approaching. I give her a quiet, ready? I tap the bracelet. A dark figure swings into view. Barbara is grasping my hand tightly, he must see us, my mind is yelling at me, he passes us at a steady trot oblivious to us. I note he is looking side to side as he goes, checking shadows. We wait then I pull Barbara on to the path and we walk slowly following his direction. The rain is still falling lightly and the sky is starting to brighten with dawn. Ahead of us our watcher has stopped at a four way junction. He is accessing his best move. He turns right with a phone out and jogs off. Good, we wanted to go straight anyway.

'OK? ' I ask.

'Well it works. It's not a magic mirror.' I grin. I can't see her, only feel the pressure of her hand. We are talking in semi whispers. 'Yes, weird to get confirmation like that, funny not seeing your feet isn't it? I'll turn it off soon.'

We keep going through the junction; our friend is out of sight. We cross another road. As we reach the broad grassed area, the sound of the surf is around us. The sea lays just over the sand dunes. The sea is a rolling calm and the sound of individual waves can be heard. To our left a number of pines are dotting the shore. We walk towards them hand in hand, the surf murmuring.

As we reach the pines I stop and look behind us. We appear to be alone and I tap my arm. We are real again. Barbara looks at me and grins.

'Now that is really bloody weird! I walk but no feet!' I laugh. 'Now where?' She seems to be enjoying the adventure. The smell of the pines just taints the air.

'Towards the point on the beach at the water's edge. I don't know if you will see it. Actually, thinking about it, you won't. I don't know if you can come with me. There are things here I am not sure about.

What I thought was, you wait in the scrub under the pines and watch, out of sight. Once I get a real handle on what we are dealing with then I come back and we reassess. Does that work?'

It is a genuine question and I do want her to know our team is still working. I look from where we have come but can't see any one around, even the early morning dog walkers are absent, rain lightly drifts.

'OK let's go.' She leads the way down the sandy path in the small set of dunes, through a gap and on to the beach. We turn left again and walk a hundred meters or so. Above a low part in the bank of sand, where dunes meet the high-tide mark, there are a set of low wind-blown bushes.

'I think this is the right spot, can you wait here?' I ask her looking at the beach. She nods and hugs me. 'Be careful. Please!'

I look up and down the beach to check for walkers then turn, face the sea and tap the sequence on my arm. The square appears before me sitting on the waves. It is an icy blued translucent cube. Through it I can see islands in the far distance. As I walk towards it over the wet sand, a gull calls a single cry down the beach. I am now walking on the water. There is no difference in feeling through my sneakers than walking on the sand. The tall doorway is open before me. I turn and look towards the shore. The beach is framed as in the dream. I can just see Barbara is perched under a dark green bush.

Chapter 6

I turn and walk into the entrance, a door closes and the sound of the sea and surf is gone. Silence.

I am in a hall shaped space and light is coming from the ceiling. The walls are dull green, the floor a brown color, earthy somehow. The room is about the length of our lounge. I feel strange making the comparison but somehow I am calmed. In front of me, floating in the air. are the same hieroglyphs as the ones on my tattoo, bigger. This word I can read.

'Welcome.' These fade as another set appears. 'Follow the light.'

The symbols are replaced with a blue green globe. The globe moves through a door that slides opens in the wall. I follow and walk through into another room, which is also a corridor. There seems to be storage either side of this room. I am unsure. In front of me another door slides open. I am in the room I have seen in my dreams.

The chair is in the middle of the room. The wall opposite is curved and it is like looking into a vast colored cosmos. It seems every part of the universe is shown on an infinite screen in four dimensions. The globe rises about the chair and I hesitate then take the seat. As I settle into place, my arm fits into the arm of the chair. Symbols again race, flash and pulse cross the screen then slowly a phrase appears.

Which reads simply. 'Who are you?'

My new knowledge comes into play. I press two buttons on the chair and roll a globe that is seated under my hand, in the right arm of the chair. I use the globe to create symbol in the air over a floating cube, a miniature of the outside, that has appeared. I am now connected to this ship. I sit back in the chair wondering about the next part of this journey but let the communication begin. There is no fear, I am not sure why. I had made a decision so, just do it.

When reflecting on this step, late at night as I stare into the black, into the recent past. I have wondered why I took this incredible leap of simple trust. I will never know. That this situation is beyond strange did not occur to me. I trusted that it, the next 'now' will be OK. I believe that this is a fickle part of the human element that is a deep buried psychic fingerprint. Humans believe the future will be better than before. Hope is in the future. Or the very next minute.

I am connected to the ship but not its library. Not exactly a computer, not exactly a library and not exactly, Artificial Intelligence but an amalgam of all three. This is the ships core, that has travelled, supported its pilot and bided its time over our planet, waiting.

My connection to the chair starts a sharing, oddly calming, a chat between two friends trying sort of a point of view. My whole of life experiences and knowledge are seen and stored. There is no analysis, no judgment. It is simply a cut and paste of who and what I am. As my experiences are taken, a new flow of knowledge arrives within me.

Much information that flows into me is beyond my ken or doesn't match my world, it comes and I am blank. Pieces of a jigsaw that do not fit; I know things that are unknowable or understandable. The vastness of knowledge before me, my mind cannot take in. The exchange is limited to my small capacity. Puzzles of knowing, float, then recede.

The wall before me is changing and in this change I recognize our solar system. The moon is closest in three dimensions with the planets and their moons, as I look at each one they become, larger, easier to see. If my focus stops to inspect one planet, it slowly becomes more defined, features become more clear, like a telephoto lens slowly zooming in.

My sight line is from the earth, through our system, past our sun towards the Ort Cloud at the real edge of our system. Beyond this lays the further infinity of deep space. My eyes shift to the sun. The brightness is dulled, I can see the swirling cloudy mists of heat and vast arms of reddened energy reaching away into the void of space. My sight moves again to Saturn with its multiple moons and its definable surface gas. The rings come into view; ice and mini moons.

As my view widens back into the room, symbols arrive in my view and they are in my language, English. The partnership is now confirmed. I understand and am humbled that the bridge of two species separated by thousands of light years is crossed.

'Welcome Bill.' Will ever float in my mind's eye.

I tap 'Hello' on my tattoo. There are so many questions but I simply write.

'What do I call you?' The reply floats before me:

'Bill, the best label that would suit is Island.'

The words float then softly fade as the space view behind sits waiting, the longer sentence surprises me, I wonder if the more I communicate the better 'Island' will get.

'Hello Island. Do you know where your pilot is?' The answer comes back a touch quicker.

'The engineer left 1186 of your planet revolutions around your home star ago. They did not come back. The engineer must have passed into the void.'

The words sadden me, I would have liked to have met this engineer who travelled so very far, who passed into the void, as we all do. As I ask another question I also start to wonder about time, how long I have been and how Barbara is doing.

'How long would you wait for another engineer, Island?'

'If the controller you carry is destroyed, Bill. Island will go into the closest star. Into the void.'

I am shocked. 'Why?' I tap quickly. The reply is again quicker.

'The controller is the first key to communicate with Island. Information stored here cannot be used without enough intelligence to use the key. It is the rule.'

I sit and watch the words fade. The answer has raised many more questions. But I feel I need time to digest what has happened here and to me. I am tired. I am a stranger here. While I know of them, I am not them. I carry some knowledge but am still very human. I feel small and alien, a dichotomy that isn't lost on me. Simply I want to go home which seems close yet far away. I have walked off our beach into a close distant world.

'Island, how did you know we, I mean our race was worthy?' The words that float in front of me are another startling shock.

'Without searching a races memories Island would not know. Your race is questionable. There are issues that your memory holds that are troublesome, Bill. In your world there are the balances within it that Island needs more knowledge. Island requires more information on your world. You are right for this task of opening the knowledge between us.'

I tap the words 'Thank you' as I watch the words float away as the solar system becomes further into my focus behind it. I feel smaller still, completely minute in the vastness before me. I write:

'Island, I need time to work through what has happened here. I shall return.'

'Goodbye Bill.' Floats before me.

Moments later I stand and walk down the island's corridor and as I reach the door I tap the sequence to make me unseen.

As I walk up the beach, the sound of the surf and gulls remind me of where I am. I feel numb with thoughts of what this encounter has laid before me. The tide has moved up towards the small dunes. I see Barbara standing by the bushes and she is not alone.

The dog walker I had run into a few days ago is standing with Harry the dog, his wife absent. He and Barbara are chatting. Damn I think. Harry's tongue flops side to side as his head follows the conversation; his tail slowly wags waiting for acknowledgement. Unseen I walk past them up the gap between the dunes and look around me through the open pines. There are no other people in sight. I lean against a larger pine, the rough bark gives me an odd sense of being grounded, of being back in the real world.

I tap my arm and become seen. I then walk back through the gap towards Barbara and her new companion. Barbara face shows shock, relief and a stoic grimace as she sees me.

'Hi.' I don't know what else to say, I lift my shoulders in a sorry but we have company shrug, which she interprets with a limited nod.

'Ah, there you are.' Barbara quips brightly.' Bill, this is Neil. One of us locals.' Neil turns and then recognizes me. The rude chap on the beach, his eyes go from happy to meet you to and oh it's you, in a slip of time. I am vaguely amused but his presence I find frustrating but then it is a public beach.

'Ah yes. Hello.' He nods vaguely then he just can't help the question. 'Are you feeling better?' Barbara's eyes rise in her own question.

'Yes, a lot better. Thanks.' I turn my head to Barbara. 'It was that bleeding after the operation. Bit of a shock really. Gave us both a fright. I may have been a bit short, sorry.' As I deliver this lie and apology rolled into one, Neil brightens. Barbara nods in agreement, eyes still, one eyebrow raised. Neil leaps on to the topic. Well-worn I am guessing.

'Ah, they can be bloody hard. I've had two. Won't go into them, bit unpleasant but they can be longer than you expect to get over.' He pauses waiting for a query to expand his details. We both are quiet. I pat Harry's head to change my gaze, bobbing my head in agreement. Neil moves on with his thoughts.

'Yes, it can be a bit of a road but you come through you know. Yes, quite hard.' The words run down and he arrives at a new subject not wanting to lose his new audience.

'Shame about that fire this morning.' He offers this into the breach. 'Real shame. The whole house has gone, I understand, owners must be very upset.' This banal observation at this loss of someone's home annoys me but he carries on.

'Yes, siren went up early, there was a lot of smoke. We could even see it from our place. Our neighbour's son is a volunteer. He told them the whole house is gone. Such a shame.'

He stops having placed this gift out to be discussed. I am now concerned, most of the local call outs are medical. A handy Facebook page tells us the job they do. Houses here rarely catch on fire here, too new, too modern, a section of my job was fires. I ask the question.

'Yes, a real shame.' I ask mimicking his banality. 'So where was the fire?' As he bends to scratch Harry's ears, he hums that he forgot such a vital tit-bit.

' Oh Lake road. Poor people.' Barbara and I stare at each other. I break the silence.

'Damn. Sorry, forgot. Time to take my pills. Should have done that half an hour ago.' Neil nods his head in understanding, pills are important. We all take pills, flits across his face. Looking at Barbara I say we should really get back. Barbara takes my arm, her grasp very firm. Neil's disappoint shows as we say goodbyes and the nice to have met. Harry is happy to move on though, nose already turned towards the freedom of the beach.

'Yes, well. Have a good day.' Follows us as we walk across the grass under the pines. We head towards one of the public paths between the houses. As the shrubs that line the walk enclose us. Barbara asks the obvious.

Chapter 7

'Our place?' Her tone has fear, anger and a touch of despair. My reply is hollow, angry and I echo her fear.

'Yes, I would guess so but we need to see.' We walk on. As we approach the street, which will end the relative cover of the path, I say tightly.

'We can't be seen.' She gives a quick grasp of agreement. I tap my arm and we are under cover.

As we walk I give Barbara a quiet run down of what I had experienced in my conversation within Island. I am having trouble absorbing the last hour. I had been on a craft that 'spoke'. Experiencing and believing can be very different. My words come in short bursts, trying to explain to myself, as much as Barbara. One car passes us, the driver obviously doesn't see us. He is a local we vaguely know and locals wave at locals, part of living here.

As we round the bend in our road towards our driveway, the various vehicles, a police car and a small fire truck tell us about the disaster that has occurred. I pull Barbara into the shelter of a fence.

'There are too many people around for Dan and his friends to be a problem. We need to know exactly what has happened, what we are left with. What do you think?' I wait I know she is struggling. A small voice says. 'We need to know.'

I tap my arm and we walk up the road. Oddly, Gary is the first to see us. He is coming out of the drive from our house.

'Christ, where the hell have you been?' He is highly agitated. Concern and worry etched on his face. I think I know why but try to put a cool face on it.

'We've been on the beach, what's going on?' As I say this, I see the tangled wreckage of our house, blackened and burnt. The roof has collapsed. There is a larger fire truck backed into end of the drive, uniformed figures are sorting hoses. Barbara has tears running down her face and she has buried her face in my shoulder lightly sobbing. Gary continues, he is angry with fear, the situation, the unknown.

'I thought you were in there.....we've been searching for you.' I stand stone still looking at the remains of our home. Memories, photos, family reminders, small beacons that had stitched our lives, and us, together. A handmade guitar, Barbara's Old Man painting, the list in my mind endless, connections with past lives that made us, us. I turn my head and look deep into Gary's eyes.

'You created this. I will never forget. Now. Fuck. Off.' Gary face is whitened with shock. He opens his mouth but I turn away as Barbara and I walk down the drive towards the ashes to see what is left. The fire crew, are rolling hoses, one looks up and sees the shock on our faces.

'Are you the owners?' I nod dumbly, the closer we get the worse it has become.

'Lucky you weren't in there. We thought you were. Had the doctor here. He thought you were.' He stops, watching us, he shifts with embarrassment. 'Look umm, sorry about the loss.' I look over his shoulder at the darkened mess, a police uniform comes into view.

The senior sergeant walks up and the fireman is happy to return to his task. The sergeant's gaze is very keen, as he looks from Barbara to myself.

'We thought you were in there, good to see you weren't. I tried your mobile just in case.' He looks at Barbara and can see the grief.

'Can I call someone?' She shakes her head eyes locked on the ashes. ' Ah no..no sorry. Shit, what a mess.' With a blank stare, Barbara uncouples herself and slowly walks towards our own private ruin. His eyes turn to me and asks the inevitable.

'Where were you both this morning?' His question is police mode but gentle. He is unsure. Playing good cop for now. Still watching Barbara. I reply.

'We went to the beach early, just for a walk, been a bit strange here. The surf was very calm for a change.'

He stands watching me closely, absorbing the reference to our call to his station.

'There were people very worried you were in there.' I nod and watch Barbara talking to a fireman. There are heads shaking, tears are falling.

'We are pretty sure the fire was set. We believe it's arson.' I look with a blank face then nod slowly. This is what I expected but the airing of the words still painful. He believes in what he saw. What that hole in the now incinerated couch told him. Somebody wants something. His instincts tell him there is a deeper story here.

'Did you see anyone at the beach?' The question is alibi seeking but fair enough, a man doing his job. I see the fire crew is about to leave. Job done. No sparks, wet everywhere. Fire contained, neighbors houses protected.

'Yes, a chap walking his dog. His name Neil, older guy, the dog's name is Harry. He was the one who told us there had been a fire. Not sure where he lives but it can't be far. He saw the smoke.' I look towards Barbara again.

'I need to take care of my wife.' As I move away, he says. 'We will be investigating who did this.' I look back.

'Good, find them, because right now I would be happy to shoot the bastards.' My vicious reply has surprised him, his eyes narrow.

'I will be in touch about a formal statement. Are you insured?' I glare at him but he is still doing his job, I guess. I steady myself.

'Yes, full replacement of the house and our stuff but not of the things that really matter. Thanks for your concern.' I turn abruptly on my heel and walk past the fire truck to Barbara.

The house is completely destroyed. Years of the small things that are the interwoven fabric of our lives, ash. Old bottles that I collected over the years can be seen blackened. The corrugated iron of the roof, a jumbled jigsaw that over lays everything.. The stove stands in the kitchen peeking through a mess of roofing.

I put my arm around her and we contemplate our little burnt world.

'We are OK. It's only a house. We can rebuild, just going to miss our stuff.'

Barbara is talking to me, and herself. This is the person that has always seen the bright side and walked into the future without fear, trepidation certainly, but knowing it will come out OK. Her simple strength has always amazed me and now all I can do is smile.

'What?' She asks with quick glare. I start to laugh and she knows what I am thinking.

'Oh, shut up.' The reply comes with a grin, we will be OK. We are, OK.

The next few hours is a strange mixed event of amazing acts of kindness, stupidity, nosey neighbors and dealing with long waits in phone queues. My truck was parked far enough away from the house to have survived. Barbara's car is black on one side, with bumpers dripping plastic, two tires blown. We both had our phones on us when we left the house.

I ring our neighbour Troy next door and he offers us his small house as a refuge for the meantime. An Air BNB rental that is ready for clients at any time. One of the fire crew had grabbed our car keys at the front door when they smashed their way in. Checking for occupants. He had also grabbed our laptops that had been on the table. He pulls them out of the cab of the fire truck with a 'I'd be lost without mine.' I could have kissed him.

My wallet has always lived under the seat of my truck. A blessing, which will stop the wait for a bank to re issue cards. It has been possibly a bad habit to leave it there but years ago I had got sick of it leaving it at home, hence it's spot under the seat, safer there than under the arm rest. Also under the seat is Dan's pistol. I had moved it there for no better reason than getting it out of the house. The swirl of people and phone calls became smaller. Troy has given me the code to his house. Barbara has been to town and bought some clothes, food and the small stuff of living; toothbrushes, towels and other things that make life tick. Life goes on but not the same.

As the sun sinks, we are sitting on the couch at Troy's one bedroom house. A forced holiday, I think. We have showered to get the smell of smoke out of heads more than clothes. We are both tired and happy with the quiet. Barbara offers her thoughts into the evening.

'Will they try again or was it a warning?' She is calm but the observation tells me where her thoughts have gone. I had noticed that she had locked the doors.

'I think a warning. It's a 'Be careful you are playing with the big boys' thing.' I shrug.

'I don't know but the next time they will try to take the guinea pig, I guess.'

She is shaking her head in what I think is anger and asks.

'When?'

'Soon, they will think we are in shock. They don't know really know what the bracelet is or any clue about Island. I wonder if what they don't know frightens them. I just have no idea. But we do need a plan.' The dusk is settling in. My phone rings. The insurance inspector will be over tomorrow but of course any final outcome will be once the police investigation is completed. Of course, I reply but the inference is hardly subtle. I say goodbye politely. Angered, I am now fidgety.

'You OK? Barbara asks reaching for her drink.

'Hmm.. they think I set the fire of course. Why would we? We had nothing to gain. I get why they are asking but just pisses me off just the same. They will look for reasons.' I stand.

'I am going for a walk just need to clear my head a bit......' Barbara interrupts with:

'And so you can check for watchers.' We look at each other. I lock the door on the way out.

The dusk is now night and the air still. I tap my arm and become unseen. There is a rustling in the hedge and a hedgehog appears rolling from side to side on stubby legs, nose snuffling for worms. Leaves twitch under its dark little paws. The gate is part open and I walk carefully up the driveway to the street. A dark vehicle is parked some 80 meters away and two figures can just be seen inside, the side window is open. I walk very slowly and quietly, as I get closer the conversation becomes clearer. I walk on to the grass off the path and stand and listen.

'I'll be glad to get home, my sister gets married in two weeks.' A male American voice just shooting the breeze.

'Oh yeah, I'd forgotten, he's a marine, right?' This voice I know. Evening Dan, I think.

'Yeah, just graduated from officer training, he's a good guy. I gave him the 'if you hurt my sister talk'. He told me to fuck off. I've known him for years. He's OK.' The speaker shifts in his seat. 'What time is it?' Dan replies with 9.10.

A late dog walker passes on the other side of the road. Two heads turn inspecting but no words are spoken. The walker passes on, the dog pulling her forward.

'The waiting we do in this job.' The speaker puts his head back on the headrest.

'Still a 10.30 go?' Dan grunts an affirmative reply. He is inspecting his phone and the light is illuminating his face, he taps a message.

I walk quietly back the way I have come. This time very carefully. I pull the gate closed and wrap the lose chain in place, a simple alarm. I unlock the door to Troy's place and relock it. I tap my arm. I can see my feet.

'That is really bloody weird to watch.' Barbara is still on the couch. She has watched me appear. The TV is going, sound low, a distraction. 'So any there?' I don't want to tell her but it is, what it is. I sit down.

'Yes two. They will be here about 10.30.' She looks at me head cocked on the side.

'You have a plan.' Telling me, not asking. 'A bit of one but not sure until I try it. I want you away from any danger. I don't want you hurt and if they do get me I may need help. If we are both caught, there's no cavalry.' She doesn't like it but gives me a carry on nod.

'OK, so I take you to Kevin and Susan's unseen and I want some cable ties from his shed. We know where the key is and they offered us the place anyway. Then when our friends arrive here, I will meet them.'

Barbara hums. She really doesn't like it but sees the logic. Kevin and Susan's beach house is on the other side of what was left of our house. They had long ago told us where their spare key was hidden just in case they needed something done. From time to time I had measured things for alterations or grabbed forgotten food from their fridge. Good people, they had offered their place until we had a plan but simply Troy offered first.

'We can't stay here, they will be here soon. These guys are dangerous. We attack or run.' Barbara nods, the resignation on her face plain.

Standing in Kevin and Susan's I tap my arm. We had turned lights out, left Troy's and quietly come through the front gate. The key was easy to find. The curtains are drawn but we don't turn any lights on. In the darkened room Barbara asks.

'How long will you be?' Sitting here alone isn't appealing, which I get.

'Not too long, not sure. Back as soon as I can.' She sits on a couch as I rummage through Kevin's bits cupboard. He keeps screws, nails, spare tools and what I was looking for, cable ties, great. I hug Barbara with a see you soon. She holds my face and looks into my eyes.

'You be bloody careful, you're the only one of you I've got.' I nod and tap my arm and am now unseen. As I leave, I lock the door. I walk quietly to my truck, which is still in our driveway and retrieve Dan's pistol from under the seat, which is slipped into a pocket. In the garden I pull out a garden stake that I have used to prop a tree we have planted. It is over a meter long, a solid batten. As I return to Troy's the moon is just starting to rise. There is a hedge that runs across two sides of the property that it protects from wind and neighbors. I sit down close to the gate and wait. A slight breeze is moving the air and a dog barks off in the distance. Time passes. The hedgehog is still shifting leaves. I enjoy my time waiting, being part of the sounds of the night. In the past few days I have had little time to think or plan.

Just as my formulation is on the horizon. The gate is rattled. I stand up, very tense.

Two figures, close to black, are in the drive. One shifts the chain on the gate, the other is standing back. The gate is opened and the chain carefully hooked in place. The first figure moves forward, the second three steps behind. As the second figure passes close to me I hit him with force in back of the head. This bastard burnt my house down. He collapses with a grunt face down. He is down but not out, at his moaning, the first figure jumps sideways and pulls a knife from his sleeve turning towards a danger he can't see. I wait. The hedgehog shifts leaves again and the figure moves towards the sound. He twists as my foot crushes a leaf.

His stroke is wide, the tip of the blade slashes my arm as my stroke takes him full in the throat, a dull thud and he is struggling on the ground both hands grasping at the damage, knife forgotten. The first figure is trying to rise. I kneel on his back and pull one, then the other arm behind him and cable tie his wrists. I then quickly tie his ankles. I recognize this is Dan.

I tap my arm, there are things I don't want these people to see or know. The one with the damaged throat is slowing his struggle, as I reach him, he stops moving and breathing. He has gone. I have killed. I am angry and hate what I feel, what I feel I have been forced to do. I am staggered at what I have done. I have no words. I sit on the grass, holding my arm and feel the blood run through my fingers. I look at this man who now won't be going to any wedding. I pick up his knife and cut a strip off my tee shirt and wrap my arm.

Dan starts to move and groan. He is testing his ties. I go over to him and roll him over on to his side. Struggling I pull him up against a fence post. I check quickly for weapons, another small automatic and a knife in the left sleeve, a dangerous man. I pocket them.

'You made this happen, Dan.' He moves again shaking his head trying to clear it.

'I said. You made this happen.' I repeat what I have said, angry and feeling very human and washed with self-loathing.

He stops and listens and asks. 'What, what happened?' Still fogged.

'Your buddy is dead, Dan. I hit him and killed him.' He is very still, as am I. Finally understanding he snarls at me.

'You fucking bastard, I will kill you, I will kill you!' He is struggling against the ties. I move forward and slap him hard across his face.

'Shut up Dan! Don't hand me that crap! You could have killed us in that fire and don't fucking say you couldn't. If you had caught us I bet I would be alive but Barbara would be dead. Anything as a lever, right?' He is now silent but the truth of my words sit in the night.

'Me as the wife killer and no place to go, and your bosses offer sanctuary. I bet the story goes something like that.' Again silence. 'I remember your words Dan "anything that can be done to study me *will be done.*"

I stand walk to Troy's house and open the door. I turn a small light on in the lounge and return to Dan. I put more cable ties on his wrists and turn the ones on his ankles into hobbles. I then pull him to his feet. I push him slowly into the house and bundle him into a low lounge chair. I take out Dan's pistol and cover him. I phone Barbara, give her assurances I am OK and ask her to come back to Troy's.

I am trying to wash my arm, watch Dan and re-bandage it as Barbara comes through the door. I am struggling with this. She takes in the scene and sees Dan in the chair.

'You said you were OK' as she takes over my poor try at first aid. I grunt. 'It needs stitches. I'll put some steri-strips on it and look later.' She says in nurse mode. Troy has a good first aid kit screwed to the wall for his clients and Barbara starts rummaging in the box. Over her shoulder she asks.

'Is the other guy tied up?' Before I can answer, Dan answers for me.

'Your fucking husband killed him.' Barbara's head snaps around looking at him then back to me, the shock and the horror evident, her mouth slightly open. I note the look on Dan's face, cursing him, sardonic bastard, still playing the game.

'He's dead?' She looks at me shaking her head 'You're sure? Maybe he's unconscious. I need to check.' She pushes past me out to the prone body. I follow her out. She drops to her knees on the grass and starts her examination. I watch her sit back, her skills not needed. She turns to me, tears glint on her face from the light at the kitchen window.

'What now? I mean.....' She trails off. But I know what she means. I have killed another human being. The game is completely changed. Whatever game we are in, nothing will be the same. A crash in the house brings me back to the now. I go inside and find Dan on the floor. The ties have done their job. I pull him to a sitting position but leave him on the floor leaning against the chair.

'Still dead is he?' He snarls at me. Barbara has followed me in and is standing the doorway. She has her arms wrapped around her, face white, staring at him.

'If you hadn't come here he wouldn't be dead. If you hadn't come here we would still have our house and our life. Yes, Bill killed him and what was he going to do? Be controlled by you or whoever you represent? You sicken me! You just follow orders and your bosses are overcome by greed!' Her tears leave shining tracks down her cheers. I walk over and put my arms around her, my blood drips on to her new sweatshirt. She whispers to me.

'Did you want to kill him?' There is a fear in her voice, which makes complete sense. I shake my head against her hair.

'God no! Jesus! I .....' I stop. She grips me tightly her empathy palatable. I turn towards Dan, walk across to the couch opposite and sit down. He is eyeing me warily.

'OK. No words. You listen. You and I are going to talk. I am going to sit you on the couch. Barbara is going to cut the ties on your hands and re-tie them in front of you. I will be holding your gun on you. I have checked the mag and there is one in the breech. I will shoot you. I won't kill you. I will shoot you in the guts and I will watch you die. Do you understand?' Dan looks at me and snaps a look at Barbara, her arms are folded across her chest, her strong stern look says it all.

'OK.' he nods angry but not stupid. I help him up on to the couch. I pass some cable ties to Barbara who brings a kitchen knife from the drawer. I stand to one side with the pistol directly aimed at Dan's midriff. Barbara cuts his ties and he shifts his arms in front of him, he massages his wrists.

'Enough, hands out, be careful'. He looks at me then complies. Barbara puts three ties around his wrists and another around all three ties in between his wrists. She fears him. She steps back then moves to the kitchen and puts the jug on, normal things bring normality, maybe. I start.

'So here we are again. I am talking to you because I don't want to harm you. Your friend was an accident.' Dan snorts. 'Believe what you want. That is true. What did you expect? Your first contact was a bunch of lies. Our house has been burnt down and we fought back. You under estimated us. Frankly, you fucked up.'

I sit watching, seeing how these words take effect. Dan just sits, eyes on mine listening, angry.

'For the second time you and I are talking, while you are faced with your bad decisions. The only reason we are talking again is because I don't want to kill you. It is the easier road but you will be replaced, there will be another Dan, you are just one in a line of Dans. You know I am right because of your reports to your boss and your background.

I know a soldier boy when I see one. I worked for a government too long not to know how orders work.' I change tact to see if I can rattle his thoughts.

'Your friend won't be going to his sister's wedding, were you going too?' Cruel I think but my house is in ruins. This bastard planned and executed its destruction and possibly ours. Dan's head shakes his head, look plain hatred.

'Fuck you.' He speaks slowly. 'His name is John.' He stops, glaring. I stare at him, the person I had killed has a name. He just became more real, there is more guilt. Barbara comes and sits beside, me placing cups on the coffee table.

'Why did you destroy our home?' She asks quietly, her gaze intense wanting to understand.

Dan stares back and Barbara waits, I sip my tea, sweet again I note. Finally Dan starts speaking, angry bites of words.

'I get told to put a plan into execution. I do it. I follow the orders given. That's it.'

Barbara's mouth opens and closes, she is thinking. I listen to his excuses, angry.

'Was,' I say.' Dan looks at me. 'What?' He is confused, eyes narrow.

'John, he was, he isn't now. Your plan killed him. The orders you followed, killed him. Oh, I am not excusing myself but you set the path and I pushed back.' Silence. Then Barbara speaks.

'You followed orders and set our life ablaze, all our memories, our work gone because you followed orders. I think I could kill you myself.' She stops abruptly and sits back, weighing her words, wondering about killing, I think, but not sure. I continue.

'So now I just want you to watch.' I tap my arm and disappear. Dan's mouth falls open. I leave the couch and quietly walk behind.

'Yes, amazing isn't?' I touch him on the shoulder and he tries to spin around, his ties slowing him. I move to his side and touch him on the face and he pulls back.

I move back to the sit opposite and tap my arm and snap back into his vision. He is visibly shaken.

'This is only a part of what I can do.' I take Barbara's hand and rest it on my leg and tap again, we are both gone to sight.

Dan's 'Jesus.' really says it all. Tap again and we are back. I sit and watch Dan, his eyes switch from one of us to the other, believing but disbelieving. I nod.

'Yes, hard to believe I know. I was standing next to your car when you and John were talking, when the dog walker went past. He was telling you about the wedding.' Dan's face is slack, the shock obvious, complete.

The words I say now are just to give us time. Barbara and I need to talk, plan, decide what we are going to do, there are things I need to explore on the bracelet. I need to talk to Island. There too many things I don't know. But the clock is ticking. No matter what I say or do, Dan is just a military robot and where are the rest of his team I wonder.

'We could just leave and you really would never find us. If you did, we go again. The thing is, Dan you really don't know what you are dealing with. So here is your choice. You take John, your team and disappear.' I slow, watching Dan's face.

'We will meet you at Holland Air Force base in 7 days from now, at 12.00 Midday, then what I have and what I know I pass on to your guys. Any sight of you here in the village. I mean any, no deal. Someone has my number. Send me a text 24 hours before to confirm, my phone will be off until then. By the way, I warn you; play games and I may go to someone else. There will be other people who would like to meet me. I will let you think about this. I know you can't make that decision. But your bosses won't like that idea at all. I will let you go and you can use your phone.' Dan says nothing, his eyes shift between us.

Barbara is quiet as she leans against me, her sadness emanating. The realization of the life we are about to have, as a life, sinking in. She puts her head on my shoulder. Dan looks directly into my eyes, I read nothing, this man is order driven, un-trust worthy. He is trying to be more human than he is, a pawn in someone's game.

'I will ring. I don't know what they will say.' I nod and lean forward to make my point.

'We are leaving. I may be here, I may not. You will ring your people and remove John. Wait in your vehicle. Remember I still have your pistol.' Dan snaps his head in agreement. I look at Barbara.

'OK, let's go, I will be back to free you.' I tell Dan, as we move towards the door I tap my arm and we become unseen. We walk over the mown grass to Kevin and Susan's quietly. There are no words.

Once inside I tap my arm. No lights. I pull back a side curtain to relieve some of the gloom. Barbara gets glasses of water, passes me one and sits on the couch.

'Do you believe him?' Fair question, I shake my head.

'No, not at all but we need time. I need to find out what I can actually do with this.' I rub my arm.

'I also need time with Island. It has only just occurred to me to ask if I can get rid of the bracelet. I mean can it be removed? There are too many things I don't know. Besides you and I need time to plan.' I sit beside her and take her hand.

'I just want our life back really, just to do what we were doing, I don't know if we can ever have that, I am sorry. I just hate it.' Barbara puts her arms around me and we hug in silence, in the gloom. Soon I stand and look out the window to the dark, nothing is moving.

'OK, time to sort Dan, he doesn't know where we are but he knows it's close. I will free him and then we will see. I don't trust him or whoever his bosses are but we have to try.' Barbara stands and hugs me again. 'Be very careful.' I nod. She locks the door behind me.

Dan is where I left him. We had left the door open and I have arrived very quietly watching for new players around the house before I enter. I move in front of Dan and quickly cut the ties between his wrists and leave his knife in his lap, I stand back across the room, pistol in hand and tap my arm as Dan fumbles with the knife to get the rest of the ties off his wrists then his ankles. He is rubbing to get circulation going again. I motion with the barrel of the pistol.

'Drop the knife on the floor. I will disappear. You leave, bring your car here and pick up your buddy, then, you ring and send the message. If they agree, flick your lights twice then drive off. Remember, you will never know where I am. If I see any of your team or anything that remotely looks like you, watching anywhere in the next 7 days. We disappear.' Dan stands and drops the knife, his hatred is palatable. He stands waiting, his face a grimace.

'I warn you and your friends to be careful, very careful.' I disappear and quietly walk outside and stand by the hedge. Dan puts his head out the door and then walks down the drive, minutes later returns with his car. He then opens the back door grabs John by his shoulders and awkwardly puts him in the back seat. He slams the door chest heaving.

'Fuck you, you son of a bitch.' Dan yells into the night. I stand watching but don't reply. My sympathy for Dan is zero.

Dan gets back into the car and finger punches at his phone. I approach the car and stand behind the door pillar just in case Dan gets clever. I hear bits of the conversation as he has his window up, it is emotive and Dan's voice gets louder. About 2 minutes later the call is ended. Dan hits the steering wheel with a closed fist. I move away from the car, he sits quietly then flicks his lights, twice. He then starts the car and slowly backs up the drive. I return to a waiting Barbara. I tap on the door and say it's me. I tap my arm as she opens the door.

'All OK?' Her worry is evident. 'Well, it seems to be. He took his buddy with him. I heard bits of his chat with his boss. But who do you believe?' I yawn. I am dog tired and I need food. Barbara catches the yawn bug.

'I'll get some food from Troy's. Eat and sleep here and we start planning in the morning. Oh and phones off. They will look for us via them.' She nods wearily and I tap my arm to do my food run.

Chapter 8

There is heavy rain through the night. I wake fitfully and sink back into sleep. The rain is still hammering down the next morning as we wake. It is late in the morning for us, the microwave tells me it is 9.47 as I put the jug on.

'Coffee?' I hear an affirmative groan. The room we are in is bedroom, kitchen, lounge combined. The rest of the night has been uneventful. I had done a quiet walk around earlier, to look for watchers but found nothing. We sit in bed and drink our coffee, instant, which I do not like; such is life. The rain is lashing the iron roof and I am tempted to go back to sleep. Barbara interrupts this idea.

'So, now what? Any thoughts?' She is leaning back in the pillows sipping her coffee but like me, she isn't happy, our routine has gone and this isn't home.

'For a start we go to the café and have a decent breakfast. I need to call Kevin about using this place. We need new phones that can't be traced, at least not for a while and we need some more clothes. Contact the insurance company. Be normal. They will be watching or they will be asking locals to watch and report. I don't like the idea that neighbours are spies but people are people. If it's not for money then it's for a line they spin. Who knows.' I make moves to have a shower.

'But straight after breakfast, I want to go and see Island. I need to know exactly what the bracelet will let me do. I have an idea but I don't really know and I need a place to practice.'

Breakfast isn't that pleasant. The local gossip mill had been running full steam. Lots of peering over shoulders or "So sorry to hear about your loss." But really wanting more gossip to pass on or the nudging and "wait till I tell you." looks sidle across the tables. One dear lady had the fortitude to ask when did they think the insurance would be settled? With a "such a shame they take so long", added on for good measure but given her son is the local insurance agent I knew that this was her way of being a bitch, nicely. People can be a virus on the earth who are waiting to pounce over the half drunk coffee cups. We sat and chatted about nothing, ate and watched for watchers that we may not recognize. We then went to the shop for food.

The shop owner is sympathetic about the house, a serious, honest guy. We had walked up for the exercise and just to have something normal in our abnormal life. I am annoyed with myself about looking for watchers but I can't seem to stop. Still, no one is obvious. We go back to our nights haven and tidy up. I send a text to Kevin and Susan to thank them but no explanation on why we needed the house. A little later, sitting back at Troy's, we start our planning. Barbara has found some paper and pens just to formalize the situation and keep our thoughts on track. The manager coming out in her and it makes sense to me. She looks at the paper and asks.

'Why, with the knowledge you have gained, don't you know more about the bracelet?'

'I have asked myself the same question, I just don't know. I had wondered if the wearer needed to be checked out or tested to see if they are actually worthy. I agree it is odd but I know there is more to the bracelet. It feels like an answer I should know, but just don't.' I shrug.

'My knowledge is like a block of Swiss cheese. Lots of holes and sometimes no connections to things that seem to sit next to each other.'

'So we list stuff then sort a priority?' She asks. I nod in agreement and look into space. After an hour we have our list split roughly in half. I go to communicate with Island and find out exactly what the bracelet is capable of. Barbara deals with the insurance and rings the police to find out where their investigation is sitting. Without some sort of outcome we have no home and can't plan for another. When I ask Barbara if we stay here, she is very quiet and still, then asks.

'Where else would we go?' I shake my head and remain silent. Our future is looking uncertain, she knows this as much as I do. The question is left for another day but the future is welling up like a wave on a beach. Just before Barbara gets into the truck to head into town, she turns to me takes my hand and asks.

'Are you OK? I mean last night, that guy, I mean.' I finish the sentence in my head, how am I feeling about killing a person? Lousy, terrible, should I have done something different? Yes, maybe but I didn't. I look back at her eyes, they are earnest, probing.

'No, not really, I have been over it and over it. What does one do against your attacker? My answer was fight back.' We stand hugging. She looks again at me and nods. Barbara gets in the truck to do the shopping we need. Phones, some more clothes, food and a stop at the police station. Some calls to the various insurance people is also on the list and a couple of stops to see friends who have left messages of support.

I go inside, have a drink of water and pick up my list that I have made so that I don't forget the detail. I put on a sweatshirt as I find Island's atmosphere a bit cooler than I would like and this session may take some time. I am keyed-up. I am feeling the pressure of being alone in a strange world. While I have been given knowledge of these peoples world, I am no less human. A waking dream with consequences that I am becoming more and more aware of. I have this unpleasant feeling that I am trusting Island more than my own kind and I don't get it, or like it, but I am unsure where to turn. The pressures of Dan and the cloud of his visits have left their mark.

As I leave the house, I tap my arm and become unseen. When I reach the beach a light breeze drifts seawards and the sea is very calm. I should be fishing I think.

Island is there, waiting, floating quietly. I tap the opening sequence and the door opens. I walk to the chair, sit and place my arm in its seat. Symbols appear.

'Welcome Bill.' I tap back. 'Hello Island.' I sit and ponder for a few seconds then start my questions. My hesitation has been that this really is the last step to bring me into the world of being a human interface. But the reality is I am sitting in an alien craft, the simple world I knew has become a place of fear and distrust, but then what are the choices? Only my questions may carve a path. I start.

'Island, can you and I communicate verbally? Our communication is very slow. My writing is I should say.' The screen of stars flashes with letters, the answer surprises me.

'Put this sequence into your controller, Bill.'

A number of symbols appear that match the hieroglyphics on my arm. I tap the symbols and a voice says.

'Hello Bill.'

The voice is in English clean and pure, not female or male, a voice of everyone but no one. Strange. I reply and am aware this may be the first time a human has spoken to something from another world. One small step for human kind. I feel the uncharted swirl around me.

'Hello Island, it is good to be able to talk to you.'

'Yes, this a good thing Bill.'

'Why didn't we talk before, Island?' I am curious about the reasoning, if this option was there, why not use it?

'Bill, Island needed to know more about you and your race. You have trusted Island with the information in your memory. You have shown trust by not bringing more of your race to Island. This meeting you and I are having now, is important. Island believes you have questions that you feel are unanswered. Island has questions too, about you and your race.'

Island is right. I have a vast number of questions. And when answer Island's questions, how do I for all of humanity? I take the honest path. Island will find out at some stage of the multiple facets of the human race. Diamonds nearly always in the rough.

'OK Island. I have some simple questions. Firstly, are you OK with me starting?'

As my eyes wander over the cosmos in front of me, the task I am involved with suddenly becomes immense. I am speaking with the ship of another race and am trying to balance what I have found out about Island and my beliefs on our people. I shiver and think about walking away but then Island replies and breaks into my thought trajectory.

'It is good to talk Bill. Please ask your questions.' This ship has been waiting for over one thousand years, how can I leave now?

'Island, I will be very honest with you there are people, humans, who will want to control you and want to hold all your knowledge for themselves. Did my memory let you understand what countries are, what nationalism Island is and how our politics works? These concepts are important Island.' There is a silence and the cosmos glows before. Island finally answers.

'Yes, these concept's Island understands. If Island does not understand what you are saying Island will ask Bill to clarify.' I nod, fair enough so I start.

'OK Island thank you, my first questions are about the bracelet. What more will the bracelet let me do to protect myself? It must be possible to take the bracelet off, I say this, as your engineer took it off and buried it in the sand.'

'Bill, the controller has two basic functions, to communicate with Island and to survey the planet that Island arrives at. The controller is designed to protect the engineer. It also to enables the engineer to travel the planet that Island arrives on, so a survey of the planet can be made.' I am shocked by this and blurt:

'What? you mean I can fly?' Island slows but carries on.

'It will allow you to become unseen for a period of time approximately 2 of your days, should this be wished. It is a light-bending device the light bends around the wearer, which also protects the wearer from harm. Objects cannot penetrate the field. The engineer is able to use the controller to move around the planet, once the correct link is made. The engineer uses their mind to regulate where they wish to go. So, yes you can fly.'

Island stops, I sit and absorb this information. So I become superman! Good God. I keep going with the questions but am struggling with what I have been told. I also have more than enough child in me wanting to try this new toy.

'Island what other protections are in the controller please? Actually what are the full range of...of ah, tools are in the controller?' I am getting that I have to be more precise with my questions. The craters of our moon come into my vision as I sit watching the worlds in front of me and I think about the time, energy and money that humans have spent just getting to that point. The vastness of space and how advanced Island's makers were when they sent Island's ship on its way is completely staggering. Now I am the conduit between two worlds. I feel frightened.

'Bill, there is a defence devise that will defend the wearer, similar to a laser on your planet. The mechanics you will understand once you link to Island. It is line of sight but it is very effective. The bracelet enables the wearer to move anywhere on the planet should this be required.' Island stops and seems to be waiting but I am not sure for what. I ask the questions that has been bothering me ever since I walked aboard Island.

'Island can the bracelet be taken out of my arm or do I have it for life? Does the removal of the bracelet kill me? Why did the bracelet pick me?'

'Bill, the controller picked you, because you picked it. If you had not put it on your arm then it would have self-destructed in a short time after you picked it up. It had to be part of the finder, the controller is designed as a key between Island and the race that picks it up. Once touched, it is activated but this creates a time limit. It was important to my race that the contacted people had the understanding to use the knowledge that is presented to them.'

So it was pure luck Harry and his walker came along, blind luck. I am feeling like a pivot point to a new world and yet the direction of where my life will head now is hard to grasp. I am not sure I want this, though I am partly down a path and there is no turning back.

In another place, at another time, I have lain on the grass at night looking at the stars and thought about the simple word 'up'. If I look 'up', 'up' never stops unless it hits a planet or a star. My mind finds this impossible to grasp.

So here we go, just "Up."

'Bill, the controller can be removed if you wish this, it will not kill you, damaging life forms is not what Island and the controller were designed to do. Should the controller be removed it will sit with Island and Island will go on with the search for another race.'

Island stops. Island seems to know the rate of information that I can take on board.

'Island, why didn't the bracelet self-destruct when the last engineer took it off? I don't understand.'

'Bill, the engineer was possibly passing into the void and thought this planet was suitable. The engineer had set the controller but did not communicate to Island before they left, Island does not know. Island believes this was strange but has no answer.'

I nod but the answers create more questions. I can be free but at what cost to my race. What opportunities do I, just one person, lose for my people?

'Island, I have two more important questions. Can I bring other humans to come on board Island and will Island go to another place on the planet and will Island become visible to other humans?' Island does not answer for some minutes. Then Island replies.

'Yes, Bill, this is possible but only with your collaboration while you wear the controller. You are the conduit for all communication to Island at present Bill. Island can change this, should Island believe this is required. There are information streams that Island will now follow to become more knowledgeable about your planet now that you have opened the path.' I lean back in the chair. I feel tired and over exposed to information but then I think, I have to move forward.

'OK Island, please give me the final sequence for the controller.' It is time to push into the future. A set of symbols arrives on the screen and I tap my arm. A new world is about to begin. My arm warms slightly and my mind feels flooded. New channels appear in my mind, I know now, what I didn't.

'Island was this the real step of trust between you and I? I mean if I can arrange for humanities leaders to accept what Island has to offer, will you accept what is decided?'

I had to ask, if I have become the fulcrum of this and I wanted to know what I am faced with. The world has no world government power. The planet is in constant flux everywhere across the planet. Nationalistic ideas are pushed and every religion has its own agenda, doctrine or both. I am no expert but the foibles of the human race seem to be in complete conflict with the needs of the race. But at that point, sitting in that chair on the edge of the greatest opportunity that our race may ever see. I think: I must try. Island speaks across the array of space before me.

'Bill, Island believes Bill will do what he feels is right for his race. Island will listen to what your leaders say. Bill, you have some idea of Islands library of knowledge but not all. There is knowledge here that will change your planet for all time. Your race is not unlike Island's, power and control of power is the coinage here but this is dangerous for the human race. Island will listen then Island will see.'

I am now tired, I need time to work through what I have learned.

'I am tired Island and I need to think on what to do. I will try to arrange leaders to come and discuss our world with you and your library. One very last thing, can I bring my wife here to meet you as I think her perspective would be good for Island and myself. I need a person I completely trust, you understand?'

'Bill, that will be good to meet Barbara. It is much for one being to take on but it was planned this way. Island was to contact one being of the new planet first. It is good to talk to you Bill.'

I stretch in the chair it has become oddly familiar and yet oddly alien. I am but a man in a beyond vast universe and I am the contact for the world. I feel very small, privileged and very alone.

I stand, think unseen, and it is so. I walk through the hallway with the beach framed in open space of the door and on to the sand. A couple have a small child in a buggy, they walk past, not seeing me. They are talking about their new house they have just bought, happy with a future ahead. I like people planning ordinary things, it is simply, nice.

I think fly and I lift up and move towards the sea, I think left and I am drifting across the waves towards the mouth of the inlet. I am 30 feet above the waves as they roll in to the beach. I see a small shark wandering in the shallows, next a school of fish flicker as the wave drifts over them. I lift higher, I laugh. I am my own personal drone.

In a fit of craziness, I lift myself towards the small local town where I know Barbara will be. The speed that I travel amazes me, I think, therefore I am there. I slow and drift over the town, looking for a car from above is odd, they all look much the same. My search ends at the supermarket car park. My truck stands out with the flat wooden deck. I float down, land and wait in the shade of a tree. When the car park is quiet I become seen again. Just on queue Barbara is pushing a trolley towards the truck.

Chapter 9

'Can I help you with that?' She looks up startled.

'What are you doing here? Did you get a lift? Have you finished with Island?'

Her surprise is obvious but she is happy to see me. The last few days are wearing thin, the continuing change and dangers have become a burden. I see this and wonder what to do.

'Yes, I had my visit. It was strange and amazing. All OK with you?' Her eyes show I am referring to watchers. As I help her load bags of groceries I look around the car park but see no one of interest. But then watchers are good at not being seen I remind myself.

'Yes fine, no problems. Lots of people asking about the fire. If they could help. There really are some great people here. I saw Di, she knows there has been a bit of a falling out with you and Gary but doesn't seem to understand what happened. I glossed over it. I gather Gary is upset.' Her look quizzes me to find my reaction, I shrug.

'Not sure what he expects, his lack of thought has lost us a house and put you and I in the firing line. Which I suspect was driven by some sort of greed. Look, lets head home there are some things we need to chat about.' She nods and asks.

'Do you want to drive?' I laugh and shake my head. I think I could fly and laugh again. Barbara peers at me knowing there is something going on. She gets in the driver's seat and as we get onto the main road out of town she asks.

'Alright, give, what have you learnt from Island?' So I start a blow by blow account. The steering wheel rocks with my first little surprise. 'You can fly? You're joking! I mean superman, all that stuff?' She concentrates on the road then a 'Laser?' She interjects my tale. Then head shaking and a 'I just don't believe it.' I agree it's hard to come to grips with.

'So that's how I ended up in the car park.' Barbara swerves slightly as she turns to look at me. 'What? You flew? From the beach to there? Really? Good God!'

'Yes, trial flight. Bloody odd, but what was really strange, I wasn't scared. It felt OK almost normal I......' I trail off, not explaining myself well, but I am also trying to understand the changes the bracelet has made to my personal world and my mind.

'The only way that I can explain it, it is like being a drone. I am it.'

We fall silent for the last part of the journey. As we drive through our little village it is just the same, a couple of old folks on electric wagons going to the shop, work trucks going to new houses being built but the 'feel' is different. We have changed, our house is gone. The world has expanded beyond belief and danger lurks. I feel sad and out of sorts. I put my hand on Barbara's, she squeezes it then takes her hand away to change gear as we pull into the driveway. We unload the truck and quietly put the goods away. The jug goes on and tea is made. We sit on the couch and watch the geese on the lake.

'How you doing?' My question is also directed at myself.

'You said Island was OK about me going aboard. So I would like to do that. I need to see. I need to know. I mean....' She drifts off but I know what she means. You need to experience the unbelievable before you believe. I agree. I feel I need to share this wholly, completely. I have started to wonder about my own sanity, what my eyes see. Is it what I experience actually real, will I wake up?

'Yes, you are right, you are part of this. You need to see, to believe, to really believe.' Her eyes are piercing as she watches me and says.

'Yes I do. It's not that I don't, it's I can't. I see you disappear. I think I have but I feel nothing. I mean, it just doesn't compute here.' She taps the side of her head. 'It makes no real sense. This is the impossible.'

I see her anguish, I nod and also understand why I want her to meet Island, to relieve my own questioning. Distrust in myself still lurks.

'OK, no time like the present. We'll go now, but first I want to try something. Come outside.' Barbara looks at me puts on her Brave Face and follows me outside.

'Stand close, arm around me.' She looks at me then follows my lead, I put my arm around her and think, Unseen and Fly, and we do. Simple really. Barbara grasps tighter as we rise.

'Jesus Christ! this is.....impossible.' I laugh. 'No, it is possible and we can! I'll show you the harbor.' We drift across the lake in front of the house and towards the habor beyond. Over trees, over houses then over the water. A pair of gulls are flying towards the habor entrance and I follow them. I get close enough to touch them. They don't see us but sense the air pressure imbalance and turn away.

'This is amazing, unbelievable.....I...' Barbara is stilled with what she is experiencing and I fill the gap.

'Yes, bloody incredible isn't it?' We are flying over the sand point at the harbor's mouth. An array of birds are sitting on the sand, in the shallows three eagle rays are slowly moving through the clear water like dark butterflies with sharp pointed wings. The crystal waves raise and lower as schools of fish manoeuvre through the sparkling water, over the pale light dappled sand beneath. The air is pure and clear, there is no rush of wind, the air is clean through the field that seems to surround us. We are in a floating box of magic.

'So starting to believe?' I ask Barbara and I feel her nodding.

'I do but I can't.' Then she sees it.

'Oh My God!' Her exclamation I feel through her body as she sees Island for the first time. The transparent light blue cube floats on the beach edge below and ahead of us. I steer us towards the beach and alight on the sand facing the cube.

'It is bigger than I thought it would be.' Barbara is just staring, I have looked around us and we seem to be alone.

'So what did you think of your first flight?' My voice is laughing, not at her but the situation, which I am still equating.

'Actually fantastic! I could do that again and again. Why weren't you scared, when you first saw Island?' She is awed by the cube and unsure. She is in wonder at the transparent blue space standing at the water's edge, which towers above us.

'I don't know, maybe the bracelet gave me a certain amount of trust but scared? No, more curious and apprehensive at the same time, I guess. Are you ready?' She looks at the cube and then takes my hand.

'As I will ever be.' we walk over the water to the open door of Island. I walk Barbara through the entrance way, her hand is clutching mine tightly and we walk to the Library. There are now two chairs facing the cosmos. The controllers chair has the contoured rest, the other does not. I seat Barbara and as I do, Island welcomes us.

'Hello Bill, Hello Barbara.' Barbara is looking at the vastness of the stars and planets in our view, the beauty undeniable. Barbara turns to me, the question on her face obvious. I smile.

'Sure, say hello.' She turns towards the starry world and makes her first contact.

'Hello Island, Bill has told me about you but it seems very strange to talk to you.' She stops and her gaze wanders the cosmos in front of her, the surprise at how the visions before her, react to her sight. I smile, it still amazes me, always will I suspect.

'Hello Barbara. It is good to talk to you too. Bill has given Island a lot of information about your race and your planet. It is good to meet his mate.' Barbara glances at me with a small smile, mate, a new term for her.

'Would you let Island search your memory Barbara? This would give Island more understanding between Island, your race and you.' Barbara sits and thinks and then asks.

'Will you give me information about your race and your planet, Island? I mean could we swap thoughts at the same time?'

I am staring at Saturn, probably seeing more than any astronomer has ever seen. The longer one stares the more magnified the surface becomes, truly incredible. Barbara hasn't been through the experience I have, she doesn't know that this will happen as part of the connection. I wonder if different people have a different reaction depending on their makeup of their memories, then Island answers. I also didn't know that Island can transfer knowledge without a bracelet, I wonder on the how.

'Yes Barbara. Island wishes you to understand Island, as Island wishes to know about you and your race.' Barbara nods the Brave Face takes hold and she replies.

'Yes Island. I am scared, can I trust you?' Her question surprises me, then makes sense. I never asked. Island replies.

'Barbara, I trust you and Bill to do the right thing with the knowledge that Island is here and what that brings. Island believes this knowledge will change life for your race and your planet. It would be good for Barbara to trust Island.' Islands simple reply strikes a chord in my mind.

'Island, please read my memory for the last few days. I believe this is important in your and my relationship.' Barbara looks across at me and then understanding crosses her face.

'Very well Bill. If this is important to you.' My arm warms and I feel suddenly tired as a transfer happens.

'Barbara, Island would like your knowledge to help Island understand what has happened with Bill.' Barbara nods, Island wants another point of view and she replies.

'Very well, I want to know more about you Island.' She looks tense but settles back in the chair and the transfer takes place. Barbara closes her eyes and seems asleep. As I wait an asteroid passes close to Neptune and moves towards the sun.

'Wow, that was....Thank you Island. Now I see. I feel that I have lived in a darkened room and the dawn has arrived. Thank you.' She is looking at me with tears on her cheeks.

'Bill, now Island has an understanding of the situation Island's arrival has created in your lives. Island is sorry.' I sit and listen but don't really know what to say, the empathy in Island's words are clear, I had not expected this. Barbara is quiet, contemplating. I try to explain not only to Island but to myself as well.

'Thank you Island for your words. Yes, your arriving has been very strange and difficult but also the most incredible thing that has ever happened to us and our world. The problem I .....we have is how to present Island and this knowledge to the world. I am but one person there are eight billion people on this planet. There are many risks, but somehow Island, I need to present you to this world as the gift your people intended. Through my and Barbara's thoughts and memories

Island will have an idea of the complex world we live in. Does Island still wish for us to proceed with passing the knowledge of Island's arrival on?'

I sit watching one of Saturn's moons circle its giant sphere, Barbara has heard me and she looks at me and asks.

'You are asking Island to make a choice on just our experience? Which is vastly different to a local in Paris or a Brazilian rain forest or ...well, anywhere else.' She is earnest and I sort of agree but my doubt lingers.

'Isn't the human experience much the same everywhere though? We grow up, work towards a life of some sort, then mate, have children, grow old and die. The culture of where we live and how we relate to our religion, if we have one, is much the same. Generalisation, I know but I guess what I am saying is why not us? Instead of why, us?'

At this point Island interrupts our discussion.

'Bill is right Barbara, the more individuals that are involved, the harder plans may become. Island has made a choice. Island would see the knowledge passed to your race. It is up to you how this should occur so that there is the best outcome for all your race.'

We sit and watch the colored infinity of space, it is easy to sit and get lost in the performance of worlds. I shake my head trying to shift away from the enormity of the task and ask Island.

'How is there two chairs in the controllers room Island? I have only seen one before.'

This is really idle curiosity I know very little about Island, what the make-up is of the craft Island is in or is how many parts are there, how is it propelled, what makes it tick?

'Bill, Island will pass on Island's knowledge of the actual Library through transfer, there is a lot of information and Island feels this will be quicker. This is a picture of the library, not the information held here, it is far too vast for any human to hold. Barbara, this will interest you too, does this suite you both?'

I look at Barbara and ask OK? She nods and sits back again, I agree and the transfer takes place. The shock is almost physical, a space craft beyond thought or invention in human terms. The passengers are held in limbo for centuries. While the craft, with Island as its crew guides the craft for light years, searching for a place to receive the gift on board. At each stop on the journey a passenger is awakened to see if this planet is suitable. If not the passenger returns to sleep. There are thousands of investigations. Some passengers don't return and the number dwindles, the stop here on our earth is the last passenger, Island has waited for them, they never return.

Island controls and maintains the library. The systems partly are organic, partly manufactured. Island was the crew and now the captain. A lot of what is passed to me in the transfer I don't have the knowledge to understand, I am not a physicist nor space engineer, things here are way beyond my ken. I am a blind man asking what is sight.

Barbara stirs in her seat.

'So now we know some, but I sure don't understand a lot!' I laugh. Island speaks.

'There is much for your people to learn about Island and the library. It is time to prepare your people, Bill, Barbara.' Barbara turns to me.

'Island is right. We now have to face the real world.' There is a smile on her face, she feels reassured by meeting Island and is ready for the next stage. I am not so sure, but smile back.

'OK, let's go back to reality or do we live two realities now?' We walk together from the control room, as we stand at the door to the beach Barbara says.

'Thank you Island.' I take her hand and think unseen and from Island I hear Thank You Barbara as we walk across moving water to the beach.

She puts her arm around me with an order "fly me home" I laugh and we do.

I do a slow careful flight over the streets checking beneath us but nothing out of the ordinary stands out. We land on the lawn unlock, get water and collapse on the couches. Balancing the unknown is a trying business. I know the look on Barbara's face, each time we have been ready to plan another stage in our lives, it appears.

'Yes, I know. What now?' She sees humor and smiles.' So? Now what?' Echoing my question.

'Well, I have one idea. I go and see the Prime Minister.' She looks slightly dazed and then slowly nods, then asks.

'How do you get to see the PM? Quick note to her secretary?' Barbara question is mocking but fair. Leaders of countries are hard to contact even one as small as ours. I am about to answer when there is knock at the door. Through the frosted glass I can see the blue and tell tales of a police uniform. I turn to Barbara.

'OK? This guy may not be real.' She nods and stands as I open the door. The sergeant turns his gaze to mine, his look is wary, not hostile but careful.

'Hello sergeant, how can I help?' I am also on guard. He nods.

'Can I come in? I have some news for you both.' He can see Barbara standing watching us. A 'sure come in' and he is standing waiting in the lounge. Barbara moves to the kitchen bench.

'Have a seat sergeant, would you like tea? Bill do you want some?' Barbara is being normal, clever I think, it covers both of our agitation. I nod a yes.

'Thanks.' He sits and waits, watching, He is looking for reactions, minor but telling to the sleuth in him. Barbara busies herself with her task and I sit and stare back. He looks around.

'How long do you have this place for? Does the owner use it much?' Probing chit-chat.

'He uses it short term. It's Air BNB mostly, so we can stay for months if we need it.' I don't ask why, he has an answer. He hums and nods, he has noted the caution but then I guess he gets that in his game.

'OK. Well, the investigation has found that the fire was set but.' There is a slight hesitation here.

'There is no evidence to suggest that you or your wife were involved. So there will be no charges, unless more information comes to light. Someone did set the fire, while you were away. Arson can be a difficult journey for the victims. The point is, our investigation leaves you out of it. I am not sure how this leaves you with the insurance company, of course.'

He stops watching our faces. I know both of us are relieved and we show it. Barbara comes around the breakfast bar and hugs me, there are tears in her eyes.

'We can rebuild, we can get a real home back.' The sergeant's eyes are watchful but he has the courtesy to look away. I do wonder whether we can ever just have a home again but the idea of being even semi normal again grabs me. I like the idea a lot. I grin at Barbara.

'Yes, yes we can.'

'There will be a letter sent to confirm what I have told you but I thought you would want to know as soon as possible. But as I say, the insurance will be another issue. It may take some time.' And you will watch the ripples in the water around us, I think to myself.

The Sergeant stands to leave and as he passes me, he nods a goodbye to Barbara and asks could I have a word? Barbara thanks him for coming with a bright 'you really made our day.' His smile widens, he is wanting to help. I follow him out to his car, which is sitting in the drive.

'You have friends in high places.' He rolls this accusation at me as he watches Barbara doing dishes through the kitchen window. I look at him in surprise, because I am surprised. My face betrays it.

'I have no idea what you are talking about. You will have dug into my background, where I worked and so on. I was hardly at the top of the pile. Why are you asking?'

He looks directly at me and I can see he is either angry or very annoyed. He can't find answers and he doesn't like it. I think he believes my shock but I am unsure.

'Someone from the capital wants you left very much alone. That's strange.' I look back at him and feel very uncomfortable. I don't understand it either but I don't like what I am hearing.

'Listen, I have no bloody idea what is going on, we lost our life in that fire. It's the small things that make a life, photos, all sorts of things that can never ever be replaced. Jesus! I actually don't care if you don't understand, because I bloody don't either!'

My anger and frustration are dripping from my words. I stop. No point, I think, but the strangeness and tension of the last few days is very apparent. He stares again, nods and turns away towards the car, as he gets in to the seat he looks through his open window at me.

'By the way, we have had an enquiry from the SIS about you.' He has thrown the bait and my stillness tells him about my surprise but not complete shock. We look at each other. He starts the car.

'Be seeing you.' He puts the car into gear and reverses down the drive. Yes, maybe. I ponder this thought. As I walk through the door I get Barbara's:

'Well, what more did he want?' as I run through the conversation on the couch, Barbara sits quietly taking it all in. I finish with.

'So someone in the capital has been approached and wheels are moving, they have ignored my warning. Very strange that he has had an enquiry from the SIS.' The SIS, are our Secret Intelligence Service are a tiny MI5 or CIA .

'There are things here he doesn't like. I am not sure if it was a warning or he's annoyed with being played for a fool by his bosses or someone in the capital. I believe he is pretty straight, a good cop doing his best but doesn't like his toes stood on in his patch. He does know there's things happening but not what and he's unhappy about it.' Barbara sits back and starts questioning.

'There's lot happening here we don't know. You are right, things have obviously got to another level. There is nothing we can do there. OK, so what plan have you hatched regarding the PM? I know you have an idea, does what the sergeant said change that?' As I sit pondering, a pair of ducks take off from the lake in a series of quacks. The rushes on the lake edge move slightly in the breeze.

'The idea is to show the PM what the bracelet will let me do and then see how she reacts. I am not sure if she knows anything from the Americans or whether the SIS has spoken to her. I guess what I am trying to do, is to see if we can get someone with some power on our side. I think she is OK but then she is a politician, everything is a balancing act. I don't know her, but I can't think of another person in government that I would trust or who has the power to make solid decisions. The ministers I worked with have gone, besides not their gig, really. Very different departments, too low on the pecking order.' I stop again, watching clouds, Barbara asks.

'So how are you actually going to do this? Walk into her office and have a chat? These things aren't that simple, surely?' Her gaze has followed mine then looks back questioning. I make humming noises.

'Well, actually that's pretty much what I am going to do. I can, fairly simply, just appear. Yes, I know it will scare her. But if done carefully, at the right time, I think with some quick explanation that I am an OK person, it may work. I'll use Chris James as a reference. She can ring him.'

Chris had been a Minister in government some years ago, we had been friendly for a while. I liked and trusted him. I think the feeling had been mutual. One way to find out. Barbara hums in her turn.

'How much will you tell her? I mean this is world shattering stuff, if a large country really wanted ......ah...you..' This expanding thought had only just occurred to her and it isn't pleasant.

'What would they do? Put so much pressure on, that our government hands you over? Invade? I mean the information you have is beyond price.....once it is out, the world, will, change. Some industries may completely disappear. Fortunes lost, others made, I mean....' She slowly stops, as she looks in to the clouds, seeing a different world and I reflect how much better I think the world could be but it is so very difficult to judge. The future is the hardest nut to crack. She is very right.

'Another thing, who makes the choice for the human race? You? The PM? Do you take this to the United Nations? The list gets pretty long.' I nod in agreement.

'One thing you forgot.' She peers at me and then says 'Well?'

'We, you forgot the 'we'. You've met Island. You know nearly as much as I do. No, you don't have the bracelet but you are clued up. You may be on their shopping list, maybe because they don't know, what you know. But at the least, just as a lever.'

She smiles and laughs. 'Bastard.' Then more seriously. 'I suppose you are right. Bugger! I am a wanted person!' But her eyes betray her thoughts. We live in dangerous territory.

'So, I think I need to get this plan moving soon. We have made a little time with the Holland Air Force Base meeting but Dan and his buddies won't wait. I think there will be a lot of planning going on but I am really more concerned about their action. I am not sure how much push Dan has with his government or how far up the line this has gone. Aliens and discussion of aliens can make the shutters go down. I just don't know. He has no real proof, that I know of. Poor copies of X-rays that could be made up or counterfeit. Not much to hang to hang your hat on. That will make things harder for him. Lots of questions, I guess.' I stop and consider as four ducks return to the pond and ski to a floating stop on webbed feet. Quacks confirm that this is their pond.

'Parliament is in session. Everybody should be at the capital, so I guess I just wander around Parliament until I find the PMs office and say hello. Yes, I know it's pretty basic but simple enough I think. I also believe it would be good for you not to be here. My trust is running out. So what about I drop you on Plank Island for a couple of days? You won't be seen, there's no one there at this time of year and it has cell coverage. What do you think?'

Barbara is watching the ducks, thinking through my words. I get up and get us both a glass of water. Plank Island is about 30 kilometres off shore, rocky, steep and uninhabited. It has one Rangers house. Th island is used as a bird breeding ground and sanctuary. The island only has Parks staff through the summer. I had been there for work on a number of occasions. Barbara had joined me a couple of times. A perfect place to disappear to, no watchers and certainly no neighbors, a safe house of sorts. Time passes as her gears turn.

'Yes, I agree but not for long. A couple of nights maybe? Ah, what happens if you don't come back? I'll be stuck there, marooned. It isn't exactly a tropical paradise.' She is making light of it but she certainly has a point.

'Gary fishes there all the time, give him a call to pick you up. I really doubt that I will be that long. Anyway they have to catch me. It's difficult to catch what you can't see but I just want you safe. It did occur to me to take you with me but I think better that you are on the outside. I am not sure if I'm not going into the lion's den. We'll see.'

She is sitting, seemingly absorbed in the ducks, slowly nodding counting the points off in her head. Then asks.

'If I need to, how do I get hold of Island? If everything went wrong and you get caught. I mean really caught?' Funny, we have an alien craft as an ally. I think this and am oddly comforted by it. It is a good thought. Barbara may need help and Island is the one to ask. I have only ever contacted Island via the bracelet.

'Fair enough, I don't know, let me try from here.' As an experiment I tap my arm and Island answers in my head somehow. I ask my question. Island answers in my mind, it is very strange.

'Hello Bill, yes this is possible. I will contact Barbara. Goodbye Bill.' I start to say what has happened but Barbara holds up a hand.

'Hello Island. Yes, it is good to talk. I understand, thank you.' She speaks out loud, sits quietly, shakes her head then finally says.

'I am not sure if I will ever get used to that. Anyway, Island has given me a path to Island, if I need to.'

The interaction has left her nonplussed. Doors have opened to another world. The ducks don't seem to notice. The sun is starting to lower and swallows are dipping over the lake taking sips of water on the wing, leaving ever widening rings on the glass calm.

'Ok, we seem to have a plan. Are you happy?' She looks up and nods.

'Let's grab some bits, put them in a couple of bags and go before it gets dark. I know it seems like a rush but I would like a good night's sleep. I feel the watchers are everywhere, stupid but....' I trail off. Barbara comes over and hugs me. We stand rocking in quiet understanding.

'Five minutes and we go. One bag for food and another for some clothes.' Again I have been organized, which I don't actually mind, I grin and do a duty nod. There are a couple of recyclable supermarket bags that I tie some rope between the handles to loop over my shoulders. Our backpacks have gone in the fire and I grieve about my old one. I had carried it many miles over the whole of the country, my old friend is ashes.

The trip is quicker than I expect. We have arms around each other as we drift up. I then mentally set the course. A rush over the thirty kilometres of sea. We are float above the green house set back into the hill in a clearing in the trees. Sea birds wheel around us, as we land on the long grass by the path up from the beach. I collect the hidden key just as the light is about to completely fade. I light candles, it has been surprisingly simple, another house but a safer haven. Candles flicker as the dark surrounds us. We can hear the surf on the rocks and in the distance penguins are calling. One of the odd things about our country that I have always liked. The smallest penguin in the world sound like donkeys braying in the dusk.

A great night's sleep is a wondrous thing. The phones had been turned off before we left. We have a simple cold meal and listened to the night noises before drifting away. The quiet, the candles, the simplicity adding to the pleasure.

The hissing of the small gas stove wakes me, Barbara is sifting through the stores left by the staff for some sort of coffee.

'Try the big one on your right.'

'Decided to join the group did you?' She throws this over her shoulder as she checks the cupboard on the right, then closes it with triumph a jar clasped in her hand.

Breakfast, with coffee again. Simple, slow and relaxed. We are both liking the lack of pressure that the last few days have carried.

Time passes as we organize our small amount of belongings and sort through what has been left behind by the last seasons' workers. Small chores are done.

'OK, so what are your plans?' I ask Barbara. We are sitting on the veranda facing the sea and three thousand miles away is an unseen Argentina. The view is just beautiful. The oceans wide vastness before us, again simplicity strikes me as a good thing.

'Very little, there are some books here, will see what they are like, watch the birds, maybe beachcomb and wait.'

'Don't worry, I will be fine. I will send a quick text on the new phone to yours, once I know the lay of the land. If, on the off chance someone does arrive with rangers, say you're from Head Office and they obviously didn't get the email. If you think it's a watcher, go to the small hut at the other end of the island, where we went last time. A stranger is very unlikely to find the start of the track. Send a note either way. I will come.' The wind is starting to pick up and we move inside.

I have gathered some bits together. Two phones both turned off, a washed tee shirt stuffed in one pocket, wallet with identity. We stand close and hug. Barbara kisses me.

'You be bloody careful. I do love you, you know, my superman.' Her hair smells of shampoo, nice. And I love you I say.

'One last thing, you may not like it. One of Dan's pistols is in the bag. It's loaded, a last resort.' She looks at me, nods, but says nothing. We go outside into the breeze. Barbara is on the veranda as I think 'unseen' and she laughs.

'That really is weird, come back to me.' I give an unseen wave, which I realize is stupid. I call, see you soon.

Chapter 10

I think fly and drift away with the breeze. I turn and fly down towards the rocky beach where there is a large block of concrete that the rangers boats use as a wharf for delivering people and supplies. I land on the block and think seen. I can't be seen from the house, which is hidden from view up on the hill. I look around me for a target, down the rocky shore is a piece of driftwood shaped like a shark. I lift my arm and point at it with one finger, I think light, and a stream of concentrated light hits the wood, it explodes into flame. Bloody hell! I try again at an old part pallet that has escaped commercial slavery. This time I use two fingers. The pallet is incinerated with a flash, the power at my control frightens me. I am also shocked that Island trusted me with this.

I walk down the steps at the back of the block, pick up a length of driftwood and then think fly. I fly around the lee side of the island at about 50 meters above the waves. I drop the wood and watch as it hits with a small splash, where it floats moving on the clear greened water. I fly up and away until I can just see my target about 300 meters away and I aim a single finger, the wood leaps burning. I am bloody Superman I think, good grief. What I have been trusted with has, completely shocked me. I am not sure this power should be in one person's hands. I float, drifting in the breeze, thinking lost thoughts and then awake to my plan.

I think unseen and fly south towards the capital. I am at about 1000 feet following the coast. The speed I am travelling I can't tell but the coast is flashing by, as I fly higher my perception changes. The ground speed seems to slow the more my altitude increases. Greenery and squares of farms and the dark of forest are below me, small towns come and go. Off to my right a domestic passenger flight is heading north. There are scattered clouds and I avoid them. I want to see my travel path. I am not sure what would happen if I hit an aircraft but I feel it wouldn't be good for either party.

A few minutes later the outlying smaller towns that surround the capital come into view, then my destination, the city. I drop lower and spot the parliament complex which is surrounded by the towers of commerce and apartment blocks. The clear grassy space in front of the parliament building is nearly empty. I land softly on the neatly trimmed lawn. My thoughts are rolling with the journey and how it has happened. I feel as though reality is a dream but it is reality. I steady myself to concentrate on my task.

A couple, with phones at the ready, pass me, heading towards the wide steps that reach up to main entrance. I follow them, snippets of architectural exclamations and minor stops to take photos slow their progress. I stay in step feeling vulnerable and highly visible. At a long stop for a smiling selfie I realize that I have flown, actually flown here and my feeling of distrust in the bracelet is stupidly misplaced. I turn from watching the photo shoot, walk up the stairs and into the vaulted main foyer. I am ignored. Security are stationed at intervals but not wary. I walk over to an information desk that has a map of the internal lay out of the building and the various offices.

A middle-aged woman with a bright colored dress is tapping away on a keyboard. I tap on the counter and say a quiet 'Hello'. She looks up and through me, she stands and peers around a column at the end of her counter, she looks around again, suitably puzzled. I am happy with my test. I wanted to be sure. I go to the map and work out my route to the offices I am looking for, the Prime Minister's suite.

As a staff member goes through the first security check I simply follow through the small waist high gate, then another. A ride in a lift with a young smartly dressed guy who has a quick argument with his brother about money on his phone, then into a corridor and I am outside a room with a sign 'Prime Minister's Office'. Shortly a woman comes down the corridor into the office. I follow. In this office there are three desks in what I presume is the antechamber to the Prime Ministers actual office. I stand watching, a few minutes later the door opens and the Finance Minister walks out. He is shorter than I thought, the door is left open.

'Thanks Jan.' to one of the secretaries, who looks up, smiles but says nothing and returns to her screen.

I take the chance and walk through the door. The room is smaller than I expected, photos of past Prime Ministers. A new photo of the king surrounded by our national flag with a wide window that looks across the old wooden Parliament buildings to a harbor in the distance. A couple of bookshelves, a wide desk, computer-armed with three large chairs in front of it with more chairs lining the wall. The Prime Minister is sitting concentrated on the screen in front of her. As I stand to one side taking this in, a secretary puts her head through the door.

'The Ambassador will be here in fifteen minutes, he seems a bit agitated.' The Prime Minister looks up.

'OK, thanks Jan, the last one was more relaxed, pity he went home. Close the door will you? I just want to finish this.' Jan nods and the door closes. The Prime Minister returns her focus to the screen.

She is about fifty. Oddly motherly, not slim but not fat either, she is known for her sharp wit and the ability to grasp the basics of an issue very quickly. She has risen through her party slowly, learning the balancing act of politics from early student unions and internships. Known to be blunt and a drive to do well for her people has put her in this office. I had vaguely followed her career, her evaluating of the political need and what the people have wanted has seemed impressive.

Named 'The Mother of The Nation.' By some idiot in the media, the title has stuck. A person who is liked or disliked, not many fence sitters, when she is discussed at local BBQs. She wears very bright colors, which I have rather liked. An odd way to pick a Prime Minister I think as I watch her work. She is better than most that have been behind the desk but my opinion is just that; an opinion.

I have been standing and thinking on how to reveal myself. I am just about to when there is a tap, the door opens and Jan puts her head around the door.

'Sorry, the Ambassador is on his way up. Seems pretty uptight, from what I gather, rude to security, blustering. Thought you should know.' She stops waiting for her bosses' thoughts. The PM looks up and takes this in.

'OK, send him through. Make some of that awful coffee he likes will you? Tea for me I think. Let's show our differences. Oh and get hold of James. Ask him to come in as soon as he can. Thanks.'

I stand still, I am thinking damn it and wonder how to approach this, when the door is opened by another secretary.

'The Ambassador of the United States, Prime Minister.' The secretary holds the door open and a man about my age marches in to the room, he waits standing, as the secretary retreats to the other office. I am stock still, the wheels are turning faster than I thought. I could be wrong but I am sure that my situation will come up here. Sometimes timing is everything. I wait and watch.

'Mr. Ambassador.' The Prime Minister stands and leans to shake hands over the desk not walk around in welcome. Her coldness evident, even to me.

'Prime Minister, thank you for seeing me.' She nods and motions towards one of the leather chairs. She leans back and surveys him. The military stance has never left him, greying, tanned and pompous. Known for having the President's ear but not his trust. The post he has is a reward for raising money in his state for the party but our country wasn't the place he expected to be rewarded with. I had read an in-depth article in one of the papers when he arrived and I remember being surprised at the insider knowledge it portrayed and now I am in the same room. Life has it's surprises.

'So Alex, why the rush and why were you rude to our staff? I don't like that.' I am surprised at the verbal slap from the Prime Minister but the power balance is made plain; this is my house, watch your step.

'My apologies Prime Minister, you are right.' Alex drops his head slightly but the words are smooth and weightless.

'This is a delicate and difficult matter, Prime Minister, and highly important to both our countries.' He stops and mulls his words then just spits it out.

'I have had credible intelligence that there has been a contact with alien technology here in your country.' The Prime Minister says nothing but she sits back in her chair and sighs, face disbelieving. The Ambassador moves forward in his chair.

'Please hear me out. Look, I know this will seem far-fetched and frankly unbelievable, but this information has come directly from the President's office. I have been tasked to pass on this report from one of our people who was in Australia when this situation arose. Incidentally, the Doctor Jeffery Shanes mentioned is a leading

Australian Orthopaedic surgeon amongst other qualifications. He lectures at their medical school in Sydney. Could I ask you to read the report now? It is only a couple of pages. Please note the clearances required on the report. Had I not had military experience and the clearances, I doubt I would have seen it.'

The pompous lean is hard to miss. The Ambassador produces two folded pieces of paper from his jacket pocket, unfolds them and places them on the leather desktop.

The Prime Minister looks at the two papers and reaches forward and picks them up.

'Aliens? Hard one to swallow Alex I...' There is a tap and a younger man opens the door and Jan walks through with a tray filled with cups. The Prime Minister turns the papers over deftly. The tray is placed on the end of the desk. The Ambassador is still and tense, waiting.

'Thank you Jan, can you see that we are not disturbed please? For no reason at all until the Ambassador has left.' Jan's eyes widen and she nods, direct orders are not normally given here I think. I have been watching this interaction with a feeling of dread, the wheels have certainly moved. Dan, or his bosses, have more influence than I thought. Which department do they hail from, I wonder. I don't know but the information seems to be at the highest level. Shit!

The younger man closes the door behind Jan and stays in the room. The Prime Minister looks at the Ambassador.

'I think you know James, Alex?' The ambassador gives a terse nod in James direction. James stands watching but says nothing.

'Prime Minister I cannot stress how highly confidential this information is, it has come from the White House with an "eyes only" classification. Given the importance I......' The Prime Minister interrupts quietly.

'Alex, please, I will say this once. Until I have read what is on this paper I cannot make any judgment on what I am about to do. You are in my office and my country, thank you. James please take a seat.' The Prime Minister turns the paper over and starts to read. James sits one seat away from the Ambassador and the Ambassador waits, red and obviously angry but silent.

I am amused at the interplay and would like to move behind the Prime Minister to read over her shoulder but I am pretty sure I know what is on those pages in essence. James watches the Prime minister, he is late thirties not wearing a tie, rather a designer tee shirt, jacket, expensive jeans. His Apple watch hums and he presses it without shifting his gaze. The Prime Minister rereads the pages and turns both over to check the back, her gaze over her desk, intense.

'You are sure about the information on here, Alex?' The Ambassador gives an affirmative nod.

'As much as we can be, we don't have the umm subject to verify of course, our investigator has done as much as he can.....' He stops. I have now become a subject, a target. I knew it but hearing the words somehow makes it even more unpleasant. The Prime Minister continues.

'The "subject" is a citizen of this country and your investigator worked under cover in a foreign country, namely mine.' The sarcasm washes around the room.

'Not only that, our local police are involved in an investigation of arson that involves our citizen whom appears to be your subject.' The Ambassadors head twitches. He didn't know I think, ah ha!

'Someone at your intelligence service asked questions about your subject at a high level in ours. We are a very small country Alex, and that has it's draw backs but also its advantages. Your people don't talk to our people for no reason and never the way this was handled, bells ring. When bells ring, I get called.'

She stops and turns her chair and looks out the window. She turns her chair back, her anger dissipated. The Ambassador leans forward to speak but she holds her hand up.

'I have not finished. Not only that, but someone burnt your subjects house to the ground. Don't you think that is strange, given the circumstances?'

The Ambassador sits back in silence, mouth working and the Prime Minister presses the point.

'The subject.' Sarcasm underlines the point 'is a long time government employee. Our Intelligence Service being quizzed by yours about a person with any government background makes our people nervous Alex, so we ring people and ask questions. Which is why James is here.' As she passes James the pages, the Ambassador puts his hand out.

'These are eyes only!'

'And this is my office, I make the rules, don't annoy me any further Alex. I warn you.'

The Prime Minister uses the voice that has won admiration on both sides of parliament, cutting and clear. The Ambassador subsides. James has taken the pages and is reading, ignoring the outburst. He reads and then rereads. He looks at the Prime Minister and passes the pages back to her. She passes them back to the Ambassador. He quickly folds them and they disappear into the jacket pocket. James sits both hands peeked, fingertips together against his lips but says nothing, a thinking pose.

The Prime Minster looks at James.

'First thoughts?' James sits and then places his hands on his legs he looks at the Prime Minister his voice oddly a lot lower than I thought it would be.

'Likely we are dealing with a real situation but I don't know. Your boys under estimated him and fucked up. He is angry and with good cause, I think. We need to talk to him if we can. I would call your people off, if you can, but that's not your call is it Ambassador?' The Prime Minster is silent and appears to be weighting James' words. The Ambassador opens his mouth but James continues.

'One of your team died I believe Ambassador. Did you know?' The Ambassador starts and snaps his head towards the Prime Minister then back to James. I feel grim and angry and I rock on my feet watching my tale unfold.

'What? No! How do you know this? I would have heard if...' He slows, realising that agents working in another country aren't really welcome, particularly if caught. It is one of the real no noes and he may have been left out of his own countries manoeuvring. I wonder about this stupid man's understanding of inter country politics.

'The flight that brought your people and Dr Shanes here, had a corpse on board when they arrived back in Australia. The Australian customs had some very awkward questions I understand and some are still being asked. I have contacts there. As the Prime Minister points out, we are a small country and we are very close to our neighbors.' James is baiting and the Prime Minister lets him. She watches this and then asks.

'OK Alex, you came here to ask something, what is it?' The Ambassador looks from one to the other purses his lips, then starts.

'He has agreed to a meeting at Holland Air Force Base in two days' time. We want your permission to run the operation and have him taken into protective custody.'

There, he said it, what I had figured all along, Jesus. I almost burst out loud with laughter. I put a hand over my mouth, just to remind myself to shut up. There is a deep quiet in the room. The Prime

Minister turns her chair to the view and James sits back and puts his hands behind his head and looks at the wooden panelling that runs across the ceiling. He asks.

'That is Holland Air Force base here?' The Ambassador nods slowly. Then sees what he is asking. An American led operation in another country against one of its own citizens. He goes very quiet. My future is being balanced, a very strange feeling. The Ambassador is now looking at a bust of Churchill on the desk, time passes.

The Prime Minister turns her chair back to the desk, her lips in a very straight line.

'Well, thank you Ambassador. I will consider your request and you will have an answer tomorrow by twelve o'clock. One thing, under no circumstances is any and I mean, any, of your armed forces to land on our soil prior to my decision. Do you understand? Should that happen they will be taken into custody and I will hold you personally responsible. One other thing, I expect a call from your President between now and twelve p.m. tonight. Do you understand? Now this interview is over.'

The Prime Minister presses a button on her desk phone. The Ambassador is white with shock, he rocks in his seat then stands and opens his mouth but the Prime Minister has turned her chair to the view. James watches and, like me I think, fascinated. He stays seated.

'Prime Minister I protest!' There is no answer from the chair or the view. James stares at the back of her chair and waits. I am smiling broadly and wish he could see me. Well done Prime Minister!

The Ambassador turns on his heel, opens the door and keeps walking, the stiff march showing his rage. The outer office is completely silent. James stands and closes the door quietly.

'Was that wise of me, James?' The Prime Minister has turned her chair half way back towards the room. The question has a wondering tone.

'They started an operation on foreign soil. Our soil. They didn't even have the courtesy to try for some sort of permission, which I am surprised at, given our relationship over the years. Which is why I am fairly convinced that they are right, that this is the first contact, or at least they believe it is. Who knows how but this chap Bill Sheppard has outwitted them.' He stops, running more data through his mind. The Prime Minister pours water for them both from a decanter on her desk, the tea and coffee cold.

'How did you get the information about the corpse?' He shrugs.

'My counterpart from Australia was pissed about the strings the Americans were trying pull, after a plane returned from here. He contacted me to find out what I knew about the plane, which had brought the doctor and his friends. I did some digging. It was easy to track, very few ever land here. It arrived, waited then went back and landed in Sydney. A customs guy there got annoyed by someone's attitude and they turned it over. They found the dead guy and people were arrested. The doctor screamed blue murder when he found out he was up to his neck in something he had no idea about. About the same time, the states were asking questions here about Bill Sheppard. It appears those questions came right from the top.' He stops and drinks some water. I am thirsty myself.

'The dead person had to have come from there as part of their team and died here, as they had the same number of passengers, including the dead guy. So Bill Sheppard was probably involved, if we meet him, I will ask. I also checked with the local police, which is how I knew about his house fire, which I passed to you.'

The Prime Minister turns fully back to her desk.

'James, I want everything you have on Bill Sheppard. Some maps of Holland Air force and also get hold of the Air Vice Marshall. I don't care where he is, get him here by eight tomorrow morning. The first, I want back here in one hour, please. Put your full SIS on standby, everyone. Also ask all the staff in my office that have clearance, to stay. I need some space to think. There are more questions but we will come to that in due course. Are you happy?' James nods and stands as he walks towards the door, he half turns.

'I will increase security here as well.' The Prime minister nods. 'Yes fine, nothing too obvious do you think?' James gives a quick flick of the hand in accent and closes the door behind him. The Prime Minister gets up and opens a small bar fridge that is hidden behind a panel, takes out a sparkling water, pours it into a whiskey glass and turns and stands looking out of the window, with her back to me. This is her thinking place, I guess.

Chapter 11

I walk to and fro a couple of times to get my stopped circulation moving. I then take out my old ID card and place it on the brown leather desktop, as my hand moves away from the card, it appears. Magic.

I stand back and wait. A couple of minutes later the Prime Minister turns and sits in her chair. It is now her eyes are glued to the card, the look of surprise then goes to curiosity and she picks the card up reads it. Now her look becomes shock. She looks up and around the room, she looks again at the card. Tentatively she says.

'Hello?'

I have made my choice. I need to trust my instincts, in for a penny I think.

'Hello Prime Minister.' Her head snaps up with a 'Bloody hell!' The complete shock is evident but not as bad as I thought it would be. She is looking around the room at no one.

'Prime Minister, I am going to appear, please keep your hands on the desk. I am not armed nor will I harm you, but if people are called I will go and we won't talk again. I would like to be able to trust you. Trust is one of the main reasons I am here.'

I wait, she sits staring in the direction of my voice, hands not moving.

'Very well, surprise me.' As I appear her right hand goes to her mouth.

'Unbelievable, truly, unbelievable.' Her face shows the shock.

'Um, do you mind if I have a drink of water? I have been here a while.' She nods towards the water on the desk, small things can be just wonderful. I drink one then fill a second glass, she watches quietly. Out of a pocket I take a small piece of paper and place it on her desk.

'That is Chris James phone number. you know him of course. I worked with him and knew him personally, please call him. A reference if you will, he has no idea of the...ah circumstances I am in, of course. But I thought it may help you feel happier. Just an idea.'

She looks at me long and hard, coin spinning. I sit down in one of the chairs and wait. I am on very high alert. I doubt many leaders wouldn't call security but I have flipped the coin and it is still spinning. We will see. She reaches across her desk and picks up the mobile, looks at the number and taps the screen. I drink more water.

'Hello? Chris, yes Ruth. Look, I need a quick favor. Do you know a Bill Sheppard? Good. Can you give me a quick run-down on him? I know he was in your department but simply put, do you trust him? This is important. Chris, I can't explain but it is very important.'

Suddenly I feel strangely out of sorts I look across the Prime Ministers shoulder towards blue sky and think about going home. I can hear Chris' voice as the Prime Minister listens. The babble is broken. I can't decipher the words. The concentration is absolute, her eyes on Churchill. I somehow wander to the fact I don't have a home and with that thought I turn my mind to Barbara, I am missing our simple life. I miss her. That too, is simple.

My wondering comes to a close with 'OK Chris thanks.' The phone call has ended and the Prime Minister puts the phone on the desk. She gives me a look then gets up and crosses to the bar fridge, gets another sparkling water, pours it and sits back down to face me.

'So you are trustworthy. Chris was pretty forthright, not like him really but then he has retired. On the other hand that was before whatever happened to you, happened.' She stops looking at me then pondering. I look back.

'I am still the same person just with.....'I hadn't thought about this before. 'with added extras.' I stop. I am not happy about the wording but what does one say?

She is watching me and some decision is made, she looks at me and says.

'I am going to tell the staff to leave us completely alone. I'm telling you, so you don't jump to any conclusions, when I pick up the phone.' I nod an affirmative.

'Jan, can you make sure I am not disturbed for exactly half an hour please. No one at all. James is coming back. He will have to wait, no calls either, thank you.' She sits back in the chair. She looks at me intensely, investigating what she sees.

'Chris tells me you are completely trustworthy. I was only three weeks into this job when the Adele affair developed. You ran it I understand, no one off the hook, all evidence presented, very well executed and you made the government look good in a dirty little nightmare. Even losing the staff that you did was efficient, given the circumstances. Not hushed up, the media handled exceptionally, with no loose ends. And you turned down promotion, interesting. Why, by the way, didn't you take the job offered?'

I shrug. The Adele Affair as the media dubbed it, was a drug smuggling operation within the Parks Department from off shore islands. The Adele had been the boat that was used. When the operation came to light I had been amazed, angry and shocked all at once. The blemish across the department had made me see red. I wanted all those involved and I finally got them. People I had known and trusted. I spent a lot of hours perfecting evidence files for the Public Prosecution. Now a number of those people are in jail. A result but one I could have done without.

'Simply, it was my job to see all of us worked within the rules and they broke them. I didn't see that I should get promoted for doing my job, too close to a payoff for my taste.' She nods slowly and sips her drink.

'OK, can you give me the story of what is going on and how you have ended up in my office, the abridged version, given our time. One thing, you were here for the whole of the Ambassadors visit?' I nod slowly.

'Yes. I heard it all.'

'Right, please begin.'

I start at the beginning and run through the last few days. Trying not miss detail, make it human, losing a home. The mental work it takes to hold one's self together when faced with the seemingly impossible, the unworldly and alien. I wondered if I should leave out Dan's buddy but it is easier to tell the truth. Her eyes raise and look into mine then return to Winston. The story rolls on for another few minutes then I stop with.

'And now I am here in the Prime Minister's office.'

She stands turns and looks out the broad window. I wait as gears whirl. Her phone buzzes and then again. She picks it up stares at the message then puts the phone down with a hum.

'That is the Presidents people insisting they talk to me urgently. That is also interesting. To be precise the Secretary of State. Do you know Bill, how many times he has contacted me in five years Bill? No, you wouldn't, but actually, never.'

I feel that the clock is ticking and I am being forced into a corner. I know this a mental state but it doesn't change what I feel. So I sit with the trust.

'Prime Minister, I am feeling the time pressure of the meeting at Holland. I did this simply to buy time which is running out. The Americans have put a lot of pressure on me personally, worse, my wife. It would be easy for you to pass me to them and see how the game plays out. Provided your people could actually catch me. I am aware of this. Big countries push or punish little countries for what they want. I would be stupid not to recognize this. One thing that stands out is their ability to react so quickly, in another country and my country. That bothers me. Really it means they obviously have tight networks that are across the globe. You may know this. I don't. I was just detecting on a beach. I guess my point is; I want to know if I can trust you. I like things simple.'

I reach for my water as the mobile on the desk buzzes again. Her hand hovers over the device and then rests on the desk.

'I will not throw one of this countries citizens to the wolves. The only thing that holds any country together are the rules that govern us. Trust in the law...I,' I interrupt.

'Sorry, but what the Library holds may be the greatest repository of knowledge ever imagined. What the bracelet lets me do and mechanics of how it works, is there just as a small example.' I pull my sleeve back to make my point. 'What that means Prime Minister, is power beyond measure on our planet.'

She is staring at me, eyes drilling into me. Then they drop to my arm seeing actual evidence, she looks back.

'What are you suggesting, exactly?' I shrug.

'They don't know what the bracelet or I am capable of. The fact that I can actually disappear is worth more than a lot. If they actually knew what I can do and add that they have no idea about Island, should they find out, I don't believe they will stop.'

I breathe a deep sigh, the target on my back feels bigger somehow.

'This isn't just the Americans. They just happened to be in the right place. Any of the bigger powers, China, England, Russia, France. Take your pick. Power is a hard tool to put down. Seems to me Nationalist governments just aren't designed to pass off knowledge to the people of the world for the peoples benefit. The United Nations is a farce; the Security Council controls it but will never act out unless for their selfish perspective. The number of humans torn to shreds by their own governments where the UN either doesn't act or is just far too slow. Rwanda, the Balkans. Anyway, if the Americans find out about the depth of what is on offer. I believe they will invade.'

The Prime Minister bangs her hand on the desk, hard.

'Don't be so bloody melodramatic....' At this point, I become unseen and there is silence. Out of the emptiness, I ask.

'Could you open the window please? I will come back. I just want to point something out.' She is stunned, I can see but also curious. She goes to the casement window and lifts it.

'Please stand back.' I drift out the window twenty feet away. 'Prime Minister.'

I call and am now able to be seen. I am now floating eight stories in the air. Her amazed face is a picture. I go backwards some distance then go unseen. I am too aware of the universal mobile cameras. A few seconds is one thing, minutes is another. I go back through the window carefully and become seen standing by the bookshelf. The Prime Minister is shaking slightly and is holding the back of her chair. She twists to look at me as I say.

'Sorry, I didn't mean to shock you but I wanted give you a real idea of what the bracelet is capable of. Seeing is believing, all that stuff.' She nods and drops into the chair.

'You disappearing is one thing but seeing you flying, umm levitating? Good God. It is just amazing I....' she trails off looking in the places I suspect I have been as well. There is silence in the room. She looks across at me.

'Yes, I see what you mean about the Americans. So what they don't know is an advantage. I do get your point. I think we need James in here. He is an exceptional strategist and before you ask, he is completely trust worthy and I do mean completely. Are you happy with that?' I don't want more people knowing, I sit thinking.

'OK, but only about the bracelet, lets avoid Island for the minute, in fact, Prime Minister I insist. Anyway oddly, it is protecting him to a degree. His networks are fairly wide or at least the discussion with the Ambassador proved that.' She looks at me then to a corner of the room asks.

'You don't trust my judgment?' I stare at Churchill and reply.

'I trust your judgment Prime Minister, it's whether I trust his.' She turns to her desk and presses a button on the desk phone as she lifts the receiver.

'Jan? I presume James is still there? OK, good. Send him in. Please keep the phones quiet. Yes, I know about the Americans. If they ask tell them I am not able to be disturbed. Yes, I know about the Secretary of State. If he gets very pushy, tell him I personally said he has to wait, all right? Thank you.' She looks at me.

'Your situation has upset my office staff.' And she smiles, some of the tension leaves the room. Just at that moment as the door opens. I become unseen. James walks into the office, he has a file under his arm.

The Prime Minister sits looking at my chair and shakes her head.

'James, sorry to keep you waiting. Please lock the door.' James is surprised by this but turns and flicks the lock. She motions to another chair. Not mine.

'Sorry James but the situation we have here is difficult and must be kept within this room. Do you understand? I mean completely. Never to be discussed without my express permission.' I doubt that he has heard the Prime Minister so serious. He is completely focused on her. He nods and swallows. Time to appear I think.

'Jesus Christ!' He has jumped partly out of his chair, face white.

'Sorry, didn't mean to scare you but it seems to make a point.' I stand and reach out a hand.

'Bill Sheppard' James' mouth is open but he automatically puts out his hand.

'Ah James...James Brandon.' I nod, look at the Prime Minister and wait. It is her office after all. The Prime Minister starts talking. There is a vaguely amused look on her face. James sits but is still staring at me, a freak show I think to myself. I could make a fortune as a magician: Bill Magic, great.

'James is the head of the SIS. To be precise, the acting head but he will be head. You know how it works.'

Yes, I do. Prime Ministers get who they want in their top roles. I say nothing, nothing to do with me, she trusts him, fine. I reserve judgment. He is very young for the job but I don't know him, her call. The Prime Minister continues, looking at James.

'Bill thought it would be better to have some support from his government, which is why he is here. He is being targeted by a foreign country. I will let him give you a run down on what has happened to him and how the Americans got involved from his point of view. It is interesting and fills in gaps but before he starts. I do want to tell you that there may be more information he will pass on to you, if he feels you are trust worthy enough. I am saying this as I want to be clear that I trust you but it is Bills decision and I don't want any vestiges of doubt between you and I. You understand?' I smile, that was well done and fair, not many bosses go that far. James looks back at me.

'I think the Prime Minister is pretty fair, your relationship has to be strong. Anyway this what has happened to me so far.....' I speak for about ten minutes. When I stop James stands and goes to the bar fridge and passes the water around. He sits back in his chair and puts his hands behind his head, thinking, a small glass bottle dangles from his fingers. The Prime Minister is looking at the view, chair back towards me. James starts.

'Pity about the meeting at Holland. I understand the why, just a pity really, your doctor, the GP. Not paid by anybody, do you know?' He asks this obliquely, I shake my head but there is doubt there.

'He was after brownie points for his ego, just stupid I think. He might have been paid, I don't think it is his style, but then I really don't know.' James makes a humming sound and drinks water at my answer. The Prime Minister turns her chair she looks at James.

'OK, we have a timing issue and a pressure issue. I am curious to see what the Secretary of State has to say and I have to give some sort of answer regarding Holland. I will not let any foreign country run their own operation in this country against any of our citizens. It is that simple. But there are balances, I also don't want to involve any defence forces until we have a plan and a reason exactly why we are running any operation. Of course, the other consideration is the pressure the US is going to bring to bear. I suspect a lot.' The Prime Minister turns her gaze to me.

'Have you put any thought at all with what you what actually are going to do with the changes that have been made to you?' I am slightly annoyed by this question. It almost forces me to expose Island to James and yet I am still unsure. I let it ride.

'Well, no. Not really. Look, I have been pushed and threatened, what would you do? This is alien hardware in my arm. Think about that for just one minute and see how you would react. The whole thing, situation, call it what you will, is rather outside my experience. I would add those bastards burnt my house to the ground. I don't like being pushed.'

The Prime Minister arches an eyebrow but she has taken the point. James has watched the interaction just as he is about to speak the Prime Ministers mobile buzzes. She looks at the screen.

'It is the President of the United States.' She then does, a thing that I feel few, have ever done.

'He can wait. No, I will ring him back!' I laugh and James looks stunned then starts laughing as well, the Prime Minister sits smiling.

'OK. A plan I think. You are lead in this James.' She looks at James then at me.

'Are you happy to go ahead with this meeting? We will arrange for you to be protected as much as possible. I know your trust is limited. I understand that. On the other hand it may give you, and us, a way forward. The point is Bill, you won't be alone. You and James can sort the detail, if you aren't happy, just say so.'

I had come here for support and I am surprised at what I have been given. I can't go back. I nod in agreement and the Prime Minister turns to James.

'OK, we say we are going ahead with the Holland meeting. We are in charge and it is very low key. They have no choices, as you say, this is our soil. So our rules. I will get in touch with the Armed Forces but they won't like me seemly to take any lead. Can you speak to them to smooth feathers?' The Prime Minister nods and taps notes on the keyboard.

'I know I am being pedantic Prime Minister but specific orders please. Any wiggle room and there will be arguments that will cost time. Turf wars is what the military is very good at. I don't need it now, please be blunt.' I am a little surprised at James' attitude and my face shows it, the Prime Minister laughs.

'James was in the Navy. He knows the system, that's why he works here now, wasn't that good with orders for orders sake.' James says nothing; he is looking through the file in front of him.

I look across the Prime Minister's shoulder, a helicopter is delivering something to a building to the right of my view, the building has a scaffolding skeleton around it with a white covering. The helicopter slows, it has a sling with a bag attached underneath it, an electric hook is released and the rope disappears out of sight. I stand and go to the bar fridge for more cold water. I grab three small bottles. Put one in front of James, who grunts, he is still reading. One on the edge of the desk, in front of my chair. The last one slips from my fingers and drops on the carpet by the Prime Minister's feet. I bend slightly to pick it up but the Prime Minister gives a quick 'it's fine' and bends forward to pick it up.

Chapter 12

At this point the back of her chair and her computer explode. I grab her shoulders and pull her towards me as another bullet follows the first. We have fallen backwards and I am scrambling to pull the Prime Minister by whatever clothing I can grab, getting her away from the window towards the wall. Shards of glass, chair foam and computer screen are scattered across the desk and floor. James has dived to the floor and is yelling.

'Are you OK? Are you OK?'

I have pulled the Prime Minister to the corner of the room closest to the window. She is shaking and in tears, not surprising, I think. There are two holes punched through the window. James has crawled to us.

'Are you OK?' His face is white, not fear, just extremely bloody angry. I agree. The Prime minister is nodding her head 'Yes! Yes I am OK. I wasn't hit.' I struggle to a proper sitting position and snap at James.

'James. Listen, we need that chopper and the people in it. We need proof of an attack. Open the window. Now! James now!' I stand and move to the towards the window.

His attention goes from the Prime Minister to me then he reacts as I become unseen. He stands to one side of the window and quickly slides it open. The helicopter can be heard moving away. I grab a curtain and pull it until it rips away in my hands and bundle it up against my chest. I then think fly and vanish at the same time. The helicopter is moving quickly as I come level with it.

I want to know if I am right. I have spent a lot of time working with helicopters over the years, shifting gear, shooting pest animals, searching for lost people, doing medevac's and searching for aircraft that have gone down.

This one is brand new, dull black with the doors off. It has two pilot crew that are dressed in black, this is odd, civilian aircraft generally only have one pilot, in the rear are two people also dressed in black, one has a rifle upright between his knees which is long due to the suppressor at the end of the barrel. Both have dark masks with microphones. The helicopter is an Airbus 130 with a fantail, which means it has fan instead of a rotor at the back, good I think. I am under the rotors but feel no wash, I am looking directly at the passengers. The rifle is a snipers professional kit, I had spent hundreds of hours shooting pests from these moving platforms, the tools of the trade are discussed and argued over and I know more than enough to recognize the set up.

The pilot has set a course and is dropping lower to camouflage his path in the higher hills that surround the capital. As he drops between two hills I drift towards the rear of the craft and the fan. The chopper is over steep open farmland heading towards the coast. I am still clutching the curtain from the PMs office. I get as close as I dare to the fan and throw the bunched material into the fan.

The effect is almost instantaneous. The fan sucks the fabric into the spinning blur and chokes it solid. The helicopter lurches, drops, and slues around in an ever tightening circle, the pressure of the rotors increase so quickly that the tail section rips off the helicopter and spins out and downward. The main part of the craft is spinning and spiralling faster towards the ground, then as in hits the side of the grassy slope, explodes as the fuel ignites, rotors disintegrate in clouds of earth and grass, shards of rotor spread through the air as the fuselage rolls burning into a stream. The tail has landed further up the slope.

I hover over the crash site. I am horrified at what I have created and yet oddly aloof, justified somehow, hunters have to be careful they don't become quarry. The anger of what they have tried to do is still sitting with me. As I get lower to the site I see a backpack lying on the grass. I land and rummage through it. There is a water bottle, a first aid kit, a knitted black hat, a mobile phone and treasures of treasures, a wallet full of annoying evidence. Unbelievable arrogance I think, and stupid. Stupid is as stupid does!

I leave the site and fly back towards the capital. I fly past the Parliament building and see the window is closed but the two holes are visible. I fly back to front lawn and land. I walk back into the entrance, as before, I am surprised the building isn't in lockdown and things seem normal. I retrace my steps to the Prime Ministers offices following staff on their movements. Just before the Prime Ministers offices there are staff toilets. I look both ways before opening the door. I quickly become seen and then head to Prime Minister's office. There is a security guard outside the office. He presumes I have permission to be in this part of the building as I have got through two other checkpoints.

'Hi, I have an appointment with the Prime Minister, Bill Sheppard.' He nods, glances at the backpack and asks me to wait. He returns and says the Prime Minister isn't seeing anyone.

'Can you please tell the secretary that you spoke to, that the Prime Minister rang me from her private phone and has asked me to come. Tell her that James Brandon has asked for me as well.' He stares at me. Two names are harder to argue with, he shrugs and asks me to wait again. He comes back and holds the door open and I enter the outer office. There are a number of people in the office besides the normal staff. Jan is looking very harassed, she clicks off from a mobile call and walks towards me.

'Jan, please take me to the Prime Minister' She looks surprised. 'She hasn't been injured has she?' She starts and shakes her head. 'I was asked to come.' I state this and wait. She walks to the Prime Ministers door and taps. James opens the door. The gatekeeper now I think, he sees me and with some control gives a slight grin. Three young men who are obviously not part of the office furniture, watch carefully.

'Bill ah....come in. Thanks Jan.' Jan looks uneasy but just nods. I ask the question as he closes the door.

'How is she?' The answer comes from the corner of the room. The Prime Minister is seated there with her feet up on a poof. The area has been cleaned and her office chair and computer have been replaced. Fast work.

'I am OK, thanks. That was a bloody surprise. Yes, I could have moved but those bastard's aren't going to push me out of my own office!' I smile at her. I agree with the sentiment but am not convinced it is wise.

'I am sorry to have put you at risk. I had no idea they would be that stupid. Anyway those people in the chopper won't be able to again. They are all dead.'

James and the Prime Minister say "what?" at the same time, their faces mirror surprise, disbelief.

'Your curtain, it got sucked into the tail rotor fan and the chopper went down.' There is silence then James speaks.

'Curtains for them then!' we are then all laughing at once. Bloody hell!

'Where is the crash?' He asks.

'About a kilometre off highway 30 on a farm about three kilometres from Ashland; still burning as far as I know. Won't be hard to find.' James taps his phone and sends orders. I wait until he has finished.

'You cleaned up pretty quickly'. I note, looking around the room, James answers.

'Didn't want the media crawling around the place, too much to explain and who do we link an attack like that to and why? There has never been an assassination or an attempt in our history, so better to avoid it I think. The Prime Minister agrees. There are our people on the building now, by the way.' He twitches his head towards the office block through the window.

'Will the staff stay quiet?' I ask. James and the Prime Minister look at each other, the Prime Minister answers.

'Pretty certain, they are hand-picked, Official Secrets and all that.' She looks tired and I don't blame her, getting shot at isn't fun. She needs rest and I say so.

'Well, it would be nice but the President is calling in fifteen minutes' She looks sour.

I slide a wallet out of my pocket and pass it to her. This may help in your ah...negotiations.'

She looks at me then opens the wallet. There is an ID card, a driver's license, money, some random pieces of paper and the golden chalice, a CIA card. I pass the small backpack to James.

'Good God!' James' mouth is open and the Prime Minster stares at me.

'How the hell did you get this?'

'I found it on the hillside in amongst the wreckage. Very lucky. Shows the arrogance with which they hold our little country I think. But the real point is does the President know? He may, he may not but it is real proof to show the world how the US does business, which I guess is pretty rare. I would say they are wondering where their chopper is right now. It must have come off a navy ship somewhere out there and not that far away. James nods and picks up his phone, more requests are issued. He stops talking, grimaces then passes the phone to the Prime Minister and she listens then snaps at the phone.

'Listen Air Vice Marshall, you work for the people of this country and you will do as Mr. Brandon has requested. I will send all Defence Heads instructions including you, covering this. I do not care what else you have on. Just do it with no delay or I will replace you. Good bye!' She slams the phone back into James' hand. 'Pompous prick!' She shakes her head. The tax on the Prime Minister is being more apparent and I can see James' intensity has grown; they are both feeling the strain.

'One thing I would add. I had other means of taking that chopper down. But the fabric will show in the crush analysis. It's a bit strange but it means there is nothing to link our forces to the crash. No external explosives.' The two faces are looking at me. Wondering what my 'other means' actually is, I suspect. I change the subject.

'Do we have a few minutes for a bite and a change of scene? Frankly, you have no idea what the President is going to say but given what you have. I think the discussion will be reactionary. I need food and I am sure getting out of here will be good for us all. What do you think?' The Prime Minister tilts her head in thought and finally nods. James opens the door and speaks to someone.

'OK, we move.' James leads and I am behind the Prime Minister and a young man I don't know, is behind me. Our procession is watched by the office staff and I can see the questions about me in their glances. I smile at them, we go to a lift, then left down a corridor and into a rather bright conference room. There are hatchway sliding doors in the middle of the wall that open to a kitchen, a couple of people are busy doing kitchen things.

An older lady waves at the Prime Minister and she waves back with a 'Hi Anne.'

The young man has stopped outside the door, acting as guard. I note another young man has appeared in the kitchen standing watching. James is being careful.

At the end of the room is a medium sized screen with attending speakers and at one end of the conference table is a computer. The Prime Minister takes the seat in front of the computer. Anne calls to James that the food is ready. Tea and coffee trays are set out with sandwiches and savouries and the doors are closed between the two rooms. I note James locks the doors and draws the waiting curtains over them. There is quiet as we all eat and drink. After a few minutes James taps at his phone.

'Shifting the venue.' He explains. I just sit and wait. I am on the sideline. It is good to eat and just have time to be. The jerking flow of this has become my life and I don't like how little control I have. Barbara comes into my thoughts again. I take the new small phone that I have never used out of my jacket, power it up send a short text and turn it off. James is watching.

'Texting my wife, it's a new phone. I didn't trust the old ones.' he hums, head nodding, he gets it.

'Is she safe?' he is asking if she can be picked up and used as a lever.

'They won't find her.' and I believe that to be true, just the same, I am still concerned. I wonder where that grey line between concern and worry actually is, and how wide.

The Prime Minister has eaten and had a cup of tea. She has been listening I think but in fact probably thinking about the conversation to come. Out of her carry bag she has put the wallet and its contents beside the computer, she has also added the file that James had. She writes notes quickly on a small pad. Preparation finished she looks at us both, her head goes up and she taps the table top. The leader is in session.

'Under no circumstances will you say anything unless I ask you. And then keep those answers brief, if you don't know, say so. Mr. Sheppard, I doubt very much I will include you. I do not want the President to know you are here. He may know, I am not sure. I am the only person in sight of the camera. Please shift to sit beside James, they will follow eye contact on the screen and I don't want them to know who exactly or how many are in this room, are we clear?'

We both nod in unison as I move to the other side of the table. Her thinking is clear and precisely detailed, I like it and very wise. The room goes quiet again, each with our own thoughts, the screen buzzes and a face appears. Our eyes glue themselves to the screen.

The face is known right across the world. Tanned with a Hispanic black background, this man had defied the odds even more than Obama. Handsome with a comic seed in the eyes, he has brought his country together. How, a wide range of political commentators can't quite understand. He started as a Republican then became a Democrat. He has managed to reach over the vast divide since the 'Trump' years. Described as a kaleidoscope of a man, uniting a torn country. The people love him and the comments about Kennedy and Camelot are often played but there seems to be more to him, more substance somehow.

I wonder about the shattered glass kaleidoscope of people who make up the power base in Washington. Shards gathering in the light. Then I wonder who is hiding what from that light.

The President speaks.

'Prime Minister, good to see you again.' they have both obviously met somewhere before he was President maybe, I didn't know. I must have been fishing, I think. The President is sitting at a desk, which seems to be the Oval Office with windows and curtains behind him and green shows through the windows.

'Mr. President. Yes, it has been sometime since Lisbon, we have both had elections and we are both here. Your first and my second, congratulations.' The Prime Minister smiles at the screen and the President smiles back.

'Yes, I seem to have the support of the people. It is unfortunate that we could not meet in person but still, needs must.' The Prime Minister shifts in her chair and her face goes hard.

'Interesting term Mr. President "Needs must!" Tell me, what is the all fired hurry from the White House to contact me? Urgent calls from the Secretary of State and now one from you. Please explain the urgency.' Her tone is as hard as flint. The President is obviously surprised and questions ripple in his eyes. The complete change of tone has puzzled him. He continues.

'Well, Prime Minister. We have had credible information that there has been a contact made between one of your citizens and an alien entity. I know this may be difficult to believe but…' The Prime Minister cuts over him. She is snarling now, her anger lashes the screen.

'Is that why you ordered one of your black operations forces to have me assassinated? Was that 'Needs must' Mr President?'

The Presidents face is a complete picture. The utter lack of knowledge and surprise is evident. His face snaps sideways to someone off camera, when it turns back his anger is very plain.

'I am assured that is not true.' The Prime Minister smiles and waits for a second and then says.

'Whoever has told you this, is lying.'

She puts the ID card to the camera, then the driver's license, then the CIA card. The President is completely silent. The Prime Minister then taps her keyboard and a spilt screen appears with a photo of her office chair, she then replaces the first with another of her office desk and computer.

'The helicopter that your team arrived in, is scattered across one of our countries hillsides. It is being delved through by our police and military aircraft inspectors as we speak. Those on board are dead, Mr. President. All four of them. Unfortunate, as I would have liked to have spoken to them. But personally I have other thoughts. Not that I want people dead. Still, there is a lot of anger here.'

The coolness and calmness of her reply almost has me shivering, this is the edge that is felt in our parliament and is feared; now I know why. The President says nothing for seconds and time passes.

'Madam Prime Minister are you all right? Have you been injured in any way? I have no knowledge of this operation, if indeed it came from our country. It is something I never would have ordered. Should I find any proof that this is so. I will hold these people to account. I am honestly very shocked.' The Prime Minister shakes her head.

'No, I have not been harmed but not for the want of trying.' Her point is pushed home. 'Nor were any of our citizens.'

'I am deeply, deeply sorry for this. I need to ask some questions. Can we reconvene in one hour, please? There are still things we need to go through but I need a little time. There are now, of course, more urgent issues to check.' The President sounds genuine but then they make a career out of that, I think.

'One hour Mr. President, we will talk then. Thank you.' She reaches across the keyboard and terminates the call. We sit quietly. I stand, open the curtains and the doors to the kitchen, collect dishes, plates and trays place them on the counter. Anne calls.

'Thank you, would you like more tea and coffee?' I nod with a smile and a 'will do dear' reply returns, I slide the doors closed.

The Prime Minister is sitting back in her chair turning over the CIA card in her hand, she asks the room.

'What do you think? He ordered it?' I say nothing, this is James' territory, James shrugs.

'Frankly I doubt it, he seems very pissed. On the other hand, is he pissed off about having his hand caught in the till? He is going to try to verify everything you have said, this is after all, a highly embarrassing situation for him and his presidency. He is relatively new at the job, he will want a second term and the house elections aren't that far away. He wants complete control to develop his policies. Being caught sending a black Ops team to a desert somewhere is one thing but to an ally who they fought with in World War one and two, is another. He's got good reason to be very careful on how this played. The cards shook him, as did your chair and knowing the team are all dead. We have bodies that can be identified. And of course, there is nothing like bullet holes to make an elected official realize the risks they run.'

The Prime Minister gives him a piecing look then she laughs.

'Well, it was a miss. Bill, your thoughts.' I am surprised she has asked; this level is beyond me and I am very conscious of the various pressures.

' I really don't know. My trust is limited, frankly I am tired and I....'

There is a tap on the sliding doors and they open. Anne is standing there with tea, coffee and a plate of biscuits, I almost laugh. I stand and pass the refreshments around. Anne closes the door and James stands and locks it and closes the curtains. I sit and start again.

'I just don't know and I don't believe that you will ever know, unless you go to the horse's mouth?'

'What do you exactly mean?' James asks me, the Prime Minister has an idea of what I saying, her eyes are sparkling. She answers for me.

'You mean sit and listen in his office? I grin back at her and shrug. 'I can try. I have never been so far but I can try......Hmm.' I end with thinking sounds.

I lift the sleeve of my sweatshirt and tap the tattoo. Neither person has seen this and their eyes are glued to the raised gold hieroglyphs. Their eyes raise to mine and at the same time an answer from Island arrives in my head.

'Sorry, just needed to concentrate a bit. Yes, I can do it, with a little help.' James echoes and asks the question.

'A little help? help from who?' I look at him and then the Prime Minister and I think, in for a penny, besides my trust has grown.

'Prime Minister, can you fill James in on the further details, on Island? I will need to go to see if we can get some clarity. I will stay in his office until I think we have established what has happened and what any further moves should be. From there I am going home to Barbara. I will send a text with a short message with my thoughts. But I will be back here in the morning. Ten am suit? What have I missed?'

I sit back 'Oh and can you sort a pass or something? It would make life easier coming here.'

James looks from me to the Prime Minister. He is annoyed, heading to angry.

'You didn't trust me. I needed all the information to make the right decisions.' I stare back then say.

'James, I have met a hundred like you in my time. I gave the Prime Minister my thoughts and what did I know about you? Nothing, I watch and I learn. I trust you now. The information that the Prime Minister will pass on is beyond belief. I would add the Presidents boys know nothing about it. If they had, they would be in this office now.

Anyway, I have an appointment at 1600 Pennsylvania Avenue. Even I, know that address.' I stand and stretch I need to get outside, fresh air will be good. I look at the Prime Minister.

'Good luck with your chat. James, everything you ever learnt is minor to what you are about to learn.' He stares and nods, he isn't convinced, the Prime Minister nods.

'The pass will be there, see you tomorrow at ten.' I turn and open the door, one of the young men is still there. James asks him to escort me to the lobby.

It is good to get outside. People are finishing their working day the sky is clear and bright, I missed it. Always amazes me the life that rushes to and fro in cities. I have spent much of my adult life in isolated places, with communities where I have known most people, cities are a foreign animal that I am not particularly comfortable in. I walk into a bar and go into the men's toilet. I sit in a cubicle and examine Google on my phone. A plan of the White House is found. I think I can find my way in but there is only one way to find out, I become unseen. I hear a patron leave the bathroom. I slip behind him and then out on to the street. I think fly and using Island's formulae I am close to space.

Chapter 13

I am not scared as such, it has been so fast, just very surprising, a second later I am bearing down on Washington. It feels like I am in a Google Maps Search dropping through the clouds; then I am on the lawn right by the West Colonnade.

I walk down the path and simply try the door; locked. I stand there wondering my options. Then I think it's a door. So knock. I knock on the door and stand to the side, a man in a suit with an earpiece opens the door and looks out, does his appraisal. He looks, questioning and closes the door again.

OK got it. I knock again louder. The door opens swiftly and the same man emerges. He walks forward several paces and looks carefully around, as he does so, I walk into the hall. I turn right then right again through a short hall into the secretary's office. I have seen no one and the desk in front of me is empty, to the right of the desk is an open door, raised voices can be heard. Bingo! I think, the inner sanctum.

The office is bigger than I thought it would be, the desk oddly smaller, there are two couches opposite each other in the centre of the room holding four men and there is a woman sitting on another chair obviously taking notes. As I walk into the room, the President is in full flight.

'Fuck you Harry! I am beyond angry, you made decisions that are way beyond your brief and your job is finished.' Harry stands up, face red and turns on his heel to leave.

'Harry, if you even think of leaving, I will have you arrested and you will be held until I can get you to court for treason. I will tell the world you tried to murder an allies' leader. I might lose some support but I doubt it, and if I do I'd rather have no support! You and your family will be finished and you, Mister, if I can force it, will be shot. So sit the fuck down!'

Harry stops, face completely white, mouth working, I recognize him. Harry A. Hoffman Secretary of State. Wow I think, interesting. So the President didn't know. There is a small chair by the President's desk, I sit down. This is going to be enlightening.

The other two are very quiet. The President looks at his watch.

'I have exactly thirty two minutes before I have to look that woman in the eye, so I want some ideas of how we are going to mitigate this. I do believe that she is a reasonable person but she is no fool. The aircraft will lead her investigators to our forces no matter which branch, even without the proof she already has. Which includes four dead US personnel. Any idea how the chopper crashed? It must have been shot down but I am curious how. Their air force is third world.'

A man with very blond hair answers.

'We don't have any more information than the last radio contact which was "Bird 1 job done. Heading home" they may have sent something else but they were very low under the hill line. We don't know. The Omaha is steaming north and should be away from the country proper in about 6 hours. The captain is very unhappy about losing the chopper. For some reason one of his flight crew were on board helping out.' The President is following this closely, he sits looking at the coffee table top and starts talking, eyes fixed the table.

'So we have a whole ship's crew who know that one of our aircraft has disappeared with one of their buddies on board. Todd, would you ask questions if it was one of your friends? Like, why aren't we checking up? Like, what happened to the chopper? Are they going to look for it? What happens if it's us? Jesus Christ!' He stops pauses and then asks.

'OK, we need a game plan and we need one now.' Harry speaks his eyes smouldering.

'Firstly, can I remind people here the operation is about the actual first contact that we have confirmed with alien presence. You have all read the file, we have no idea what this Bill Sheppard can do or is party to. One of our people has died.'

He holds a hand up as mouths open.

'Yes, I know we are a little grey on how but it does seem that this Bill Sheppard was involved. The guy we lost was a SEAL. Anyway that aside, something happened and he died. It is proven that this guy has alien technology in his body. We have the witnesses, an X-ray. Is he still human or something different?'

I think about this, it is a good question. Am I controlled by Island I wonder? I doubt it but shelve it for later examination. Harry continues, the others are looking thoughtful. The President is staring over his shoulder at a portrait on the wall.

'OK, I fucked up but the point remains, this may be the biggest risk our country or the world has ever been involved with....' A guy with no tie and longish hair speaks, interrupting Harry.

'Or the greatest opportunity. There has been no invasion that we can tell. All this is around one guy who lives at a beach in another small country. One guy. I can't work out why your stupid spooks just didn't pass this off as a maybe and get someone to knock on his door and ask him what's happening, and.'

He heavily emphasizes the "and."

'Include his own government. These people are long term allies and he was a government employee for decades. I will add that your guys on the ground were out manoeuvred, twice. He ain't stupid obviously. He recognized they were a threat right at the start. You saw the report. You pushed the wrong person and now you have his government on his side or at the very, very least wondering what happened. Or why they were targeted and why so extremely. We still don't know what they know or if Mr. Sheppard been in contact with them. Given his background, I would lay money he has. Our Ambassador there is poor material. You know him. Their Prime Minister would have eaten him for breakfast. For the record, I agree with the President, you should be arrested Harry.'

Harry starts but no words come out as the President beats him to it.

'OK, OK. We will sort our own issues later. Right now we have to solve the problems that are before us, you've made your point Sam and I am inclined to agree but still no plan.'

Sam sits back crosses his knees and speaks.

'Simple. Trust the Prime Minister. Put the cards on the table, rogue person all that stuff. Personal apology with assurances, see what they want, if anything. Tell her who you are sending to the chopping block but not the details. Ask to help clear the crash site and walk forward in collaboration. Ask for us to be involved. It will be a balance though, they have never ever had a politician assassinated, the closeness of those bullets will have pissed her off. Can you blame her? No. One thing I find interesting, there is no media coverage at all, they have covered it up. At least for now, which means it is more likely that Bill Sheppard has been in contact.' He stops and uncrosses his legs and puts his hands behind his head waiting.

Todd clears his throat and puts his hands palm to palm.

'I tend to agree, if the attempt on their leader had worked what would have we actually gained? Not much, the country is very stable. Change of leader and they would have screamed blue murder. The world would know and this presidency would be finished and a lot of our credibility in the world. The Brits would be very unhappy, they still hold sway there and have very close ties to the region. China is waiting in the wings. The democracies around the planet would be wondering privately who is going to be next. Lots of support will disappear and who fills the vacuum, people we don't like.'

'Frankly, Mr. President the ball is firmly in their court. One thing though, we really don't know the risk here. The Secretary Of State is right on that. We have no idea what we are dealing with and how far do we trust the Prime Minster to give us answers? If this alien technology is as far advanced, as we are lead to believe. Where exactly does that put us? You're the boss. Your call.' The President sits back and stares at the Seal on the ceiling. Harry turns to the President.

'This may be the biggest decision you have ever made, leaving this guy in a tin pot country, where we can't control him or the outcome is madness. If they control something that is beyond anything we have ever seen, this could put our country and its people into a risk situation that may be unprecedented. Our whole way of life, for us and maybe the planet, is being put at risk. That is on the record too.'

The President holds his hand up, he looks across at the woman taking notes.

'Mira, what do you think about this?' Mira looks up from her I-pad a bit stunned. She lifts her glasses off her face and turns towards the President.

'I actually think you just talk to her, sir. She seems like a nice person. That's what I think, she seems fair to me. Yes, just fair.' She puts her glasses back on and sits looks back at her I-pad and waits. The President says.

Thank you Mira. Fair.' and stares back at the Seal.

The ticking of the Grandfather clock can be heard. I am feeling very tired and have had enough, I want to leave. Time passes. The President pulls his phone out and taps a text. He looks at the immediate reply and nods. A few minutes later through the secretary's door two suited men appear and all heads swivel towards them. Then the President speaks. Heads turn again.

'What would you have done if you caught him, Harry? What would you have used this guy for? What would you have used this unknown technology for or how? These questions really concern me, Harry. Maybe you will tell me one day.' He looks at the two men waiting.

'Please place the Secretary of State under arrest. The charge is treason and an attempt to assassinate another countries leader.'

Mouths fall open, including mine. The two men walk towards Harry, who is now on his feet screaming. The other two are dumbfounded, stuck to their seats.

'You son of a bitch, I will have you hounded out of office I'll... get your hands off me, you fucking bastards. I'll have your fucking jobs.' One of the suits grabs Harry's arm and spins it behind his back and the other holds Harry's other arm and handcuffs are clipped on.

Harry is still screaming. The President says to one of the suits.

'As little fuss as possible please. Take him to the CIA building and hold him on my personal orders. I will have the director get in touch with you.' the suit nods and they bustle the yelling Harry out the door, his complaining dissipates and the room is very quiet. Suddenly, I am wide awake, deeply surprised. The President turns and looks at each person in the room.

'My reasoning is simple. Not only was this an assassination attempt, he used his team in a foreign friendly nation. He has put our nations reputation at extreme risk and eventually, if I didn't act, I would be seen as part of the largest cover up this office has ever seen. The Prime Minister would not let it rest and frankly nor could I. It would make Watergate look trivial. I want this nation back together, not torn apart. The conspiracy theorists on social media would break our country. Not without complete transparency. Not on my watch. To be honorable you must act with honor. I will have him tried with complete transparency and will take the flack.'

The people in the room are still stunned. Todd is the first to speak.

'You have 6 minutes, Mr. President. Should I set up the camera?' The President nods and pours a drink of water from the jug on the table. He turns to Mira.

'Thank you Mira. Fair, is a very good word' Mira looks up and smiles. 'You are welcome, Sir.'

'OK, I think we have a consensus. We are to lean towards fairness and trust. To that end I want the camera pointed this way and I want both of you in shot. If you need to, interrupt, do. I want her to feel that all of us are on the same team including her, OK? We almost killed this woman today and I want her to feel our remorse.'

The President picks up his phone and is obviously talking to the CIA Director. There is a quick explanation on his side, then orders, then a rebutting of the alternatives. He listens and at the end says.

'Mr. Director, while I am President, no one, I repeat, no one, is going to act outside this country without my understanding or directive. What the Secretary did is not defendable. You will follow my instructions as Commander in Chief. Thank you.' he taps the phone.

He stops and looks around the room as though looking at it for the first time and nods to himself. I watch him closely, he is doing what he can in a very bad situation. He is saying the right things, I think to myself. We will see. I get up and walk carefully into the secretary's office and then into the hall and walk up and down it for some exercise and some thinking time. I am alone. I need to contact the Prime Minister but am unsure what exactly to say and I need a place to do this.

I check for people in the hall again and carefully open a door to my right. I peer in, it is a large room that is, thankfully, empty. I fumble for my new phone. I was going to text but decide to ring. I feel I can convey more information quicker by a brief call. I turn on the device select the pre-set number and press call. I am not sure if it will actually work. I had added international roaming as a matter of course but I had made mistakes with phones before. Part of the sea of change that mobiles have created. I wait, it rings, my Prime Minister's voice answers.

'Bill? Yes Prime Minister. I need to be brief. I think, I am in the conference room, it is empty. They know very little. The assassination was ordered by the Secretary Of State and the President has arrested him.' The utter silence tells the story.

'He is going to apologize and wants to work with you towards a solution, have you got that?' I ask.

'Yes thank you, I will think on this. Please go back to his office and watch the call. Many thanks Bill.'

I turn the phone off and pace up and down past the long table. I am working through my thoughts then I retrace my steps into the Oval office. I see the camera has been setup facing the two couches with a larger screen below the camera. The three men are sitting on the couches. The President on one, Todd and Sam on the other. Mira is out of shot. The seat I take is an antique sitting against the wall with a perfect view. The President is reading, what I presume is the file they have on their teams work around me. Todd is looking at his phone and has a remote on his seat.

'One minute Sir' He says. The President nods. Sam is also looking at a phone, humming to himself. Todd turns on the screen and says to the room.

'Camera on and we should have connection in....' the screen comes alive with the Prime Minister in view and her voice says.

'Mr. President, gentlemen.'

'Madam Prime Minister very good to talk again. Firstly, before I make any introductions, can I say how sorry I am that you have been attacked by a rogue element in my government. You were right about where the attack came from. The orders were given from the top level of this government. The person that issued those orders was the Secretary of State. He is now under arrest and will be held to account. I will follow this through personally, on that, you have my absolute word.' The Prime Minister nods.

'Thank you. Mr. President to say this has come as a shock is understating the situation. It was also a shock that, your country, given our combined histories, was involved. One day we be able to talk in person but I accept you at your word; let us continue.' She stops and the President turns to the two men on the opposite couch.

'Madam Prime Minister, this is Todd Hamilton he is my international foreign affairs analyst, ex-military and has worked in the UAP area.' Todd nods and murmurs 'Prime Minister' The President continues.

'This is Sam Bellhouse, he is my geopolitical military analyst.' Sam nods and twitches a smile but says nothing.

'Both of these guys have been with me for years and I trust them with all and everything. I like to have some people on the outside of government structure, a thing of mine if you will. They are both apolitical, loyal to our constitution as an ideal rather than me as a person. Consequently when I am wrong, they tell me. In a tight situation, like today, they are here beside me.' The President stops and watches as the Prime Ministers sips some water.

'The only other person in this room is the head of our SIS James Brandon, Mr. President. By the way, is this conversation being recorded in anyway?' The question I see, takes the President a little off hand and he looks at the other couch, the two men shake heads in the negative. The President says.

'We have Mira taking dictation Prime Minister. It is White House protocol, that is the only record, Ma'am.' The Prime Minister just nods and then sits back in her seat.

'So where do we begin Mr. President?'

'Well, I will apologize again for what has happened. I am stunned. I have already taken steps against the person involved as I said. There will be a wider investigation in how this all occurred and why. People using military assets for such an attack and how it came to pass will be part of that and how the orders for this operation were developed....I.' He shakes his head.

The Prime Minister takes over in the gap.

'Pretty shabby I agree. I have read the report that started most of this, from your Ambassador. What I can't understand is why nobody included our government. Anyway, water under the bridge. I accept your apology Mr. President but I have little reason to trust your staff or the system that creates such people. I'm sure you get my point.' The President nods in agreement.

'How can I not agree? Prime Minister is there anything that I can do to mitigate what has happened? I note that you haven't put this to the media. I would have done the same in your place, if possible. In the circus, details get lost.' He stops. Head cocked curious, I think, to see what this woman is made of? He is not sure.

'No. No thank you, absolutely nothing. Actually, when I am in Washington for the trade talks in four months, let's have a private lunch?' She smiles genuinely and the President is charmed.

'Madam, it would be my complete pleasure.' He smiles back at the screen, Todd and Sam both move slightly, which I take as surprise. 'Mr. President you have read the report on Bill Sheppard and his situation? Take the work of your under cover people out of it for a second, what are your thoughts?' The President takes a sip from a water bottle on the table.

'Well, this actually maybe the first contact with another life form. I just don't know. In the report we only have three confirmed sightings of Mr. Sheppard and the issues with his arm I....' At this point Todd interrupts.

'Excuse me, we also have the x-ray of Mr. Sheppard's arm Sir, back of the report.' The President takes a piece of paper from Todd and peers at it intently, he then looks up.

'Thanks Todd. Sorry, I had a quick look but didn't know there was an X-ray.' He peers at the image, his head is shaking at what he is seeing.

'Frankly, that is pretty amazing. It is, after all, the first real physical proof....hmmm.' He stops, thinking.

'OK, have you spoken to or met this guy, Prime Minister?'

I had wondered how long it would be. The Prime Minister cocks her head.

'This guy, Mr. President, has been harassed and had his home burnt to the ground, lost every single thing he owns, is watched then pushed too hard. That's this guy, Sir.' She is bristling and angry.

'So returning to the point. If there is anything you can do? Yes! Your government will replace his house and anything else he has lost, and pay compensation. Am I clear about this? Your personal guarantee Mr. President or our conversation stops now!'

The woman is glaring at the screen, the Prime Minister side-lined for the moment.

The Presidents mouth works. I am more interested in the reprimand than the content. Then I realise what the Prime Minster has asked for us, Barbara and myself. I am deeply humbled by her care.

'You are right Ma'am and I stand corrected and, of course, I agree. Your anger is understandable. I am sorry.' He looks at Sam 'Please contact Mr. Brandon and sort the details. Whatever it needs to be.' Sam nods and taps on his phone.

'So Ma'am have you met Mr. Sheppard?' She sits and stares at the screen, her anger still obvious, and in part, the anger has answered his question, she knows it.

'Yes, I have met him. I knew of him as a civil servant, did his job well and retired. But I have met with him in the last few days. He came to me for advice.' The President cuts across her, the surprise in his voice obvious and laced with a trace of underlying sarcasm.

'I'm sorry Ma'am, he came to you for advice? I mean, do ordinary people just pop into your office?' The Prime Ministers face goes red.

'OK Mr. President, cut the crap! He was a senior in his department. He knows people who know people and we only have a population of five million. I could have gone to school with one of his family. We have a simple system here, mostly built on trust. Any more of your arrogance and I will lay everything I have at the feet of every news media outlet and the United Nations at the same. I still have your helicopter, four dead crew and paperwork and photos of the Omaha inside our territorial waters at the time of the attack on my person. That is also beside the proof he brought to me of your countries involvement in his own situation.'

Her voice very cold, very cutting, the President has put his head down. He looks up and holds a hand up, he is calm, unbowed.

'OK, well said and you are right. On the other hand I also have 300 million people to serve and protect. As people here have reminded me, Mr. Sheppard or whatever may control him, might be the biggest threat that this world has ever seen. Risk is what we are always worried about and how great that risk is, is what I have to determine. So what can you or will you tell me about Mr. Sheppard and his situation?'

The Prime Minister turns away from the screen. The mute is hit and is obviously talking to someone off camera, I presume James, a few seconds later she turns again to the screen and her voice starts.

'Mr. President, sorry for the interruption. I think it would be better if you spoke to Mr. Sheppard himself. But and I mean but, this will only happen if you are alone in the room. You told me there were three people there, sir. Please ask them all to leave and close all doors or the interview will not go ahead.'

My mind is whirling. I see her point, but Jesus what a risk, not really to me. I suppose when I think about it I could get out unseen but......ah well, in for a penny. I also realize that the Prime Minister has complete trust in my meeting the President. I am surprised. The President is caught completely off guard, he turns his head and looks at Todd and Sam, they both nod. Mira is already standing.

'Alright Prime Minister. One minute please.' He presses a mute button and asks 'You guys OK with this?' Todd replies.

'If you need to pass anything on to us, you will, besides I think she needs time with just you to develop your relationship. Hell, she has just been shot at by us.' He shakes his head and turns into the doorway. Sam glances at the President but says nothing. Mira has already walked to the outer office, the door is closed. The President unmutes the screen.

Chapter 14

'OK Prime Minister, we are all alone. I would like to talk to your Mr. Sheppard.' He leans forward towards the screen. The Prime Minister has a faint smile.

'OK Bill, are you happy to talk to the President of the United States?' The President looks at the screen and is about to speak when I become unseen, still sitting in the chair against the wall.

'Hello Sir.' I say. The President jumps up with a 'Jesus Christ! ..... Where the hell were you?'

I hold my arms palms up. 'It's OK Sir, it's OK. Sorry to scare you.' The Prime Minister chimes in with.

'Mr. President, Bill will not harm you. He scared the hell out of me, the first time I saw this.' The President's mouth is working.

'You were invisible? How long have you been here? Jesus! That isn't possible.'

Just as he says this I become unseen again. I am really proving a point. As luck would have it, the door opens. Sam has heard something that alarms him.

'Are you OK Sir?' He is looking at the President but has already checked the room.

The President looks at him, the screen and the chair where I am still, but unseen.

'I, ha umm, yes I am fine.' He replies. The Prime Minister jumps in with 'Mr. President this meeting is highly confidential.' as she has heard the question. The President puts his right hand up and nods.

'Yes, I am OK. Thanks Sam. I will call if I need you.' The door closes and the President sits back in the couch and waits. I give it a couple of seconds then appear. The President has watched me reappear but the disbelief still evident.

'Yes, make a fortune is a magic show.' I am not sure what else to say, I am getting a little bored with being serious. The President looks from me to the screen.

'You knew about this? I'll ask again, how long has he been here?' The Prime Minister lets it ride for a few seconds then says.

'About the time you had the Secretary of State arrested. Now let me be clear Mr. President. Yes, we were spying on you but I had just been targeted, literally targeted, by members of your government. We knew that and we had the absolute proof. Our expectation was that you or close members of your government had set up an attack on ours. Bill offered and I took the opportunity. So quite simply don't get on your high horse. Espionage is a tool of any and all governments, including ours.' She sits back waiting for the reply eyes keenly watching from the screen.

The President has been watching me.

'You don't look like a spy.' he says with a grimace. 'So how did you get here? I mean this place has some of the best security around.' I turn to the screen, I am leaving the lead to the Prime Minister.

'Prime Minister?' I am in her angle of view.

'This is your call Bill.' I note she is being careful with what information I give out. I also wonder how much she has passed on to James. I am getting to the point I have to rest. I have been awake for about twenty two hours and I can feel it. The President is watching, waiting. I am not sure about this, anyway.......

'I flew. I have that ability, at least the bracelet gives that to me.' The temptation is too much. I rise from the seat and float around the room over the desk and slowly back to the chair. The President watches with a look of fascination and maybe horror mixed.

'I cannot believe what I have just seen, I ....' He trails off. I look at him nodding.

'Yes. Well, you should try it, very weird.' he looks at me, and just laughs.

'Jesus, I bet. How do you? I mean what makes you? Umm, Just how?' I shake my head and roll up my sleeve as I do so. 'I just don't know really. But this is part of me, you saw the X-rays.' He comes over from the couch and peers at my arm. He looks at me directly questioning.

'Can I touch it?' I answer with a "sure."

His fingertips are cool and they trace the Hieroglyphics. 'Can you read this?'

'Yes, but it is really a keyboard for me to make the bracelet work.' His fingers retrace them.

'Sorry.' when he realizes he may have been too long but I do get it. Proof of an alien world. Simply wow! I say so and he glances at me then grins, then asks.

'Did it hurt? I mean when it, umm, when they put it in your arm?' I nod, remembering the nightmare of pain.

'Yes a lot. More than I have ever experienced. More than I thought I could endure. Yes, it hurt.' I finish lamely not knowing what else to say. The Prime Minister says from the screen.

'I didn't ask Bill. Interesting, I am sorry.' I shrug the pain has gone and left me, different, what else does one say? I turn to the screen.

'I need to rest. It has been a very long time since I did. I am going to go home.'

I face the President.

'The point is, Mr. President. I am the proof that you needed to see and, to a degree, understand. I am trusting you, personally.'

The President nods and stares into my eyes, evaluating, seeing the worry, the risks I have run and the ones I am still facing. I am the only one of me. I still feel like a target. And yet he has a country to protect. Maybe from me. Gears are moving.

'You can rest here. I am sure we can find a spare bed and some food.' He smiles at the screen and myself.

'Thank you Sir, but no. My wife is waiting and I need my own space for a while.'

The Prime Minister talks from the screen.

'That's fine Bill. Please be in touch at some stage tomorrow. You know where I am.'

I nod, stand and look at the President.

'I will leave you two to talk further. Prime Minister I believe further explanation to the President is required the circumstances of the bracelet and where it is from. You know what I mean. I am exhausted. I really have little energy left. I need rest.'

'Mr. Sheppard, a real honor. Please come back to see me soon. I thank you.' the hand shake is warm and the smile is genuine as he turns and walks towards the door. I look at the screen and say 'Goodbye' the Prime Minister nods and gives a small wave and as I walk to the door.

The President opens the other door into an empty side hall and as I pass him I nod and go unseen, turn again and find the door to the outside by the pressroom where I had come in. I am just about to turn the door handle when I hear muffled voices and some words from the pressroom.

'Who the hell was that with the President, and where did he go?' another voice come back with 'Check the other cameras again.'

I turn back and see the door is cracked open. I can see two people staring at a CCTV screen. The screen appears to be focused on the hallway I am in. Interesting I think. I can't be bothered but return up the hallway and go into the secretary's office which is empty, the door is open to the Oval room. The President is just finishing with the Prime Minister and Todd and Sam are back in the room. I stand back, become seen to text the Prime Minister quickly, then go unseen immediately. I slip into the Oval Office and wait by the wall.

'Prime Minister this has been an enlightening meeting. I wish you well. We will meet very soon. My people will be in touch regarding the crash site and compensation for Mr. Sheppard.'

The Prime Minister cuts over him.

'Mr. President could you ask your people to leave please? There is one confidential matter that I have missed.' the President looks confused but nods and Todd and Sam troop out again, they aren't looking happy, their faces are stiff. The door closes.

'Ma'am sorry but I don't quite...' At this point I become seen. The President jumps with a 'Hell boy' his mouth is open, head shaking.

'Sorry, but simply there are cameras watching every movement to and from this office and I was seen. Which is annoying.' I am staring at him blankly, tired and pissed off.

The President holds his hands out.

'Look there are cameras all over this building I......' I cut over him. 'Being watched from the press office? Hmmm OK, well it's your house after all, I am going this time but I find it curious.' the President goes red faced, the look of anger is plain to see.

'The press office? They shouldn't have any.....' He nods at me and turns to the Prime Minster who is still watching on screen.

'Sorry Ma'am. I obviously have a house to clean here. I would say goodbye. Again, thank you.' The Prime Ministers nods and the screen goes blank. I say to him.

'All I want to do is go home. If you will call Todd and Sam I will do that. What happens with your press office people has nothing to do with me. But you and who sees you when, seems to be the subject of their interest. It is strange, after all they should know. Why the close monitoring? I would watch your back Mr. President.'

The President looks at me very hard and again shakes my hand. I go unseen. His face twitches with a slight grin. He walks to the door and as he opens it, asks Todd and Sam in to the office. I wait until they pass me and walk out again to the outer door.

There is jabbering in the press office but I ignore it, the President can deal with whatever is going on. I look back to check for people, see no one then open the door. I walk quickly to the lawn and think fly. The flight is a blur. I land at the front of the house that overlooks the sea, think seen and walk up the steps. The sound of the waves is rising from the rocks below. The smell of salt fills the air.

Chapter 15

'Hello!' I call as I open the door. Barbara comes from the kitchen and hugs me.

'Hi, you took longer than I thought. You OK? How was your day at the office?'

I just laugh, nice to be home. As long as Barbara is there, no matter where 'there' is, is home.

'Hungry?' She asks.

'Yes very, shower first, I stink! And yes. I will tell you all the news!' She smiles and bobs her head as she heads to the kitchen. I wake up on the bed, I have showered, eaten and was talking when I fell asleep. Barbara is reading a book by a head touch, no electricity here. She looks over at me.

'Get under the covers and go back to sleep, we'll catch up with the rest in the morning.' I do as I am told. No dreams.

The morning is bright and the gannets are wheeling over the sea below us as they hunt, occasionally one will twist in the air, concentrate, then pull their wings in, neck straightened and hit the water like a huge white dart. When a few seconds later they pop to the surface, mostly with their beaks empty. I read somewhere it is one in 6 tries before they eat, a lot of work flying and diving, I think.

We have just finished breakfast, a strange concoction of tinned and dried stuff found in the cupboards and store room. We had brought our coffee, which puts a patch on most things.

We are sitting on a small veranda with a wide expansive view. I have filled in the story as much as I can. There have been particular questions on the President and what he is like? After all he looks just great on TV and he seems so nice, which I smile at. Presentation of people and the real thing have always been different I guess: Politics; the ultimate game show I think. In my musing Barbara asks.

'So now what? One thing I have wondered, are you feeling like a bit of a pawn now? I mean....well, it's something I can't put my finger on.' I nod in agreement.

'Yeah, I know what you mean. I have wondered much the same thing but I would like to think I hold most of the cards. We can disappear. Not only in reality but go anywhere in the world. Although I don't have any interest in being a fugitive. We would both hate it. They have no idea of what the bracelet is capable of and I note the Prime Minister didn't say anything about Island to the President. I don't know what her reasoning is but at the bottom of that, is it simply distrust maybe? If not of him, then his system. There are too many sharks circling and too many leaks in Washington. Power is still the ultimate game.'

As I shake my head, a school of small fish broach the surface and birds race for a feast. The surface of the water goes white with fish being chased by larger fish from below, as the smaller fish leap trying to escape, birds drop out of the sky. Joining in, a pod of dolphins rocket through the churning water, torpedoes of grey, scattering fish and birds alike, they turn and circle back. Breakfast in Washington, I think.

Barbara is watching them fascinated. I have been thinking.

'I would like to go home but I actually don't know if Dan and his buddies have been called off, which bothers me. with Harry gone is there a vacuum? Orders can take time. I am not sure we are in a better position. I think Washington will leak, not one hundred percent certain, I just don't know. Anyway I have to see the Prime Minister to get a handle on this. Are you happy with one more day here? I will bring food and stuff on the return trip. I could take you back home but I want to make sure it is safe. Even the Prime Minister has no idea where we are, by the way.' Barbara looks across at me and waves her hand out at the vista before us.

'Nice place to be really. I know what you are saying and agree. Are you going to visit Island? Island's point of view may be good.' She stops and looks hard into my face.

'Do you think the world is ready, or for that matter, actually worthy of Islands' knowledge?' She is very serious and the question bothers her and I understand why.

'Well, I have put a bit of thought into this. I can't make that decision. The world has to really. Not the Prime Minister, not the President, the world.....I just haven't got a solution...umm yet. But maybe, if we could use Island's library to make a far better world.' I look across the sea to the horizon.

'You've seen what could happen; pollution disappears, changes in industry, in transport, poverty gone, reforestation, no hunger, medical advancement beyond belief and enveloped in a fair world government. Nuclear power removed. You have seen what can be done.....the issues that stop most things, are self-interest, power, money or mostly combination of them all.' She peers into space for a few seconds and then says.

'Well, you had better discuss your plans with me before you do anything. You know how the last pergola turned out.' I laugh and just say 'Thanks!'

Chapter 16

I walk into the Prime Minister's office just after lunch with Jan opening the door. I am refreshed. The Prime Minister is looking on point, the glass has been repaired, I note and her desk has been shifted, so her back isn't towards the window. She sees my look.

'Afternoon Bill, and yes, I like to see what's coming now, if possible.' she quips with a smile. She beckons to a seat and as I sit James arrives, files in hand, the door closes. We nod to each other as he seats himself. The Prime Minster starts.

'OK, who's first? Bill?'

I give a run down on anything I think may have been missed or my thoughts on the visit with the President, ending with.

'I don't know if the hounds have been called off here. That bothers me, the crew in the chopper must be different than the ones on the ground. I think someone is watching the President far closer than he knows. I was very surprised at that little drama with the press office, it was just very odd.' I pause and look out the window to white clouds and blue sky. I then relate my conversation with Barbara this morning covering both of our thoughts and concerns and end with.

'I believe Prime Minister, that this is beyond your brief and the Presidents. The world has about eight billion people. I am just one person, at the end of it all they should really know, don't you think?'

The Prime Minister sits back and looks at us both and nods her head in understanding. A good question it seems but leaves it unanswered. She turns to James and directs.

'Your report James, please.' He nods and starts.

'The helicopter crash is now being sorted by our guys and the Americans have just arrived. There are some mumblings of annoyance from CAA, toes being squashed but it is under control. There has been a note from the White House to confirm your meeting with the President at the trade talks. The President has also asked for a meeting here in person in two weeks, which I am very surprised at. So are his people from what I gather. They don't understand why. We are rated as very small fish. I have heard the Ambassador here is being recalled and another put in place. This has only just happened. The President is moving very quickly, Washington is buzzing. That the Secretary of State has been arrested has just hit the ground and the press are screaming and social media is completely overboard. I also note that the White House Media representative has been changed. Watch this space.'

He pauses as he shuffles through the files.

'As far as I can tell, all the US agents on the ground here have gone. We are still searching departures, working through matching arrivals from months ago, simply, I don't know. It is a slow process with a lot of tourist visas and they may not use an American passport.' he looks at me. 'Sorry, all I have'. I nod, not surprised.

'One last thing though. Five million US dollars has been passed into one of the governments accounts with a note naming you as the recipient. The President is moving very quickly. That will get you a new house, I think?' He grins at me.

My mouth is open. Five million! Bloody hell! Then I realize the exchange rate close to doubles it. Wow! Not expected. Wow again.

Pays to pick up the detector I think. But then I think of the seemingly small things of our combined history we have lost, that can never be replaced. We both still mourn for them in the background. I wish it had never happened. I shake my head sad for parts of our life that have lost their thread. The Prime Minister is watching me and sees the regret.

'Money isn't everything.' her look is compassionate. I nod and comment.

'No, not everything.' I think about what was. James waits then continues.

'There is a bit of noise coming from the military, Prime Minister. They didn't like your treatment of the Air-Vice-Marshall and they don't understand why the orders didn't come through the Minister in charge. So they have gone to the Minister with a complaint, who of course, knows nothing about what has happened. You will hear from him very soon I expect.' The Prime Minister nods but says nothing. I ignore this, the inner workings of her office are her issue. But I can see there is concern there.

'So that is about it, really. Basically everything is being managed. There has been the odd question in the hallways about what happened here in the office. I have put it down to very a minor issue from the construction site across the road.'

There is a quiet hush as we work through this. I break the silence.

'OK, simply put. I still have to watch my back and we are no further ahead with how, or if, we distribute Island's knowledge. Prime Minister can you please get hold of the President and see if his people are under control here?' the Prime Minister answers but is really passing on instructions to James.

'Yes. I will contact the President. Anyway his visit will need sorting and I am curious why he needs to come here. As to the wider question of how we work with Island is another matter. I have put a little thought into it and had no real solution. I fear what the world will say or at least the governments. Who loses and who wins? Which industries will be effected, who pays for it, and where do power balances shift? Then there are the religions of the world, how will they view such a radical shift in thought? By the way, have you discussed religion with Island?' I shake my head in the negative.

'Actually no. I should have I guess, but time has been a pressure mostly due to being pushed and getting my head around the whole situation....I, no, I haven't.'

I finish limply. So much to know, to ask and every question gets replaced by another. I turn to James.

'Any thoughts?' He stares back at me, gears are ticking over. 'How or when do we meet Island?' He asks, ignoring my question.

The Prime Ministers head goes ridged 'Meet Island?'

'Why not?' James asks 'Is Bill going to be the gatekeeper forever? This Island thing, at some stage, needs to be presented to the world. As Bill has pointed out. So why not arrange further people to meet Island and work through how this should occur.'

I sit thinking about this. While I get the point of the words, it is the tone that has raised alarm bells. Gut feelings are something I have learnt to follow over the years. When you can't put your finger on something, often the answer is staring you in the face. I blandly say.

'Yes. I think this is possible, Prime Minister would you like to?' My question is not only asking the Prime Minister but I am curious to see James' reaction, something isn't quite right here. The Prime Minister is staring at me, weighting the question when James cuts in.

'I am not sure about the risk to the Prime Minister, frankly. I would be better as a trial, more secure less risk, don't you think?' He is talking to the Prime Minister more than myself. The Prime Minister is watching us both and she asks.

'Do you trust Island, Bill?' I pull my sleeve up and show the golden tattoo.

'This has caused me no harm. Well, if you ignore it becoming part of me. It has acted as a conduit to Islands world. I have actually flown with it. So yes, I trust Island. And Island's technology.' The Prime Minister nods and sits back in her seat quietly thinking. James is fidgeting with his files, his face a mask. Then his phone buzzes, he looks at it and stands.

'I am sorry but this is important, excuse me' He stands goes to the door and leaves. I look at the Prime Minister.

'Sorry!' and become unseen. I follow James quickly, he has left the door half open. I see him walking quickly down the hallway and I follow. He stops in the middle of the wide corridor, where he can see both ways. I walk up to him, stand, watch and listen.

'I have told you about contacting me on this phone. Jesus!' His tone is agitated and imperative. I can just hear the person on the other end. Words come and go but the accent American. James voice is low and his head turns continuously watching for people.

'Look, yes. He will take a person to this Island. He's talking about taking the Prime minister. Yes, yes, I know. Once I know, you will. They are discussing it right now. I need to get back. Another five hundred in the account tonight! Dan?' But Dan seems to have gone.

He taps the phone and I turn and run quietly back the way I have come. The office folks are peering at screens. The door is still partly open. I slip through the door, sit back in my seat and become seen. The Prime Minister jumps, I put my finger to my lips. She glares at me but says nothing, at this moment James comes in, closing the door.

'Sorry, update on the helicopter, some dramas with the Americans, all sorted.'

I look at him.

'The Prime Minister and I think that you may be right. Probably better that you come with me to meet Island. Safer all round, really. You are right, risk is the first issue, certainly.' The Prime Minister looks at me very hard but says nothing. James nods.

'Yes, OK. So when do you want to arrange the meeting?' I look at my phone as though I am checking time.

'No time like the present.' James' mouth falls open. 'Now? Is it that simple? Don't you have to contact this Island or something?' I smile quietly.

'When we get there.' I answer obliquely.

'Are you happy with this Prime Minister? James volunteering on your behalf?'

The Prime Minister is very still she is doing a balancing act. She then nods, she is looking directly at James.

'Are you sure James?' He isn't but just says 'Yes, it's fine.' She looks back at me and says.

'I expect you both back soon. Please take care.' I nod and ask.

'Would you open your window please?' She stands, goes to the window and opens the casement.

'James could you turn around and put your hands together please? I know it's a bit strange but makes it easier for me to fly you.' He looks at me shrugs and complies.

I take out some of the cable ties I have had in my pocket for the last few days and close two around his wrists. He struggles. 'What are you doing?' I reply with.

'This is for your safety while flying.' I then bend and put two around his ankles. The Prime Minister is watching this, looking uncomfortable.

'We will be in touch shortly, this won't take too long.' James is rather white as I put my arm around him and we go unseen. We drift out the large window. James gasps but says nothing. I fly us to the top of the tallest building in the capital, not high by international standards but the 30 odd floors are tall enough for my purpose. I land and let James go and become seen. James is looking around him he obviously doesn't understand.

'Why here?' The wind is blowing. He watches with no understanding. I take out the pistol. His mouth opens. I look at him, aim and shoot him in a kneecap. He screams and falls to the roof. I take my knife out, bend and cut all the cable ties. He grabs his knee and rolling groaning, blood drips through his fingers on to the tarred roof top. I take his phone from his pocket, sit down close to him and wait. Time passes. Wind blows. Enough time, I think.

'OK. James just listen. I may not kill you but you need to make some very quick choices. You sold out not only me, your country, but maybe all the people on the planet. Decisions have consequences. I want to know everything you have passed on to Dan or I drop you over the side.'

'Fucking prick! I won't tell you anything.' He screams at me, spittle runs down his chin. I have no mercy or feelings for him. I ask again.

'I have your phone with Dan's number, you're fucked. Treason is the only thing that you can die for in our country. Hanging isn't it? I know you are married with two kids, think about that and I mean think about it. They will carry will the traitors badge you have created.' He is moaning, under his breath swearing.

'Fuck you, Bill you ....'I press on his knee and he screams.

'No. Fuck you and all the bastards like you. You made a choice, the money or the bag. Well, I am the fucking bag.' He is sobbing. He looks at me then turns away.

'He called me days ago, I knew him from the service, offered 500k. Then said he would pressure the family.' He groans I had turned the phone to record. I say to him.

'And you kept you're mouth shut. OK, for the camera' He shakes his head 'No!'

'Do it! I have the proof anyway. This will be the Prime Ministers choice but if it goes public, your family and kids are destroyed.' He groans. 'You son of a bitch.' I say nothing. He nods and through deep breaths says.

'Dan contacted me, he paid me to pass on whatever information I had, it was for world security he said......Jesus!' He stops with the pain.

I look at him. I don't like what I have done but then this guy has sold out his own people, all people. He wasn't following orders, he was just simply, greedy. I look at him and wonder how humans have this good and bad side but then I have just displayed my own. I stand up and walk away from him and look out at the sea of buildings below me. I turn and James has managed to get to his feet. I watch as he hobbles very slowly to the edge, he leans on the parapet and looks back at me. He says nothing as he rolls over the edge into the void. The wind blows and sounds whisper off the edge of the building.

As I walk into the Prime Ministers outer office there is a buzz in the air. One of the secretaries tells me the Prime Minister is occupied and may be for some time. I tell her she will want to see me. A phone is lifted. I wait and a few seconds later I am standing in front of the Prime Ministers desk. She and I are alone.

'So what the hell happened to James? He is dead on the footpath across the road. Why did you kill him?'

She is very angry, her tone snarling. I take out James' phone and turn on the recording. While not perfect James' voice is in the room. That stops and I play the short video. The Prime Ministers face is grey, head shaking. I stop it and play it again. She waves at the chair.

'Jesus! Sit down.' she says quietly 'how did you find out?'

'When I followed him out to the hall. Why would he take a call out there? We had just been talking about alien technology, flying, me

Disappearing. So what was so important or confidential he couldn't speak in front of you? I thought it was odd.'

'So you killed him?' She is looking at me with a very blank stare.

'No, he did that himself. I may have but he actually made the choice to go off the roof. He sold his country out. I think treason is the last hanging offense? To be clear; he sold information to the person that is still hunting me. Who burnt my house down. Who will kill my wife. Also, they are people that took shots at you.' I sit back, we are eyeing each other. The Prime Minister is still angry but I just don't care.

'Prime Minister. I want you to meet Island. You will have more understanding of this situation and mine, once you have.' I stop and let the words drift in the room.

'Please, this is important. You need to see what Island holds for humanity.' She is shaking her head.

'I know what you think. I am not trust worthy, I do get your point of view. But without experiencing Island for yourself, I don't believe you will ever understand.' I stop, hunting for a solution, then.

'I will bring my wife as a hostage, if you will.' she starts to speak but I hold up my hand.

'OK, bond of trust then, call it what you like. She will agree. Barbara has met Island.'

I sit and wait and look out at the blue sky. I actually hope Barbara will agree. She may not like being a pawn. She can only say no, then we will see what plan B is.

'Bill, you are right. I am starting to wonder about you. I don't like people being judge, jury and executioner, no matter what you say. You never gave him his day in court. On the other hand the proof is difficult to argue with but I am very opposed to extremes. I take your point. Anyway, James is dead and the media are going to have a field day and my own office is asking questions, particularly about you. Odd things attract attention. But I do need to have the facts. Bring your wife; I will want to chat to her alone, by the way. Tomorrow at my house. I think it will be easier from there. It is a work from home day anyway.' Her phone is buzzing and her email has been pinging, time to go.

'Thank you, 11.00 Am?' I ask as I stand, she nods and I am dismissed. As I leave her office, heads and eyes turn but the room is quiet. She is right; I am attracting too much attention.

As I walk out of the lobby through the main doors, there at the edge of my vision, is a profile I recognize: Dan. Well, well I think. I can see across the road to where the bank building is, a number of police cars and an ambulance sit. James' rest. I slowly walk down the broad stone steps and turn towards the scene then turn down towards the port.

I feel I am being followed but unsure. I walk into a shop that sells imported home wares with lots of mirrors on one wall. I look and see Dan has stopped. I was right, he is back on the trail. I walk out of the shop and wander slowly looking into shop windows then into a clothing store. I pick up a pair of jeans and go into a changing room then go unseen. I leave the jeans in there and make my way out of the store, back towards Dan's direction. He is loitering in front of a shop waiting. I stand in front of him working through options. I turn on my heel and walk across the road. I stand and watch as Dan finally figures out he has lost me. I wonder how he feels watching a person who he knows can disappear.

Chapter 17

I have simply had enough. The day has stretched me. I think fly and head back to the house where Barbara is waiting. On the way I stop on the grass opposite a small grocery shop, become seen and get two bags of supplies.

As I walk up the steps to the house that watches the sea, I am thinking about Dan and what to do. I need a slow day I think. Barbara sees me and welcomes me with.

'Good, some different food! Nice day at the office?' A gull calls from below us and the sea is surging on the rocks.

We have been sitting watching the sea, discussing the events and how people make seemingly strange choices. Barbara can't understand James' direction. Why he did, what he did. Yet, she isn't sure I have made the right choice either; too much violence. She is right. I shelve this for later. This is a question for me, that I need to answer. She makes humming noises about being a hostage. She understands the point but doesn't like the term.

'OK, we will go. I want to meet her. Anyway, you are right, without meeting Island she will never know what she is dealing with.' She shrugs, we both understand that this explanation only comes with the experience.

We potter through the rest of the day and the night arrives with candles. Time passes quietly until the next morning.

When we land on the grass outside the Prime Minister's residence, there is a light misty rain. I look around, make us seen and we walk up to the gate and press the button.

A policeman lets us in and shows us the way to the front door. He is slightly puzzled why we didn't arrive in a car but says nothing. The Prime Minister answers the door. She is bright with Barbara over introductions, less so with me. The room we are guided into is bright with two sets of windows overlooking a well-tended garden, a comfortable room for long nights discussing the country and the world.

Each Prime Minister uses the house when in office, most say they like it and I get why. We sit and coffee and tea are offered. Barbara says yes and I follow her lead, more to make her comfortable.

'So you have had an amazingly strange and difficult time.' The Prime Minister is looking at Barbara with interest. This is more of a statement than a question. She then turns to me.

'Bill, in the office next door is the plan for the President's visit. Could you have a look at it and see what can be tweaked to have a meeting with just the three of us? I had wondered if he shouldn't meet Island?'

I just nod, stand and find a small office down the hall. This is an excuse to get me out of the room and it actually suites me. I will put thought into the President meeting Island but am not sure of the benefits. How far does my trust go? I file the thought to examine later, there is a briefing note on the desk, which I start reading.

I have jotted a couple of thoughts on the notes when Barbara puts her head around the door about twenty minutes later.

'Would you like to join us?' Her grin is relaxed and happy. She hasn't had the chance just to sit and talk with another woman for some time and it has done her good. Particularly when she is able to talk completely freely. The Prime Minister is tapping her phone as we walk back into the room. We sit and wait, a mantel clock ticks in the background. The Prime Minister stops tapping and looks at me.

'So quite a story. Barbara has filled in a number of gaps, interesting. She is a fan of yours I see.' Barbara goes slightly red but says nothing.

'Bloody difficult time all round.' She is nodding to herself 'I really don't know how I would react in your situation.' She stops, a decision has been made. She picks up her phone and calls her policeman. He pops his head through the door.

'Prime Minister?'

The Prime Minister is writing on note paper. She finishes the note, puts it in an envelope and seals it. She passes it to the cop.

'Please hold this for three hours exactly. If I haven't called for it within that time, please open it and follow the instructions written there. No questions please, just do as I ask.' He looks at the envelope then back to her face, nods with.

'Yes Prime Minster.' He isn't happy but has his orders. The Prime Minister nods.

'Thanks John.' He leaves. She turns to me, face bland.

'Insurance.' I nod and I don't blame her. She is taking a step that even an ordinary person may not. First steps are often courageous.

'When would you like to go?' her fear is there but also curiosity. it I still think that way, I get it.

'Now would be good. I will contact Island. I am pleased you are coming.'

She looks from me to Barbara, who is smiling at her.

'It is better and more amazing than you could believe.' She says. The Prime Minister nods at her, face set, determined. Barbara gives a quiet.

'See you soon.'

'Is there a private spot in the garden?' I ask. She stands and we walk out another door to a small patio. I give a quick explanation on what will happen. She nods but I am not sure about her comprehension. I quickly tap a message to Island about our arrival.

'Ready?' I stand next to her and put my arm around her. She is still surprised at the intimacy. As we go unseen I see the disquiet in her eyes. We fly, her grip tightens then slowly releases as her fear recedes. We land on the beach with the tide full out. White shells dot the wide stretch of sand. Island is sitting like a square iceberg on the edge of a low sweeping surf.

'Good God!' she says as she glances at me then looks back. Her shock is obvious. Eyes seeing but struggling to believe.

'Yes completely incredible. Nice flight?' I ask but she just shakes her head, the experience a bit too raw. I take my arm from around her and looking around us, become seen. I hold her hand. She looks at me questioningly.

'Without my contact, you won't see Island.' I explain, she nods. We walk towards Island and as we walk across the water she is looks down, mouth open. She then looks up at the transparent cube before her. We walk into Island and then to the control room. The seats are waiting. I seat her and take the larger then put the bracelet in its rest.

The Prime Minister is staring at the floating universe before us. Planets, suns, gas clouds, that are green black and blue, some a red orange. The Prime Minister is quiet as she looks at the vastness of the place we call simply. Space.

'Hello Island' I say. Island replies.

'Hello Bill. Is this Ruth?.' The Prime Minister is looking around trying to discern where the voice is coming from. I agree, it is odd, it seems to come from everywhere or inside one's head.

'Yes. Island this is my countries leader, our Prime Minister Ruth Smithson. Who I wanted you to meet and I wanted her to meet you. It will make things easier when we tell the world you are here and what you have to give to our world.' Time passes then Island asks.

'May I check your memory Bill?' The Prime Minister looks at me with a snapped glance, questioning and surprise at the same time.

'That's fine Island.' I watch the worlds in front of me, then focus on a blue world that I think is in the Ort cloud. The world gets larger and larger as I peer at it. A blue world I think! I see blue then clouds and then wonder of wonders, an ocean. There are other worlds! There are other worlds! I knew this by talking to Island but now I can see one! This is echoing in my mind. As this reality sinks in there are other planets, Island cuts across my thoughts.

'You have had a difficult time, Bill.' I nod at Island's words. Island queries Ruth.

'It would be beneficial for Island to read your memory, to further understand your world. You are in Bills memory a lot recently, he has balanced a number of decisions on your words.' Island stops and waits for an answer.

The Prime Minister looks at me and asks.

'So you actually trust Island with your memory?' I nod, not wanting to stop, I am glued, viewing this new world. I turn away to face her, she is right. It is an important step. I need to clarify.

'Yes. I wondered at first too. I still have no reason to doubt my decision. By sharing your memory Island will be better able to understand our world. I presumed Barbara had told you, my mistake. There are things I miss. There is a huge cross-over of information. You will get far more than you give. My explanation is really poor, I know, but you came here to experience the unknown. This is another door.' I pause, shift my gaze and see before me, what should not be possible.

'Look around you, Prime Minister. You just flew here and then walked on water.' I stop and wave my arm at the universe that is in front of us. It's millions of players sit across our curved view.

She asks 'Will it hurt?'

'No, you will feel nothing. Sometimes I feel a touch drained but I would bet at the end of it, you will feel elation. My only real explanation.' She sits thinking her eyes rove over the everything before us.

'All right Island. I agree.' She sits back and I go back to my blue oceanic planet. I look deeper and then deeper, there are palms lining beaches white sand and coral like reefs. I have a strong pull to go there. The Prime Minister stirs in her chair.

'My God, I ....thank you Island. I don't know what to say. It's like saying to the world; these are eyes and they ask what are eyes? I have been blind.' She turns to me.

'Bill, I owe you an apology but then how does one explain the completely unexplainable? I see your position now.' She stops as the stars and planets and worlds ride in her view, she sits and time passes. Then Island speaks.

'It will be difficult for you to introduce Island to your world. Is Barbara well, Bill?'

'Yes Island. Barbara is well and she sends greetings. I will bring her soon. Island is there anything that Island needs from our planet. I am sorry, I have never asked. I should have.'

'There is nothing Island needs. Thank you Bill.'

The Prime Minister looks across at me there are tears running down her cheeks.

'This is something I never thought of nor I would see or believe. Thanks will never be enough.' I smile 'Yes, impressive isn't it?' what else do I say?

'Island, we need to plan for our world to meet you. I do not know how yet but when this plan is made I would like to tell you of it and ask if you think it will work. You know about our wars and power struggles through our memories. We are, what we are. But I think your help may change some of that. Will Island look at the plan?'

I look back to my blue planet through a drift of stars, red dwarfs, black holes and watch waves running up the shore. A flying thing of bright red and gold flashes by and in the water glimpses of silver flicker. Fish? I wonder. Light years from earth, the palms look like coconut. Island says to us both.

'Bill, bring the plan and Island will discuss it. It was good to meet you Ruth.'

The Prime Minister looks at the depths of worlds and says.

'Thank you Island. I will remember this honor until my dying day.' as we stand she looks across the uncounted places of the universe. She looks at me and twitches a smile.

'Some things are beyond thought or imagination.' There is nothing to say.

We make our way hand in hand out on to the beach. We have become unseen. The tide is moving up the beach again and a couple chasing a ball, playing on the sand. I put my arm around the Prime Minister and fly back to the patio.

Barbara is sitting in the afternoon sun with a glass of water. She jumps as we become seen.

'Boo!' I say and she glares at me. 'You enjoy that!'

'So Prime Minister, what did you think of Island? ' She joins Barbara on another chair. She sits looking across the garden still contemplating then quietly starts.

'Please you two, don't ever call me Prime Minister again, it is Ruth!'

The change in her is marked, less stiff, more human but then meeting Island changes thoughts and one's place in the universe, I guess. Ruth sits back in the chair and looks at the clouds. She takes her phone out of her pocket. Turns it on and makes a call. Her policeman appears.

'The note I entrusted to you, John please. Thanks.' He passes the folded paper over and leaves. As he does she tears the note into little pieces and puts them in a pocket.

'It was almost beyond words. The dilemma Island creates though, is another situation. Oddly a good dilemma, I hope. We can take our race forward thousands of years but finding a way forward for all the people of the planet will be extremely difficult. There is so much here to exploit. I don't know if Island would let that happen.' She slows contemplating, then.

'I do think Bill is right. Nationalism is probably the major barrier. Democracy is one thing, then there are the dictators. Some are the leaders at the head of huge nations who are unwilling to ever leave power. Then there are the corporations that act in exactly the same way...'

She slows and sits thinking. I have sat down next to Barbara.

'We, that is Barbara and I, do have one issue. Closer to home. I saw Dan in the capital. He was following me, he was the one who turned James. I don't know who is running him or if he hasn't had orders to stop. Whichever way it goes, we aren't safe until he and his team are stopped.' Ruth looks over from her thoughts.

'I will get in touch with the police commissioner shortly. we'll see what can be done.'

I nod my thanks but feel they are unlikely to move fast enough and more to the point, who are they actually looking for? Difficult without photos, I think. I need bait and the only thing I have is me, and then I wonder where to put the hook. I grin at this thought. Barbara looks at me.

'Thinking shallow thoughts? Anyway umm Ruth will be busy. We need to let her work.' She is right, besides I need some space to think. Ruth has watched this inter play.

'I can't thank you enough but you know that. What now for you two?' She is looking at us both. I reply.

'Back to our hideout for the mean time.' her look is questioning but doesn't ask.

'I do need to solve the Dan issue somehow. Then we will see. Hopefully get some normal back into our lives.' I shrug at the plan, it isn't much.

'A new house is on the horizon of course but how we work with Island is really the top of the list.' I laugh and add.

'Saving the planet from its self, maybe?' Ruth looks at me over her quip.

'You may be right.'

As the light fades, we land by the house on the rocky shored island. There is a stiff breeze blowing and it has got a lot cooler, gulls are calling as they drift along the cliff edge below us.

'Great way to travel. No tickets, no waiting, no parking. I like it.' Barbara says as we walk up the steps. We have been to the store again and have a bag each. I recognize that we are getting comfortable here. The remoteness made ridiculously simple by the bracelet but one day I think I will be normal again, as a gull cries in the dusk.

The next day we spend together. We walk some tracks and then explore some of the shoreline, finding treasures washed by the sea, a seal barks at us as we pass then slips off his rock into the water, annoyed. Skinks scatter away from us on the high tide mark into grey bleached driftwood. They have been basking in the sun, watching for small prey.

A pod of orca pass close to a point of rock, the tall fin of the male folded at the top as he rises for breath, a calf is close to their mother's side. We sit on a very small pebble beach watching the waves where Barbara announces.

'I could live here!' I nod and agree. 'Yes, so could I but without the bracelet it would be a bit more difficult.' we both watch the sea as the waves wander through the rocks then hiss into nothing on the rounded stones.

The next morning I announce that I am going back to the capital. Barbara looks up from her book. We have just finished breakfast and wind is starting to howl.

'You are going to find Dan.' a statement. Ah well I think.

'Yes. I want some part of our life heading to a small bit of normal. Now there is one thing I completely forgot to pass on. I should have earlier, sorry.' I then tell her about the sum waiting in a government account. Her mouth falls open.

'You are joking!' I shake my head. 'Are you sure? That much?' I nod.

'So house hunting or rebuilding; your call.' I say smiling. She looks at me stunned.

'I just can't believe it. I wasn't looking forward the insurance company hassle. I wasn't convinced they would pay. This makes it so easy. I mean we....' I think about castles in the air as I pull on a sweatshirt.

I have no real plan but I am pretty sure Dan will still be hunting. James' death will have made life harder. He knows something has happened to James though no detail but not why or who. He may be guessing who. He will want to catch me if he can. He is a professional, he will believe I was involved. His stakes may have got higher but the question remains. Who is sending the orders to him?

I wonder about getting Ruth to contact the President but the news is full of the arrest of the Secretary of State and leaks in the White House Pressroom. The sharks are circling in Washington it seems. That aside, Dan has been too persistent and there is something I can't put my finger on. When in doubt, ask, I think. Barbara stops her building work and says.

'You be careful. He is dangerous, he may have other people with him.'

'Yes, you are right and I will be. I am just looking for a simple life.' I smile but she isn't convinced. She gets up and we hug.

'Say hello to Ruth if you see her, she is good people.' I salute and grin at her.

I fly into a very small park some way from the parliament buildings. It has a large tree right in the centre, with two back walls of brick that create a corner for cover. I become seen here. I walk through the streets just wandering, looking at shops and people watching. I amble towards the parliament building, walk up the broad steps and into the main entrance. I wander around, go to Information and pick up a map then turn and slowly wander out the door again. I turn left, down the steps using the map as a cover, do a bit of pretend reading. I walk around the grassed area in front of the building, wondering how long I need to play bait.

I can't be bothered with the game and feel I am a piece in someone's else's toy box, waiting to be played with. I am grumbling to myself, watching as I walk along a broad path that curves to the road. I quickly duck between the traffic crossing the road into a very small café that sports a large wide mirror on one wall.

I am standing idly watching the street as I wait to be served, when I see the bait has been taken. A profile I recognise. Dan is on the other side of the road, his head is newly shaved, he is sporting sunglasses.

I order coffee and then go to the restroom in the back, seconds later I walk out, having gone unseen.

I walk over the road and sit on a low cement wall just behind Dan and wait. Time passes, Dan walks up the road slowly, then back past me. He then crosses the road and walks past the café. He turns and walks into the café. Seconds later he is out, a phone is in his hand.

Well, well, I think. Danny Boy has friends. He waits by the café, a car arrives. He gets in and the car drives down the road. I think fly. I follow the vehicle for a few minutes. It heads to the harbour, into a private marina parking space. Dan and one other person emerge, walk down a pier, past yachts and launches. They turn down a finger on the pier and go aboard a large white launch. The name " Stargazer" is written in dark blue on the transom. The irony is not lost on me. I land on the pier and walk down the finger. Now what? I wonder about cavalry.

I go back up the pier and become seen crouching between two cars. I stand up watching the pier, wondering. I take out my new phone and dial the emergency code.

'Hello, yes police please. Hello, I am at the capital marina and I have heard shots fired on a boat at S pier. Boat 12. Yes, gun shots. I think someone is hurt.' I bang the phone on the roof of the car I am standing next to.

'Did you hear that? Yes. More shooting, please hurry...God, there is a man with gun... help.' I bang the phone again and turn it off. Some long seconds later I can hear sirens, I crouch and go unseen. I walk quickly back down the pier to the next finger and wait. I take out the pistol that I have kept as part of my kit for the last couple of weeks. A number of police have arrived and are walking slowly down the pier assessing the situation.

They get about 10 meters away. I go to the end of the finger where I am hidden behind the 'Stargazer' I then fire two shots into the water. I wait. Three people have emerged from down below in the boat, two holding pistols. One of whom is Dan. Three police officers with pistols aimed, are screaming at them to "Drop the guns" More police are coming down the pier at pace. I stand and watch as looks are exchanged, guns are dropped and hands go up. There is much yelling as a stream of uniforms converges on them. The three are pushed to the deck, guns taken, arms are grabbed and they are roughly handcuffed. I am enjoying myself.

Minutes later, after Dan and his friends are searched, they are led away to police vehicles. The area is cordoned off and the boat is quickly searched, evidently a small armoury has been found. Our country has been very careful with its gun laws over the last few years due to a couple of very sad public attacks. Pistols have been banned for many decades; automatic weapons have been banned for a number of years. Public and government tolerance of holders of illegal weapons is very limited. I get closer and listen to the senior sergeant who appears to be directing the operation. A line of weapons and boxes of ammunition has been placed on the pier.

'Is that all Mike?' a cop just getting off the boat answers.

'Not sure yet, I doubt it. Not sure what happened with Customs. These guys may have just arrived. We need to strip the engine bay.

This is just what we found in two of the cabins, I am expecting more but who knows I.......' another cop turns up with a grey plastic tube about two feet long, he has taken the taped end off the tube which he is holding very carefully.

'Hey, boss we need to move this boat.' he nods at the tube 'grenades, not sure how many or what else is here but...' The sergeant stiffens and nods.

'OK, put that back on the boat, where it can't move around, quick photo, get the rest of the guys out now. Leave everything else. Do it now please.' The cop turns and retreats back on board and can be heard yelling.

'Explosives! everybody out! Now!' the sergeant is now on his phone to an army office bomb disposal squad, chatter goes back and forth.

Four police emerge from the boat, one is carrying two assault rifles and adds them to the pile. He looks at the sergeant 'enough for a small war' the sergeant's call has finished. He nods and asks 'Boat clear?' Mike replies. 'Yes, all clear.' they have grouped around the sergeant.

'OK, until the bomb squad turns up and gives the all clear, the marina is closed off. Mike some quick photos of what we have so far and then do a list at the station of the lot, very detailed tags eh, position found, everything.' Mike nods.

'Heidi, go and close the whole marina. They will bitch about it but it is what it is. A boat has been discovered with explosives and the area must be cordoned off. Public safety, just that. Be wary of the media, the bastards are everywhere.' Heidi gives a lopsided grin, nods and walks back down the pier.

'OK, grab some of these and secure them. Gently, no hands, gloves only.' Mike has finished his photo shoot and the other two cops pick up a number of guns and ammunition boxes and walk down the pier.

Mike has three assault rifles cradled in his arms and he looks at the sergeant.

'Odd one, this job. Do you know who called it in? No one injured, can't see any holes anywhere and who fired the shots? It wasn't them, guns weren't fired.' the sergeant shakes his head.

'No, you're right there. No idea but I agree we need to do some digging. I wonder what our friends will say.' he looks at the cars in car park.

The fun is over and I am ready to move. I fly back to the small park where I have landed before. I land, watch, then become seen. I go into a café over the road and order lunch. As I eat I sit and watch the swirl of life around me. People are just doing what they do, working, shopping, chatting, catching up, just being. My possible influence on their lives is starting to weigh heavier. I sit and think as the clock ticks. On one wall there is a TV going, the world news is full of the issues at the White House. The Secretary of State has not been given bail which surprises me. The 'Press-gate' issue follows this and statements from the White House stand resolute against possible spying on the President. The commentaries are ongoing, with a lot of surmising but no facts, panels of experts who know little, then political reporters being interviewed by reporters, reporting about rumours.

My mind turns to the 'right now'. I send a quick note to Ruth about Dan and his friends. Given their situation, the new person at the SIS may wish to have a chat with them? I get a quick 'thanks' back.

I go back to the small park and go unseen then fly back to the house, where I see Barbara walking back up the path from the shoreline, I land up by the house and call out.

'How long have you been back?' She asks, she has a couple of large shell treasures, one in each hand.

'Just got here.' we go up the path into the house and I put the jug on the gas stove, as I do. I relay my tactics with Dan. She is watching me from the couch.

'So we can go back to Troy's place and start thinking about a new home?' She is obviously very keen on this idea and I don't blame her. We have been marking time and it's weight is starting to tell. This thought gives a flash of anger, not being able to live in one's own home, feeling insecure has been taking its toll. I nod.

'Yes, there is no reason why not. When would you like to go? We can pack up quick enough.' She is calculating then says. 'I do love this place but we can't stay forever so why not soon? Besides if we are going to start might as well be now.'

Chapter 18

The sun is getting lower as we arrive in the enclosed back yard at Troy's. There is a note taped to the door, which Barbara opens and quickly scans. I open the door after rescuing the key from its hiding place. I dump our new small backpack and other bits on a couch, left-over food on the kitchen bench.

'It's from Di, asking me to get in touch when we get back. Oh, she and Gary are taking a break.' she glances at me as I grunt.

'Has this got something to do with you?' she is sporting her annoyed look.

'No, not at all. The last time we spoke was in the drive the day of the fire. I was pissed off at him and said so but this has nothing to do with me, besides I have been a little busy. This is news to me.' She hums at my reply.

'I am going to see her.' I know the look and just nod with a "fine."

'I'll sort some dinner in a couple of hours OK?' I get an "OK" from the bedroom where she has gone to change. Shortly she reappears and says.

'I have my new phone. I won't be that long.' She gets in the truck and drives down the driveway. Nice to be back in civilization I think.

Sometime later Barbara is back. I have a salad on the bench and have defrosted some steak. She walks through the door and drops on to the couch.

'She is pretty upset. It seems that he has had some sort of break down. He wants to reassess and needs to be alone for a while. He has gone to his parents in the city. Hardly alone though is it?' I shake my head, hum to myself but say nothing. Barbara asks.

'So what did you actually say to him when you last saw him?' I tell her what I said or at least to the best of my memory.

'Do you think that pushed him?' She is looking in the fridge for wine.

'I don't know, maybe, maybe not. I still stand by what I said. His greed for whatever almost got us killed, then there is the rest.' It is her turn to hum, she puts a glass of beer in front of me and changes the subject.

'What's for dinner?'

With dinner over we are catching up on world news. The issue with the President centre stage in the western world channels. In local news saboteurs have been put in custody in the capital. Explosives and guns have been found on a launch in the harbour as well as a lot of cash. The explosives were destroyed and the launch, that has just arrived from overseas, has been impounded. All three people in custody are American citizens. Fascinating I think, but them getting caught does create a problem for the US. I sit wondering. Barbara asks.

'So what now? Do you think the US will ask for them to be sent home?' I stare out at the lake pondering.

'No. No, I think the US will let them take their chances as they seem to be part of whatever game the secretary was playing. The President has made it very clear where he stands. If one of their agencies puts their hand out and gets caught I would think the President would let it be cut off. Besides in the background is the attack on Ruth and the proof held around that. On the other hand, if Dan and his boys do talk it would be very embarrassing for the US. I think it's unlikely though, it would give them serious time in one of our jails. Lots of questions, not many answers but I would bet the cops are asking, what have we gotten into?'

There is silence as we contemplate our complicated little world. Barbara finally asks, breaking the silence.

'Do you have a plan to send Island out into the world?' I sit quietly, I can hear a cricket in the garden.

'Well, yes I do. I have an idea but I need to do a little work on it yet, then run it past Island. I have a question on Island's capabilities, then I will run it past you and Ruth. She has a better idea on the world level and I trust her insight.' she looks at me and then takes my hand and squeezes it and looks at me deeply.

'When it needs tweaking, I will be here.' She starts laughing uproariously at her wit and gets up. 'I am going to have a shower,' I laugh with her slightly sourly but I suspect she may be right. I have often later reflected on my own stupidity. My thoughts turn to my plan and I ponder.

The following morning is dark and over caste but it doesn't match my mood. A decent night's sleep and feeling more secure has helped. I hadn't realized the how the lack of semi normalcy had worked on me, us, in reality. I am quiet over breakfast, which Barbara notices.

'So still planning?' I raise an eyebrow and smile.

'I am thinking about starting to plan, maybe.' to this she grins as she picks up my and her plate and puts them on the bench.

'I am going to look at houses with Di. And no, you can't come!' I put my hands up. I know that she will look and then we discuss ideas. We have always had a rule when buying houses. The right of veto. If one of us hates it, we don't buy, compromise pure and simple.

'I won't get in your way. I am going to talk to Ruth anyway.' She eyes me.

'OK, I will see you later. Be careful.' She gives me a quick kiss and leaves in the truck. I get some bits together and lock the house. Soon I am walking up the steps of parliament. I stand in the foyer and send Ruth a text is she free for a few minutes? The reply is 'a few' busy, I think. As I walk through the outer office eyes follow. Ruth waves me into a seat I sit and the door opens with Jan asking if we would both like tea or coffee but she is really the one who has been sent in to see if she can garner any information for the gossip mill. Ruth says no thanks, as do I.

'It annoys them, they don't know why you come and go.' she says with a smile. 'And why an ex-employee is so important. I rather like keeping them guessing. My little game, stupid, but oddly fun.' I laugh.

'Yes, oddly is the word, speaking of which. Dan and his friends, any news?' Ruth grimaces at the question.

'The police don't like politicians asking questions and they don't like the SIS getting involved. Actually I am not sure what they do like.' She shakes her head.

'The people on the ground are fine but the middle managers. Anyway, it seems the Americans have washed their hands of them. The Embassy people came and went but didn't return. which is not normal. Generally they bend over backwards for one of their own. Orders from further up I think, but not like them to cut citizens loose. The SIS got nothing, not surprising really, the police are the ones with the levers. They are rightly taking them to court. They will be on remand for some time. Months or maybe more. I did expect a call from the US State department but not a word. They have said that the arms must have been on the boat where they hired it in Australia.' She sighs.

'Which doesn't fly really, given they came on deck with guns in their hands, I understand. The other arms have finger prints, theirs, as do the grenades and the rocket launchers that were found. Oh and packets of plastic Centex and detonators.'

I am really surprised. What I don't understand is what use does all this terrorist gear have? This was bought into the country after Dan saw me. All very odd. More orders it seems. I am also surprised at all this information that the police didn't want to pass along.

'OK, so how did you find this all out, given the polices ummm unhelpfulness?'

She laughs and says.

'I pulled the National Security card. I am the Prime Minister and that is that!' I nod and get it. I am disturbed at the amount of arms and explosive and am trying to make sense of it but can't. Ruth sits forward in her seat.

'So what are you here for? You've been thinking.' her eyes are smiling but face is serious, I nod.

'Yes I have. There is a little something that I want you to do for me, Island and the world. I do need you to trust me. In fact, Ruth, I need you to trust me, a lot. I have a plan but am not sure it will work.' I stop and consider my words, then.

'Anyway, I would like you to contact the President. I would like an emergency meeting of the Security Council at the United Nations.' Ruth's mouth falls open.

'You are joking? I worked at the UN years ago and if memory serves there has only been ten or eleven emergency meetings in the UNs whole existence.' I am nodding.

'Yes, Eleven. I checked. Oh and with just one interpreter each.' She is shaking her head and says quietly.

'Do you know what you are asking? The organization is unwieldy and full of holes. It could be done and maybe, just maybe the President could do it, even then I am doubtful.' I nod again and continue.

'I also think it would be good to have the full General Assembly there at the same time. So I want the whole lot, all one hundred and ninety three states, plus the observers.' She sits back shaking her head.

'You are bloody mad. They just won't do it.' I shrug. I have always liked the little colloquialism: 'How does one eat an elephant? One bite at a time.' I look at her and lean forward to push my point.

'Look Ruth, if not them, then who? They are a start, you've met Island, you know what is at stake. It's how Island is introduced to the world, that matters. This is the start of the solution. If one power gets Island then I can see a world war eventually. Planetary control by one state, maybe? Ultimate power corrupts ultimately. Or just a war to try to get to Island. Tell me where the population of the planet would be then. It has to be done soon. The cat is almost out of the bag.'

'I don't even know if Island can be controlled by one power or how that would happen or if Island would just disappear. I don't think Island could or would let that happen but who knows? The actual way Island is introduced, I believe, is the answer.' Ruth's lips sit in a straight line, her eyes very still. I roll on.

'There will be more Dans'. He has spoken to his people and they have a plan. Dan is still under orders, where do they come from? The US Secretary is in jail, so who else is there? That boat with turning up with its cargo should be a warning to you. It is to me. Gears are turning, soon more questions will be asked. They will dig deeper looking for answers and ultimately, me.' I am looking across her shoulder into a future of danger.

'The Security Council meeting has to be back to back with the General Assembly. The nuclear control of the Security Council has the General Assembly by the throat but they are not the whole world, Ruth. I do believe they are the conduit to the people of the world though. It is the only world forum. I need your help or I tell Island to go and leave us to our fate.'

Ruth is watching and listening intently and her eyes darken at the word, fate.

'Our planet needs this help Ruth. We just need to link Island to the people. Or where else could, or should, we go?'

I sit back, turn and look at the grey sky, it might rain again. Ruth's phone buzzes but she ignores it. She looks around the room and her eyes rest on Churchill. Her head tilts towards me.

'One thing, why the rush? There is time.' She asks. I stare back then I say.

'I have a date to work to.' She takes this in, she is thinking about trust.

'OK' she says finally 'I will call the President. You will go and see him?'

I nod 'As soon as I can see him, I will be there. One thing, I want you to know, I am going to take him to Island, if he agrees. Without his full belief he won't buy in, and yes, I believe that it is a risk. The trump card is Island and our relationship.'

Ruth sits then picks up her phone.

'Hi Jan, please get me the President of the United States. I know the time. Make sure they know who is calling and yes, they should wake him. He will take the call. Thank you' She puts the phone down. She looks at me and asks.

'When do you see Island again?'

'I am not sure, it depends on my interview with the President, within 24 hours I guess.' the phone buzzes.

'Mr. President. Good to talk to you. Yes, I am sorry to ring at this time. I have Bill here with me. Is it possible for him to see you soon? He has a question for you and the implications need to be discussed in person. Yes, we both think it is very important. Excellent, very well, I will. Thank you and good night.' She taps the phone and sits looking at it.

'Ten in the Rose Garden, in the morning. He will be alone.' She turns and looks out the window then says.

'Say hello to Island for me, please.' Her voice is quiet, I stand and nod.

'I will, Island becomes part of you. It is a strange thing, you gain something and lose something with the memory exchange.' I look at her, she nods.

'Thanks Ruth' I turn and leave the very still, quiet office.

In the foyer of the capital I go and look at a street map to find what I am looking for. The Central Police station. I walk two blocks then up the stairs into a horribly designed Nineteen Sixties building, through a self-opening door into a lobby with open cubicles. A young policeman is at the one I approach.

'Hi there. Bill Sheppard I would like to talk to one of the American gentlemen you have in custody please.' The identification I show him had been issued by James. It has SIS all over it. The policeman looks serious after reading the card. He asks.

'Can I take that through sir?' and he puts his hand out for the card, I shake my head.

'Sorry no. Would you give me your warrant card?' He goes red and turns away. Presently he arrives back with the sergeant that was directing the team on the pier.

'Hello Mr....' I show him the card and say 'Sheppard, Bill Sheppard' and I smile.

He nods and points to a door. I head there, the door opens and the Sergeant says.

'Senior Sergeant Roy Peters' and shakes my hand and he directs me in to a bland interview room and motions for me to sit down.

'OK Mr. Sheppard, what are you looking for?' I look around and smile.

'You picked up three Americans at the marina. I would like to talk to one of them. Dan, the older of them. Thick set, shaved head and probably uncooperative.' I wait as he takes this in.

'We had two of your guys here yesterday, they didn't seem to get any information so why are you here now? And do you mind if I ring to check on you?' He smiles blandly and I return the same smile.

'No problem, can I give you a number? Just so it doesn't surprise you, it will be the Prime Minister.'

He stops, looks at me, head still, grey eyes piercing. He takes the number and taps it into his phone. I look blandly at the desk and am hoping Ruth will back me. I know I will get a roasting the next time I see her, maybe.

'Yes hello? Prime Minister? This is Senior Sergeant Roy Peters. I have a Mr. Bill Sheppard here from the SIS. He wants to talk to the Americans that...umm yes I see, alright. Thank you.' He carefully taps the phone. A second later his phone buzzes and he reads a text.

'I am to give you as much help as you need.' He quotes but he doesn't like it, I understand why. I have been in his shoes. But needs must. I try to soften the blow.

'Look, I have been watching this guy for a while. I can't tell you why, but anything that I get for your case, I will pass on.' He looks at me, trust is limited, but he says.

'They had only just arrived' I shake my head.

'No. Dan has been here for a couple of weeks. I am not exactly sure how long, the other two, I gather, were his back up for something to happen here. I don't know what. I would bet you have had absolutely nothing out of them? Right?' Looks are exchanged, he waits, then nods.

'They asked for consular help and they ran a mile. Odd for one American to be left to take their chances but three?' He is watching me quietly and then finally nods.

'One thing if I could, do you have an interview room that has a glass panel? Dan knows me and does not like me. He will want to attack me, if he can. Once we get over that, I think, not completely sure, but I think, he will open up. We'll see.'

The sergeant sits and just looks at me, I glance at him then stare at the desktop, hands in my lap and wait. After a few minutes he stands and says.

'I will be back shortly' I nod. Ten minutes later the sergeant puts his head through the door. 'Follow me' which I do. He directs me to a door, he has his hand on the handle, he turns and looks at me, distrust is floating in the air.

'He thinks you are from the embassy. He hasn't spoken to any of us since he has been here. No name, nothing, I think he is ex Special Forces, has the look, tough guy. His passport is very good but I am told not issued from the US, at least at first run through the Immigration Office.' I nod my thanks. I am surprised he has told me so much.

'So what's he looking at time wise?' he shrugs.

'With what they had on the boat, under the new terrorist legislation, real time? Ten years, depends on the court, maybe more but about that.' I nod my thanks.

He turns the door handle, opens the door. I walk into a small room with a thick glass divider that has holes drilled through it. There are two chairs facing each other. Dan is seated in one, his surprise is very obvious. He stands turns and pounds on his door. He glares at me over his shoulder and pounds on the door again. I sit in the seat opposite his and say through the glass.

'They won't come until I say Dan. Not until you and I have talked. So sit down!' My voice has got loader close to shouting. Dan turns and snarls at me.

'Fuck you! Lucky you have the glass! Fuck you!' I sit back in the chair and reply.

'Fuck you too Dan! Takes a real man to burn a house down but you know what? You have been left to hang. You will do ten years real time, you bastard! I am, right now, the only fucking friend you have on the outside, the only one! You are going for the terrorist high jump. Yep, we have a new law here that they will try out on you guys. You will get twenty maybe thirty but still you will do ten. So sit down!'

I sit and wait. Dan paces up and down glaring at me from time to time. He stops hands on hips.

'Bullshit!' his mouth is working and he is breathing deeply, I relax and open my hands and I shake my head.

'No, no bullshit. The embassy boys came and went, didn't they? And where are they now?' he glares again and paces, then stops and sits down. He is turned away from me but listening.

'I am not lying. Why would I? But I do want you to answer two questions and in return I will talk to the President on how to get you and your buddies home.' His head goes up and looks at me directly.

'How? That's complete bullshit, you can't talk to the President. You're lying!' I shake my head, look directly in his eyes and smile.

'No, again why would I? I could have killed you. You know that. I let you go and for what it's worth, I didn't want to kill John either. I do what I say I am going to do Dan. You know that.' I sit and wait while he thinks about this. Gears are whirling and to make them go a bit faster, I throw a stone on the pond and wait for ripples.

'Sam Bellhouse hasn't helped has he Dan?' Dan's head snaps up to look at me eyes boring saying nothing but very still.

'He is right next to the President and yet here you are, looking at a lot of years.'

'You don't know.' His reply is angry defiant but questioning; the uncertainty hovers in the under tone of voice and look.

'He was pretty close to Harry, Dan. The Press office stuff has yet to come to light fully but when it does, Sam's name will be on the list, Harry will see to that. You know he will, even if it isn't made public and you will still be in our tin pot jail. You know it, I know it' I stop.

I have said enough. I will let those thoughts mature. If I was in his shoes spending years in a jail wouldn't appeal, but I am not him, maybe he is that tough. Time passes and there is a knock at the door, the sergeant's head appears.

'Your time is about up.' I didn't know there was a time limit, but I'll bet he and others have been listening, subtle pressure. I just nod my thanks. I wait then enough, I think.

I stand and look at Dan.

'We won't talk again. This game is over.' I turn to the door and just as I put my hand on the door handle Dan says.

'You can talk to the President?' I turn and wait, then sit back down.

'Yes.' I say mildly, this is no time to antagonize. He looks at me, eyes wide staring, weighting things I am not sure about.

'When?' a snapped answer but he has just crossed a bridge. I toss a ball on to the court.

'Tomorrow morning 10.00am. I already have an interview.' I wait as his eyes flicker into a choice.

'OK.' I turn and sit.

'NASA monitored the UPA program but the CIA has people, us, watching it. Harry and Sam are some of the people unhappy about the direction of the government. We came because you are the first real lead we ever have had.'

He has stopped and is glaring at me, gears still turning, balances still forming. 'Go on' I say.

'Our contact here gave us real proof. The X-rays, well, we paid for it. Anyway a world first. You. And what you have. You became the must have.' I nod, Gary was paid. I had wondered, shame for Di.

'We didn't know how much that thing in your arm could do but we were directed to get you or it. Your vanishing act sealed it, after you killed John. Then you went to the Prime Minister. Harry went nuts. He was scared of where you and your knowledge would end up.' I look at him thinking about Ruth's office, holes in a window and the luck of a miss. I also think about a young man who didn't get to his sister's wedding. I stare at this military robot and try to fathom any of his moral code. I shrug at my waste of time and prompt Dan.

'He ordered the hit I know. But why? what was the motive?' I still don't get the why. Dan shrugs I can see he wasn't sure either.

'If she was dead, your government in flux, her knowledge went with her and James would help get you to us. You had disappeared and the only place you seemed to turn up was her office.' I just shake my head and I look at him and ask.

'So why all the explosive crap on the boat? What was the point of that?'

'Set a couple of lots of Centex off around the country for the shock value. Maybe a grenade attack, a diversion until we had you.' He stops and I watch him thinking. I wonder, if in speaking, letting this out, the stupidity becomes obvious to him. I think about greed and power and how people are so easily bought or somehow worse, just follow orders. My mind wanders to Gary. I stand and stretch. This guy just makes me very angry but I say.

'OK. I will talk to the President tomorrow. It will be his situation to deal with. Dan would you, or the other two, testify against Harry or Sam? I am asking because he will ask me. I personally, don't care either way.'

Dan is still sitting he folds his arms across his chest and then says.

'I would really like to kill you.' I shrug and as I do, I go unseen. Dan's mouth drops open and he jumps to the glass staring. I leave it a couple of seconds and become seen. He falls back in his chair, mouth still open, I am standing looking at him blank faced.

'I told you Dan, you will never ever know where I am. You forgot. This isn't all I have available. One warning. If I ever see you again here in my country or hear of your buddies being active here. I kill you first.'

As I walk out of the room the sergeant is walking down the hall, he nods and directs me to another small room. He sits in one of the chairs leans back and laces his hands together, eyes very steady, drilling into mine.

'So, you know each other quite well?' His tone casual, as I shake my head.

'No but we have met.' He is watching closely.

'We listened to all of your chat. Who is John?' he is still casual half smiling.

I look at him, I knew they would be listening and I just didn't care. Knowing and thinking a thing then proving it are vastly different. I say nothing. He then says.

'You seem to have been flying in rarefied circles, Prime Ministers, talking to Presidents, how do I get that sort of treatment? I rang a friend at the SIS. They don't seem to know you and yet you have the PMs number and SIS ID, bit odd don't you think? What would you think if you were in my shoes Mr. Sheppard?' I sit and say nothing. He tries another tack.

'What hit was ordered? On who? You both seem to know about the subject. You knew his pressure points and now you are talking to the President, what tomorrow? And you are the first what, exactly? Maybe you will still be here tomorrow. Mr. Sheppard.'

He has emphasized the name with a nice roll of sarcasm. I have now had enough. I get he is doing his job but I am not going to be part of his play. I watch him and wait.

I look at him unblinking in the eyes. Time to go.

'Sergeant I am leaving. I don't have to explain anything to you. If you are going to detain me, do it and suffer the issues that that will raise.' I stand and walk towards the door. He stands and snaps.

'I will find out you know.'

His look is perturbed, questioning. I shake my head but say nothing. He pushes past me, opens the door and then another to the foyer. As I turn towards the entrance he holds my elbow and says.

'If these guys are let go, they get away with it. I don't know what political game you are playing but they are still scum. They could have killed a lot of people, you heard him. Think about that.' I stand there looking at him for a few seconds and say.

'I know.'

I turn and walk out the door and walk towards the small park. I pass a McDonalds. People are looking out of windows and kids are playing on bright colored slides. I think about what bombers do to innocent people and the kids laughter echoes. At the small park I sit on the only bench and watch people for a while. I want to go home but time is starting to press I need to be in the Rose Garden shortly, half a world away. More games I think.

I walk behind the tree and become unseen. I fly towards home and fly slowly across Troy's place wishing I could stay. The truck is home. I should have called Barbara I think, with this thought I head towards my meeting with the President.

Chapter 19

The day is clear and cold. I check my watch as I slowly descend into the garden. I see the President standing on the grass, there are a couple of secret service agents wandering around watching their charge. I wait and when they are both out of line of sight, I become seen.

'Mr. President!' I call, as I do one of the agents hears me, he pulls a gun and jumps into action.

'You! On the ground now!' The President calls out to him and waves him away.

'It's Ok! It's OK, he's here to see me!' I have raised my hands. Another agent has appeared who is also looking for action.

'It's fine, he's here to see me!' The President is coming forward. By this time the first agent has reached the Presidents side.

'Sir, where did he come from? We haven't been notified of any visitors. Where has he come from?' The President turns to him and says. 'He is here to see me. I will not repeat myself, thank you. Now, please leave.' as he turns towards he puts his hand out.

'Hello Bill, nice of you to drop in' I drop my hands and smile at the President's choice of words, and his grin, as he sees they haven't been missed. We wander across the lawn both agents are watching like hawks.

The President asks laconically. 'Nice flight?' I laugh.

'Always, you should try it.' He grins and nods.

'I would love to, one day.' I hum to myself. We walk towards the office and by tacit agreement, say very little. The President shows me into the Oval Office and we sit opposite each other.

'Coffee? Or tea? It's tea you guys drink, right?' He seems relaxed and I wonder how a person stays relaxed in his job, like anything I guess, you just get used to it.

'Thank you, no, maybe later?' He nods.

'So what is the pressing issue? I know you have at least one. Early morning calls make me nervous.' I start.

'You may know that there are three US citizens in our capitals police station. They haven't been charged yet, but it is likely they will be with our new anti-terrorism laws. That is my understanding.' He is watching me carefully and I am sure he knows but I continue.

'I have spoken to who I think is their lead, Dan. He first approached me at home then he was involved in burning my house to the ground. Incidentally, my wife and I want to thank you for the money that arrived. And I do, thank you.'

The President nods but is still looking for detail, he says nothing and waits.

'Dan and his friends are unhappy about their circumstances. They arrived with arms and explosives, got caught red handed, so the case is pretty easy to prove. They are looking at a ten year stretch maybe more. I said I would speak to you on their behalf.'

The Presidents surprise is apparent he sits forward.

'Why would, you, of all people, do that?' I open my hands, palms out.

'I wanted to know who else was directing them. Harry is unlikely to be, given his situation. I don't know but I would bet he is watched fairly closely. So there has to be someone else. Like it or not your Presidency has been unpopular. The last few years created hardliners.

You know that better than I do. Anyway, the internal politics of your country has nothing to do with me. Dan's team attacked us. We lost our home! I believe that they would have killed my wife or used her as a lever!' I am angry, I calm myself with a shrug. I sit, playing with the next sentence, then just say it.

'So Dan has confirmed that Sam Bellhouse was pulling his teams strings.'

I sit and wait for the explosion. The President goes stock still, then starts shaking his head. Anger and shock are working across his face.

'No! You are wrong! I've known Sam since he was an intern! He is fucking loyal!'

'Sorry, OK, but to who?' I ask quietly, I know he is hurt, broken loyalty is a very bitter pill. The President's look is rock steady, hating the words.

'Can you prove this? Seriously? If you are wrong, I think I would like to have you shot!' I look at him steadily and nod, I get it.

'Dan will testify, he knows without your offices' support, he will be there for a long while. Harry can't help. He is pretty pissed. He thought his back was covered I guess. I don't know how these operations work but....' I let it slide, the President is still glaring at me.

'This is simple enough. Sam will be here somewhere. I would bet a dime to a hundred he has been very close to you since Harry was arrested. I will ask him.'

The President has stood and is pacing stiffly his anger a cloud around him, he turns to me, looks me in the eyes and says.

'You know Bill, I don't think I like you.' I say nothing, his anger is understandable.

He taps his phone.

'Hi Sam, can you drop into the Oval for a minute? Something we need to cover. Yes now. Thanks.' He sits and looks at me.

'God help you, if you are wrong.' I nod. I get it. I feel for him but also think I didn't make choices against my own government, I say nothing. We wait. Shortly the door opens and Sam arrives walking quickly into the room.

'Mr. President, sorry I was on the other...' he looks at me there is a 'where have I seen you before' look on his face but no real recognition. The President waves a hand in my direction and says at the same time.

'Have a seat Sam.' I sit, saying nothing, just watching. Sam puts his hand out.

'Sam Bellhouse.' I take it and say 'Bill Sheppard.' Sam snaps his hand back in shock, the surprise stark. His head swivels to the President who has been watching.

'Sam, I guess you have seen a photo of me.' I say.

'One of Dan's maybe? No matter. I have been talking to Dan. He is in a jail in my country but you know that. Anyway, he wants out. Simply put; you are the price.' I stop. I want a reaction. Sam is white shaking his head.

'I don't know what you are talking about ....' I cut in.

'Dan will come back here and testify Sam. He has agreed. Like I said, you are the price.' Sam is still shaking his head and his body rocks.

'He wouldn't .....!'

I look at the President, his face is deeply saddened.

'Jesus Christ! Sam you know him!' Sam's mouth is opening and closing.

'You set up the Pressroom watch Sam, or were part of it, I heard your voice.' my voice is quiet. His head snaps towards me. Fear and surprise in equal amounts.

'How, how did you know?' I shake my head and watch the President as he walks to the door of the office. He returns with a secret service agent who follows the President into the room then another arrives.

'Please take Mr. Bellhouse under arrest to the Attorney General's office.' The agent looks at the President, he swallows and nods, the other agent moves forward.

'Yes sir.'

Sam stands shakily and faces at the President.

'This country is better than your kind. We will beat you.'

His anger and hate drip out of him. The agent puts handcuffs on Sam. Taking an arm each, they lead him towards to door. The President is rock still, watching. As they leave the President flops on the couch. He takes out his phone and speaks to the Attorney General. The conversation is terse on both sides, I gather. The room then becomes silent. The grandfather clock ticks quietly.

'So much hate.' He says finally.' Skin color, back ground, where you were born, which school you went to, the money you have. Does that make the difference to how good you are or how worthy for office?' he falls silent again. I shrug and say.

'I believe somewhere at some stage that man got told a lie and he has lived it. And Harry helped. It is going to be a very tough time for you.' he looks at me and nods.

'Yeah, the media and the Party. One arrest in this house is one thing, two? Christ! There will be questions about my sanity. Can you speak to the Prime Minister and ask her to arrange to have those three guys to be sent home? I would have transport sent to pick them up but more orders from here will be questioned now. I will need them to save my Presidency.'

'As soon as I get back, I will see her face to face.' he is looking at the painting of Washington in the wall.

'There is more to say Sir, more important than Sam.' He turns towards me. His look ranges over me, balancing and then says "shoot".

'First, the culture that gave me the bracelet have sent a library, a cache of knowledge that is so vast it will change the world. It may completely rearrange life on the planet, not for the better. I believe for the best.' I wait then.

'I am not sure what Ruth told you or how much you believed. But I am the proof that there is an entity that takes care of the library who has taken the name 'Island'. I stop then.

'I want to take you to meet Island before I ask the next question.' The President is staring at me.

'You want me to go with you, alone, to meet an alien?' I look at him.

'Yes. For the planet. For all mankind. And yes, I think you'll do it.' As I say this he bursts out laughing, head shaking.

'Sir, just to make a point.'

I float across the room to the chair behind the desk and then go unseen. The President twitches slightly and grunts. He sits staring.

'OK, point made.' I become seen again. He is thinking about trust and he looks at the desk I am sitting behind. I wait watching. He looks at me.

'Now?'

'Sure, now would be good. About an hour I would guess will be enough.'

The clock ticks and his phone buzzes twice, which he ignores. He then reaches for his phone and issues instructions about not being disturbed. A very tense short discussion is held about media, he then stands and tells me to follow him. We go through the secretary's office down the hall outside and towards his residence. We walk down the colonnade, through a door and into a room then through into another, where there are doors that open out on to the grounds.

'Nice room' I say. He opens the doors to the grounds. We are alone. We walk on to the lawn, I check again for watchers.

I give a quick run-down on what will happen. He nods, questions ripple across his face, more curiosity, I think, than fear. He stands beside me as I put my arm around his waist. I can feel the tension in his body. His face is close to mine and is about to speak when we go unseen. I hear "Jesus" beside me. Then we fly.

It is just before dusk as we land on the beach. Island is floating quietly, waiting. I take the Presidents hand and we walk over the water into Island. The President staggers slightly with walking, not being able to see his feet. We become seen as we walk down the entrance hall towards the control room. He is looking around him and follows my lead sitting in the other chair. The wonder of the universe is slowly turning in front of us.

'Hello Bill.' Island welcomes.

'Hello Island. The person I bring with me is the President of the United States of America. Ralph Gomez. I have brought him because he is the leader of a large country on our planet. I am hoping he will help me to bring your wisdom to our world.'

The President is looking bewildered but I guess I was as well at the first time here. The view of the immensity of space and the vast array before us is almost too much to take in. Yet as you focus, worlds become real, stars get bigger. It is a telescope into infinity, yet each single thing real, a duality of the impossible and the real. He looks at me and answers.

'Hello Island, I am amazed, I did not know that, you, this was possible.' He stumbles to a halt.

'Welcome Ralph. Island has some knowledge of you and your place on your planet. I have read Bill's memories and passed on knowledge of Island's world. Ruth allowed this process to happen. Would you permit this Ralph?'

The President looks at me, I nod and shrug.

'Simply you get far more than you give, it is why I brought you here to this place, and no, it doesn't hurt. The only thing I can say is: You are now blind, with this you will see.'

The President is looking deeply into my eyes then turns and looks around him, minutes tick by and I look at tongues of flame from two vast suns in deep space.

'Very well Island. Please go ahead' He looks tense but never the less sits back in the seat. The worlds wander in front of us both. I look again at the blue world I have seen before, then deeper. I look until I am again watching the waves on the shore, deep red birds slowly drift through the scene, then a huge green ape like animal appears on the beach and walks into the water where it sits lazing, its hands playing in the water.

The President turns to me and says 'I was blind and now.....' he sits quietly watching the view of worlds. He slowly says.

'I thank you, Island. I did not know a world could be what you have shown me. Your world was just wonderful.....I... All the population happy, cared for by each other and by the all. No war, jealousy worked through, all potential developed. The planet and its resources honoured. Every animal given the right to live in its own space. A place where money has no meaning. Ask and ye shall receive. Heaven on earth? I ......' He stops and tears are falling on his cheeks. He looks at me.

'Could we do this? Is this transition possible?' I look at him and then at the shoreline of the blue planet, the wet green ape is walking back into the trees.

'Well, I think we have to try. Island's people took millennia. The distance of deep space was the issue. You have seen this. They have given us the opportunity to by-pass this. The path we are on will kill us all. You know that better than I do, you have the worlds' destruction in a suite case. Sooner or later someone at your desk or one in China or Russia or somewhere will start it. Our seas are starting to die. Less than one percent hold all the wealth, people die of lack of food, others die of too much. We have to try.'

Out of the vastness in front of us Island says.

'Your world is at the cusp of the end Ralph. I thank you for your memories but they show much difficulty. Bill is right, time is short. Island is here for peoples like yours to become better than they are right now, also to bring them into a different future.'

I sit back and say no more. I am enthralled with 'my' blue planet and go back to watching the waves curl and things shimmy in the water, the palms are a light pink, odd but rather nice.

The President has been lost in the stars.

'Bill, I think it is time. I have to get back, needs must.' he twists a smile. I nod and understand, I rather like it here too.

'Island, thank you. I will return soon with a plan I hope.' I say. I stand and watch the President take in the surrounds. He seems to be storing the scene to review later. As we walk down to the beach entrance I take his hand and we go unseen. It is dark as we walk over the water. I put my arm around the President's waist and shortly we are coming to a soft landing outside the double doors of his residence. The doors are shut. I look around me carefully and we become seen.

The President walks forward and opens one of the doors. A woman who I recognize as the President's wife is just walking into the room.

'Ralph! where have you been? There's been a lot of people looking for you. This business with Sam....'she stops eyeing me. The President turns to me and makes introductions.

'My wife Estelle, Estelle, Bill Sheppard' She nods with an automatic smile.

'Pleased to meet you Mr. Sheppard.' her gaze wanders over me questioning then goes back to her husband. He glances at me then says. 'Yes, I thought they would be, but Bill and I had something to discuss. Sam's situation was part of that.' Estelle turns her gaze to me again her look is stern and searing. A power here I think but say nothing. The President turns to me.

'We need to talk further but I have some people to placate in the meantime. Can you wait? You have thoughts and I want to know them. I may need to talk to your Prime Minister to get the ball rolling her end.' The President is saying he is going to be up against the wall very soon, political pressure is building rapidly. I nod and say of course. I don't want to but I think it will be quicker. The President says to me. 'Follow me, stay at my side, and say nothing. I may want your insight.'

The first lady gives an intake of breath. 'Ralph! I mean I am sure Mr. Sheppard is capable at whatever he does but we are heading towards an emergency beyond anything I think that...' The President cuts over her.

'Estelle. Thank you. I do know what's building but I am still the President and Bill's advice is what I wish to have. Please excuse us.' He turns on his heel and we walk towards the Oval office. Estelle's look is unpleasant to her husband, bloody to me. I follow the President.

Chapter 20

As we emerge into the hall from the colonnade a striking woman approaches.

'Sir, we really have an issue here. The party has gone mad and the Attorney General is angry as hell. The media is howling and I have no idea what is happening and frankly I should!' She is obviously angry. The President tosses me an introduction.

'Lee Bradley, White House Press Secretary' I nod she looks at me with a who the hell are you and where did you come from look. The President continues.

'Bill Sheppard' I look at her. Quiet, is good right now.

'Umm Hello. Sir we really need...' The President, silent, keeps walking through the adjoining office, into the Oval Office and sits at his desk. Lee is hovering looking very unhappy, with her mouth working. She starts talking but the President lifts a hand and cuts over her.

'Lee, please call the staff in here, you know who. Our team only. I will explain to all staff once they are here. Please do it now.' She opens her mouth but the President puts his hand up.

'Lee, you work for me, please don't argue. Just do as I ask. Now please!' Her mouth snaps shut and she turns and stiffly walks out of the room.

Within minutes people start coming into the office. Five minutes later there are about twenty people lining the walls. I have moved to the back of the room and stand waiting. They are uneasy, the rumour mill has been rolling I see, uncertainty and fear are in the room, the guarded looks, quick bursts of nervous laughter cut off. There are looks in my direction of curiosity but no actual questions. Lee is standing at the front of the group, clearly put out but unsure what to do about it. She has seen me and has filed me into the trash. The President starts.

'Hello and thank you for coming so promptly. I know things are very busy, too busy and difficult at present. I want to give you some explanation around what has happened in the last few days. I need your help, it is only right you know so that when the full information comes out you, we, as the White House team, can stand together against what will be thrown against us. I am speaking to each and every one of you as part of this team. I hand-picked each of and every one of you for exactly a time like this. So as this will take a few minutes. Please take seats where you can or grab a piece of floor. I want you to be comfortable to take this in.'

There is some movement and nervous shuffling as people do as the President had asked. No words are spoken, the air thick with questions. The President waits, looks around the room then starts.

'Thank you. This may be one of the most difficult periods this institution, this office, and this House has ever seen. That our country has ever seen.' Attention gained.

'In the last couple of days you have seen me request the arrest and detention of the Secretary of State and now one of my top advisors for treason and other offenses yet to be filed.'

'I want you to understand some of the reasons around why I took these unprecedented steps.' Ralph looks around the room, face grim.

'Firstly, the Secretary of State ordered an assassination attempt on one of our close allies in the South Pacific. The attempt was just that, thank God. The bullets missed the Prime Minister only by luck.

The helicopter that was involved with this attempt, crashed and all four people on board were killed. At least one of these people were CIA, the rest US navy. The country involved has one person's ID and the other's dog tags. May I add, the attempt was actually made in the Prime Minister's actual office.'

The room is completely silence, mouths are open, hands rub across faces.

'This helicopter left the USS Omaha and was returning to the ship when it went down.' The President stops and looks carefully around the room.

'Add to this, surveillance was set up in the Press Room in this office. Now I find Sam Bellhouse was involved with that and he was also involved with the assassination attempt, there was cross over there. But I will come back to that shortly.' Ralph slows and lets words sink.

'This attack was generated because information was received, by a group controlled by the Secretary of State, that one of this countries citizens had found an artefact. A tool if you will, that absolutely proves other life forms from space, exist.'

There is movement in a wave around the room. Faces turn to each other, mouths open.

'This artefact may change world history or the world going forward. The leader of this country wants this kept quiet at present. I hope this underlines my trust in each one of you here today. This information cannot be repeated out of this room. To anyone.'

This has heads turning towards each other in utter surprise. I am now curious to see where the President is heading.

'NASA has been looking for UFO information pretty intensely recently and, as such, has published a number of sightings from the navy, amongst others, as you may know. The artefact that was found proves beyond any doubt that alien life exists. This information was passed on and but not exactly verified. Unfortunately, instead of going through normal channels, the Secretary of State ordered an undercover operation to find and recover that artefact.'

I am watching the President very carefully, as he says this, he looks me directly in the eyes, the creases tell me he wants to smile. Oddly, I think of the man I killed and just feel intense anger and shame.

'That operation did not go as planned, one of the operatives was killed. Others are now held in a jail in the country that the operation was under taken in. After the Secretary of State was arrested, Sam Bellhouse continued to give orders to these people. They were directed to undertake terrorist attacks in our allies' country to bring confusion and to lever the Prime Minister or create enough confusion into passing over the artefact. While working towards that end, they were arrested. Incidentally, had this artefact not been found, it is very possible the conspiracy in this office would not have come to light. My thoughts are, that once this artefact was brought under control, the intention was to change the power base in this country.'

The President stops, watching the disbelief and amazement in his audience. I am surprised where his thoughts have led but the calculations make sense. My fear factor shivers.

'Sir, have you seen this artefact? I mean what is it? How can someone just change so much?' the questioner is a very young man with excellent reasoning. I am slightly amused and think I am the artefact in the room and I am also interested how this will be answered.

The President nods slowly and looks around the room then his eyes rest on the questioner.

'Yes, I have seen it. I am not going to describe it here, as there really is so much to go into. I believe that the artefact will change the world as we all see it, may I add, for the better. But the unveiling if you like, has to be done in such a way that any power opportunities from other states are negated. The Prime Minister and I are very much in step on this.' the President has stopped, waiting. I look around the room and see there are a lot more questions but they are unhappy with the answer. You tell us but you don't trust us.

I put my hand up.

'Mr. President could I say a few words?' The room turns and looks at the interloper, a man with a different accent, a few heads turn back as the President introduces me and I walk up to stand beside the desk. The President stands and shakes my hand, which I think is odd but then it is politics.

'This is Bill Sheppard, he found the artefact and is his countries representative regarding this situation, might I add, I trust him equally with you all.' The looks are curious like a new feature in a classroom, a new exhibit at a museum.

'Hello. I found the artefact. My wife and I were the targets of the undercover operation. Just to make a point here these guys burnt our house down, we were out at the time but.....' I let this linger I want these guys to know it has been no game.

'No. I am not going to describe the artefact either. Like it or not there can be no leaks about this. This may upset some of you but frankly this is too important.' I see faces harden around the room.

'This needs to be disclosed to the whole world, or as much of it as possible, all at once. Yes, I know that has challenges but with a little luck and I think with your help this can be done. The basic reasoning rapping around all this comes back to what the President has said. This will change the entire world and I completely agree, for the better. Completely for the better. But should one power take the artefact for their control, world domination is not too far a term to use.' I turn and look at the President he looks at me and nods and turns to the room and continues.

'Bill is right. I want you all to know what is about occur is more important than the next election. This may be the most important step in the history of the world. I joke not.'

The looks are now incredulous, Lee blurts.

'More than the coming of Jesus?' The President looks at her and I think, now this is dangerous ground, you could lose parts or all of your team here. For me it is simple but for others, this is deeply serious.

'That is not for me to judge the teachings of Mohammed, Jesus or Buddha or any of the faiths. That is beyond me but, I would say, this will change the way we live and the corporeal world in which we live.' He stops and looks around the room.

'OK, more questions?' The young man puts his hand up again.

'Bill are you an alien?' There is some laughter but some are peering at me pretty intensely. I shake my head and smile.

'No. I was in our Parks Department. I got to just under capital level then retired. I found this artefact, I wanted and still want, a simple life. Check Google if you like, there's some bits about me there. To be very honest, I just want this over. Umm for the record, if I didn't think this was utterly worthwhile I would not be here. I trust Ralph and I trust my Prime Minister. This is world changing. I am deeply aware that this is a lot to ask of you. This is so much you are taking on trust.'

I stop look around the room then say.

'But if you want to see red blood, I can offer some.' A few grins appear, some think about that The President looks at me sideways. A young woman with a checked dress stands up.

'Mr. President, when do you want to tell the world about this and what's your timing, I mean, will it be soon?'

'Bill and I will have a chat around this, directly after this meeting. Yes, it will be soon, very soon. Days. The pressure is going to mount from the arrests made, with the whys and wherefores. I see no reason to keep you under any pressure longer than you need to be. I know there will be more questions but timing is now critical. Can I say that I sincerely thank you for your trust and' He stops and looks around the room slowly eyeing each person.

'There is no greater team, than those who are in this room right now, that I would rather have by my side in this test that is to come.'

The room is completely still. Then Lee gets up and hugs the President, who is completely taken by surprise and deeply moved, she then turns and hugs me. That sets the tone each person shakes our hands or gives us a hug. It is a show of trust and solidarity that I had never expected or experienced.

As the door closes I sit down on the couch and put my hands behind my head and look at the grandfather clock, it ticks slowly.

'OK Bill, what's the next question? I know you have one there.' Ralph has sat down opposite me.

'OK, but, I am not sure you will like it. I want you to call an emergency meeting of the Security Council, no representatives it must be all leaders. No ducking, no diving, all leaders, one interpreter only. That's it. Difficult but it can be done. I checked the rules. There has only been eleven since the war but to make it work the full assembly has to be there ready after our presentation.'

The President looks at me with a wide complete smile.

'Jesus that's simple! The Security Council is one thing but the full Assembly is another thing completely. It isn't meant to meet for another three or four months. Why the whole assembly as well? I will need a reason and a very good one.' He stops thinking about a task that may be beyond his scope. I shrug.

'I don't know what you use, or how to make it work. Time is getting short, be diplomatic. In other words, lie.' Ralph grunts as I go on.

'When they are told about Island I believe that one or more of the Security Council will stall. They will want proof and then the arguing will start. It may mean someone would go to war for the prize as soon as they know what it is. Telling the Security Council or even showing them me, is one thing. Island is completely different. I don't need to quote power struggles or nuclear arms races to you.' I press my point.

'Christ Ralph! People in this building wanted me as a pawn and they had no idea of what I was part of or capable of. Neither did I, really. Two of the biggest players on the council are dictatorships. England used to own half the world and would probably like to again. All I know is most leaders are so power mad that they can't let go. All the people on the planet need to know, not just a small handful. Do you really trust all the world leaders? Of course not! At times I am not sure I trust myself.'

I am feeling the pressure of being alone with what I wear, I rub my arm. Ralph stares at the table.

'Why now?' I know he is testing the theory. Good, it needs testing. 'Some reasons just walked out that door, they responded well but their own ideas and fears will break them. The guys arrested will talk and we may have missed conspirators in their lot. Then there are the people running them and how many are there, who are they or is it one? Questions are being asked in my country, as well.' I look at the clock and then at Ralphs face.

'I want my simple life back.' He looks back at me.

'What happens after the General Assembly?' I shrug slightly. 'It's televised, the world will know. Media storm, besides I think it's more around what happens during. I do my party tricks maybe and I think we introduce Island. Island will fit in the room. The size of the building is online, I checked.'

I smile at this. Ralph looks at me and just shakes his head.

'At the same time we do a complete social media blitz, everything. Every platform that can be thought of in every language, including breaking into the Chinese ones. Timing will be everything. We break all the rules but no laws. Well, not the big ones. Once it's over I doubt anyone will care. If they do, tough.' I stop and think.

'You will need to black mail, lie, cajole, payoff and even use diplomacy to get them there. I will talk to Island and see how that will run. At least, I think Island will agree. I don't know really, what Island will do or can actually do. I mean Island's actual capabilities. The team will need to sort the media, they will need to flood, and I mean flood, the world in a few hours.' At this point Ralphs phone buzzes.

I stand and walk around. I need to get moving. I have to speak to Ruth then I want to go home. I really need to speak to Island. There are questions I have avoided and now is the time. I feel drained, I also want to see the blue planet with the palms and the flickering sea. The dichotomy of thinking about an alien world, standing where I am makes me laugh. I must tell Barbara. I am missing her and I need to talk to her, I turn.

Ralph is looking at his phone thinking, he looks up and grimaces.

'It had to happen. Harry is out on bail and he drove directly to a TV station. It will be taped for prime time of course. Silly really, he doesn't know Dan will talk. We have the Omaha's captain's interview and I hear his Admiral is very unhappy on how those orders arrived. How long Harry stays out is another matter. Moves are being made to arrest him again. I am surprised the court freed him.'

He stops and sees I am ready to go and he needs me out of the way. He has to direct his team.

'I'll walk you to the garden, by the way, did you have a date for the show?'

'Actually, yes. The 24th of July' He looks at me and hums but says nothing.

We walk back the way we have come through the building and out the garden doors. Ralph orders his minders well away out of line of sight. 'I am going directly to see Ruth. You need this solved and I want you to have that insurance.' He walks up to me and hugs me, which I didn't expect. I nod and smile. I step back go unseen. A short time later I am outside the gate of the Prime Minister's residence. I press the button and a sleepy looking policeman arrives eventually. I sent a text to Ruth while waiting. She opens the door and says.

'Don't you ever bloody sleep?' The policeman laughs and I grin. 'Come on, tea.' I follow her into the kitchen. She is in a light blue dressing gown, she potters making tea. She doesn't ask what I want, just plunks a cup down with far too much milk and no sugar. Ruth looks at my face and says.

'It's three in the morning. What can't wait?'

'Ralph needs the boys we have in jail back in America as soon as possible. The Presidency will be at stake, also his credibility around any revealing of Island. I know this is a long shot but could you send them on an Orion? Chained then dropped off on the East coast by Langley maybe?' Ruth is blowing on her tea thoughts swirling with the steam. She says slowly.

'You have thought it through. You know, when this gets out I could lose my job? Interfering with the judicial system is normally a step too far? The press will roast me.' I nod.

'Yes maybe, but not if they were given the SIS National Security excuse, they won't question far and you say you simply can't reply, not with it being operational. They will bitch but not against 'not allowed to.' Ruth laughs and shakes her head.

'OK, well done, still I am taking a risk but you knew that of course. One thing, I have told my husband, I thought you should know. He's jealous! Wants to meet Island.'

She has paused, thinking about a glass box on a wide beach floating on clear waves, I am too.

'I will ring all the people to get things moving. I will have those people on the plane by midday tomorrow. Whatever the cost.'

She looks at me 'What now? For you?'

'Me? Home, sleep. See Island in the morning and back to the States I think. It's important for Ralph to know what's happening. One thing, have the Air Force or whoever escorts their charges, directly into their jail at the other end. Full security lock down I think. Please ask the President, and him only, for the exact place and time. These guys are now targets, any leaks, they may die.' She nods, not liking the information but understands.

She stands and leads me to the garden door 'Good night, Bill' She says as she pulls her phone out of her nightgown pocket.

'Good night Ruth.' I go unseen and fly home. The night is clear and there are a cloud of bugs flying around a light Barbara has left on as I land.

Chapter 21

As I walk through the door, I hear the call.

'Nice day at the office?' I have missed that voice. I put the jug on and go into the bedroom where the voice is propped in bed where she has been reading, a great smile on her face as she gets up hugs and kisses me.

'What are you doing awake?' She moves through to the kitchen bench. 'Don't sleep well with you not here, you know.'

'You look beat, I know, food, sleep then talk!' Mind reader so she is! In that way I made it to the next morning. I wake groggy and slow but that's OK. I am where I should be.

Over a very slow breakfast and general catch up with local gossip, amongst which a house is mentioned twice, I agree it sounds great. We need to look. Then the conversation changes to the last day and the 'what happens next'.

I am slow as I work through my thoughts as I lay them out. Barbara says little, she watches me, nods, and reviews. She asks at the end.

'Is this possible? The timing. Have you thought about the world reaction? The change is beyond imagination.' Her face is twisted in concern and she is completely right. I stare at the lake and shake my head.

'Yes, you are right. I simply don't know. I think, or at least I hope, some of this planning will mitigate some of the dangers. I don't bloody know. I believe that without this opportunity for change our world may be gone, eventually. I don't know. You've met Island. You know Island, as I do, what do you think?' Her voice trembles as she answers.

'If this isn't done we may have lost the greatest chance to move the world to a better place. Heaven on earth. I know its trite but, you know. You have seen. Or Island is asked to leave and we forget this minor blip in history. That could be done. The real question is .... who are we to make this decision for all the people on the planet?'

My girl makes the case and we both watch three geese swoosh on to the glass surface of the lake with some mild honking; ripples flow outward.

'OK, do you think what I am thinking is the right way to go?' I ask her. She knows her opinion is the one that I will work with, the one I balance out of all others or simply; trust.

'It is the right choice.' I look at the coffee table and nod.

'OK, shower. Another tea then I go to see Island. I may be some time. Island's input here is the lynch pin of all of this. There is a lot I don't know about Island's power and what Island can, or will, do.'

Just as I am walking out the door I say 'I will be back here before I go to see Ralph.' Just as I turn my phone beeps. Ruth. They have gone home' is the text. Ralph informed. I tell Barbara.

'Woman are very organized you know!' I laugh.

'Don't I know it! We'll have a look at that house tomorrow eh? Soon, we might miss out.' She smiles and nods.

'Be careful' follows me as I go unseen. The day is blustery, greyed waves are breaking and Island just sits reflecting the green grey and white of the foam. I could watch the scene for hours. A tern then another patrols the waves and I can see the black white of their shapes behind the cube; fantastic.

'Hello Bill.' I have come to value Island's steady greeting.

'Hello Island, it is very good to be here. Could you search my memory and thoughts first? It may give a better understanding to the plans I hope may work.' I think I may be asking a lot of Island but I really don't actually know what powers Island has available.

'Yes Bill, it is good for you be here. I will search your thoughts.'

I watch the star systems and once again go to my favorite little planet. I wonder where this place is. How far away, what and who lives there.

Island pulls me from my reverie and I file my questions. Island says.

'Thank you Bill'

'Is what I am thinking possible Island? I mean, could you do this, would you do this? And do you understand why I am thinking this way? You have seen what I know of our race. I couldn't hide what we are, nor would I want to. You have seen, Barbara's, Ruth's and Ralph's memories and thoughts. No, they are not all humanity but.........' I wait and I can see the moons craters bright and stark under a strange cloudless sun and beyond our home planet.

'What you plan is possible for Island to do.' Island answers.

'Will Island do this? You have seen my reasoning and it is mostly centred around the distrust I have of my own race, that is true. But it is balanced against the needs of us all. I do not know if I am right but I believe in the help Island offers our planet. I need Islands help to bring about your introduction to all our world.'

I stop, feeling and fearing the balances. And, strangely, I deeply fear Island's rejection.

'Island, I believe and as do the other people you have met, that Island will change the direction of our planet for better for all of us. I have thought about the choice of your help or not. But I believe you are our planets chance at long-term survival. I would also like your evaluation of this.'

I wait again. A gas giant spins and slowly closes; a planet starting, maybe I wonder.

'Island agrees with your assessment. Your planet is unlikely to have life in another five hundred rotations around your star. Certainly your race will not survive, other life forms may. Island sees your plan, sees the risks but Bill is correct, without islands support, the planet may die. Island will support your plan. Help and education are Islands primary directives.'

Island stops and I don't know what to say. Then I think about the people that made Island, these people who may be our saviours. I have seen part of their world but my own distractions have got into my mental line of sight.

'Island, how long have you been travelling from your home planet?'

'Island has been travelling over thirty millions of your years, searching for planets such as yours.' I may be wrong but there is an echo of sadness in this endless journey.

'Island took approximately half that time to reach another galaxy and then to the next. Space is a very big place.' the silence after 'big' draws my tears. A small vast word. A meteor streams across a desert in China and explodes.

'Island, how do I set my plan into place once ready? Do we contact through the bracelet?' I have a concern about one person having so much power. Then I think the plan is made. Make your plan and follow it through. Island answers.

'Yes Bill. You will have control to do what you require.'

'Thank you Island. When this part of the journey is over I will give you the bracelet back. It should be held by you, I think, or destroyed, you know why I think this.' I have regrets about the simple travel. Ah well, I think.

'Yes Bill. I have seen your thoughts; Too much power!' I laugh. Island continues.

'You do not trust yourself, Bill' I laugh again.

'Island is very, very right. I will go now Island. There are things to do. I would like to bring Barbara back before the plan goes into action. She would like to talk to Island before Island becomes known to the whole world.'

'That would be good Bill. Barbara brings different thoughts that Island enjoys. Barbara is different to you.' I smile, now there's the truth of it I think.

'Thank you Island, until we meet again.' I am sad, soon this too shall wash away. Relationships change but some change you and they echo in the mind for all time.

The day has brightened and a dog is running at full speed down the beach, its master off in the distance whistling, shortly I am at the back door. The truck isn't parked where it normally is. I have just sat down when Barbara comes through the door with a shopping bag.

'Tomatoes have gone up and there were no peas. I need my garden back!'

She grimaces and starts putting the bits and pieces she has bought away. I smile at the cross over of the day. Tomatoes prices and the planets change of direction that, I guess, is life.

'Hungry? She asks still fossicking.

'No thanks, not really. Tea and talk I think' She looks and nods as the jug goes on, I fetch cups and we sit down. The geese have been replaced by a group of mallards who bob in miniature grey green waves.

'Island has agreed to the plan we discussed. If we say no to Islands help, we have five hundred years left here, maybe, or we take this chance. At least that is the simple version. I am going to miss Island. I said I would take you back to see him.'

She looks at me and smiles. 'I would like that very much.'

'After the cuppa, then back to see Ralph. Time is ticking. I may be sometime. I did think I could take you to Ruth's for a change but I don't know. What do you think?' She watches the ducks just be ducks.

'No. I would like to stay here. Ruth has a country to run. The world may change soon but not much here and not us. Once that happens Island will be doing what he is designed to do and we can walk on the beach, go fishing, do the garden and that's OK, I am happy with that.'

We have landed on the beach and I take Barbara across into Island. Once she is seated and we have said hello to Island I remain standing, looking into the swirl of the universe then say:

'I think it would be good for you and Island to have time together. I will be on the beach.' Barbara says nothing but gives me a twitch of a smile.

I wander up the beach searching the sand for treasures amongst the colored variegated shells and pieces of smoothed stone. A gull is pecking at a small dead fish who does not look very happy. Another larger gull arrives and there is quite an argument until the big black backed gull flies off with its prize. There is our planet I think.

Barbara walks over the waves towards the shore and then turns and meets me on the beach as Island floats.

'First time by myself. Well, Island helped. It is strange.' She is happy.

As we walk up towards the trees a man appears from the tree edge.

'I saw you walk on the water' He is looking very intently at Barbara. I laugh, my continuing smile seems to annoy him.

'I know what I saw.' He glares at us both. I look at Barbara and ask.

'Are your shoes wet wife?' Barbara is smiling, then laughing 'I have told her not to get her shoes wet.' I look at him and say nothing. To Barbara I mock an order.

'Home with your dry shoes, excellent!' we both turn and walk off, the accuser is unhappy, good, I think. We turn into the shrub lined path go unseen and fly home through the trees.

'Did you see his face?' Barbara is laughing as we open the door.

'Yes odd, don't you think, his first reaction was anger, not amazement. Guess you can't change basic instinct, he must live an angry life.' Barbara looks at me and raises an eyebrow.

'Hard for his partner, I bet. Anything you need before you flit off?' I laugh and hug her. I shake my head and collect my travelling bits, a small water bottle. I look at Dan's pistol but leave it where it is. I get some cash, my wallet stays here, no ID and the new phone. I send Ralph a text and wait for a reply. I stand and watch the lake. Hills are mirrored in the water with a line of blue above.

'Are you OK?' She is watching me. I turn and look at her and love what I see.

'Yes, calm oddly. The right thing, is the right thing.' My phone buzzes, a TXT. Lee Brandon will meet me at the front entrance to the White house in one hour. Once more into the breech, I think.

'OK, I love you. I will be back in about two days I think. I may need a ride from the airport.' I laugh and so does Barbara then she says 'Have you got your passport?'

'I'll wing it, if something goes array.' I leave the sentence unfinished. She nods.

'You come back to me, we have a house to buy. I do love you'

We hug, I simply walk out the door into the dusk and fly to Washington. I had checked a map and found Farragut Square and finally a place out of sight to quickly go seen. I then find Connecticut Ave and walk towards the White House complex. I can see I am going to get lost so when in doubt I call the President and explain, his reaction is what I thought it would be.

'Jesus! Where are you? Hay Adams OK, right. Lee is on her way.' Silence, the pressure is on I guess. The dark SUV that turns up, is driven by a young man in a grey suit, Lee is in the back seat. I climb in and say hello.

'Hi, how did the cab leave you at the square?' Idle chatter maybe, maybe not.

'I thought..... anyway I got it wrong. I don't know Washington at all or the States really, just a visitor.' She hums and her phone buzzes and the chatter starts.

'No, if you want the biggest story of your life you will free your channels. No, I am not joking. Put it this way Donna, you do it and your career is made .... it is and will be ground breaking. If I am wrong never take any of my calls again. No, I can't go into it and I won't. Risk makes or breaks Donna, your choice.' There is gabbling, Lee is staring intently at the back of the grey drivers head.

'I know, look Donna this is bigger than 'Watergate'. I promise you.' the call has ended. She turns to me and looks steadily into my face. 'Am I right? I am risking it all you know. What I said there I have repeated a dozen times, the head of my career is on the block. I know you have convinced the President but.....' We arrive at a checkpoint into the White House compound. I am spoken for, after a question about luggage to the driver who they know. Sweeps are made under the car, we are clear.

We drive around to an area by the Oval office. I thank the driver and say I appreciate it. His deadpan face splits in a happy smile and returns with the 'have a good day, Sir.' Lee watches this inter change and hums.

As we walk to the office I ask Lee.

'Could we have a private chat before we see Ralph?' Her head snaps towards me more for the familiarity regarding the President, I think, than the suggestion.

She bobs her head and we arrive shortly at a small crammed office, Lee's name is on the door. I close the door behind us.

'Yes, I know its crowded but it's an old building. Go ahead.' She sits on the other side of the desk and starts opening her laptop.' I watch this and she looks up with a question on her face. I look back and say.

'Full attention on me, OK? I want to give you some very small idea on why the President has asked you to risk your head. You are right. You are a key element here, you need more faith in us both, not only us, but an idea why this mission is critical.' She looks at me and I can see her slight smile of dare, go on shock me.

So I do and go unseen and Lee faints. That I didn't expect. I go seen again and duck around her desk. She is laid back in her chair, I shake her and pour a little water from my bottle on her lips.

'Jesus! What the hell?' She is pushing me away.

'Sorry, I didn't mean to shock you.' She just stares then says. 'You disappeared, you fucking disappeared!' I nod.

'Do it again!' she wants to believe, so I repeat my performance. 'Can you hear me?' she asks

'Of course but makes it hard to read my face don't you think?' I am smiling as I become seen.

'So how?' I shake my head.

'No, that I won't answer and, to be really honest, I don't actually know either but it seems to work. I have done this because we need you and you need to have faith. Simple really.' She looks back at me.

'I heard the President's speech and I knew he was telling the truth. I saw he trusts you but I didn't like your aloof approach I ....' I nod. 'Trust is earned, not passed about like a football, you and the President are the only ones here who know of this here. Not more than ten in the whole world. You need to have that trust Lee, we need your expertise.'

Lee looks at me and stands. 'I don't normally swear you know.' I nod, I get that.

'The President is waiting, thank you, I will... I am not sure what to say.' I shrug.

'Let's talk to the President?' She laughs 'yes lets!'

She leads the way into the Oval office. The President's head snaps up as we walk in.

'You guys been out for lunch?' the pressure is certainly on, I get it but I want to concentrate on my ball, he has his own. I ignore the bite. He waves us to the couch. One of his team I recognize from the talk says.

'I am on to it, should have it locked in in an hour.' the President nods. The guy leaves and Ralph stands and stretches and comes to join us on the couch.

'You may not know but the whole world is starting to buzz. A twenty four hour meeting is rare, though not unheard of. But the Security Council is one thing. When you ask the rest, as the next step, it creates serious questions. They are rushing now not to miss out. Of course, the council is pissed off.' He looks at us both.

'OK, you two have been up to something.' I nod and say.

'I showed Lee this' and I go unseen, then back again a few seconds later, they both jump slightly at least Lee doesn't faint. Ralph's look is searing. I hold my hand up.

'She needs faith, some understanding to give the best performance of her career. We are relying on her to bring this together. It's fair Ralph, its simple really. Trust.' I stop, he is watching Lee. He looks back at me and nods.

'You are right, fair enough. Amazing isn't it? I mean incredible!' Lee smiles.

'I fainted.' Ralph nods 'I nearly did too' and they both laugh. I turn to Ralph.

'Do you know when the plane arrives here on the east coast?' His face clouds.

'Seven hours maybe, what are your thoughts?'

'These guys are a bigger target than Kennedy. They have an escort that will not let them out of their sight until they are locked up in a jail. Those are their orders. They are SAS or our SEALS. Be warned they are tough. Let them do their job, don't argue about jurisdiction. Just get them safe and get Dan on tape ASAP. If they disappear or die then....' Ralph is watching me then turns to Lee and she nods.

He takes his phone out and makes two calls, both to generals. Lee and I sit and wait. He finishes the last call and says to me.

'I bet you are over insured.' I laugh.

'Actually no. I just went through it before we lost our house. We were right on the money.' Ralph smiles and Lee says 'Oh, your house!' and looks dismayed. I look at her and say.

'You should meet my wife Barbara, she would like you.' Lee colors and smiles back. Ralph then turns to Lee, face serious.

'Media stakes?' Lee nods and gives the update.

'I have the social media guys all working on the timing, they are really happy. We are having issues with TikTok but that's expected and they will hit with a combination reroute once needed. We are looking at about 42 channels. That is encompassing the majors and a number of minors. I have lined up most of the major players. Fox is playing hardball but Bill has given me an idea that I believe will work. I have all the larger papers and their channels sorted. If this is not close to the minute, I will never work again and they will roast you for time at the next election or not give you any. What I am saying is, if this goes wrong, simply you won't get any air time to win.' She stops and looks into the air, takes a breath and starts again.

'The European channels have been difficult, oddly the French are the hardest. Russia has taken the bait well and the old Eastern Block is more or less following. Germany is asking questions.' She shrugs.

'Asia has been difficult. China won't really play ball but once Hong Kong came on board along with Singapore then the rest got curious, so simply, on China, I don't know. Australia and Pacific were fine they generally take their lead from us but they hate Sky so that raised some cross over issues.' She looks down at her phone and hums again.

'Africa has been difficult but I got Larry to work through most of that, he is cool. He has bribed people and you will have to pay, not money but visits and trade discussions. He said something about you wanting to head in that direction anyway. Good call by the way, we don't look that way enough.'

'South of the border has been patchy but the bigger countries OK, central difficult across everything, still looking there but.....I simply doubt we will get anything high but who knows.' She stops and scrolls her phone.

'We are pushing all TV satellite stations of course, this has been hard, mostly controlled by one or two players who want exclusives. After Bills show and tell, I am going back to them.' She looks at both of us in turn a very steady gaze that says 'do not argue' then goes back to her phone.

'It is simple; I will lie and take the flack. In fact, I have decided that is what I am going to do across the lot. This may destroy us or make us. I really don't know. But you know I do believe in what I saw and in you two, God help me. So that is about it. Oh, the numbers. With this all piled together. I am guessing about half the world population in the first 15 minutes, eighty percent in 12 hours. Balance in the next few days.' She looks up from phone. I shake my head and clap my hands. She looks at me hard and sees there is nothing but admiration. The smile is wide. Ralph is nodding, smile wide.

'I need to double your salary! In fact can you please tell the team that there will be an extra month's salary this pay? The cost to you all could be catastrophic but they have done it anyway. Sorry, change that to three months. I will sign it off and wear it.' Ralph is smiling and very pleased. I can see he loves teamwork, hard to argue.

'OK, when do we actually hit the air? I haven't got an exact handle on the security council's timing.' Lee goes back to her phone.

'Pretty much 24 hours. I am doing a bit more wash up and then I am sending the guys home for rest for a full eight hours. Your bonus will have them smiling but, you are right, they are worth it. The next day will be the hardest of their lives.' She looks at us both.

'Our lives?' She is asking if she is right. I nod.

'Yep, quite likely.'

Lee stands and nods to us both and heads to the door. Ralph turns. 'Lee' She looks back. 'You are the best I have worked with or will ever work with. I thank you.'

She nods again and wipes a tear and leaves us alone. I look at Ralph. 'She is bloody amazing!' He nods and grins.

'Thank God she is on our team. So what are your plans? I presume you are staying in town?' I nod.

'OK, you are staying here. Anyway it will be easier, things always come up and I mean always.'

'Thanks, will your wife mind? I mean short notice, all that?'

Ralph laughs.

'We have done the campaign trail, Now that is where you learn short notice and change. All things are subject to change. Now I have had Enough.' He stands and stretches and we walk towards the door, as he opens it he asks.

'So do you fish off that beach of yours?' he is serious but a sly grin.

'Well yes, you can, but I normally take my small boat out.' Eyes gleam at me, the nodding is enthusiastic.

'How small is the boat?' and it is with this chatter we wander our way to his residence. Ralphs tie is loose and we both have beer before us when Ralph's wife, The First Lady arrives.

Chapter 22

'Mr. Sheppard. Pleased to meet you again.' her tone is curious not cool but neutral. I stand but she waves a hand.

'Please sit down and it is Estelle!' I return with 'and I am Bill' she dips a smile then Ralph chimes in.

'Bill may be with us for a couple of days. There are things moving very quickly and things you need to know. I am very sorry; normally I would be further along in passing this on but it has been a very hard and difficult balance.' Estelle has stopped at the bar fridge her hand frozen for a split second then takes the wine bottle, pours the wine, and joins us. Sitting so that she can see us both. She sips the white.

'OK, let's have it.' Ralph starts and as the story unfolds Estelle looks as though her husband has gone completely insane. As the minutes pass I get up and refill her glass, which she takes from me but hardly notices I am there. Ralph tells her everything including me taking him to meet Island. I get more beer and watch as my glass slowly empties, Ralph's doesn't, he talks. Finally Estelle looks at me and I know what is about to happen. Her look is so intense and disbelieving that I even doubt myself. She looks at me, then her husband, and back to me, eyes narrowed.

'Prove it!'

So I go unseen. I drift towards the two doors that look out to the lawn and hang in the air and become seen.

'Estelle over here.' her words aren't what I expected. Her head snaps in my direction and she has leapt to her feet.

'Fuck off! Jesus H Christ!' The shock has her completely frightened and Ralph jumps to her side.

'It's Ok It's OK! He won't hurt you. It's OK!' He has his arm around her, holding her. He is watching me and rubbing Estelle's back at the same time. He grins.

'OK, that's enough, does look bloody odd though.' I drift back to the couch and pick up my beer, actually it was fun. She is shaking slightly and she has a good gulp of wine. She sits and Ralph sits beside her, holding her hand 'It's OK' He repeats. She settles herself, more surprised at her own reaction I think than scared and looks at me and asks.

'How do you do that? What makes it happen?' I lift my sleeve and show her the tattoo and then she leans across to touch my arm after I give a short explanation.

'Weird!' Is her diagnosis. I laugh.

'You are so very right! It takes a bit to get used to but, oddly, not as long as you may think. Umm no airport line up though.' Estelle's head stiffens and she looks at me intensely.

'You mean you fly? Around the world? You are joking right?' I shake my head.

'No. I came here from my back door.' Her mouth opens Ralph buts in.

'He took me to meet Island. I flew with him, guess you missed that part' She looks at him.

'I didn't believe you! I thought that ummm......Jesus! You hate flying!' At that I really laugh and look at her.

'He never said anything! Ha!' Ralph looks suitably uncomfortable. We are now relaxed. Estelle says nothing and disappears into her thoughts, we all do. A few minutes later there is a knock at a door and an older man looks around the corner. Estelle answers.

'Hello Herman. Sorry, we have an extra guest for dinner, if that is all right. Anything you have, anything that is easy for you. This is Mr.......'But I cut over her.

'Please, 'Bill' Herman, nice to meet you and thank you, anything will be fine.'

Herman returns the smile and looks at Estelle.

'45 minutes Ma'am' and the door closes. Ralph seems lost in thoughts but Estelle asks.

'What does your wife think of all this?' So, I answer for Barbara as much as I can or what I think she is feeling. I end with a shrug and say. 'These things are happening to me, being the second wheel is a hard road. But I guess I don't have to explain that to you, of all people, you know far, far, better than most. Your support makes him.' I nod to Ralph. Estelle looks at me quietly.

'I think I would like to meet to meet Barbara.'

'She would like that, I really think she would.' I smile back. Dinner is simple; steak, salad and fries on a large kitchen table not formal, exactly what I wanted. I had rung Barbara and given her a run down on the day. She really likes this house and there is some deal to be done with our insurance that has been sticking with minutiae and paper work. I sigh but hardly unexpected it is what they do. The call ends with the 'I love you and miss you and the not normal 'The first Lady wants to meet you' and I get a 'don't be ridiculous'. I laugh.

We are back on the couches. Ralph has been bouncing calls from the Party, the Vice President, an unhappy general, some person close to a very large social media company who insists that something is happening tomorrow does he know? It's big evidently. Ralph smiles into the phone. Where needed, is serious, careful and simply lies where needed. Get it. It's all balances. He looks up at me from the little screen.

'The balls are in the air. One thing, the markets are getting very unsure. They know there is something about to happen. Some will get burnt or maybe wiped out' I nod, this I know and I shrug.

'Ralph, the Americans have led a completely open market system for the world, that is bad for little people and very bad for the planet. Un-stemmed competition uses far too many resources on this planet. How many models of cars do we need? They are now a fashion item, fashion incidentally is another nightmare for our world. Most stuff people wear you can't recycle, so goes into land fill. China has poured more concrete this decade, than in the previous hundred years in the whole world. Concrete is one of the world's biggest polluters.' I look at the coffee table and slowly shake my head.

'If we don't adapt on a world scale then well......so yes there will be a complete change but if no change, soon no world.' I pick up my cognac and Ralph looks back thoughtfully and nods. But I can see the trepidation.

I have a better sleep than expected. I wake as the dawn breaks and I tap my arm and contact Island. We communicate for some time. I wanted Island's perceptive on how and what we are going to do. I am now very conscious of how time will play such a part in telling the world. Island is quiet, solid with the thoughts passed across and not phased, but then I am not sure stress comes to Island's world. I just worry.

I shower and have taken some advice from Estelle. She has lent me some of her brothers clothes who stays from time to time. Light packing can be too light!

We reach the Oval office and the full team is there. Everything is a solid go for 3.00 pm this afternoon, I check my mental timing and still worry.

Lee is at full force and doing a job that knocks it out of the park. One of the team stands and waits just as the debrief from Lee comes to an end. Lee looks across an the older prim woman.

'Robin?' Robin looks at the President.

'Sir, is there going to be a world war? If there is, you should have told us.' She is grim but I agree a fair question. The President looks back and nods.

'I understand why you ask that question Robin and that question should have been part of the situation here. I would have told you and I would have told the American People. No, I do not believe that this will happen. But what you all do here helps in maybe mitigating that possibility. The reason we are doing, what we are all are doing, is to share what we have with the widest amount of people in the world. So simply Robin, no. But I should have said that earlier, so thank you.' His smile is warm and genuine, the relaxation in the room palatable. Side looks tell me this was an issue and we were stupid to have missed it. Good question Robin, I think. Robin has sat down no longer grim; calm and focused.

As the team stands to go I can feel the air is lighter, the mood more reflective on this big day. The excitement is there but the strain as well. Yeah I think, I want it over too. I want to go home. Ralph taps me on the shoulder and draws me across the room. Odd, no corners here.

'The interrogator says Dan is being quiet.' Ralph is worried. I nod and ask for his phone he passes it over after a quick introduction.

I listen then ask to be put on to Dan.

'Dan? Bill. OK this is simple. You start now and miss nothing out at all....no.... just listen...everything. You have one hour. If you do not do this I will come and kill you. At the end of that hour I will arrange for you three to have one million dollars each paid wherever. Yes, all three. It must be done on video. You have one hour. One minute over, deals off. You have seen what I can do. Please pass the phone back now.'

I relay my message to the interrogator. I mention the one hour far too much and then say.

'Tell Dan the clock is ticking from now; it is 11.06 am.' I hit the off button and hand the phone back to Ralph. Ralph asks the question.

'Where or from whom are you getting the three million from?' I look at him with a steely look.

'He came to my home threatened my wife and burnt my house to the ground. He made a deal to leave and didn't. I lied. Simple. I will kill him if I have to Ralph.' Ralph looks at me then down to his phone, at me again and nods.

'By the way, I have a phone recording from him, so even if he plays hard ball it really doesn't matter if he lives or dies. I will send it to you now. Insurance.' I grin and Ralph's lips twitch, I can see the shadow in his eyes, talk of killing bothers him. He says.

'Insurance.'

I am taken by one of the team to have photos taken and an ID sorted for the trip to the UN building. The security will be the highest for anywhere in the world. There are eyebrows raised but the words 'at the personal request of the president' seems to open nearly every door. One gentleman is huffing and puffing then just says "no". Henry, the team member, is getting unhappy that we are running out of time. I ring Ralph.

'The President for you.' He nods and snatches the phone 'Sir I... yes this way above my... National Security, right. Yes Sir!'

The two security passes are bright and new and swing on nice strong lanyards. I am part of the team I think, but not as good as being at home. As we get back to the office Lee motions me over.

'Everything is set, the Security Council meeting is a touch late at about 3.30. Will that make a real difference?' I think quickly and shake my head.

'Maybe better, I need a very private place to make a call now though, and I mean now.' Just I turn to follow her Ralph takes my arm. 'You know we are late? We have the tapes, all three. I have seen a very quick flash. The interrogator said is it is the most damning thing he has heard in his career. Shocked and awed.' I nod.

'Good, pleased about the tapes, I need a minute Ralph I need to contact Island. Sorry important.' He looks and nods 'OK?' I nod again and follow Lee. She takes me to an office the size of a broom cupboard. I smile my thanks. As the door closes I tap my arm and begin my request of Island. Time passes as we communicate. I step out of the broom cupboard and see Lee and Ralph rapidly approaching down the hall. Ralph's face is grim and angry.

'Inside' and he pushes me in to the tiny office and slams the door.

"You Son of a bitch! Why did you kill those guys? We have the tapes! We had some sort of deal you.....!' His shouting is loud in the small room I put my hands up palms out.

'Hey, hey easy tiger! I did not kill them, Ralph! I have been here talking to Island.' He tries to cut over me.

I tap my arm and a group of letters appear, they float over the desk. Both Ralph and I move back in surprise as I ask my question. Ralph is peering at this new aberration, his mouth moves and he licks his lips. I am surprised, but then, I have seen this before. I didn't know this could happen on the other side of the planet. How far do Islands powers run? I shelve this reflection in the needs of the moment. As I tap my question my letters appear, float then Islands reply appears below.

'Island have I just been talking to you? Have I used the bracelet to fly anywhere since arriving where I am now?' Islands voice comes out of thin air.

'Speak, I will reply.' So I talk to nothing.

'Island can you answer the questions I just asked please.'

'Hello Bill. You have not moved from your location with the controller for approximately one of your days. Yes, you and Island have been discussing Island's introduction to your world. Hello Ralph.' I say nothing Ralph looks at me then replies.

'Hello Island, ummmm how are you?'

'Island is well. Thank you Ralph' I tap my arm and the letters are gone. We both look at the space where they had been. Ralph sits on a small chair.

'OK. Sorry, get it, and yes. I should have been made to look a prick. So that leaves Harry right? Jesus Christ!' I nod and I sit in the other chair.

'I am as surprised as you are....umm For the record I was probably going to kill Dan.' Ralph's head rises and he stares. I shrug.

'Where were my choices? One day he would come back, he was the type. He knew where we lived. I will not run, too old.' I stop and look at a waste paper basket, there are a lot of empty paper coffee cups. I go on.

'He would use something as a lever. He would want some knowledge about Island or the bracelet even if I didn't have it. Ralph, you know what you do when you have mould in the kitchen? You clean it! I am pleased I don't have to, but I don't have one second of regret about his situation.' Ralph looks at me and twitches his head.

'You can be a callus bastard.' Where my wife is involved I think, but say nothing.

'How does Harry have the clout to do this inside an army jail? That is the interesting question, given his personal situation?' I nod, my gears are turning then Ralph looks at the desktop changing the subject.

'How does Island do what he does?' Simple question said with awe and I am in the same boat, I shake my head slowly.

'I guess I will never know. Island amazes me, will until my dying day. But you know what that is like. You've have met Island.' I go quiet and still. I look at Ralph.

'One thing, I am going ask Harry soon why he set this entire situation going. One other thing, Mr. President. If he hadn't, we would never have met and that would have been my loss.' Ralph sits for a few seconds and then says.

'We need to go fishing.' And he is right, we do.

Lee is on the phone as we emerge into the hall, she does ending noises and looks from one of us to the other.

'Friends again?' We both grin then she says.

'It's time to go, we are more or less the last in. The atmosphere is hot out there. The media is beyond crazy and I mean beyond. All countries security are on very high alert. God help anyone who makes any move, anywhere today.' She is scared I see, and understand.

'Lee. It will be OK. I mean seriously, it will be OK.' Lee and Ralph are watching me. She nods not convinced. Ralph leads the way to the waiting helicopter. Secret Service agents are everywhere and the head of the detail comes up to the President where he and I have stopped.

'Sir, is this gentleman riding with you?' Ralph turns stares and asks.

'Good question. Bill would you rather fly alone?' Ralph's eyes are rock steady. The agent is nonplussed he does not want any changes in plan and the "fly alone" has him. I look back and say.

'Maybe tomorrow, now timing is everything.' Ralph nods and looks at the agent.

'He's with me.' the agent nods and stands back. The President walks to the steps of the helicopter. Salutes the guard, we wait then Lee and I follow side by side. In the deep distance cameras are flashing and I let Lee in the doorway first. The flight to the New York airport is lost in our own thoughts. We land. As soon as we board Air Force One we are airborne. It's a well-oiled machine. But I suspect there has been a lot of better than normal care from Lee's team here. The flight crew are professional, friendly and very tense. Quiet is the name of the day. Some of Lee's crew have boarded first and are in seats huddling with her directing calls and answers.

Ralph is reading notes from a laptop, he glances at me, looks down and then says.

'You don't seem to be that flustered given you are giving a speech to the biggest group of world leaders ever assembled.' I look at him and feel guilty but only just and I shake my head.

'I don't think I will be talking. We will see' Ralph leans forward stiffly 'I may be the leader of the United States but a lot of people, don't follow our lead, let alone trust us. Without you as proof and what you can do, I may be up creek without any paddle. Why haven't you brought this up before? In fact, why are you on this fucking plane if you are not going to support me?'

He is shouting now. A Secret Service Agent is right by his side glaring at me and Ralph waves him away. The cabin is very still. I sit and look at his hands that are clenching the arm rests.

'Ralph, I take your point.' He opens his mouth and snarls

'You have no single idea what I am putting on the line here. Not just for me but for my country.' I sit and then turn to Lee and wave her down to our seat and I move over.

'Lee, a question. If the world saw, even in the UN council or General Assembly a person flying around the room or disappearing what would they think? Yes, fully televised, live. What would they actually think? Scam? Bullshit? Vegas magic? What would you think?' I ask her steadily and quietly. She looks back then looks at Ralph, who is listening with high intensity.

'If I didn't know what I know. Scam. Big scam. Yes, maybe Vegas wires. I saw a show there that I still can't believe.' Ralph sits back slightly, still pissed.

'This plan you have, what part haven't you discussed?' I turn to Lee, she gets the point and she slips back to the huddle.

'I think it would be better if Island spoke.' Ralph's mouth falls open.

'What? How?'

'I don't actually know. Not what we saw in the office. We need something else. The trouble is there are lots of things I don't know about Island's capabilities. But I take your point, you, as the President can't introduce Island, it has to be a neutral party. You are right. Sorry, you are very right.' I watch the huddle of the Presidents team.

'I will talk to Ruth. She would be better doing it. A stranger, an unknown wouldn't work. It has to be a leader. Ruth is going, of course. Our country is better. I should have asked your thoughts earlier. The United States is one thing, you as my friend, is another.'

I sit back and watch as Ralph processes. He is still unhappy then asks.

'How will Ruth get before the Security Council?' I smile.

'I think they will open the door.' Ralph grunts, still unsure. We get coffee, which I hardly ever do during the day. Ralph watches me stirring milk and three sugars.

'You drink that?'

'Normally one in the morning but today is special.' he humms. My call to Ruth is a little difficult. She does not like surprises, not at this level and she certainly does not like what I am proposing. It will put us, our country, in the gun sights of every other country on earth. If Island is not there, or in fact anywhere, then the trouble begins. Just introduce Island and Island will come, I say. I get a snapped.

'How? When?' I tell her I will see her in there. Call closed.

We land at La Guardia, transfer to a helicopter. Lee is still with us. Eyes are everywhere, I do wonder how anyone gets used to being so watched and followed. So much risk and ceremony on a guy going from place to place. I know I would need far more than coffee to boy me up. I think about my simple life and I think about Barbara.

Cars like tanks are waiting, as well as a small army. We travel towards the UN building past the river, we are closely watched. Not far away from the building I say to Ralph and Lee.

'I will go unseen very soon. I need to talk to Ruth so I will go to the General Assembly before I get to the Security Council. I know there is a half hour difference. I will follow you in Ralph. I am doing this so Ruth knows the detail. Please trust me on this. Before this starts, I want to say thank you for what you are doing for our planet and its peoples.' Lee squeezes my hand. Ralph looks at me and says.

'You would have made a good insurance salesman.' I grin my thanks.

'One last thing Ralph. Can you tell the driver I am in the back seat feeling unwell and please to go to the Trump Hotel. If anyone is feeling sick, that is the place to be.'

Ralph and Lee really do laugh. I send a quick text to Barbara and as I go unseen, I know we have a new house. Good.

Chapter 23

This will be one of the strangest experiences, of a list of strange ones, that I have now lived. I follow on the heels of Ralph into the UN building then turn towards the Assembly room. I have to dodge people continuously and once tap a security person. He jumps and looks around but I have moved on. I am annoyed at my carelessness and slowdown.

The door is watched and watched by more security. An African guy walks up shows his pass and I quickly slip behind him. The room I enter is huge. The symbol of the United Nations rises round behind the podium and screens either side. The room is designed to take all the world's leaders and their support people. There are about one hundred and ninety seven countries represented here at last count but then there are also a couple of observers which I had read about. I don't get the politics around it all. Some countries that aren't countries, I support but don't understand it. The air is tense and I note everywhere seats are filled. I see the Security Council people are missing. I had asked Lee where Ruth would be sitting and after a small delay I pick her out. As luck would have it, she and her team are at the end of a row, towards the right wall.

I walk across carefully avoiding people. I slip behind her and tap her shoulder, put a note in her hand and quickly move out of the way. She turns, looks around and looks at the note. Ruth quickly snaps instructions at her people and reading the note again, she stands and moves to the back wall, where I join her.

She is standing very still, very unhappy and as I tap her arm again she says very quietly.

'I am not on the speaking list, you idiot! This is going to be impossible! The Secretary General starts and no one has the right or the ability to override that. Jesus!'

'Ruth, all I want you to do is stand and walk to very middle of the main isle as he starts speaking.'

'What and make me look like a fool? I could murder you right now! Why the hell didn't we go through this earlier?'

'Because Ruth you wouldn't have agreed. This is to save the world not your face. We are making history right now and I need you as the focal point to introduce Island.'

'What? Island? The Security Council isn't here! Christ!'

'That's the point Ruth. Please! The Assembly has to understand their choices without them. Ruth with all you have seen and experienced with Island. You and I flew, went invisible and visited a blue cube on a beach. Trust your thoughts of Island, if not me! Above all, trust your heart.'

The room is now very quiet as the Secretary General of the United Nations moves to the podium. Ruth's people are watching and concerned. An older man, who I think is the Ambassador, stands and starts walking towards us. Ruth glares at me and returns to her seat. She sits, waits, then stands.

She leans forward presses the button on her microphone which she lifts to her mouth then speaks. Her voice cuts across the silence and the meeting. Her standing figure all eyes focus on, the shock and quiet roll through the vast room. I am lost in the seconds.

'Mr. Secretary General, before you start this meeting. I apologize. There is no simple way to do this. I have had a message from an entity from another world. I introduce, Island.'

As Ruth stops speaking Island's floating hologram appears; a cube of cut diamond and ice, sapphire blues and light rainbows of drifting colors that are beautiful, evoking early morning light and above each desk a small exact copy floats.

Islands first words come to the world.

'Hello Planet Earth. My name is Island.'

The voice runs and ripples across the deep silence. The voice is almost musical every tone pitch perfect, listening is a strange joy. People are leaping to their feet, others cry out in surprise, some pull back, some are just routed to their seats. All are stunned. Fear and amazement is mixed and panic is close. Ruth shouts into the microphone.

'Please. Ladies and Gentleman! Remain calm. Island is a colleague. Island will not hurt anyone. Please just be calm.'

Island's voice flows through the crowd, the calming effect following. The easing modulation of Island's voice cloaks the room. The shock is over, settling begins, seats are taken, faces are intense, accepting but wary.

'Thank you Ruth. What Ruth says is truth. I am not here to harm. I would speak to the leaders of the world is this forum, in peace.'

Ruth has kept her feet, eyes are flitting between her and the cube.

'My world colleagues. I was asked to introduce Island to this meeting a few minutes ago. I did not know Island was able to speak in this way. I have had the opportunity to speak to Island before this. I do not know what Island will say. I have no idea. I do believe that this is in the interest of all the peoples of our planet. Simply put; I trust Island.'

The Secretary General has been stock still at the podium, his hands gripping the edge. He looks at his notes then at the floating beautiful creation that is before him, his throat clears, eyes directed. It is time to take the lead.

His voice is voice deep and warm, perfect for the history of the moment. He says the words that will echo over the rest of our human age.

'I welcome Island, traveller from another world to the United Nations Forum and we will listen to his words.'

The quiet seconds of history ripple across the world. The room is bound in silence and awe. Island speaks:

'Island's speaks to all peoples of your planet. To each of you as a person, all people will understand my words, language will be no barrier. The words spoken here will be heard across your planet by all your electronic devises, in every city, in every time zone, everywhere.'

Eyes in the forum flicker to phones. A man in front of Ruth hesitates then takes off a translation head set, others follow suit. An Asian person turns and looks at an African woman next to him, they smile quickly. It is true. We can hear and we are the same.

'Island came to this world many of your years ago. Island is not a 'Being.' Island is part organic, part Technology. The engineer that came with Island has gone into to the void. The planet where Island came from has long gone.' The collective sigh is a sweep of sorrow that drifts across the people before the podium. I can't help feeling surprised at the empathy.

'Island is a repository of all the planets knowledge from where Island was developed. There were a number of Islands sent to the vastness of the everywhere. One of your people found the controller, which is the key to speak with Island. This person brought people he knew to talk for Island to have some understanding of your planet.'

The world is listening. These words are logged and lodged and recorded and rerun from now until the worlds end.

I stand unseen and watch the sparkling floating cubic jewel in front of me that is Island but I am also interested in Island's direction, not in fear, a wondering of curiosity is increasing and I think of Barbara's 'You're up to something' Quips. I miss her, on the stage of history I would have had you with me.

'Island was allowed by these people to search their collective memories. Island has monitored all your planets electronic devices and has looked into and down loaded all the databases across your planet.'

The shock of this vast thought and indication of the knowledge of thousands of terabits of information in the one place rocks the chamber. Faces turn, mouths open and close, heads shake.

'This has been Island's directive. Should island arrive at a planet that may be helped. Should be helped. Island is not a judge of a planet, or it's people. Island's directive is to help that planets environment and organisms survive to be the best they can be.'

'This blue planet is one being. Balance is the all. Island's planet had a similar issue and the population of the planet went close to the void. Island's directive is to bring hope and direction.'

Island stops, and the words drift. Time passes the assembly of the world waits.

'What direction would you have this Assembly take?' The Secretary's question rumbles around the world. Seconds tick as the world waits.

'Island would see a plan for each person in the world to hold hope for their own future. Island believes that the people of this planet need to reject power and a number of the controlling factors in their world. This needs to be decided here at this forum today. To that effect, Island has balanced the power in this building. People here will have noted that the Security Council is not part of this Assembly. Balance cannot be dominated by complete power.'

'Island has closed use of all nuclear weapons everywhere; all the ones scattered throughout this planet are now unusable for all time. All stock piled weapons, all those stored, all in every form of transport can no longer be used, ever' There is a tremble of humming slips around the room.

'Island has sent the dangerous, poorly covered, power station Chernobyl into the void. Island has cleaned the vast number of nuclear parcels of waste that is leaking in the blue oceans into the void. The stored broken and rusting nuclear submarines at Vladivostok have been sent to the void.'

'Island has done this to help the planet survive and show what Island can do. Island will wait until what Island has said is verified. Island is passing this information to the Security Council and asking them to join this full assembly.'

'Before they come here Island believed it is important for the representatives of the world here, now, not to have the pressing of power and the trappings of nuclear military power oppressing them or their people. This example of removal of the nuclear weapons is a small one in Island's scope to help the planet.'

'But there are others. Constant power from renewable resources with no harmful by-products. A shifting of the monetary system to fairness of wealth. Water and food for all peoples and education. Which is the key to balance.'

The wholesale, stunned silence of the chamber is obvious. Ruth turns and looks towards me but not seeing me, she castes her gaze around the room looking for me in the shadows at the back of this huge chamber. Island continues with a clear aloofness.

'Island will wait thirty minutes for the information to be verified.'

Island goes silent and the chamber is buzzing to a loud chattering hum. The Secretary General bangs on the podium.

'Please order! Order! We will work to verify Island's claims. The Security Council will be asked into the chamber. We do not know what information they know. We will confirm this information shortly.' As he stands waiting, a murmur of conversation is drifting across the room, it starts to rise.

He is tapped on the shoulder and a person relays a message in his ear, another man behind the first is nodding vigorously. He bends to the microphones and the talk drops away.

'It appears what Island said is true. All devises across the world have carried his words and messages in all languages. The message came through phones, televisions and all computers, anywhere, anything that could produce the message has come through. It is being repeated everywhere as we speak.'

The room is now a rolling whisper as colleagues confer or are on phones confirming the news. Ruth walks along the wall towards my spot calling my name very quietly, others have stood in little knots. Ruth gets to me and I say to her.

'Stop there. I am here. Just wait.' I have my back to the wall, I look quickly across the room then become seen. Ruth's face peers into mine.

'Did you know anything about this? I mean anything?' I shake my head and cross my heart at the same time, an old childhood manoeuvre but effective enough.

'Jesus! You are joking! I had no clue. I don't know what to think or what the implications are. Shit, you know about this stuff better than I do! Christ, the world just changed. The world powers have had the rug pulled. Ralph will think I was part of this. Well, I wasn't. Simple. But Island has a bigger plan; that much is very obvious.'

Ruth has been watching me and she turns and leans against wall.

'The world will want to know about my part in this. That concerns me but the loss of the nuclear winter? Who would have thought that was possible?'

She takes my hand as we watch the dance of nations before us, her grip is dry and tight, her face turns to mine, tears stream down her face. 'For that alone this has been worth it.' I nod and feel my own tears. We hug in the swirl of the room as I look up others are towards our understanding.

My phone buzzes, a text appears. Barbara; 'Holy shit! Are you OK? Where are you?' I tap where I am and an OK note. Have I spoken to Island? Is Island OK? That is my girl I think. And it is a very good question. So I tap a note and ask. Island replies in my head, strange is not the right word but it will do.

'Thank you Bill. Island is good, Island believes things will be well. Thank you for asking. Are you and Barbara well?' I reply, we are fine. The room is in a controlled chaos, a mumbling hum of disquiet and disbelief and yet oddly the sea change of history holds these people in the palm of revelation. They are seeing an unknown horizon with awe but no fear.

It is into this space and time that the Security Council enters.

Each member is stiff, tension a walking cloud that surrounds them. The chamber knows the truth now. The nuclear broad sword is not theirs to wield and intimidate with, the so-called balance has gone. Fear is part of the procession, the process of change that may happen, to them terrifying. It is the glint of light on the swords edge.

The room grows slowly quiet as the group takes their seats. There is one man who doesn't. He waves a lackey away and walks towards Ruth and I. The chamber watches as Ralph moves to stop in front of both of us.

'You knew?' He is on the edge of violence just controlled yet lost, grasping at whys. I shake my head. Ruth is still, she sees the signs of where this man's limits are, and rightly scared I think.

'No, I had no idea.' the gap between us inches and a thousand miles. 'You helped this.' He watches.

'And so did you. You know Island. Island's course is beyond you or I Ralph, our world is on the knife-edge. Your countries control or any countries control of the fate of humanity is now beyond nationalist lines. We now have a maybe for the whole of humanity, don't get lost in simple politics or borders. Politicians, Kings and Dictators all come and go. Borders shift in alliances or in theft. Humanity just rolls on Ralph. People want to feed their kids and let them have a better life. It is that simple; it really is, just that simple.'

Ruth is watching and she puts her hand lightly on his arm. 'He is right, Ralph.'

Ralph turns sideways to us and then looks around the room, across the peoples of the world. The rest of the room is waiting and the seconds tick. Ralph's look ranges over me.

'I wanted better for my people. I wanted opportunity for them, I wanted a better future for them. Is this it? I never ever thought of all peoples of the world but now .....we shall see.' He looks at Ruth and walks back to his seat. A light whisper moves through the chamber, eyes are watching Ralph and then flicker to Ruth and I. Ruth moves to her seat. I stand and wait.

The Secretary General is taking charge and bangs on the podium and his words run through the chamber.

'Ladies and gentlemen, while verification is still coming in, the information that we have is as follows; the Chernobyl plant has been removed. A satellite over view has just been completed, the site is empty and the complete building complex has gone. A number of nuclear submarines in Vladivostok have disappeared. Tagged stored isotopes have disappeared from their facilities. Island's voice has been directed to over eighty percent of the world's population and Island's message is being repeated across the globe.' He stops and looks across room.

'What Island said would be done, from this first analysis, has been done. At this stage there is no reason to think anything else but our investigations are on-going.' he stops as the words race through the silence of the room. For such a small word I think, awe is a profound statement, I finally understand the word.

In this gap I am surprised to hear Ralphs voice.

'Mr. Secretary, please forgive the interruption. My advisors are against what I am about to say. But I believe this is the right course. To build trust in this meeting and for all the peoples of the world.'

The room goes deathly still. Someone drops a phone on a desk and the noise rattles into the air.

'I would like the Assembly to know that the Unites States of Americas' nuclear strike capacities are unable to operate. It is also my understanding that all of our strategic allies are in the same position. In other words, what Island has said, is the truth.'

There it is, a simple word, truth. Not often heard in this chamber or with such pure conviction. Ralph sits back, I note a quick side bar from his Ambassador to the United Nations his face raging. Ralph is snarling at him in return. The content I will never know. Another microphone clicks and the British Prime Minister leans towards the microphone with:

'Sir, the United Kingdom is in the same position and our forces on patrol are returning to their assigned bases.' He sits back eyes on the podium, dazed and staring.

A man of the Israeli delegation lurches to his feet screaming. The thin-pitched words lash across the chamber.

'We will be wiped out by the Arab scum!' The room starts to rumble and a person leaps to their feet, another from further up the room is yelling in a language I don't recognize and yet another from an Asian cohort, there is now screaming and pounding the desk in front of him. A very tall African woman has stood and is yelling, for what I think is calm. The chaos ripples and gathers strength. People are on their feet and the Secretary has joined in. Banging the podium with 'Order, order!' which is useless. I stand and watch as this mob starts to unravel, everyone is now on their feet.

A sound echoes in the chamber. It is the pitch of a deep bell, the sound of the sea, a rippling roll of thunder and a sound of joy, the room in its vastness, goes silent. The crowd is stopped. I see a young guy who has his arms extended in anger, fists clenched, look at them in confusion. A woman in a dancing multi-coloured dress has stopped, mouth open. She puts her hands slowly to her lips and sinks, shaking her head, into her seat. A man with a pure white turban drops his arms to his side, turns and bows to the man next to him. Who in turn presses two palms together and returns the bow, they sit. There is a shuffling whisper as seats are taken, silence returns.

I am reminded of children caught in a folly by a parent. The power of that moment sits with me still.

Island speaks.

'Each individual on this planet is different, every single one, but the focusing on those differences may destroy your species. Each part of your planet is completely interconnected with the other, all life, everywhere.'

'This goes well beyond the human level. Island knows all life is part of the place of life, and the balance of life is only as good as each being in its own place. Humans must be one with balance of their planet.'

The words are rolling quiet, the etching of truth in the sky, on the dawn, on an ice lake.

'Life on this planet is not indivisible, each is part of the all. The thing you call environment is part of you and you are part of it. They are not, nor can ever be, separate.' these words lay in a crisp light before us. Some heads are bowed in possible prayer.

'Island has the ability to help your planet adapt and move forward. The removal of the constraints of a monopoly of power is an example to this end.'

'Island would have the peoples of the planet make this choice. Island would stay guiding the planets change until Island is not required. The choice the peoples of earth would make is a universal oneness. This will mean change over a period of time. Free energy, environmental reestablishment, pollution removal, industrial change, and monetary reforms, where the quality of life is balanced.'

Heads are nodding, some cocked sideways, questions are across each face, the ideal wanted. The reality underlined with a cynics 'How'? 'The start of this would be a Planet Wide Government. The petty squabbling of each government's national view is not a good basis for the planet. Rich countries protect themselves and override others. This is truth.'

The words roll on, with truths and shocks, mouths are open, lips licked, implications are trying to be measured. Arguments light then kindle and die as the words move on.

'The basis of that government is in this room, today. Now. This group may vote for world government. Then each person of the planet may vote for Island's support.' Island stops and the utter stillness sits hanging, in the quiet the room waits.

The Secretary general finally asks.

'What do you propose?' We wait on the edge of the future. Island says.

'Each person who can see hear and listen will have one vote. All people, all children, all humans on the planet regardless of age, race, or belief, each will be asked for change or not. Island has stated every human on this planet is part of every other. Parents do not own children. It is their right to vote; they are a being regardless of age. Political Party, country or religious politics are not directions in this choice to vote. It is each person's choice to make for themselves only and wholly.'

Island stops and the glittering cube floats.

'When do we do this?' Ralph has asked the question he is looking directly at Island.

'And what if we refuse?' The question twists and turns through the air, the world is still as Island's voice drifts across a tide of time.

'Refusal is your right. At that refusal Island would leave and your planet will move towards its own destiny.'

Island stops as the information is gathered and taken in.

'Island will wait for this room to accept the planetary vote or not. Island will wait 30 minutes. Thank you.'

There is a bubble of noise, then a mumble, then a swirl. It is contained but tense. I walk up and down the wall making still legs move and find my mind is as numb as my legs. Ruth looks across and shakes her head. I turn my gaze to Island floating quietly. I want to go home, and I think about the beach. The gulls drifting on the wind, white flecks riding above blue green waves. We are in a vast building where there is no real reference to the world of forest or plain or sea or sand. It is a man-made box of minimal design with no attachment to the real planet; the diversity of the planets beauty and state of being is not part of this space and yet the decisions being made here will affect every living being. I look at the gabbling faces and feel an infinity of sadness.

Ruth and Ralph are now standing talking and Ruth waves me over. As I join them one of Ruth's team is speaking quietly and intensely in Ruth's ear. She nods twice and the woman turns away, clearly shaken.

'I can't believe how fast the pressure came on. Calls, emails, every God damned information device, including hand delivered letters, are flooding parliament and every government agency. A crowd is gathering outside the parliament buildings. The message is simple enough, though: 'We want our vote' If you vote against having a world vote, your Party and you are finished. One Vote One Human is the cry.' Her mouth closes and she looks at the floor. Ralph hums and nods his head.

'Yeah, us too. Same thing. France, Germany and the whole Europe are alive. Brits as well. I gather China is and most Asian states.' He stops and watches Island for a few seconds. 'South Americans.....there is news out of Columbia that the army is on the move.' He shrugs.

Ralph looks at Ruth 'I have my own ideas, what are yours? I like your calm opinions Ruth.'

'The democratic ideal is pretty simple. One person one vote. Choice is a powerful freedom. Our parliamentary system actually takes that away. As does yours with the Electoral College. People can't vote for a President they picked, they get what they are given by a smaller group. Same as ours.'

Ruth rocks from side to side on sensible shoes that are an intense bright blue. I like them, they make me smile. Ralph looks around the room as one of his team approaches and he nods acceptance of the advance. He looks at Ruth and then at me Ralph then turns to the man asks. 'OK what? Everything please.'

'We are over run by people wanting the vote. Both parties are hedging and want more time. The party has said, if you vote for the vote, they won't support your next term. I quote Sir: 'You will be finished. America does not bow to any pressure.' that's from the Party President, Sir.' Ralph nods and he looks at the man and asks 'What do you personally think in your heart of hearts?' The middle aged man stiffens slightly looks around the room and at Island's cube floating.

'One man. One vote. Sir. A lot of my people never had that choice, Sir. You know my background.' Ralph nods.

'Ain't that the truth!' He grins and as he looks around to us, then grins again. He nods and touches the man's arm in thanks, who moves away.

Time has moved, the chamber is settling, there is tension; which is overlaid with purpose.

The Secretary General asks for order and waits, then.

'Ladies and Gentleman of the world this is simple. For clarity I will ask each member to stand and record their vote of either Yes or No.' 'Island has asked that each leader in this room give Island the direction to help our world. We are meeting now, to allow a planet wide vote and agree to a planet wide government.'

As his words disappear Island speaks.

'Thank you, It is simple; allow your people choice or not. Please vote now.'

The first to stand in front of the podium is one of the Security Council, France. I wonder how they pick the first, the thought annoys me that I don't know. The French President stands 'Qui!'

The vote roles on the Russian delegate hesitates then votes 'Da!' I am surprised.

China 'No!'

The United States President stands and looks up at Island.

'The United States of America votes, Yes' There is strange collective hiss through the room and the voting continues, the Security Council is almost split.

A man from Ghana votes Yes! And he bows to the podium and then looks up at Island above him and nods. A man seeming to talk to a being from another star system. He turns to his colleagues, smiles and calls something in his language. There is nodding agreement and simple joy.

As the vote moves, the numbers appear on the screens that are set either side of the podium. I glance a couple of times but it is the smaller countries that are holding my gaze.

The whole of the planet is watching and then after long dripping seconds it is done. The votes have been caste. The world has changed. The Secretary General stands at the podium.

'The vote is 149 for with 44 against, the 2 observer states have voted for the motion'

It has sometimes been said that these words 'will be heard around the world' on that day. They were. In my spot, leaning against the wall, I noted that the states against were mostly dictatorships. Letting go of power was not in their plan. I wondered how Island would face that and what Island knew of humans intense personal craving for control and power. I wondered how Barbara was. Time to go soon I think, my part in this is closing. I want the return of a simple life.

The room is in tumult, there is high joy, there is silence at some desks, others angry and banging at their desks. The Secretary General and two men I don't know are hugging. Ruth walks over and takes one of my hands in hers, she looks me in the eyes.

'This is because of you.' I shake my head 'No Ruth, never. Was I in the right place at the right time or was it the wrong place? I may never know. I think someone would have found the bracelet and then who knows?' I am very uncomfortable about what she has said. I stand looking at the room missing my wife, missing being normal. I look back at her. 'It is time to go home for me Ruth. She looks at me, nods her understanding but says nothing I smile at her and say.

'When you are passing, please drop in.' Her smile is wide.

'Say Hello to Barbara.' and when I get home I do.

I walk through the jostling crowd towards Ralph, he is being harangued by three people. He sees me, returns some comments, lifts a restraining hand off his arm and I guess is rude to the man. An aide blocks his protagonist as Ralph sidles towards me.

We stand below Island in the central isle, people are avoiding this area. The fear of the unknown is still strong.

'What do you think?' His eyes are grave, as if my opinion matters.

'I think for the first time in my life I am personally seeing a brave man with real convictions for his people.' His mouth opens and I raise my hand palm out.

'And I never thought I would see that day.' He looks at me, then the floor and then up at Island.

'Ralph, I want a thing from you. I want to see Harry. I need you to arrange this, please and I would like you to do that now.' Ralph and looks deeply into my eyes.

'Will you kill him?' I shake my head.

'I simply don't know, but do I doubt it.' Ralph looks at the podium as he asks 'Do you believe in justice?' I nod in the affirmative.

'Yes, and I don't believe in fear or the continuous black mail of fear, Ralph.' He searches my face then finally nods and heads to his seat as he reaches for his phone.

There is a noise from above us and Island speaks. People watch the cube and listen.

'Humanity, your leaders have taken the immense step of agreeing to a planet wide vote. Some countries did not agree. People will be able to vote in those countries anyway; each person across the planet will take part. This vote will take place 48 hours from now. Each person will be provided with their own hologram everywhere, each language will be provided for.'

The words sit in the chamber as I walk towards the main doors heads are touching and plans are being made, the whirling of gears very obvious; the stink of conniving is in the filtered air. My phone buzzes I will be picked up at the front door by Ralphs' people. Harry has been arrested again with new charges.

'Any person or government or group that tries to stop people voting will be sent to the void.'

Heads pop up and are looking around them; the questions in their faces almost comical. I want to yell at them "Actions have reactions!." I tap my arm and Island echoes in my head. We converse. I had never heard Island head in the direction of humour before. Yet it lingers as I put my plan to Island. Island agrees with my thoughts. I turn and walk back down the aisle towards the podium as Island starts to speak.

'Island has spoken to a number of people of your planet and Island has conferred with all databases. Island understands the grip and flow of power within humanity and how this emphasis on control, wealth and power for its own sake is cultivated. This will pass away. Island does not lie.'

The room is still. The warning is implicit but faces are poker stiff, some with scorn and I wonder at the stupidity of my fellow humans. As I walk past Ralphs' seat he stiffens and looks to rise. I glance at him and minutely shake my head; he sinks down. The secretary General and his group are watching me, questions in their eyes, the security move forward on guard.

I walk to below the podium and Island says.

'This person is a threat!' and as he says this, I rise into the air. I move to below Island facing the assembly forty feet in the air. The shock and complete amazement flashes across the room as every single eye is on my body. Phones rise, as I hang in space then go unseen. I am not sure if anyone got a photo but the image will be blurred. The vanishing act is complete. The room is deathly still. Lesson learnt, I hope. I wonder about this as I drift across the room. Examples can be looked at in many ways.

Chapter 24

I have drifted to the door and security is watching, not sure how to act. I duck past between two burley men then walk towards the main entrance. Three minutes later I have become seen in a shadowy corner and a secret service man asks 'Mr. Sheppard?' as I walk up to a waiting limousine that has little USA flags on it.

I am very tired. There is a small cooler with bottles water and beer, water will be perfect; bliss. One of the agents in the front seat talks into a microphone.

'We have orders to take you to Langley, Sir. There is a navy helicopter waiting for you to board.' He is watching me in the mirror. I just nod, give him a thumbs up and I lean back in the seat.

The helicopter ride is non eventful. I could have flown myself but I wanted the legitimacy that the little flags on limos bring. I have dozed on and off. The greeting I get is sour and wary. It doesn't help I am obviously not an American. Not in the forces, or the FBI, or the Secret Service. They don't want me nor do they trust me, no matter what the President of the time says. I am an alien and sitting in a Mr. Brad Smithson's Spartan office he dances around it. I sit and say nothing and wait for the question.

'So why exactly are you here, Mr. Sheppard?' His eyes are piercing and he is holding anger back.

'To talk to the Secretary of State. As you well know.' I look at him and smile.

'Look, Mr. Sheppard the President may ask for this but there are other priorities at stake, of which I am the gate keeper.' He smiles very thinly.

I smile again broadly.

'Fine. You know the President requested this?' I ask in a neutral tone, I am actually thinking I wish I had come here unseen but this place is a rabbit warren. It could take me days to find him. I want to go home. I am bored with this man. I sit quietly and wait.

'Yes, but things take time you understand.' I see a flicker of teeth, the shark feeding on power. I nod and take my phone out and send a text. He watches.

'Just sorting transport.' He nods and the smile widens.

'I am sure that at a later time, we may be able to accommodate you.' and he stands, interview over and he moves around the desk. I stay seated, time passes, he is still standing. Mr. Smithson is annoyed.

'So if you will excuse me I have....' There is a knock at the door and two men appear. Mr. Brad Smithson is caught off guard.

'Mr. Director?' It is a question and a statement. I turn in my seat but don't stand. The director looks at me.

'Mr. Sheppard?' I nod. 'Please come with me. I am Director Shahib. I will take you to the Secretary of State.' Brad has gone slightly pale and is again, angry.

'Sir, I have explained to Mr........' The Director cuts over him.

'Brad, you didn't obey an order from the Commander-in-Chief of the United States of America, a very simple one. You are relieved of duty, pending a review, which I have little doubt will cancel your contract.'

The shock on Brad's face is complete. His mouth falls open, then snaps shut. He is stock still, the Director continues.

'Agent Roberts will escort you to an interview room where he will take your ID and all department property.'

I am looking across the desk and I wait. I want no part of this. I just want to do a simple task. I think about complications that people create. We all create, but then, it's picking the time.

'Why? I have worked for this department for more than 20 years!' Brads voice is edging higher and louder. 'This is bullshit! I am getting a lawyer! I have my rights and you are trampling on them!' His voice is very loud and snarling now. The director puts his hand up and waits.

'Mr. Smithson I am not sure if you ever read the fine print of your contact but it was certainly explained when you joined us. You were under orders, failure to undertake a fair and reasonable order is grounds for instant dismissal. Simple. Please go with Agent Roberts or I will have you arrested. Make your choice now.' Agent Robertson is ready for business and I could be wrong but I would guess he is enjoying Brads position.

Brad Smithson walks around his desk glares at me, picks up a phone off the desk and walks out the door followed closely by Agent Roberts.

The Director watches then turns to me.

'If you will follow me please, Mr. Sheppard.' I nod, stand and follow the Director. At the set of elevators while we are waiting I throw a pebble in the pond.

'You are happy to see him go. Give a man enough rope'

The Director slips a glance at me, snorts, but says nothing. We walk on in a compatible silence. As I had surmised, this place is difficult to navigate, corridors, large hallways, elevators and stairs.

Ten minutes later we arrive in a complex within a complex. Guards are evident and security is high. The Director shows me into an office that has the feel of an anteroom. He waves me into a seat and takes one opposite.

'OK, that little issue was unfortunate and I am not going ask why the President has asked for this interview. That's between you guys. But I am responsible for the Secretary of States' security. I don't want him damaged or worse.' I nod, but say nothing.

We sit in silence for a couple of minutes.

'OK, have it your way but be warned Mr. Sheppard. We will be watching'

'No, you won't. Nor will you be listening. Everything I do or say in this room will not be recorded. You are more than welcome to contact the President. If my requirements are not met I would guess you will follow Brad Smithson.' The Director is angry now, the subtle signs show are on his face, red with tense lack of movement.

'Look, I don't want to argue or piss you off. You saw the Island broadcast. I will say that my interview with the Secretary is concerned with that. Which the President would confirm, no details I guess but that broadcast is a turning point in history. I am just crossing 'Ts' and dotting 'I's' He sits looking at me.

'I don't trust you.' He states this simply and I nod and understand the drivers. He picks up his phone and issues some requests. Once that is done he drills me with his eyes.

'What do you actually want?' I shrug the truth is easy really.

'I want to know why he needed to threaten myself and family. Then tried to kill the Prime Minister of our country. He didn't need to, it was a vastly over the top reaction on both counts.' He is watching me, his mouth moves and then his head shakes.

'I would have heard.'

'That chopper that went down what? a week ago? One CIA and three navy guys on board, ring any bells? You heard of that and I bet you had a lot of questions but no real answers. That was the team.' His mouth works again and he watches my face, then nods.

'Those guys were following orders, his. Mr. Director, I think it is better I don't tell you any more to protect you and your position. If you are questioned you can genuinely say you did not know. On this point, please trust me.' Time passes and he finally nods, he picks up his phone, instructions are again issued. We wait.

The door opens and the Secretary is standing there with an escort. Harry is smartly dressed but casual he looks around the room and then his gaze settles on me. He then looks at the Director.

'Who is this? Another one of your lying investigators, looking for clues to hang me? I formally request you release me so that I can answer any charges in a proper court of law. I also request a lawyer to be present, this is my right as an American citizen. I will not answer any questions without one.'

The Director looks at me and shrugs, this has obviously been an ongoing gambit. I look at Harry and I don't like what I see. A person over run with ego and the semi trappings of power even in these circumstances. Ah well.

'Harry, I am not an investigator nor am I any part of your government. My name is Bill Sheppard. You know my name. Will you sit down, now please?'

Harry is now rather white, deeply still, lips moistened and his eyes narrow.

'I don't know this man, I am going back to my room.' He snaps this to the room and turns on his heel, his escort blocks his way but the escort isn't happy, conflicting loyalties I wonder.

'Harry, if you don't sit down, all the evidence I have will be turned over to your justice department via the President's office. You will end up in a cell for life or maybe being executed as a traitor. I have Dan's evidence on a video file.'

Harry seems to droop but catches himself. He turns back, now is an odd mixture of white and flushed. He takes two steps forward, waits then drops into the chair in front of him. The Director castes a look at me and then leaves us. The escort is unhappy about his charge being out of his sight and I hear the Director snapping a reply just as the door closes. Seems Harry has special treatment and I wonder about power, privilege and loyalty.

'OK Harry, you know who I am. There will be no hesitation or games. If you don't tell me what I ask fully, you will never reach court. You threatened me and my wife and you tried to kill our Prime Minister. The full story and any more people involved or you may die here and now.' His gaze is fixed on me. He is shocked but still defiant.

'Show me your evidence. I don't believe you.' I look at him and smile and then go unseen. Harry jumps in his chair, he is looking around the room wildly, he even looks under the table we are seated at. I wait a few seconds then stand by the window and become seen. Harry jumps again but stays seated. I suspect his legs wouldn't hold him.

'Something for you to think about Harry.' I sit back in my seat, pull out my phone and scroll through until I find Dan's chat. Dan's voice ripples in the room, a bit reedy but recognizable enough. Three or four minutes pass. Harry is looking at the desktop he then makes a lunge at the phone in my left hand. My fist hits Harry on the nose not squarely but enough to make his eyes water and his nose start to drip blood. He sits back holding his face, red dripping on his chin.

I sit and wait. Dan was more honest than this piece of garbage I think and this ordered Dan's death. Harry has rummaged in a pocket and found a hanky, monogrammed of course and is holding back the drip of blood.

'Last chance Harry! You have exactly one minute.' and I concentrate on my black divers watch dial. Seconds tick. Harry squirms in his seat and dabs at his nose, the blood has just about stopped.

'Ten seconds, Harry.' I call quietly then 'OK, times up.' I stand and say 'You are a dead man Harry. You will never reach court. The evidence will reach the media. You will be tarred with a traitors brush and your family will be destroyed. Your son is at Westpoint isn't he?' I walk to the door and open it, there are now two escorts there. Interesting.

'Alright, alright! I'll talk to you.' Harrys voice is rising and he has turned in his seat. The escort who first brought him to the office moves forward.

'What's going on? Why is the Secretary bleeding?'

'He tried to take my phone and it's none of your damned business.' I snarl at him.

Over my shoulder Harry calls.

'It's OK. Sheppard come back.' I wait, eyeing the escort, the other one is just watching but says nothing.

I close the door and sit down. I then get my phone out and put it on record. I look at Harry and say.

'Everything now, no gaps, I will know. Remember, I have Dan's words!' Harry nods. I ask Harrys full name and position. The tale takes about 50 minutes. Some I know, some people I don't. All of it stupid and sickening. A small conspiracy gone mad but the fulcrum to move was the bracelet and what it represented. They thought power, control and much more. Ah well. But no rights and wrongs. Just power really.

Harry has finished. I quickly forward the long clip to Ralph then drop the phone in my pocket. I stand. Harry's head turns towards me.

'So now what? When do I get out of here?' I look at him and have an urge to shoot him. I shake my head, an act of "why bother" to myself.

'Not up to me. I don't know how it works. Bye Harry'

'What? What do you mean?' I open the door and the first escort is standing stiffly waiting his face grim glaring. I look at him and then step aside and he walks into the room eyes on Harry. As he passes me I say.

'He named you for killing Dan, of course.' Face stunned, he glances at me. I close the door and stand in front of it. The other escort is against the opposite wall watching me.

'Is there a problem?' He shifts his weight, looking concerned. I shrug.

'I don't know'. This is the truth. There is shouting in the room, furniture moves and more shouting, then a shot. The escort pushes me out of the way and just as the door opens there is another shot and we are in time to see Harrys escort fall. He hits the edge of the desk then rolls to the floor. Harry is lying across a chair and blood is dripping from his open mouth on to the carpet. The escort has a wound in his temple, brain matter is stretched across the wall.

'Emergency! Emergency! Interview 140, Interview room 140!' He is yelling into a mike in his sleeve, face tense and angry. He is glaring at me. I just hear a gabbled reply from his earpiece. Men are rushing down the corridor, some have guns pulled. I move up against the wall. Men are keyed up and shouting, one pushes me to the blue carpet, a knee is placed on my back and handcuffs are locked on to my wrists tightly. I say nothing, what is the point, I wonder. Guilty until proven innocent.

Time passes and the Director arrives. I have been hauled to my feet and one guy is shouting questions, which I ignore. He just shouts louder. Unhappy people crowd around.

The Director says in a louder voice to shut up and waves people away. He looks into the room and sees the dead occupants. He looks at the other escort and beckons him over. The group in the hallway edge closer.

'Back up and back off. I want twenty meters either side of the door. You and you. Set up a perimeter. No one comes within the lines without asking me first. No one! Do it now!' The shouter moves forward and takes one of my arms. The Director looks at him.

'He stays and get the cuffs off.' Shouter stiffens and opens his mouth.

'Now Delaney or get another job.' the cuffs come off with a glare and I smile back, fuck him. The Director motions myself and the escort over to him so we are both facing him.

'Alright, in simple English what happened?' He points at the escort. 'You first.'

'There was a bit of shouting then this guy opened the door. The Secretary was bleeding like he had been punched. Keen asked if he was OK and he said he was. This guy then said it was his fault for trying to take his phone. The Secretary that he would talk.'

'This guy closed the door stayed in the room for about 45 minutes. This guy then opens the door. Keen was pretty uptight; pacing and agitated. This guy said something to Keen as Keen goes into the room. I didn't catch it. Keen and the Secretary start shouting. He stood in front of the door and then one shot followed a couple of seconds later by another. I opened the door to see Keen fall on the desk and then to the floor. I called emergency.' The Director looks at him and nods.

'OK, thanks. Go and get a coffee. This is tough. I then want you to write a quick report. Just what you told me and anything you think you may have missed. That can be the blue print for the big one in detail which can come later. Do you need a doctor? No? OK. They are available at any time. Take three days off, longer if you need it. The only office calls you are required to answer are mine, OK? I doubt if I will ring. OK, Levy and thanks.' Levy looks from one to the other of us then his gaze stops on me.

'Did you know this would happen?' His look is level searching for answers at the horror he has seen, looking for someone to blame.

'No. I knew there may be an argument. Possibly a fight but no; not this. No.' I shake my head, I want him to feel my regret at his situation.

He holds my gaze then turns to the Director nods then walks through the watching barrier of people. The Director looks at me intensely.

'You lied.' I shake my head.

'No, I didn't expect this. Something, but not this. I am not sorry Harry is dead but I would rather have seen him on the stand, that was my motivation.' I stop then add.

'I wanted him off my back, sooner or later he would have made another move against me, I believe. Now with Islands discussion out in the world, I just don't know.' I am talking to myself, really. I put my hand in my pocket and bring out my phone.

'What's your number?' Head cocked he looks at me for split seconds then gives me the number. I forward Harry's recording.

'You now have what Harry told me and what happened from his orders. I will tell the President. I have no idea if he will agree with me but I think you need to know. By the way, Ralph already has it. Just to be clear. It may help protect you from the wolves in the capital.' The Director looks at me and then at the waiting crowd in the hall. I see there are white cover all's in the line-up: Forensics. There is impatience in the group who are shifting from foot to foot, faces grim.

'Time to get this cleaned up. I will give you an escort to get you out of here. Where will I find you?' I shrug, as I don't really know myself.

'Possibly with Ralph or at my home. No matter what happens, I will be around if you need me.' I actually doubt that he will but reassurance is better. This guy is going to get a beating by most people on the capital. The Secretaries death is too convenient and in custody. The wolves will the howling in the next few minutes, few months. Questions will be a flood, a tide that will be hard to stem. Scapegoats will be looked for. He looks at the floor, gears ticking, pressure building.

'I should hold you.' I say nothing. He looks across the gaggle, stands looking reflective, then motions to one of the group waiting.

'Agent Roberts, take Mr. Sheppard to the main entrance, he has a car waiting.' I turn and put my hand out.

'If you need me, I will come.' The Director's eyes fix on me, hesitates and he puts out his hand and gives my hand a firm shake. He turns to the group and starts issuing instructions. Agent Roberts is at my side and we wait as the white suited people move past us and others are sent on their way with tasks. Roberts points the way down the hall and I follow.

At the main entrance the limo is still waiting. I am vaguely surprised but then what do I know about limousines and Secret Service orders, nothing. An agent climbs out and says.

'We have instructions to return you to the President, Sir' I wonder about the wisdom of this.

'Where exactly is the President?' The answer is simple enough; a hotel in New York. Better that than the floor of the Assembly I think. Time to lay low.

And so time passes and finally I am shown into the Presidential suite, my tiredness is showing. I feel stretched and hollow, I do need to go home. Ralph and Estelle are in the room with two people I don't know. Nor do I want to meet them. I have had enough of people. I did think about going home immediately but knew that would be unfair and simply rude to Ralph. Ralph looks at me, his eyes still. I suspect his is mood angry, his cool greeting cuts across one of the men that is talking.

'Hello Bill.' Estelle smiles with more warmth and bobs a 'Hi Bill' Ralph snaps.

'Harry is dead and I know you were there. I have seen the Directors first report. He didn't die by your hand but I know this was at your pushing.' He is angry; pure and simple. I did warn him, I think. Ah well.

The other two men are watching this interchange and both faces are ranging over me trying to place me and annoyed they can't. Ralph stops and introduces us.

'Bill Sheppard, Arch Moorland Security advisor from the CIA and Hal Bedford the FBI.' I say hello and sit on one of the couches. I just don't care who they are from. I am dog tired and as far as I am concerned I am not going to discuss anything with these people particularly the CIA, lesson learnt. Ralph is nonplussed. I turn to Estelle.

'Sorry Estelle, I am just about shot. Could I get a cup of tea?' She looks at me, her amusement obvious. She smiles an 'of course' and disappears from the room.

'Ralph, if you think I am discussing anything with these two, you are wrong. The CIA in any form is bullshit. As far as I am concerned anything to be said will be said to you, and you alone. These what-ever-they-are don't make my trust list. Simple.'

I have given my speech. Arch opens his mouth but Hal beats him to it.

'Mr. President, the Secretary of State is dead. If you think this person was involved then that's good enough for me.' I am tired and I laugh and as I laugh Estelle comes in with tea and coffee on a tray. Nice, I think. The three men in the room are watching me. I put my hand in my pocket, rifle through the phone and find Harry's last words. As I turn up the volume Harry's voice fills the space. The men stiffen and eyes are glued to the phone. Estelle pours tea for me.

Ralph fills a cup with black coffee and sits on the edge of a seat. The other two follow suite. Harry's voice rises and flows, the words run across the table, drip to the floor and seem to stain the carpet. Faces are focused. Mouths open and close, then heads shake. Arch gives involuntary "Jesus Christ" and looks at Estelle and mumbles sorry.

Ralph is stern, his eyes flicker to me from time to time, he ages strangely and Estelle reaches over and squeezes his hand. Finally, Harry's voice stops but the words are still here. Sometimes I think it is better just not to know. Trust is a delicate thing that is built over years like a home in one's heart; the collapse of that home is something that will never be rebuilt.

Ralph has said nothing, a few minutes tick past then he looks at Arch and Hal.

'OK gentlemen, please keep this to yourselves for the mean time. I will discuss this with you tomorrow morning at 10.00 am on how we will proceed. I will need your advice. Now, please excuse me. I need to talk to Bill.' With two 'Mr. Presidents.' they leave more than subdued.

The door closes, Bill is still looking at the phone and he wipes two hands over his face.

'I sent a copy through to you. I thought you had heard it. Sorry.' Ralph shakes his head.

'No, no time. I saw it....something.....but it has been quite a day. Jesus. I really didn't think he was so, so.....misguided. Jesus! I know I had him arrested but I really thought in my heart of hearts he was on the side line, a bit player. At least I wanted that but.' He nods towards the phone, hating it.

'He was my friend.' Ralphs face is grey and the coffee cup trembles slightly as he takes an absent sip.

'Ralph, I want you to know what exactly happened. You should know. The wolves will be baying for blood but witnesses can't be refuted.' He nods slowly the grief of a broken trust too easily seen. Estelle looks at me, she is also quiet, feeling her husband's hurt. Reading her thoughts I say.

'Better now, Ralph needs to know the facts.' She nods and takes Ralphs hand.

I relay what happened and how it played out simply, no embellishment.

'Did you know Keen was involved?' Ralphs question is quiet, slightly hollow, a touch of despair. I shake my head slowly.

'No, not really but he was too keyed up, too attentive and the issue of who actually killed Dan has been in the back of my mind. It had to be an insider that was close to Harry. I baited the hook. I would bet a little investigation will put Keen close to Dan and his friends. I guess the Director will find the how.' I slow and stop. The room is over-the-top garish American classic to my mind. Not my taste. I have had enough.

'Ralph. Simply, these people gambled for power, control of a nation and maybe the world. But to what end? No winners, billions of losers? I don't really know. We know now Island can't be controlled. I would add this conspiracy may have happened without me or Island coming along. Then what? At the end of it they lost.'

Ralph slumps back in his chair but the gears are moving, he is planning. The grief dissipating with the needs of the moment.

'Now what for you?' he is looking over my shoulder. He wants me gone. I have brought too much strange and bad news. The world is now a different place. You may not shoot the messenger but then you really don't want to look at them. I get it. Estelle has seen it too, she glances at me and nods.

'I go home. I have been away too long, and I stay there. I will ask Island to remove the bracelet and maybe go fishing. I miss Barbara. I miss my simple life.'

Ralph looks at me and then to Estelle.

'Could I ask you to show Bill out? I have some calls to make.' he stands and I follow Estelle to the door as I reach it Ralph says. 'Bill, Sometimes the cost of a thing is difficult to bear. Anyway, thanks.'

I nod but say nothing, he turns away, phone in hand, already back in his world.

Estelle takes me to a large balcony with a view across the river. I see she likes it here. We stand watching the flow as lights flicker and reflections shimmer, her eyes are calmer, happier.

'There is a lot to be done. Ralph has a State of the Nation broadcast tonight. This may be one of the most important speeches that any President has ever made. He and I will be writing this. Our writers don't have the information and, frankly, trust is in short supply.' She is speaking to excuse but I do understand Ralphs wanting me gone, besides I don't belong here.

'Thanks for everything Estelle. I wish you both well. You two are good people.' She takes one of my hands in both of hers, kisses me on the cheek and flashes a quick smile. I smile, step back and then go unseen.

Chapter 25

I land in the very early morning. There is dew on the grass and a slight chill is in the air. I can hear the surf on the beach in the distance. I tap on the door. 'Anyone home?' I ask. Barbara answers the door in her pyjamas and holds me very tight.

'You took too bloody long!' I can feel the tears on her cheek and she is very right. I took too bloody long. I sleep deeply after breakfast and wake about two, groggy, disorientated and happy to be home. I go and scrub myself in the shower and think about food. The smell of our soap and just being here makes me smile. Barbara comes in from the shop with a bag loaded with groceries.

'Good! I thought you might sleep all day. Feel better? You look cleaner!'

She piles her bits into the right cupboards and the fridge. I put the jug on and find some biscuits in the pantry. We settle on the couch and I relate the story slowly. Barbara is laying on her back on the other couch, staring at the plywood ceiling. From time to time she interjects with a question to give balance to something I have missed or doesn't make sense. She likes the detail. As I wind down and I tell her about my leaving of Ralph, she stirs and turns her head to look at me.

'Are you OK about Ralph?' Her eyes very direct. I nod quietly.

'I didn't realize how it had effected him, but yes I am OK. I get it and who can blame him for being pissed off? He likes things to be right, not wrong, he likes balance. He believes in honesty. He believes in trust.' I stop, I don't know what else to say. Barbara hums. Three geese land on the lake honking softly to themselves, I like watching them ski to a landing.

'Have you spoken to Island?'

'No. Actually I am not sure if Island is here or in the UN building. I can contact Island of course but I needed space, and I needed to be home. I needed to talk you and be normal.' She snorts a Ha!

'One thing, I want Island to remove the bracelet. Soon. I have to be normal. I need to be normal. The world can do what it does, but for me I need that. What are your thoughts?' My words hold more intensity than I expected. Barbara has sat up, she is peering at me and then says.

'You don't like airports!' A quick grin and then a serious face. 'You are right. We need to be normal. Your part or our part is over.' Good, the pact between us is made and I love her for her simple understanding.

'When?' she asks.

'When is the vote?' I haven't caught up on world news and know nothing of the ferment the world has been in.

'The vote is here at 5.00pm tomorrow. The news has been frantic, every single service is full of it. Social media has exploded and the various news agencies have taken sides, in some capitals there is rioting. Some very odd things have happened. A number of hard line dictators have disappeared. As in, vanished. Everyone is blaming Island, which may be true. I don't know. Ruth gives a speech at 6.00 pm. The interesting thing is Island has said nothing since the Assembly. The cube is there but no words.' She doesn't like the uncertainty. I get the feeling she is troubled about Island and the path Island may have taken.

I turn on the TV and wander through the channels. Every single program is focused on Island in one form or other. The before, the during and the after, and of course, the Assembly vote. Then what happens after the vote. Island is a saviour. Island is a devil. Island is preparing the way for an invasion of human eaters and so it goes. Experts are giving knowledgeable opinions. Experts who start at astronauts and end up as UFO chasers. Christ, what a mess. I turn it off, numbed. I check my I-pad exactly the same, but much worse. I toss that aside.

Barbara has been watching.

'Yeah, a nightmare! No one knows who to trust and in typical fashion, if people don't know, they make it up. But who can blame them? The news of Island has been dumped on them. People don't trust what they don't know, it's basic human nature.'

My turn to hum. I don't have any answers. Instead I change the subject. I need more normal.

'So when do I get a chance to see this new house?' Barbara brightens.

'We pick up the keys next Friday, they are still packing. I pushed for ASAP and that's what we got. We can walk past it though. Here are the photos.'

She digs through the I-Pad and sits with me as I scroll through. She is watching tensely for any twitch of disapproval. It's actually really great and I am impressed. The house is homely, not too, big not too small. I don't like the kitchen but we can change that. The setting is perfect. Nice trees, private and it looks across the sea to our island. That home away from home, on the edge of the blue green horizon.

'Wow! Well done! No, I am serious, it's close to perfect.' She hugs me and says.

'Yes, we will change the kitchen! Why do people have blue kitchens?' We both laugh at our shared pet hate.

'What time is it? I want to see Ruth's speech then there will be Ralph's.'

'It's just before four.' her face is a question then she says 'Island?' I nod.

'I want you to come. If removing the bracelet is a bad as when it went in, I will need your help.' The pain I still remember and am scared of the removal. Barbara nods, not looking happy. She looks at the arm with its shining symbols.

'You could lose your arm.' I had thought of that but there is only way to find out: Ask. I tap my arm and Island echoes in my head.

'Hello Bill.'

'Hello Island. Are you still at the beach? I would like to come and see you. I will bring Barbara.' I wait and the reply comes.

'Yes, Island is at the beach, it will be good to speak to Barbara too.' I think of the lonely space in which Island is and feel sad somehow.

'Island, will you be able to remove the bracelet? The world knows about you now, so there seems no reason to keep it. Besides I want my life back. I am not cut out to be an ambassador.' I stop and then ask the question I have been dreading, oddly my palms are sweating.

'Will I keep my arm Island?' There is a long silence.

'Island understands, Bill. Yes, you will keep your arm.' I am very relieved. I nod 'Good, good.' I didn't realize how simply scared I had been. I sit slightly numbed.

The drive to the beach is very short but I figured if I am in pain, easier for Barbara to get me home. We walk down the path through the overhanging bushes. And just as the beach comes into view, Barbara comments.

'This may be the last time we talk to Island.' I glance at her and nod. In this melancholy state we walk to the beach. The surf is very small, only inches high and the sea seems still, waiting.

The cube is there floating, the sun is going down towards the horizon. Dusk is not far away. A very light mist is moving up the beach and there is no one to be seen. Too close to dinner time I think. Oystercatchers give their piping call at us, this is their space. We walk into the cube and then through to the seats that watch the universe. We sit quietly. I watch our system and concentrate on the planet I had found in the vastness. The blue sea foams on a shore I will never see and silver fish are playing in the shallows, out of the jungle an animal like a deer walks onto the sand then to my amazement a two legged being walks out then another, they are holding hands! At that moment Islands voice ripples through the space.

'Hello Bill, hello Barbara.' we both echo hellos.

'Island I am curious. Does Island believe that the contact with our planet has gone well?'

'It is better for some people than others, Bill.' That hasn't answered my question, some others? The statement shakes me but I ask the question in the front of my mind.

'Has Island removed people?'

'Yes Bill, Island has. Do you disagree?' I am not sure. I guess I am scared of how far this may go, not only for me, but the planet.

'You have become the judge, jury and the executioner. Island, humans don't like that.'

'There are some humans that hold their fellows in bondage by the power of weapons or the number in their army or both. This is not balance. These humans rule by greed only.' I look at the rings of Saturn as a large meteor races into them.

'Greed is part of humanity, balance is difficult. Balance can be an opinion, Island. I am not defending greed, I guess I am defending choice.' Barbara reaches over and touches my arm.

'Island, how far will your balance reach? If I don't agree with you, will I go into the void?' I don't like that Barbara asked the question but this is the nub of where we are at. It is the right question. Silence prevails. I watch Saturn, but I am tense. I know Barbara is too, her glances at me are part of that.

'Barbara, you are right. Balance is difficult, opinions vary. Not agreeing with another being is no reason to send them to the void. Island sees a lot of human endeavour that Island does not agree with but simply that are part of the uniquely human situation and ethos. Yes, choice is one of those. Island does make those choices it is true and Island is the judge.'

I sigh and shake my head.

'But' Island stops to emphasize the point here.

'If a leader allows excessive greed and the accumulation of personal wealth when their people are hungry, where people are not given medical attention or refuses education then Island will intervene. Your history shows many examples of this. There are countries that are either in collapse or on the brink of this. You know of a number. There are more than you may know that are headed in this direction, Bill.'

'Island sees that your United Nations has not worked in the full interest of the whole world. Wars and massacres have happened because of a lack of intervention or lack of interest by states that should be, and know better.'

'World government is the answer for the planet and Island is able to help with this but when the vote was taken at the Assembly this passed influence to Island. Some of that influence is also balanced judgment.'

I see a comet slowly curve towards the Ort Cloud; this view is an astronomers dream. I am still uncomfortable how this going but I get the point and I can't but ask.

'Was this judgment what they signed up for?' Island's voice is balance itself.

'The choice has been made by the nation's leaders and simply put; do the people of the planet want peace and a fair, balanced life?' Island stops and Barbara watches me, she too is unsure. Island continues.

'Bill. You have made similar choices in your own situation. James is an example.' I nod, not liking the parallel but see the point. I have to agree.

'What people vote for will be an open option. An explanation will be part of the Hologram when voting. Like you, Island believes in fair balance.' I wonder what that description will be but I get the feeling Island will not answer. Barbara asks one that shakes me. Simple, direct and right.

'What Bill and I are asking simply; can the whole of humanity trust you to change our personal lives and our whole planets direction?' We wait then.

'This is what the vote is for: 'Trust' and oneness throughout your planet. At the end of a period Island will go on and this planet will continue. Then humanity will be balanced. After that Island does not know.' I think about not having Island here with whom I have been through so much and how Island has changed me. I personally will miss my alien friend about whom I know so much and so little about.

'How long will you guide the planet, Island?' My question is part sadness, part straight curiosity.

'Approximately fifty of your years Bill.' I watch the vast array of the Ort Cloud millions of suns, millions of planets and feel small. It is time to change the subject. Island is right. The choice will lay with the people of the planet.

'Island can you please remove the bracelet? It is time. I like you Island and the bracelet is amazing and curious but I am just a human. Too much power is bad for us, for me. It is your cultures, not mine. I want my simple life back.'

Barbara is watching me closely and now she sees the dilemma. I was getting used to the bracelet and it's addictive power. Some of which I never used because of the possible changes in me and for us.

'You never said.' I slowly shake my head. A feeling of loss, of need and addiction sweep over me. I clutch at my arm. I will never fly again, tears run down my cheeks. The grief of loss ripples through me. I shake with the fear of loss.

'It was just now I realized how much I want to keep it: It has to go.' Island breaks into our discussion.

'Island sees the issue Bill. This is part of the human condition.' My arm grows warm then goes to hot, my palms start to sweat and I feel light headed. I tear off my sweatshirt. I am feeling cooked then suddenly I start to cool. I feel my arm and I feel bones through the skin and muscle. The bracelet is gone but the golden tattoo remains, a scar of days past. Barbara is by my side, she runs her hand over my face.

'You OK?' I hum.

'I feel as though I just lost you, my best friend and everything all at once.' I look around me, shaken, grieving. But I got what I asked for.

'Thank you Island, it is very difficult to bear. I feel……' My words drift.

'Bill made the right choice. Now this done, Island will go to the Assembly and replace the Hologram that is there.'

I stand and walk around the chair massaging my arm, very odd. I sit back in the chair.

'Will we talk again Island?' Spots on the sun curl like dragons breath I look away I have had enough of heat for the day.

'You have made your choice Bill.' Island answer is cryptic, I nod. Deeply sad. Barbara is in tears.

'I will miss you more than I can say, Island.'

'It has been good that Island met Bill and Barbara. Island wishes them well.'

As we stand and I turn and look at the beautiful vastness of the space that is before us and in that split second I see the shores of the little planet I have been following, a bright rainbow bird flits out of the jungle across the waves and dives back into the dappled green pink of its home.

We walk down to the entrance way hand in hand. The sound of the sea is louder. Waves are moving as I step off the edge of the cube and into waist deep cold water. Cold shock as I laugh, normal! I turn and see Barbara standing on an invisible platform. She jumps beside me and as she does, we both get pushed under by a wave. We surface completely soaked and I start to laugh. Normal.

Waves swirl around us and our wet clothes are dragging. I take Barbara's hand and we wade to the beach. We are both cold now and struggling a bit with the dripping weight. The dog walker, Neil and his dog Harry are on the tide edge. He is watching us with his mouth open.

'You seemed to appear from nowhere.' His nosey attitude still annoys me but I don't care: normal!

'Well, we didn't! Stupid swimming at this time don't you think?' I quip this as we walk past him, up the sand towards the trees and the vehicle. He stands watching us wondering. Harry's tongue hangs out, tail moving slowly side to side but unlike his owner, keeps his thoughts to himself.

The keys are still in my pocket, lucky I think. We head straight to the showers, one each. Hot water, bliss. We were getting too cold. As Barbara appears, I have made tea. Wrapped in dressing gowns we sit to watch Ruth. Perfect timing.

Chapter 26

There is the standard start to the news. An announcer importantly tells us what most of the country will already know. The Prime Minister is going to discuss Islands vote, this is live, from Parliament in the Capital. She will make a speech and then take questions.

Barbara is staring at the screen 'Any ideas what she will say?' I too am glued to the bright coloured screen.

'No, no idea. She voted yes to the whole planet vote but I don't know...party politics brings a lot of pressures. Behind the scenes?' I drift off as Ruth walks to the podium.

'My fellow citizens welcome! Today may be one of the most significant in the world's history. I will welcome questions after I have finished. A good portion of the audience tonight are from the news media. To be clear, if I am interrupted by any person, they will be asked to leave. I will pick the questioners at the end of my statement. Each of you will be answered. I bring this up, as this particular point in our history is too important to be turned into a free for all.'

'There are a number of members of the public joining us today who will get the opportunity to ask questions. These people were asked to take part are from across the country, not just the capital. I would add, that these people are a random selection of ordinary citizens who were asked to join us from across the political, religious and cultural spectrum. I would personally like to thank them for coming and being part of this historic day.'

Ruth stops and takes a drink of water; the rules are set. There is silence in the audience. There are our countries flag on poles behind her and two microphones either side of the wooden podium. A camera flicks to the waiting audience. There appear to be two halves. One comprising the press and then the rest. Well known politicians sit in back rows. Faces are tense but curious, then the shot returns to Ruth. At the right of her, in camera shot, a person is translating in sign language. Before Ruth starts, she signals to someone off camera and one of our Supreme Court judges walks across the stage. The judge is a woman, she is carrying a Bible. Ruth turns to the podium.

'My fellow countrymen, there will information passed to you today from myself that may be difficult to believe. It has not been in any forum before. I have asked Supreme Court Judge Joan Whitney to take my oath, so that you may have assurance of how seriously I view today's announcements.' The room is deathly silent, the Judge is standing to Ruth's side and Ruth turns and places her hand on the Bible.

'Has this ever happened before? I mean ever?' Barbara is asking the question that will be answered the media later. Simply, this has never happened in this country's history. A cloak of solemnity is laid across the room as Ruth takes the simple court oath. She then thanks the judge and turns to the podium once more.

'Some days ago I was told about Island by one of our citizens. This was the very first person Island had been in contact with anywhere on earth. I struggled to believe this story but evidence was shown to me that was irrefutable. What I am telling you today, is known by only a small handful of people. Members of my caucus and my MPs have no idea. This will be news to them as well.' There is a hissing shocked babbling in the room, a camera shot sweeps the room. One person has stood in the back row. The camera shot returns to Ruth.

'One of our citizens became the contact for Island. They came to me, to tell me of Island and show me the proof that Island existed . A short time later they took me to Island's craft. I spoke with Island in Islands craft. This is and was to me, one of the most amazing experiences of my life. I have not seen Island. I have only seen Island's craft and heard Island's voice, much like you have. I can tell you that Island arrived on our shore more than a thousand years ago. Island has been waiting for a pilot that never returned. Island does not know what happened to the pilot. Island waited. Island described Island, as not an alien being, rather a cross between a computer and organics.'

A voice rings out 'Why isn't this person here Prime Minister? Why weren't the public told earlier?' Ruth stops and nods at someone behind the camera shot. The camera angle changes and a man is being hauled out of the audience. There is some noise and shouting. Ruth waits quietly then she says.

'As I said at the beginning, questions will be answered but I will not under any circumstances tolerate interjections or be bullied. The people of this country deserve and will get, clear and concise, transparent information. If I have to clear the gallery I will!' She looks very hard around the room seemingly weighting the idea then continues.

'This person has chosen to remain anonymous. That is this person's choice, which I respect. I will not answer any questions on who they are or any of their circumstances. To be clear, this person was the first to contact Island in the whole of the world.'

'I am telling the country now, as much as I can, which is I believe the right choice for transparency going forward. I don't believe in skeletons in cupboards. Islands contact also contacted the President of the United States. Circumstances of national security made this wise. Yes, it will annoy you regarding the lack of information here but I will not go into that area further. Choices were made which were, I believe, the right ones.'

Ruth stops and has more water; thought gathering, I suspect. I am surprised at the information she has passed over but then tell as much as you can, I guess. I am not a fan of the media. Ruth looks into the camera.

'I have spoken to the President of the Unites States about Island. Of course, you know about the General Assembly and how this has gone. In the next few hours he will speak to his country, as I am speaking to you now.' She looks around the room and then back to the camera.

'When I said meeting Island was amazing. It was. It was deeply profound and I am still processing this. I would say that I may be processing this for rest of my life. Which brings me to this point. I will resign as Prime Minister tomorrow, at twelve midday. The reins of leadership should go to another. It has been an honor and privilege to do this job but I believe this to be the right choice. I make this choice freely to become an ordinary citizen of our wonderful country.'

'Holy shit!' Barbara has shock on her face, mine too, we look at each other. I am saddened.

'I also do this, so I can say what I say now: My friends, we are on the verge of one of the most important decisions of this planets history. I am not here to tell you how to vote. This is not my role. You vote as your conscience and thoughts require. I do not believe any one person, group or organization has the right to direct your thoughts. This is above party politics or national requirements. This is quite literally about the earth and the whole of the human race. This is my opinion and my personal belief. We have been given a freedom of choice humans have never had. I believe in the power of that choice, whichever way this goes, is your will, pure and simple. I wish you, our country and the whole of our planet well.'

She pauses and looks around the room, tears are in her eyes. The complete and utter shock and stillness in the room is obvious even to us camera watchers.

The camera shot shifts to the audience and a tall woman with red hair has stood, she begins to clap. The rest of the room follow her lead. Everyone is on their feet. Barbara claps to the screen and so do I. Wow! I am surprised saddened but happy for Ruth. I get it. I do know she will get pounded to reveal who Island contacted. Reporters will work on that. Barbara asks.

'Did you expect that? I mean Ruth resigning? Great speech though, the party and the deputy PM will be rattled, the knives will be out.'

'No, I am as surprised as you. Wise move I suppose. I suspect that once the vote happens, and if the vote is a yes, then countries leaders rolls will change dramatically, though that will take some time I guess. Besides she wanted as close to the whole truth out. Meeting Island changes you, one's perspective. I think you become more 'whole world, more whole universe' does that make sense?' I am grasping to explain the experience. Barbara is still looking at the screen then she turns her head and looks directly into my eyes.

'Yes. We became less human, more universe and more global at the same time.' She reaches out and takes my hand. As the questions to Ruth start, our words are stilled.

Ruth now looks around the room. Arms are being held up by the press and the audience. She points to the woman who first stood.

'Prime Minister, what was it like meeting Island and this person who took you to Island. Why did they pick you?'

'It was frightening, amazing, awe-inspiring, and life changing, all at once. You walk into the cube and it is possible to see, not only our solar system, but also huge vast stretches of the universe but strangely as you looked into this they got closer, it is the only way I can explain it. You only hear Islands voice, you do not see Island.' Ruth takes another drink.

'The person came to see me as they had been a government employee and they believed that I was the right person to take this forward. I am very glad they did.'

'Let me be very clear to you, Joyce and everyone in this room or who is watching. I have said I will not breach this persons confidence and this also this includes my staff or colleagues. Any questions that are even obliquely aimed at finding out further information about Islands contact, I will have banned from Parliament permanently, so tread very carefully.' Joyce nods, rebuke taken.

'To further answer your question; at no time then or later have I felt threatened by Island. Island did ask to read my memories, the person that took me had been through this, so I consented. You may see this as foolish, as the head of a state but I believed it was the right decision. I have reflected on this and still believe it was the right one. I would say I made this choice after talking with Island for some time and with the person that took me. I felt it was important that Island had as much information about us as possible and no, I did not, nor do I perceive Island as a threat.' She looks around the room and point at an older man in the middle of the gaggle.

'Ruth' there is some smiling at this, instead of Prime Minister. Ruth smiles as well.

'Jock Henderson from Hampton Downs. I know this is a personal question and you can refuse to answer of course but will you vote yes or no?' Ruth has expected the answer but not from a private citizen. She ponders, then.

'Thank you, Jock. You are right, I could refuse and I will say again that this is a conscience vote. One's choice is one's choice. In saying that, I will be voting yes. Thank you for your question.' Jock sits down his face thoughtful.

'Jesus! I didn't expect that one! Her saying which way she was going to vote. Bloody hell!' Barbara is bouncing up and down on the couch. She is right I didn't see that coming either. I wonder if Ruth's resignation has given her that freedom. Her party will be shocked, I think, but way too late now. I go to the fridge, wine for Barbara for a change and beer for me. She looks across and raises the glass.

'Glad to have you home, you know.' I smile and nod. I had spent too much time away.

Ruth is pointing to a very sharply dressed young man with a "person going places" look.

'Rodger, your question.'

'Prime Minister, so are you expecting the people of the country to follow your lead with a yes vote?' Cocky question from a cocky person but not unfair I think.

'Rodger, I trust the people of this country to be able to make up their own minds. They don't need me or your channel to tell them what to do. Do you have another question or do I move on?' Bang on the nose.

'Are you worried about the political fallout throughout the world with coming of Island? And secondly, now that the world knows you met Island prior to the General Assembly. Do you think that you should have disclosed that earlier? ' Excellent questions I think, astute.

'Worried, no. I do not believe disclosing my meeting with Island would have made any difference. Island wanted to be introduced to as many people in the world at once. That should be obvious with Island's arrival at the General Assembly. That is my understanding. Actually, thinking about your question I know it would have muddied the waters. Island is more than capable of introducing and explaining Island. Island is a repository of a whole culture but there will be marked changes and this will depend on how the General Assembly reacts. World government could be a vastly different thing. Only time will tell. Thank you.' She smiles at him and oddly he bows slightly and sits down.

The questions roll on, much the same, some more pointed some annoyed with a 'why were we not told more, sooner, theme' hanging somewhere in the back ground.

Then Ruth gets bored and she says at the end of a rambling poorly framed set of dribble.

'Well, that isn't going to lead us anywhere and I am rapping this up. I won't be able to answer the unanswerable.' She smiles grimly at the obviously shallow young girl from a social media platform.

'To close. My meeting with Island, I saw then and see now, as a meeting between two beings, not as a leader of a country. I know some of you will disagree but I will say that I did not disclose this meeting with any of my government nor any of my staff. I did discuss it with my husband and the person that took me to meet Island. Strangely, after meeting Island you don't discuss so much as stand in awe at a shared experience. The choices I made, I still believe were, and are, the right ones for this country. I wish you well for the coming vote. Thank you for allowing me to be your Prime Minister.'

Ruth then walks quickly away from the podium. Calls are made from the audience. Some people are shouting, some clapping and others are sitting contemplating. There is a touch of confusion. The camera we are watching shifts to an announcer in a studio. Barbara hits the off button.

'Well, well. Surprises all round I think.' She stares at the blackened screen 'How long before some enterprising reporter comes sniffing, maybe from a lead from the PMs office? Police?' I laugh.

'Not long, sniffing and proof are different things. We will see. Anyway we have furniture to sort and I need to send some sort of rent to Troy. ' It is my turn to stare and think into the screen.

'More importantly, Ruth has spoken about Ralph and that he knew about Island before the General Assembly. I do wonder if she contacted him before speaking. I suspect she did but there will be fall out for Ralph. A roasting I suspect. But the world is running towards change, no matter how the vote goes. World government is on people lips and seen for the first time as a possible choice, odd to think a couple of weeks ago it wasn't.' Barbara nods. My mind has turned to details here I need to sort. The end of change, I think.

'Is Gary back here do you know? I have to go and clear up something with him.' She looks at me. Barbara nods.

'He came back yesterday, the surgery was over run. Why? You're up to something.'

'Don't be rude!' I grin and shake my head. 'No, just blunt. Some things just need to be said.'

She snorts ' I'll start dinner.' But her eyes are serious

As I pull into Gary's driveway I see Gary is fiddling with his boat engine. He straightens and walks up the drive. 'Gary' I say as he walks up he puts a hand out, which I ignore. He drops it to his side.

'Umm how are you?' He asks warily. I stand and look at him, not liking what I am seeing.

'I now know you got paid and where the money came from. 500K, then more. You sold us out Gary. Our house up in smoke. You not only sold us out but your friend Dan was an agent under orders from a traitor in his own country. Things have happened which make you an accessory to treason. Which is still a hanging offence. I have checked.' I let this thought settle. Gary is now white, eyes glazed looking into a future of horrors.

I just can't be bothered, the man sickens me. Somehow his being a doctor makes it worse. The hypocritical oath, I wonder. I look over his shoulder at his boat and his personal world beyond. I see a good comfortable life. Strange.

'The information in your office, you will destroy. Anybody who asks any questions, you will deny. Any hint of anything, ever, coming from you and the evidence will go public. You will sell up and leave here. You have exactly one month.' I am staring. He stands eyes fixed on me, as Di opens the front door behind him.

'Anyone Gary, and I mean anyone. Your friend Dan is dead and all his team. You have no friends. I will see you hung as a traitor. Do you understand?' I stand staring.

'Hi Bill, how are you?' She waves. Gary turns and vomits in the driveway. Di's hand drops and she walks towards Gary, concern on her face. I wave, get into the car and back down to the street. She is looking at Gary and then back to me.

'You weren't long.' Barbara says as she stirs something on the stove. Her phone buzzes. I wonder who? Barbara wipes her hands and looks at the phone. She looks at me.

'What did you say to Gary?' I look back at her think about lying but can't.

'I told him to leave; if any information is leaked I will find him. He worked it out from there.' I shake my head at the situation. I am just saddened. The disappointment of what I thought I saw in the man and then found out through his actions.

Barbara stands facing me and then looks at her phone again, looks at the screen again then nods.

'I do understand you know.' and I see she does. She stares at the screen, evaluating balancing. 'Poor Di.' She shakes her head.

'So pasta OK?' I smile then laugh and hug her. Yes, she does understand. She untangles and turns to the stove. I go on a wild wine hunt in the pantry, nice to be home.

Chapter 27

I have set the alarm for the televised event that will be Ralph's speech and just as I put my phone on charge a call comes through. Ruth.

'Hello Ruth, good to hear from you.'

'Hello Bill. How are you and how is Barbara?' Polite as always but I know this is meant.

'We are both well, thanks. Good to be home to be honest. I was sorry to see you are resigning. We watched the broadcast. I understand.'

'Yes, I knew you would. Island changes you in ways only a person who has met Island can understand. I am ringing to say I have spoken to Ralph. I knew you would be concerned. Things have moved quickly in the General Assembly but that will get announced later.' She stops not wanting to say more I guess, in the gap I tell her my news.

'I saw Island for the last time I think. I asked Island to remove the bracelet and Island did. I am, what you would call, normal.' I chuckle into the phone.

'Did you? You gave away a lot of power. But well done, I think I understand. I wonder if I could. One day when things have cleared we will discuss this. Interesting.' She is quiet then says.

'I meant what I said about meeting Island. It was the most amazing experience of my life. I rang to thank you.'

'I wanted our leader to see what I saw.' I pause then.

'Ruth, let me be clear, had it been your deputy or the leader of the opposition in Parliament, I doubt I would have approached them. To be honest, I am not really sure what I would have done. You made the choice easy.' There is silence then:

'Thank you. Good night, Bill.'

'Good night, Prime Minister.' and I hear a chuckle as the phone call ends. Barbara has been eavesdropping.

'Ruth?' I hum agreement. 'all OK?' I nod.

'Yes fine. She has spoken to Ralph. Just the same, the heat will be on full bore at the White House at the minute. Poor bastard. And Estelle.' I undress and get into bed. I am shattered. As I drift off Barbara says:

'Sleep well. I love you.' I am in the right place and so very lucky.

The alarm scares me awake. I hear a groan beside me and then a 'shut that thing up!' as I try to do just that. I finally find the right button, put the jug on for coffee and turn the TV on. I am not a TV fan as a rule. TVs do not live in our lounge as a focal point. We have always made the lounge a people place. This is an oddity in our world that I am looking forward to changing when we move.

Sleekly groomed announcers are sitting at glass-crafted desks with perfect clothes and gleaming teeth, carefully chosen for their expert knowledge. Which in this case is completely nil but their opinions we will be given as though it is fact. I sort the coffee and tell Barbara her wake up coffee is being served at her seat. There is some complaining about time zones and early mornings and finally a happy face appears above a rumpled dressing gown. She sniffs the coffee and nods that I got it right.

There is a furry of anxiety and annoyance at the clear bright desk of the announcers. The President's speech will not be held at the White House but at the United Nations General Assembly. This has not been planned obviously. There is breaking news of a security breech coming out of Washington at the White House but with very little detail. The White House is in full lock down but the President is OK and will be in New York for the televised event, stay tuned.

'Not good, glad I don't have his job.' I am talking to myself. Barbara looks across at me.

'What's he like? I mean the man you know?'

'I like him. I didn't expect to. I was hoping he was honest when we first met. I wanted to trust him and I do. He believes in the job, he has the power balanced I think. He hates greed. He wants good for people generally not just his country. He tries to look globally within the constraints of his position. Simply, he has a good heart.'

I am not really that happy with my answer. But then it is what I think. Judging people is a point of view; an opinion, not right or wrong. Barbara shakes her head and hums then nods.

'Yes, difficult to judge but that's the way he seems.' my turn to hum.

There is further chatter of no importance from the teeth at the desk then there is an announcement that we are crossing live to the General Assembly building of The United Nations in New York. I have always wondered if the TV stations ever cross to a place 'dead'. Their wording makes me twitch with a touch of annoyance.

The Assembly interior comes into view and the podium has a line-up of the leaders of the world. In the foreground just above them floats Island's cube. At the centre is the Secretary General he is flanked either side the top world leaders. At his left is Ralph. Barbara looks at him closely.

'Something is wrong, he looks terrible.' She is right, he is grey and shocked. He has aged but oddly strengthened, no. Determined and grim. A man on a mission.

The Secretary General starts.

'People of Earth, I welcome you all to this meeting. This is being beamed around the world to as many people as possible, in as many languages as possible. The thoughts here today are from the leaders you have chosen. They are giving their point of view in this historic time for our planet.' He stops and looks around the vast room to emphasize the point.

'Some leaders are not present. They have been replaced by other people Island believes better represent their nations and their peoples requirements. The Assembly has not, nor will it comment on this. Some of you will disagree with this intrusion into national politics. The Assembly is not going to comment. The questions before us are globally changing and quite possibly planet saving.'

'This is going to be a new world we are shaping today. The consensus in this room has never, I repeat, never been as directed nor as single minded as I have seen or known. I thank the party states and leaders for being so proactive to move beyond their own national issues. To the people of the world, thank you for listening. I wish you well for the vote. I pass now to the President of the United States of America. The President was not going to speak first but things have come to pass that require this. Again, I thank you all.'

There is a standing ovation for the Secretary General and some garbled comments from the glass desk. The question is, why has the order changed and who was going to speak first? Barbara gets up and puts the jug on for a refresh.

'You Ok?' She rubs my arm on the way past.

'Something isn't good at the White House if the speaker list has changed...don't know.'

The chamber settles and Ralph is standing behind the podium. He is obviously struggling and he takes a drink of water before starting. He looks around the room and then at Island.

'People of the World and people of the United States, I welcome you all here. Firstly, I will struggle tonight, please forgive me. Just before leaving for this meeting there was a domestic attack at the White House. An assassination attempt on myself and my wife Estelle. My beautiful wife of twenty-eight years has passed away in this attack. I am bereft and lost.'

He is gripping the sides of the podium. The tears are obvious now. He brushes them away. People are standing and the groan fills the room. The announcers give intakes of breath and a very clear 'Jesus Christ!'

Barbara's head has snapped to me 'Hell what?! You liked her! Right?' I am shaking my head. I don't know what to say. She was a very good person. I liked her a lot, she had a quick vibrant intelligence. Poor bloody Ralph. They have two children at University. God.

'A good person who matched her husband.' I am stunned. I watch as Ralph holds up his hand to this vast chamber, to the world.

'Please! I am here at Estelle's last request, had she not asked, I would be able to stand before you.'

The words ripple across the room and across the globe, a man in his grief but one with a message.

'The world has changed. We need this change. Opportunity lies before us all. Our small national disagreements, if not solved, will send us into oblivion. We have been, and are, poisoning our planet. We are starving some, allowing over feeding of others. In my own country, medical aid isn't reaching those who need it, because of profit first. Across the world, woman carry dirty water for miles, a daily routine. Women and children have carried the burden of men's lust for power and control through arms and misogyny. Children are not being educated. They live in poverty, mostly due to theft of their birth right by money hungry thieves, whom we name corporations.' he stops and sips water. Silence.

'Corporations and companies across the globe have put continuous profit before the environment and the people they are meant to support and ultimately serve. Staggering personal wealth is a metaphor for success. The worlds banking system has turned people's daily lives into slavery through high profit loans, including the simple home mortgage.' He stops again and looks across the great room and then directly into the camera before him.

'The over powering burden that the various religions have sown through war and hate of our fellows throughout, our history is too well documented and seen daily on our screens. This is one of the great problems that beset us and is ignored. I do not judge nor do I have any comment on any God or persons choice of religion. That is your affair. But this must be remarked on. Manipulation is a strong force in any religion but for what gain and who's gain? Reflect on this. Reflect on this elephant, in the vast room of our planet.'

Ralph is stronger; a great orator finding his feet. The world listens.

'Our planet is a place of great beauty. Our human race is an amazing mixture of greatness, hope, of opportunity for all people. We are part of the great puzzle of all biodiversity of our mother earth. We have come from this earth, we all return to it. The preservation of the earth and our race is on the edge of the knife. I believe in humanity. I believe in the basic goodness of humankind and your power, your power to do right, to overcome our human issues to preserve our home world. Our truly Mother Earth.'

'I thank you for listening. I wish you all well for the vote. I for one, will be asking Island for the help we need.' He stops and closes his eyes and then says.

'Estelle believed in the beauty and the right of our human race. Her last wishes were to pass those words to you all. I thank you and I thank her for the courage to stand before you today.'

Ralph bows and turns away into the arms of the Secretary general. The leaders have crowded around him. The people in chamber are on their feet and, in the strange way of some the European countries, there is a clapping in low timed unison. It is hypnotic and respectful, the sound rolls through the room and out into the world.

'Jesus!' Barbara is bouncing on the couch. 'I mean bloody, wow!'

The Secretary General is back at the podium Ralph has left the stage.

'I would like to pass on to the President his family and his country our sadness and thoughts from the nations of the world.' He stops head bowed then looks up.

'There will be a number of leaders make their thoughts known over the next three hours. Their time is limited to the same amount. At the end of this, Island will be talking to the world. I now invite the leader of China to speak.'

A dark haired man with a black suite and red tie walks to the podium. But Barbara is not in the mood for more politics and the sound disappears. I agree. I am feeling Estelle's loss and Ralph's pain. Poor bugger. Barbara sorts more coffee. I feel numbed.

'How are you doing?' Barbara's voice comes across the kitchen bench. I ask myself the question. How am I doing? What have I introduced to the world?

'Should I have brought Island to the world?' The question has started to haunt me even before today's events. I hear the cups being put on the counter and then comes Barbara to sit beside me. She is looking into my eyes.

'I have a question for you.' Her face is very serious.

'You put the bracelet on by accident not design, right?' I nod in agreement, the pain oddly still sits with me like an old scar one can trace.

'The first meeting with Island convinced you of......' she searches for the phrase then says.

'The rightness of your discussion with Island. Is that the way you saw it at the time?' I nod and open my mouth but she holds her hand up and I close it.

'Whatever choices were made by other people. Gary and the rest were choices they made mostly for power or just money, orders. I don't know. But what I do know is the choices you have made were what you believed were simply right. For that is the person I married.' we hold each other for a long time.

Barbara's bridge of support will hold me for the rest of my days.

The dawn is coming and I head to the shower. Time and history is passing but sometimes you just need hot water. When I return, the TV is back on and the addresses are coming to an end. Island is meant to speak in thirty minutes.

'Shower time for me too, sort some breakfast will you?' so I head to the kitchen and find bits to do toast and eggs. A speaker from Asia is talking; the translation is at the bottom of the screen. I am not sure where he is from but his words are thoughtful and caring. He sees hope in the future but is trying for balance in the number of religions that are part of his culture. A tight rope that most countries are trying to tip toe over.

I have noted Island has ignored or side stepped this issue and I wish I had asked but then I wonder if I would have liked the answer. Damn! I have burnt the first lot of toast. A smoke alarm screams, which I flap at with a tea towel. I hear a 'Ha ha' from the bathroom.

There has been a discussion on the lousy toaster at this house. Time to have a home.

We settle down to tea. The coffee has got a bit much, with scrambled eggs and non-burnt toast, which is actually good luck I suspect.

The General Secretary is now thanking the speakers and the World for joining this historic event. He stops and looks around the chamber before him.

'People of the World, I introduce, Island. Traveller from another world.'

The cameras focus on the floating crystal blued cube, a strange beautiful hologram that has travelled the vastness and is now part of our future. It is familiar and yet not. I miss the tide around the cube and, to me at least, it is out of place.

As Island's voice comes across the screen, most of the world is locked into these seconds of history. From every place people are watching from home, at work, in crowded bars, hospitals, in the ice bound north or south, Tokyo, Khartoum, LA, London, Paris, Beijing, Rarotonga, Vladivostok. History is being made and watched and pondered.

'Peoples of the earth. I welcome you to Island's thoughts and words.' the words are low and measured.

'Island has travelled the vast universe for thousands of your planets years. Island is one of a number of voyagers that left the home planet millennia ago. Island is not a being. Island is a repository of knowledge gained and stored over a vastness of your years at the home planet.'

'Island came to this planet some long time ago. The pilot from Island's planet came to your earth but did not return. Time passed and one of your people took up the contact that was able to bridge the knowledge between Island and your people. This happened recently.' Island lets these thoughts sink in.

'The contact gave Island a connection into your people and your history. This has been made stronger with a number of your peoples help.' There is a gap yet the world waits and listens.

'These connections enabled Island to have understanding of the intervolved life on your planet and the problems that beset it.'

'This planets situation is not different to others in the vastness of space.'

This thought is a shock. Island has seen others? I am trying to review our conversations. But then the statement answered its self.

'Intelligent beings work to protect their own tribe, their own race, how can it be any other way? But in this protection can lead to domination; balance becomes skewed with more control. Once one race tries to dominate other races or species then environmental balances are lost. Balance is always the key.'

'Your planet is on the cusp of ending, heavy over-use of your planets resources, controlling wealth for powers sake is a key human condition that has failed. Humanity is beyond the tribe with its population and yet still is tribal. This is truth.'

Island stops, there may be a commentary from the news people going on but I don't know, there is just silence.

'Island is able, with the population of earth's agreement, to change the environmental issues that lay before the Earths people. These changes will redeem forests, seas, water-purity and introduce energy solutions that are sustainable. Island is able to bring balance.'

'Island has taken steps to free a number people from the total control of the tyrants that have enslaved their future. Island made a balanced judgment and this is done.'

Changes in the desks around the room have been noted by commentators, which now are clarified. I wonder at this, not sure if I like it, but understand the why.

Island's voice stops and from the cube a noise rises. The sound of trees in the wind, water on rocks and the sea swirling on a sandy shore, the wind in the desert, birds sing and animals call. It is the sound and soul of our world. A natural primal Earth in totality, beautiful and simple, the real music of our world.

Island voice returns as the sound slows.

'People of earth, there is one more thing to add to the choice of vote that you will make.'

'Island has said that other ships like Islands were sent in different directions from Island's home world. This is truth. The purpose of each Island was not only to journey to other planets and support them but to inter-connect them. Should each planet be judged capable and wish this contact.'

The simple shock of this statement is staggering to me. Barbara heads snaps towards me.

'Did you know?' I am shaking my head still staring at the screen. 'God no! I never presumed I mean.....' I am quite lost for words. Islands voice rolls on.

'Should the people of earth decide to take Island's support, the interconnection between planets would be made possible to the people of Earth. The door of space and the universe will be opened to your race.'

'This is what Island offers. This is humanities choice.'

'Island will educate and work with the Earth's population until transition to a balanced planet is enabled. Interconnection with others in the universe will be made possible. At the end of this period, Island will be gone.'

'Each person's vote is for world government and Interconnection. Each human will have one vote. Age is not a factor. If a human can comprehend this issue, they will be able to vote.'

'Each human has a choice. People who try to force a block of vote, in either direction, will be sent to the void. Island says this as a warning and a truth.'

'The vote will take place in one hour across your planet.' Islands voice stops.

The cube again has a low sound of the Earth music. The world I believe is stunned. I am.

Barbara says 'I thought the vote was later?' I grunt, nodding in agreement.

'Island is pre-empting organized block voting. Think about what the Chinese or Cubans feel about one person voting, any of the basic dictatorships. Oddly, most systems don't have it. You might vote for a party but the voters don't pick the leader. The party does, same here. Democracy isn't really that democratic.'

'So join the stars? Bloody hell!' She is shaking her head 'I mean the implications! Who do we join? How? Do some people go there? Do aliens come here? How far does Island's control go?'

She looks at the pond, rain is drifting across the water in sheets but the two mallards are just sitting bobbing in grey wavelets, uncaringly happy.

My phone goes. I am temped not to answer but look at the screen. Ralph. I answer.

'Hello. Are you OK? I am so, so, sorry for you. I liked Estelle very much, I can't believe it.......shocked. Oh, I had no idea about the other planets, by the way.'

'No, I knew you wouldn't. But still, good to know. I am struggling. Right now the world can fuck its self.' His reply is slow and grief filled. I nod and get it, poor bugger.

'What do you need?' He needs help but I can't help thinking why me?

'Do you believe Island? You know better Island than anyone else.' I am surprised he has asked. Anyway I answer.

'You spoke to island, you have been inside the cube. You saw, what you saw. So yes, I believe. Joining the stars other planets? The implications are huge enormous. Beyond my comprehension. But simply we join or don't or worse. One thing. I gave the bracelet back. After having the bracelet experience, Ralph. Yes, I believe. How can I not?'

I stop. Ralph has already beaten me to all this, he just wants to talk to someone. Anyone outside the nightmare he is surrounded by and looking at. There is quiet on the phone.

'Thanks. She really liked you too. I….anyway, thanks.' the phone goes silent.

'How is he?' I shrug 'How would I be without you? He is in a living hell.'

Barbara gets up and puts on the jug, cups tingle on the bench, jar tops open.

'So I guess we wait. Walk in the rain?' I nod why not? Clear the head. We leave the jug to its devices and wander through pathways to the beach, in dripping jackets. The rain is pockmarking the sand and lines of surf are in darkening grey drifts. A very white gull sits glaring at its grey surrounds on one orange leg. The rain is hissing into the sand as we walk down the beach, saying little but still good to get out, wet or no.

We turn up through a cutting in the small sand dunes and down a lifeless wet pathway to home, the jug goes back on and we change into dry clothes, calmer and less over whelmed.

Barbara has put the TV on, the world is swirling with questions. Experts from every sector are being asked things they just cannot answer. Maybe this, maybe that and so time passes and in the ticking of time, it comes.

We are sitting in our lounge watching the scrabble of commentary and then the TV stops.

Two small blue green cubes appear floating in space; they are 6 inches square. They float slowly turning. On one side of the cube is a cross on the other is a circle. We both look at them, surprised, but not shocked.

In Islands voice the message comes:

'Touch the circle for Yes for World Government. Touch the cross for No.'

It then repeats:

'Touch the circle for Yes for World Government. Touch the cross for No.'

It repeats again:

'Touch the circle for Yes for World Government. Touch the cross for No.'

I lean forward and touch the circle and the cube is gone. Barbara watches me and then leans forward. I look away, it is her choice, she will do what she thinks is right.

'Done.' She says and the other cube has gone. She gets up and goes to the fridge as I sit staring out at the darkening day, another rain cloud is making its presence felt. I hear a pop and turn to see Barbara has pulled the cork out of a bottle of champagne.

'So you know the answer already?' She shakes her head. 'No.'

'But how many times has the whole world voted on anything? Let alone the direction of the whole of our planet?' So we sit and toast. 'To the world!' We say but are really a little lost in our own thoughts. I wonder about the future and what it will bring. One hour later the TV comes alive. Islands voice comes into the lounge:

'The people of Earth have voted for world government. The people of Earth have voted for world government.'

The screen then turns back to the news channel. Barbara surfs a number of them all full of the same news that Island just imparted. The world has changed, channels are doing world tours. Street parties are erupting in London, Moscow, Sydney, Beijing, in Athens people are on the streets, in villages in India and small towns in Peru. Islands in the Indian ocean, the Sahara desert. Right across the planet the world has changed and the people know it. There is a new world and it will be good, is the feeling; humanity is linked to a common realistic future.

The program now returns to the United Nations in New York. Island's cube floats in the vast ceiling of the room. The cameras sweep the huge room, every seat is filled; here in microcosm, is the Planet. The Secretary General is at the Podium. He is alone he stands straight and is smiling into the camera before him.

'Citizens of the world, history was made today! We have a new world. You, the people of Earth have voted for a World government!' There is a round of applause through the chamber, which rumbles then dies away.

'Island has given criteria to develop the direction of this world government. This will open to a new cooperative system, the members of this forum will work towards global collaboration.' The applause rises again as this closes he says.

'The universe will now open to our planet, fellow citizens, we stand together in history!' The chamber is quiet as it contemplates what has opened before them.

He stops looks around the chamber which waits quietly.

'Island has asked me to pass on this simple message.' he stops again and looks out across the podium.

'The world that humans have voted for, will be built on care for each entity and species on this planet.'

The Secretary looks into the camera and repeats.

'Care for each entity and species on this planet! People of earth this is our new Mantra! Care for each entity and species on this planet!' The chamber is silent and then a young man from an African nation stands and starts to sing in a strong base voice with clarity and joy. His fellows join him and others of the chamber follow; soon the rising song is a strange mixture of words, tunes, dialects are driving through the chamber and then into the world. The sound of the planet comes from Island. The sounds and voices of our world entwine in joy and in hope; the ever present wine of humanity.

Epilogue

Eight months later we have moved properly into our new house. What we were able to save from the old place has been resurrected, with smoke and water damage cleaned off as much as possible. Funny how the touch stones of one's life can be in a small ornament of an aunt or your mother's. A picture of family long gone gives rise to a sense of place. Where we were, as a family, does this give peace to where we are going? I am not sure but I like the continuity; a sense of place.

The house is different but becoming ours. We have a plan in place, the new kitchen is a small thing that is yet to happen but it brings us forward together. Sorting through towards a common idea. Barbara is working a lot in the garden, planting plants to eat and trees that fruit. We have built vegetable gardens that are just starting to produce our salads. Other trees we have planted to bring the birds. Simple things, good things.

The scars of tension are retreating within me. Sometimes I am flying across a lighted city, sometimes my arm aches. The tattoo is still there, silvered hieroglyphics of what is becoming a past dream. I do wake from time to time dripping in sweat, a world gone crazy. I waken in dreams of Islands cube. I am sitting in the seat, seeing the sea and sand on another planet, that has flickering diving red birds and sadness takes me. Slowly these are less; Barbara knows and in the night I hear her say, it's OK. In the morning she says nothing.

The world is vastly different in such a short time. The world government is starting to work. Complaints and glitches true, yet oddly people want solutions not arguments. A number of dictatorships are now 'Working Alliances of the People' which seems to be a catch phrase of the moment. Some leaders have simply disappeared. These vacuums are filled with better leaders. People are shrugging their shoulders at whatever fate they have had but balance is the key. The catch phrase that keeps people moving forward. It is a new, old world.

Food production has tripled and rain is falling in the right places. With food production rising, prices are falling. Re-afforestation just seems to appear, the borders of the Sahara are green, oceans are cooling and the plastic pollution islands have disappeared. Mid-Africa has had a climate change with balanced rainfall. Snow is falling on the Arctic and the white bears are happy, as are the penguins in the cold south. The great forest of the Amazon is recovering as man-made cattle grassland disappears under a fast growing new forest. Across the planet meat production is rapidly falling away, in line with humans new fascination for a plant based diet and the push to stop harm to any animal. Again, there are issues but the trend is wide spread. Sugar is well in retreat. Mono cultures are being replaced with native forests.

An energy company has appeared as part of Island's Earth Care Council and its branches are across the globe. Rare earth batteries are on their way out, replaced by a completely renewable one which has something to do with sea salt. It is being produced quickly and very, very cheaply. Solar stoves are replacing burning trees for fuel. Corporations have joined together in cooperation. Internal combustion will be gone in the very near future. Vehicles are being swapped at 'Replacement Stations'. Arms production has stopped, the changed factories are producing solar equipment. Armed Forces are becoming unarmed work groups. A hard transition for some but still, it is happening. It appears previously unknown simple ideas are remaking our world.

Oil production is dropping monthly. Oil companies are helping to shut down production while adapting to new dynamics of planting and selective harvesting. Plant based technology for large manufacturing companies is being redeveloped to produce recyclable steel like products. Desert power has become a by-line in arid countries. Energy plants that create 'Cold Energy.' which reduces global warming and uses the word 'Balance'. These natural technologies were in front of us. Just not found. These marvels are on peoples lips and certainly each media outlet is full of each new development.

The medical world is changing. Not only with new medicines but the ethos of helping each person, not profit driven, not wealth driven. Medical insurance has been removed and that wealth moved from profit to support. Medical help is free across the planet. The war on drugs has gone to a war on addiction. Those supplying are given one chance only. New training methods are appearing in schools and universities which adapt to each student needs where personal development is focused. The young are blossoming into this new world. Travel for travels sake is well down. People want to experience the world that is closest to them and make it better.

But of all things that show the real change, are the people of the planet. Attitudes have moved to caring. People wave, people smile, they take time to stop and chat. Crime is down by a very high percentages as wealth is balanced. Police are making happy noises. Co-operation is a by word across the nations and the planet.

Barbara and I are happy. I am reflecting on this, as I turn the jug on and put cups on the bench, afternoon break. I look up and standing at the wide glass open door is Ralph. He is greyer, has lost weight but smiling. I come around the bench and hug him.

'Very good to see you, my friend.' I am looking into his eyes and he knows it's true. At that moment Barbara walks in.

'Oh hello!' She looks at me with a 'did you know?' look. I shake my head to help out.

'Ralph, my wife Barbara. Barbara. Ralph, President of the United States.' She smiles and nods with a hello nice to meet you. She holds up her hands, dark from the garden she excuses herself to wash her hands and heads to the bathroom.

'Coffee or tea?' Ralph looks around the room and I wave him into a seat. 'Coffee. I want to see how good it is.' He twitches a smile.

'So what news from the centre of the world?' I am being flippant. I know he is here for a reason. But world events I want to pass me by. I have reflected on my change of interest yet I have no answers. Ralph is looking around him, taking in our home and I see him nod to himself.

'How are you?' I ask. 'I still can't believe what happened and how you coped. I don't know how to process it. Some people should not live.'

He is looking at me and nods. Barbara arrives back in the room she sees the interplay and by passes me to the coffee stuff. I join Ralph and sit down. From here I can see a guy standing on the edge of the garden. Secret Service. No doubt there will be more. Glad it's not my life.

'Yeah! A nightmare and part of me will always live it but Estelle wanted me to do what was right I........' He trails off ' Then says 'I am not so sure.' He watches quietly as Barbara brings coffee and the additives. He pours a touch of milk into a mug and sips.

'Not bad for the end of the world!' Barbara grins. Ralph looks at her then switches his glance to me. Eyes piecing, very still.

'This is what I wanted. What you both have; I got lost in my world.' the intensity of sadness shakes me. Barbara watches him then wipes away tears and tosses her head.

'You did more than anyone ever expected! I am so sorry for you.' He swallows. We sit and wait, then I gently ask.

'OK Ralph, why are you here? It's a long way from that New York forum. By the way, how is the World Government actually going? News seems positive. Is it?'

Ralph sips his coffee again, looks at the garden and begins.

'Strangely, far better than any predictions that could have been made. You know I was heavily under fire once Island appeared, after I announced my thoughts. But the reality is I don't understand it and I am seeing a lot of the detail. I thought the hardest to overcome would be the religious element. It didn't matter which. My country is as broad across it's affiliations as any country in this regard but the extremes are disappearing, as are the political divides. National borders are getting ready to open. Which is frankly amazing, unheard of. The petty wars have stopped. Polarization is a thing of the past. Looking for common ground is a standard. Actually, it's more than that. It's the people, governments are saying: Here I can give this, then they say, no. I should and can, give more! Everywhere!' He shakes his head and turns the handle of the mug with one finger slowly.

'Mid country USA to the middle east to Asia it's all: OK, let's see how we can work together. After thousands of years. The Catholic Church has started to fully integrate woman and I mean fully. Papal eidetic, one small example. Speaking of borders, now the countries are becoming more equal, people want to stay where they are, at home, in peace. Why move if you don't have to, I guess. Home is home.' He looks across the lawn towards the beach.

'There's more, the planet itself is changing. I guess you will have heard.' we both nod. 'It truly is a new age' He is quiet, I feel he is trying to grasp the rate of change.

'I will not be going for re-election. It's simple, not without Estelle.' we both nod at the same time, his eyes flicker across us and lips rise in understanding.

'I have had a couple of long discussions with Island.' I am surprised, but then, what Island is doing and how Island is working with the World Government I don't understand. Barbara's chin rises. I know that move, she is asking so what else is coming?

'How does that work? I mean one on one? It just occurred to me, that some people may find that privileged, which breeds its own issues, but I don't know.' Ralph nods and finishes his coffee.

'Completely but what they don't know.....anyway.' He holds his arm out, rolls up his sleeve and I see there is the same tattoo as mine. I am taken aback and oddly, a wave of jealously sweeps through me in a flash, then I laugh at myself and the feeling. I shake my head at me.

'I've been replaced!' Barbara looks from one to the other, not liking where this may be heading.

Ralph shakes his head.

'No. There are a number of people throughout the planet who can communicate directly with Island now. Those Island trusts. Island judges well I think; but Island judges. It is a strange thing to let a being do that. I struggle with it. I guess I always will and yet it does seem to work. One single being who actually uses their power to create positive change. God like but not.....' He nods his head and stops. Thinking, he seems to be weighing his words.

'So the reason for me being here.' Ralph taps the tattoo. A small copy of Island's cube appears floating over our coffee table and empty cups.

'Hello Island' I say. Barbara copies me, eyes wide with surprise.

'Hello Bill, Hello Barbara, Hello Ralph. It is good to be able to talk you, thank you.'

Ralph starts.

'Island, I thought it would be better if you explained your thoughts to Bill and Barbara.'

'Thank you Ralph. Your planet is moving in the correct direction. Island believes the people of the earth will develop their true direction sooner than expected. Yet it will take some years.'

Island lets these thoughts sit. We wait.

'Island believes that soon, a number humans should journey to different planets to open channels with other beings, on other worlds. This is to bring about a further consensus across the vastness of space. Communication is the key.'

'Who?' Barbara snaps the word, she is surprised and shocked at the implications. Ralphs head tilts towards her. He already knows the answer I think. Island rolls on.

'Ralph has said he will be part of this. There are others. Yourself Barbara and Bill. You are both good representatives of your world. You could go should you wish. Island can only ask, the choice is yours.'

Barbara looks over Island's cube through the doors and quips.

'I have only just planted the vegetable garden.' and Island replies. 'That is true.'

Ralph smiles and watches our faces but says nothing. I look at Barbara's face familiar, beautiful, screwed up in concentration and fear of a future that she hadn't planned for. I look at the cube, translucent blue green with the promise of new worlds. I think of a beach I would like to see; the beach in the stars, with pink palms and flickering red fish and then I think of a beach that I can hear, where I met my friend. Island.

I look at Barbara and see my answer.

'No. Thank you Island, we like our simple life here at the edge of sea.'

As I reply Barbara is nodding, she looks at me and smiles; we both get it. I look at Ralph.

'So when you can, drop back for some fishing. We will be here.'